KAMELEON MAN

a novel by

KIM BARRY BRUNHUBER

Porcepic Books
an imprint of

Beach Holme Publishing
Vancouver

This book is published by Beach Holme Publishing, Suite 1010, 409 Granville Street, Vancouver, British Columbia V6C 1T2, *www.beachholme.bc.ca.* This is a Porcepic Book.

The publisher gratefully acknowledges the financial support of the Canada Council for the Arts and of the British Columbia Arts Council. The publisher also acknowledges the financial assistance received from the Government of Canada through the Book Publishing Industry Development Program (BPIDP) for its publishing activities.

Editor: Michael Carroll
Design and Production: Jen Hamilton
Cover art: Copyright © Dennis Novak/Getty Images. Used with permission.

Printed and bound in Canada by Printcrafters

National Library of Canada Cataloguing in Publication

Brunhuber, Kim Barry
    Kameleon Man/Kim Barry Brunhuber.

"A Porcepic Book."
ISBN 0-88878-443-0

    I. Title.

PS8553.R866K35 2003   C813'.6   C2003-905868-9

KAMELEON MAN

To my little family: Twiddy, Mouse, Wolf and, most of all, Mum

ONE

The inside of the tent is a whirlwind of stockings, nubile limbs, breasts of all kinds. No time to look. A minute and a half to change.

Otto, on his way out, turns for one last glance, but the mirror's full of Sandor and his conical top hat. "Am I tucked?"

"Let me..." one of the models behind him says. He pretends to tuck it, pulls Otto's shirt out even farther. Not that Otto has a chance of winning, but it's the last routine, and why take any chances?

Everyone else is still trying to fit into their bridal gowns or tuxedos, too big or too small because there aren't any rehearsals for shows like this. Tairhun, our dresser, a young balding Pakistani with big hoop earrings in both ears, flits among us, adjusting collars and brushing off lint, telling each of us to call him Tyrone. I fumble with my suspenders, can't figure them out, search for my shoes instead.

Before the show all the clothes were neatly arranged on racks, our names and the order of each outfit printed in marker on cardboard tags. Now, after three changes, tags litter the floor, shoes are in the wrong boxes, outfits are mixed up and inside out. Two square feet of space each in which to manoeuvre, and one chair for every three models where we toss our used outfits. Tairhun told us to hang everything up after each change so the clothes wouldn't be wrinkled for tomorrow's show, but now even he realizes he was dreaming. Discarded clothes hit the ground like spent cartridges.

"Zip me?" Cindy asks. She's crouching next to me, holding one pump in her mouth while she tries to jam the other size six onto her perfect size eight. I zip her, trying not to stare.

"The jig is up," she says in a stage whisper. I nod knowingly, though I think she means "the fix is in." We both suspected it since we first saw the lineup and which outfits were assigned to whom.

"I hear Manson likes pink," I whisper back, but she has heard enough about Chelsea Manson to know I'm making it up.

"I look like a fucking flamingo," she hisses, pointing with a mouthful of shoe at her dress. A horrible pink chiffon. "And check that out," she adds, waving the shoe at Zoë.

In a full-length sable Cartier dress, Zoë, one of the newer girls from Bramalea, looks as good as she ever will with that nose.

"Don't sweat it," I say. "You're still the bee's knees, baby." I'm trying to be helpful, though I don't know what the bee's knees are, or if that's even good.

"Thanks, but I don't care anymore," she says, but I know she does. "This is all bullshit, anyway."

Zipped and shod, Cindy swishes out of the tent, her strides already timed to the music outside. A brave soldier at the Gallipoli of fashion. Which is, of course, a shame, because she's one of the few among us who actually has a chance to win. Most of the other models here are just attractive—one better than good-looking, but one less than pretty.

In this town, to say that you're dating a model is more often than not an admission of failure. Models here would never turn your head at a supermarket or inspire you to push up on the dance floor. Most of the models in Nepean are the girls in your class who sit in aisle seats and never lend their notes, or farmers' daughters, extra-large thanks to country air and potato fritters, grown too big to eat, like prize-winning cornstalks, reluctantly rounded up in trucks and sold to one of the two modelling agencies in the city—Bramalea Talent or DBMI. And Cindy and I both work for the wrong one. Cindy, rumour has it, was iced out of Bramalea for going down on the director's husband after a show. Then again, rumour has it that I go both ways.

"Stacey, shouldn't you be on already?" Tairhun says, still fussing with Sandor's hat.

I peep through a slit in the tent. Otto, on the ramp, seems nervous, keeps glancing back toward the tent. Expecting the cavalry. But my dress shirt's still on its hanger.

"Damn."

I struggle to undo buttons, zip up zippers, snap off hooks. Nothing's worse than being out there too long. It's a small runway, about twelve feet long, shaped like a lowercase t. Not enough room to do anything except walk slowly up and down, slowly because if you walk any faster you'll either look like a caged baboon or else drop off the t into the front row. And the mall's lunchtime crowd, so quick to clap at every pirouette, every new accessory, can turn ugly in seconds. You don't leave a guy out to dry on the runway—it's part of the unwritten code, like lending your socks to the model from the other agency. It's just not done, and I know this, but haste turns fingers into spoons, none of them prehensile. I miss a button and now I have to start over. My mother used to have a saying, written in neat black calligraphy on a cue card taped to the dash of the family Fairmont: "If you're late, don't rush.... You're late already." Good advice. The faster I change, the slower I end up moving. Like in those dreams where you battle to escape from sharks, but you're swimming in chocolate pudding.

I need help with my pants, but Tairhun's too busy plucking lint off Sandor with a handful of rolled-up tape. In his spare time Tairhun teaches the makeup course at Bramalea. Sandor's with Bramalea. Bramalea's affiliated with Chelsea Manson. And Manson runs the Feyenoord Faces contest.

Cindy opens the tent flap. "You know, the chair's still out there."

"What chair?" Tairhun asks from behind Sandor's hat. We all drop what we're doing and peer through the flap.

Zoë forgot to take off the huge red collapsible beach chair put up during the spring scene, and there it is, on the left end of the *t*. Otto's at the top of the ramp, cruising nonchalantly around it, pretending it's part of the set.

"Stacey! Take it with you when you come off," Tairhun says, pushing me toward the flap. "Don't worry. Here." He throws me a pair of sunglasses. "You're done. Go!"

On the mike Sandrine the announcer, cool as ever, talks about the construction of the vest, what other accessories would be hot. She's an old pro. She could go on for hours. Otto's still there, doing laps up and down the tiny ramp, opening and closing his jacket like a goldfish gasping for oxygen. As we pass each other on the stairs, he shoots me a glare that would fry onions. I mouth "Sorry" and step up onto the runway.

For some reason the runway is also called the ramp, which evokes images of takeoffs and landings. Magical properties. Models suddenly gifted with the power of flight. "Ramp" is a strange name for something that's totally horizontal. A perceptual illusion. It bends light, it's curved, it's tilted, enabling models to ascend or descend to different levels.

"And here we have the last of our outfits from Merriweather's," Sandrine announces.

Up the ramp I go, look side to side. Like a hammerhead. Trying not to slip on smooth masking-taped soles. After the show, I'll return the shoes, minus the tape, to Stetton's for a full refund, satisfaction guaranteed, although I'll probably have to go all the way to the east-end outlet because it's show season and they're starting to recognize my face.

"At work, rest, or play this beautiful jacket from Merriweather's Men's Boutique is guaranteed to impress. One hundred percent wool, double-knit, with invisible stitching."

I'm in full stride, attempting to get my groove on, but the music's too fast. Techno at two hundred beats per minute, and the treble speakers aren't working. From far away it sounds like a bass drum player on speed—*boom boom boom boom* till he's dragged offstage by the rest of the orchestra. It's like taking a stroll on a treadmill stuck on Jog.

"You'll notice the pants," Sandrine says, "pleatless with a slim line that's very popular this spring."

I'm into my pant turn, hoping the hems don't come undone. Of course, they haven't been altered for the show, and Tairhun was too busy with Sandor to fix them. In a panic I taped all the excess material to the inside of the pant leg, but I can feel it loosening with each step. Plant leg left, left hand in pocket, half-turn, hand out of pocket, half smile to the crowd, pivot, walk again.

"The trench coat is fifty percent cotton, warm but breathable, with a removable lining..." I fling off the coat and sling it over my shoulder, exposing the red lining. "Which is always handy when the weather warms up. If the weather warms up."

The crowd chuckles. Sandrine will use the same line tomorrow.

"You can find his sunglasses at In the Shades, located on the third floor, left at the escalators."

I slip them off my eyes onto the top of my head. Finally I can see.

I'm at the top of the *t*, next to the red beach chair. I ignore it, edge carefully around it, pretend it's not there, smiling the whole way. Most guys on the runway don't smile. They try to play cool: smirk, jaw clenched like a fist, hair by "stylists," attitude by Armani. They creep around the runway in a seductive slouch, or else strut a slow goose step, chest out, butt in, fooling no one. This ain't Milan. You can't be cocky in rugby pants, shirts with crests, reversible belts. A big-time model came up from New York to give a runway workshop back when I was starting out, and he told us never to smile; it shows you've got something to hide. But this is Nepean, not New York, and they book me every season for this crap, and smiling's got everything to do with it. When I'm on the runway, it's as if I'm walking past the girl at the bar who I've been eyeing all night. And just when she thinks I'm going to pass her by, *blam!* Turn and give her the smile.

My mother saved up for years for that smile. My teeth were wired in grade five until grade nine when I decided I couldn't afford to talk with bits of carrot and salami dangling from my teeth. My mother was running out of money, anyway, so she didn't put up a fight and I was left with a perfect half smile—top teeth straight like A's, bottom teeth crooked like cops. When I'm on the ramp, I ignore the guys in the crowd, who either like the clothes or don't. I focus on the women, give each a secret smile, as if to say, "I put this outfit on just for you."

When I head back down the runway, I spot an old lady sitting beside a walker. I smile. She smiles back. A group of whistling sisters are gathered near the edge of the ramp. I smile. They'll probably hang around the tent after the show, waiting for me to come out. Mulattos are a rare breed in Nepean. I see a white woman on a bench by the side of the stage. She's so obese she can't close her legs—a roll of fat hangs between her thighs like a marsupial's pouch. I smile, anyway. In the front row at the bottom of the ramp, there's a photographer—an older man, probably from the mall's marketing team, but you never know. I smile. But the camera only clicks when I turn away.

Manson's just sitting down, almost an hour late. I've never seen him in person before, but it isn't hard to pick him out. Today his hair's black. He has a black goatee, streaked with grey. Should I smile? Surely everyone else has tried to catch his eye and wink their way to first place—a one-year contract with Feyenoord.

There are no guarantees in modelling, but Feyenoord models, even the guys, can make almost $150 an hour. You never hear about that kind of money in Nepean. Girls around here make enough to buy their first CD burner, or maybe a custom-made prom dress. Our guys always have other jobs—they're cabinet makers, computer-software designers, government consultants, just modelling to say they can. No full-time models in these parts. Of course, every so often a local girl is sent down to Toronto, never to be heard from again. But a contract with Feyenoord gives any model a name that's worth something. And a name is worth everything in this business.

I decide to play it cool. After all, anybody who knows anything knows the real contest is tomorrow. Tomorrow's show is for the unknowns.

Modelling virgins, culled from travelling mall booths and blurry Polaroids. The winners from today's contest will then be judged against tomorrow's winners. We're the warm-up act, the freak show of this travelling circus. Hurry, hurry, step right up! See the skinny girl with no eyebrows... Come one, come all! Next up, the man with the permanent smile! Tomorrow Manson will beat the bushes for his new Dumbo. The joy, after all, is in the chase. Most of us have already been discovered, and put back. Too small. Too hairy. No hips. Too hippy.

Finding myself in front of him, I grin, after all, but Manson's busy examining his cappuccino. At the edge of the ramp I slip the shades back on. The look-away into the crowd. And there she is—Melody, two rows back, trying to hide behind a pillar outside Fenway Shoes.

I pause. I have to be sure. Everything's brownish-yellow through the tint of cheap sunglasses, but I'm positive it's her. Short, cutting-board blonde, well-leavened breasts swelling under her tight sweater—grey knit, short-sleeved—which I gave her for Christmas. Skin white like rye bread. What's she doing here? And how did she find out about the show? I didn't tell her. I never invite her to any of my shows. Especially this one.

The cameras flash, and I move again, walking up the other side of the ramp. Trying to forget about Melody. A different pose at the top of the t. Hands on hips, staring out into the crowd. Civil servants on lunch, teenagers skipping school, senior citizens with nothing better to do. All staring back at me. What do they see, anyway? They're not looking at Stacey—he doesn't exist anymore. Fashionable metallurgists have broken me down, smelted me, moulded me, sculpted me, into a model. A representation of an object. Perfectly to scale, proportioned in all dimensions. Worthy of imitation. Exemplary. Designed to be followed. Or maybe I'm still there. Essentially Stacey, but made up, dressed, camouflaged, disguised by the art of powerful illusionists, obeah men. Maybe the disguise is really my own. I'm a chameleon. A mimic, like a stick insect, like those yellow-and-black-striped flies that pretend to be bees. I have a recurring nightmare in which I walk down an endless runway. The audience is restless. I attempt to smile, can't stop smiling, face frozen, an impossible rictus stretching from ear to ear, but no one's fooled. The audience sees through my face, howls at the deception, rushes the stage, tears me to bloody ribbons.

Another pause, another halfhearted pant turn, as I await my replacements. Thinking of what to tell Melody. Then Sandor and some girl I don't know, tuxed and gowned, emerge from the tent.

"And that, ladies and gentlemen, concludes the wonderful set from Merriweather's."

Applause. My time's up.

"And finally, bridal fashions from June Jenny's and Tuxaco."

As I hit the stairs, I catch Sandrine's eye. I follow her gaze over my shoulder, see the beach chair still at the top of the *t*. Too late. I'm already on my way down, wondering now if Zoë left it there on purpose.

Back inside I start to hang up my clothes, only doing up the important buttons. My collars are ringed with brown sweat, armpits soggy like cereal.

"Keep them on, put them back on!" Tairhun screams. "The finale! Everyone on together when they announce the winner." He wipes his face with the bandanna draped around his neck. With twelve models furiously changing in a small canvas tent, it's unspeakably hot. But most of us are sweating from the tension.

I stare at the other male models. Otto, Sandor, and three other guys I've worked with but forgotten their names. California blonds, slick-haired Greeks, All-Canadian quarterbacks. Square jaws, undulating abs, even when they aren't flexing. The stuff of shaving-cream ads and truck commercials. I glance at myself in the small mirror. From this angle I look like a badger. Not like the black guys you see in magazines, videos, those ebony princes with strong noses, bald Negroes with chiselled features. I don't stop traffic. I've been dumped by my last three girlfriends.

I'm a mediocre model. Blessed perhaps with fair mulatto skin, fine features, a ski-jump nose, full lips, Barbie-doll eyelashes. With no chance of winning. Yet here I am, the coloured clown in this lunchtime cabaret, ready for my final tumble. Here because of what? Not because of the money. For three years now I've grinned and jigged at every mall in town. Eight-foot-long runways. Freeze modelling, heckled and jeckled by grubby kids, old ladies touching me—is he real?—hockey players flinging boogers from a safe distance, trying to make me laugh. Shoots for *National Wildlife* magazine, direct-mail catalogues, government brochures, posters for the Tulip Festival. Grocery-store mockups and neighbourhood flyers and isn't-he-cute family-friend dinners and "I saw you in oh, what was it again" run-ins at the bus stop. I'm in a model's purgatory, everywhere and nowhere at the same time. The poster boy of mediocrity. Mediocrity's a one-mall town—comfortable and predictable. Every road a dead end.

"Don't forget the props in the bag by your name tag," Tairhun says. "Briefcases or purses, kids. Briefcases or purses."

I rummage through my bag. Cindy's purse, I see, is orange. She looks at me, looks away. Knowing that, for her, it's already over. All around I hear the whispered prayers of the has-beens and never-will-bes. No time to pray. A minute and a half to change.

TWO

I have always lusted after white girls, ever since I was old enough to wash my own sheets. Megan Fegan, taller and a little wider than her sister, Lara, but just as easy. Mo, who used to pay for everything. Agi Popescu, the Romanian cosmetician who just had to see me at least three times a week. The girl who worked in the little card store at Pinecrest Mall, whose name I've forgotten. Rhonda, whose breasts bounced over me like pink water balloons. Cyanne, who came after me one night with a fork.

This girl must have been a model at some point before she gained the weight. Dark hair, pale white skin. Asleep. A baseball cap, SEX DRIVE, pulled low over her eyes. A copy of the *Tao Te Ching* has slipped between her thighs. She reminds me of Melody's ex-roommate, who I desperately wanted to sleep with. A little thicker, much of it in the right places. Once the bathing suits stopped fitting, the agency must have put her out to pasture answering phones and faxing pictures of the younger girls who haven't yet discovered the pill. I can hear the *tico-tico-tac* of her headphones from the doorway.

I'm in a small round room with plenty of light streaming in from a large concave window. There's a gnarled iron table in the centre, and a bench, upholstered in mock Kente cloth, runs along one wall. Facing me, behind the girl, is an enormous white placard, FEYENOORD in yellow lettering, and underneath it in black, PARIS, NEW YORK, MILAN, LOS ANGELES, BUENOS AIRES, TORONTO. The last city is tacked on, seemingly, as an afterthought. And all around the sign are pictures of Feyenoord's finest, plastered peanut-butter-thick on the walls, hurled at crazy angles to stick where they may.

None of these girls are nude, though many are a nipple shy or a shadow away. The girls are blond mostly, some brown, a few red, an occasional yellow or gumball-green. I see one black girl wearing face paint and a buzz cut, body harder than algebra. Girls crouched in corners, chained to rainy streetlamps, covered in webbing, fur, smoke, scarves. Girls with angel wings, devil horns, boxing gloves, and attitudes. One girl, pale, almost translucent, wearing nothing except a sailor's hat made of newspaper perched on her hearse-black hair. She's palming her small breasts, her mouth open, exposing a sliver of tongue, pierced. White teeth. Her naked pubis lurks out of view, cloaked in shadow. She glows like an erotic angel.

"You know, I could make you a copy."

The girl at the desk, awake now, arches an eyebrow, though most of the sarcasm was lost in the plucking. It's possible she was the naked sailor.

"You're late. Almost an hour," she says.

"I thought...Mr. Manson told me twelve o'clock."

"Chelsea? He's lost. I make the bookings. When I say 11:00, that means 10:45. He went out to lunch. Everyone's out to lunch except me." She sizes me up. "This won't take long. Let's go in the back."

I hoist my satchel and follow her dumbly, wheeling my suitcase down the dimly lit corridor. Along the right wall are tables littered with black-and-white prints, loupes, and guillotines. On the left, an office and a plushly decorated bathroom with the biggest mirror I've ever seen. In front of us, a glass door. On it, a tiny piece of paper taped to it: DO NOT ENTER. BOOKINGS IN PROGRESS. She opens the door.

"I'm Rianne. Have a seat."

She pulls a rolling chair toward me, sits down herself at a circular desk with four evenly spaced computers. The walls are lined with comp cards—cardboard ones. The good kind. Rows of portfolios on the shelves. Each book with the model's name labelled plastically to the spine.

"Your book?"

I fish my portfolio out of my satchel. It's a sombre black volume, with DAVIS-BARRON MODELS INTERNATIONAL emblazoned in letters that aren't quite gold. Why INTERNATIONAL I've never figured out. All the DBMI models I know work in Nepean, though rumour has it they sent a girl to Paris once. I open my book to the first page, hand it over open and facing her the way we're taught. I don't know who the hell she is. I give her a smile, but she's already thumbing through the pictures. In a Harry Rosen suit, serious, the young black executive, the caption MAN AT WORK. In a Georgetown sweatshirt and jeans, walking down the street, oozing boy-next-door, hand waving to an imaginary friend. On a cast-iron stool in black Paul Carville, legs wide, cigarette dangling, James Dean with a tan. Snarling in outrageous plaid, stuffed into a white corner, bare-chested except for a bead necklace and a peace sign. The last shot. Army fatigues, waist-deep in snow, opening a can of army rations with an expression of sheer glee. It made the cover of *Guns and Bullets*. A joke shot that my agency insists I take out, the picture I always sneak back in. So the client always leaves with a grin.

Rianne snaps my book shut. Grinless. "I'll have to be honest. First of all, it's obvious you don't have much experience. More important, the market for black guys, it's not really big here yet. Not like New York or Miami. Have you tried there?"

I shake my head, trying to figure out what's going on.

"Anyway, we already have a couple of guys with the same look." She points to a group of photos on the wall of men who look nothing like me. "They get pretty much all the work there is around here. Have you heard of Crispen Jonson? No? He's going to be really big. Huge. The next Simien."

I've heard whispers of Simien. The first black model on the cover of *New York Life*. The next Tyree.

"You know, you might want to try Maceo Power. It's a smaller agency, more runway, less print, more overseas stuff. But they're not bad. I'll take a comp card." She slips the floppy paper card with several shrunken pictures of me along with my measurements out of the portfolio sleeve. "I'll pass it on to Chelsea. Thanks for coming all the way here..." She stands and takes my hand. I feel a pang of lust so bad it actually hurts. "There's a party tonight at the Garage. Models, photographers, stylists, mostly. If you're still in town, you should come out."

Still shaking her hand, I try again. "I'm not sure...I was supposed to see Mr. Manson. He told me to come here. To work. I'm Stacey Schmidt?" Hoping my name will ring a bell.

"You're not here for the eleven o'clock open call?"

"No. I met Mr. Manson at the Feyenoord Faces contest."

"The contest? You mean...are you the winner?"

"No." Trying to decide if her emphasis was on *winner* or *you*. "I was at the contest in Nepean. Mr. Manson saw me and told me he could find me work here in Toronto."

"Modelling work?"

I don't dignify that with an answer.

Rianne sits back down, swivels to a computer, and clatters at the keyboard. "There's no note. He didn't mention anything." She gazes at me again. "Well, like I said, Chelsea's lost."

"Can I wait for him at least? If he's just having lunch..."

She laughs. "Chelsea used to have a sign up that said OUT TO LUNCH. IF NOT BACK BY DINNER, OUT TO DINNER. Trust me. He won't be back for a while." Wheeling around to her computer again, she adds, "I might as well get your measurements then. Age?"

"Twenty-one."

"Height?"

"Six-one."

"Weight?"

"One seventy-five."

"Jacket?"

"Forty-two tall."

"Waist?"

"Thirty-two."

"Inseam?"

"Thirty-four."

"Crotch?"

"What?"

"Just kidding." She grins mischievously. "Sports?"

"Tennis, skiing, rugby, volleyball, football, horseback riding..."

Rianne glances up at me, then continues typing.

"Do I have to name them all? Everything except basketball and golf."

"Fine. Any special talents? Singing? Acting?"

I think for a minute. "Well, I play the cello. And I'm a pretty good photographer."

"We'll just put no. Keep your portfolio, and when you meet Chelsea, we can talk about putting together a new book, new comp cards, and everything else."

That smacks of money.

"If you're going to be working here, I'll give you this." She hands me a Feyenoord appointment book: small, white, plain except for FEYENOORD in bold black letters. I tuck it into my satchel.

"The best thing..." Rianne looks at my bags. "Where are you staying, by the way?"

"Mr. Manson said he would take care of that."

"Figures. The model apartments are full right now. What you could do, though...I know a couple of guys who might have room. I'm sure Crispen and Augustus wouldn't mind."

Rianne picks up the phone. I search the wall for my would-be hosts. Crispen and Augustus aren't hard to find. Two chocolate chips in a bowl of ice cream.

"Busy." She hangs up. "They don't live far." She draws a rough map on the back of a cheque marked VOID. It's made out to Jeanette Grenier for $2,554.35. "While you're there, tell them Eva from Greece will be here tomorrow morning at 9:30. That means they should get here at 9:15. Make sure and tell them that. Nine-fifteen. And tell Breffni to pack a smile. He'll know what I mean. And here." She scribbles some numbers on the back of the cheque. "My number. In case you need anything."

From beneath her hat it's hard to tell if anything means a hair dryer or a hand job.

Suddenly buffeted by the nuclear winds of the subway, I sway perilously close to the pit below. Grey steel, brown pools, yellow wrappers, and I've heard there are rats. The subway skrees to a stop. Crowds lunge. I hoist my suitcase onto my head like an African porter, follow the surge and grab an awkward slice of the pole. Through a corner of the window I spot a mother, a child, and its balloon rising at the top of the escalator. The mother sees the train coming and starts sprinting, dragging the child, who goes limp with the instincts of a kitten. But three chimes, the doors snap, and "Osgoode next!" We lurch into the night, packed like cigarettes.

All around me, many hues and shades of Africans. The popcorn staccato of Chinese. A nun with a small beard circulates through the car selling cookies. A short bald man in a spotless baseball uniform cleans out his ear and smells his finger in disbelief.

With one hand I search for my new Feyenoord book, pull it out, imagine it overflowing with appointments, go-sees, shoots, contacts, names, and numbers. Sharon Davis and Liz Barron, the important halves of Davis-Barron Models International, said my smile would be worth a fortune in Toronto. Said it smiling, thinking of their five percent of everything. Peering at my empty appointment book, I'm skeptical. I don't believe much at face value. I don't accept things until I see them for myself. A glass of water drunk upside down curing hiccoughs. Energizer batteries actually lasting longer. Catalogue shoots really running more than an hour as promised. Modelling is a business built on broken pledges. They guarantee you the moon and hand you a match.

All Sharon and Liz told me before leaving was to be careful, and to be myself. Advice as useful as aromatherapy. I'm not the country cousin. I did, after all, live in Montreal for almost a year. And why would I want to be myself, anyway, when the point of leaving is to leave myself, to slough off my old life like a snake skin?

A sudden stop and I swing halfway around the pole like a stripper.

Outside, confused by the *boo-blahs* of angry taxis, the greasy streets sweating rivulets of people, the smell of onions and ketchup, I stand in the backwash of a bus and have to move. Left or right, I don't know. I feel as if an invisible man is throwing sand in my eyes. Rianne said the apartment was only about two hundred yards from the bookstore. But two hundred yards is as good as a mile when you don't know where you're going.

There seems to be no way to cross Bloor Street. Lexuses and BMWs, distracted by falling stock prices and cell phones, ignore streetlights. I follow a small knot of pedestrians. We cross halfway against the light, straddling the painted yellow lines, until the winking of brake lights promises safety. We weave between the stopped cars like hyenas among the wildebeest, nervous, skittish, ready to evade a sudden charge until we reach the sanctuary of the sidewalk.

Everywhere bums gumming for change. Some stretched out in sunny corners. Others curled up in alleyways like withered leaves.

A woman on the corner wears a DIET BY PHONE placard over her suit like armour, a playing-card soldier from Wonderland. I've never seen so many young Asians. Chinese men with walkie-talkies and cell phones. Korean women in Donna Karen mini-suits, hair tinted gold or red.

I'm almost run over by a procession of squealing kids. They're on a field trip. Arms linked with string. Behind them their teacher leads them like huskies past me through the streets.

An old turtle stands on a welcome mat strumming a banjo, croaking

"H-e-e-y, J-u-u-u-d-e." The joints of the arthritic microphone are bent at impossible angles. "Spare some change, bro?"

I shake no and smile, wondering how he can afford an amp and a speaker when he can't, according to the crumpled placard, afford a meal.

"Nigger," he mutters, and stretches his song toward the next passerby.

I'm genuinely shocked. Usually bums are the only strangers you ever meet who wish you a nice day. They know most people will pass by twice. I have no witty rejoinder. I have only my Feyenoord appointment book and shiny sneakers to testify on my behalf. I can't escape. I have to wait in front of him to cross the street.

The door opens before I even have a chance to knock. He's even bigger in real life. His pop-out chest is more impressive in 3-D than his picture on the agency wall, half-naked and oiled, posing in an old gilded mirror. His biceps bulge under a small blue Kool and the Gang T-shirt. His legs are as thick as thieves. But somehow his head seems too big for his body. And his nose looks too big for both.

"You can hear the elevator opening from inside the apartment," he says, opening the door wide. "The buzzer downstairs doesn't work. The elevator door's our early-warning system."

"In case any of his women come knocking, he has time to hide," a voice says from inside. Two male laughs.

"G'way," he says, smiling. "Come in. Rianne called and said you were coming." He grabs my suitcase with one hand, and it flies upward of its own volition. "I'm Augustus." He offers me his other hand. His grip is surprisingly soft. His voice rumbles so deep I can feel it in my ass. "But most of my friends call me Biggs. It's Stacey, right?"

"Yeah. Stacey Schmidt."

"Cool. Welcome to our house." He pronounces it *hoose.*

The apartment is small, carpeted with clothes of all kinds. The walls are bare, and there's no furniture except a wide white couch and a tiny TV as large as a parking attendant's security monitor.

"There's not much left," Augustus says, gazing around. "Most of the crap was Simien's, and he took it yesterday. Tour?"

The other two are sprawled behind the couch, opposite each other. Feet almost touching. A small bowl of lumpy dip between them. They're sharing a cigarette. Everything smells of sweetgrass.

Augustus points. "The white guy's Breffni. Negro's Crispen." Breffni, brown-haired, stubbled, impossibly blue eyes almost glowing. He's naked from the waist up. A jeans commercial. Crispen, shorter, darker than I am, bald, beautiful lips, almond-shaped eyes, and a gold earring. He's dressed as if he should be either hitting a home run or robbing a liquor store, and has a toothpick stabbing out of the side of his mouth.

"Stacey." I put out my hand, but it seems as if neither will get up for a while.

"The fresh meat," Crispen says, taking a drag, passing the joint to Breffni. "Want some? In there."

I open the fridge, hoping to find more dip, but all I see is a stick of butter, some milk, and a plastic bag of what appears to be oregano. I begin to doubt it's oregano. Without warning Breffni applies his spoon to Crispen's face, and the two roll toward the wall in a ball.

"They'll be all right in half an hour or so. Simien's supposed to be out of his room by tomorrow, so until then you can throw your stuff here." Augustus motions to a stained corner. "Shower's in here."

"Rules," Crispen gurgles from the floor.

"Right," Augustus says, barring the bathroom door with one arm. "One. When you leave the apartment, don't lock the door. Simien has the only key. Two. When you finish the milk, don't just put a new bag in, cut the damn top open, too. Three—" he indicates the toilet "—we're guys. We miss. That's fine. But either clean it up, or do it sitting down like a bitch. Got it, Pappa?"

"Sure." There are brown mushrooms growing in the carpet behind the bowl.

"Lucky Charms!" Breffni shouts, mouth full of dip.

"Oh, yeah. Lucky Charms are Breff's. Touch them and he'll touch you. Of course, he only likes them 'cause they got a picture of a little Irish dude on the cover. Keeps him in touch with his heritage."

"'Tis troo," Crispen quips in a cartoon Irish accent. He and Breffni both clutch their sides, dissolve into a pool of laughter.

Augustus shrugs. "Like I said, they'll be okay in a half hour or so. Shower?"

The shower has almost no pressure. I feel as if I'm being watered. I pump some soap from an industrial-size tube. If the black dot on the tub is moving, it's a snail. It's hard to tell what's in motion and what's not. I'm so weak with hunger, my brain is a loaf of bread. I don't even feel wet when I step out of the shower.

"You want some?"

"Sure."

Crispen hands me the joint. I rarely smoke up, but I figure if I can't get food, at least I can get high. I fumble, burn my fingers, then pass the roach to Breffni, who inhales expertly. Filling his cheeks like a horn player.

"So what happened to that girl you were with, Biggs?" Crispen asks Augustus. "She was fine."

"Gave her the boot. Possum lover. She played dead." Turning to me, he asks, "You have a woman?"

"No." Thinking about Melody. "I wouldn't mind working on that girl at Feyenoord, though."

"Specifically..." Breffni says, scooping another finger of lumpy batter from his bowl.

"The booker. What's her name?"

Scowls of collective disgust.

Breffni groans. "Shawna?"

"No. What's her name...Rianne? She gave me her number."

Degrees of laughter all around.

"She's as easy as pie," Breffni snorts.

"Rianne's not our booker, by the way," Augustus says. "Rianne books the girls' shoots. Shawna books ours. But by all means, go for it, Pappa. You're just the kind of guy who'd make her runny. Damn, I'm in the mood! Let's go out. Any of you have to be up tomorrow?"

"That reminds me," I say. "Rianne told me to tell you guys we have some kind of go-see tomorrow morning." I scan the room for my Feyenoord book, but my eyes can't seem to keep up with my head. "Someone from Greece at 9:30."

"Probably Eva again," Crispen says. "I ain't goin'. You?"

Augustus shakes his head.

I frown. "Are you guys mad?" I can't believe what I'm hearing. Elite college football players skipping the NFL draft to join the pro bowling circuit. "Europe's the big ticket."

"Europe's a sham, man," Breffni says. "Guys have to pay their own way. By the time you cover rent, food, and smokes, there's nothing left to take home. I have all the pictures I need for my book. This is the place to be, my fine feathered friend. Commercials. Movies. Hollywood without the beaches, tits, and cars. You can't go to the can without pissing on someone who's casting for something. Europe's just pretty pictures. And kick-ass herb."

"Have you ever done any movies?" I ask.

"When I was a kid in Buffalo, I worked all the time. Cutesy stuff, a couple of small roles in movies. Lots of commercials. Remember the Loony-Roos kid?"

"The kid who wouldn't eat anything that wasn't red? I thought that kid was blond."

"That was me. I dye my hair brown now."

"Damn." Impressed. "Have you been in anything lately?"

"I was Dude Number 4 in a Schlitz spot, and the guy who gets pushed out of the way in *Revenge of the Hammer*. I haven't gotten any speaking roles since high school. My career peaked at age thirteen." He smiles. "It would be funny if it weren't sad. That's why I came to TO. They don't call this Hollywood North for nothing. Forget about overseas."

"They wouldn't take us, anyway," Augustus says.

"Why not?" I ask.

He pulls up his sleeve and rubs his arm.

"What's that?"

"Skin tone."

"You're black, right?" Breffni asks.

"What do you think?" I feel the answer's obvious, even though I still can't figure out whether to capitalize black or put it in quotations.

"You're light-skinned," Augustus says. "Who knows? Maybe they'll like you."

"Like I said," Crispen says, smiling. "Fresh meat. How old are you?"

"Twenty-one. You?"

"Twenty-four."

"You?" I ask Breffni.

"Twenty-four."

"How old are you?" I ask Augustus.

"Older than you."

"Seriously. How old?"

"Seriously old."

I turn to the others. "How old is he?"

Crispen and Breffni exchange glances. "We don't know," they both say.

"How do you not know?"

"He never tells us," Crispen says.

"Put it this way," Augustus adds. "I was doing shoots in New York while you were watching Hammy Hamster."

"If you modelled in New York, what are you doing here?"

"Well," he says slowly, "too many models in New York. I read somewhere that there are more models in the Big Apple than people in Jackson, Wyoming. And there's less competition here. No offence."

"No offence?" Breffni says. "Tell him what kind of modelling you were doing in New York."

"Never mind that, Pappa. Money's money."

Breffni grins gleefully. "Biggs was a hand model."

I did some hand modelling once in an internal video for the Department of National Defence. They had to shoot eighteen takes because I had trouble opening the envelope. The client blamed me. I blame extra-strength tamperproof glue. Hand modelling, like pretty much everything in life, is harder than it seems. I crane my head to study Augustus's hands, but they're now in the pockets of his sweater.

"Don't blame me if people want to pay me serious cash to wear shiny things on my hands. And I'm doing more real modelling now, anyway. Hand modelling's just for the money. So are we out or what?" Augustus asks, standing.

I peer at my watch. Somehow it's already past 11:00. "I think I'll have to pass. I'd better get some sleep if we have to be there for 9:15 tomorrow."

"Forget it," Crispen says. "You'll have plenty of time to sleep when you're dead."

"Yeah, but if I don't sleep, I'll be dead that much sooner."

They're all looking at me. Didn't Rianne say something about the Garage?

"Well, if I go, I have to eat first. I'm starving."

"Me, too," Augustus agrees. "Starvin' like Marvin. Let's get some pizza."

"Pepperoni, Italian sausage," Crispen insists.

"Make it half and half," Breffni says. "Tomato, onion, and zucchini for me."

"Your pizza's getting nastier every time we order, Breff," Crispen says, wrinkling his nose. "Next week it'll be corn, squash, and rice. I don't know how you live on plants and still have any meat on your bones." Breffni is shorter and thinner than the others, but cut like a diamond.

"Protein's in the beans!" Breffni sluices the last of the goop from the bowl into his mouth.

Augustus, holding one end of the receiver, asks, "Do we want free pesto?"

"Throw a shirt on, Breff," Crispen says.

"I can't dress until I hear some tunes," Breffni says. "Let's hear some tunes." He turns to me. I notice one of his nipples is pierced. "C.J.'s a kick-ass DJ. He used to DJ in the States."

"Back in North Carolina," Crispen says. "I got everything from Method Man to Mozart, man."

The house bops to some old Cameo while we dress. I root through my suitcase for my dancing gear, chip a nail on my camera at the bottom. An old Canon, not the best, but good enough to win last year's Nepean Public Library Photo Competition, Amateurs Under Forty. I pull it out. "Will this be safe in this apartment?"

"Safer than if you left it out in the hall, but that's about it," Crispen says.

I stuff it back into the bottom of my suitcase. The little gold travel lock's just enough to delay a would-be thief by the length of a chuckle.

Breffni's still primping long after the three of us are done. We finish off another joint and the pizza while we wait. Both taste like tapestry. For some reason it doesn't seem the least bit strange to be sharing stories and spliffs in a strange city with three strange guys. I suppose I haven't lived long enough for anything to be truly surprising. I wonder if one can go into shock from the experience of moving. If the phrase *comfortably numb* wasn't sung about decades earlier, now would be a good time to dream it up.

"Hurry up, Breff!" Crispen shouts. "When he's doing a show, he can change from a sweater to a tux in less than twenty seconds. But when we want to jet, it takes him an hour. Go figure."

Breffni yells from the bathroom, "Big difference between modelling and real life, right?"

"Just hurry the hell up."

The men's washroom at the Garage is surprisingly similar to the rest of the club. Cold concrete underfoot, hot neon overhead, and tools as far as the eye can see. My stepfather, were he alive, would be prying pliers and spanners off the wall. Even in here there's no refuge from the black light. Constellations of lint glow on my black turtleneck. On the sleeves, long electric filaments from cats long dead. I'm afraid it may appear to be dandruff. Right now I'd trade my shoes for a lint brush.

The taps are operated by unmarked wrenches. I'd like to splash some cold water on my face, but I can't figure out the taps. I puke in the sink instead. Pieces of salami sluice down the drain. I'm tempted to blame the pesto, but I know better. My eyes are infernally red. Then I squawk with dry heaves. I feel as if my soul is passing out of my mouth. There's a young, smartly dressed man standing politely next to me. I try to ask him what pesto is, but it comes out more like "Why I'm pissed." He offers me a towel. I'm not sure if it's pity or his job that motivates him. I compromise by accepting it and giving him a quarter. His expression says that was clearly the wrong move, though whether it's because I gave him money or because I gave him so little, I can't tell.

I check myself into a stall for a half-time pep talk. My game plan is clearly not working. Focus is the key. A comeback, not entirely impossible. Crispen and Breffni are hunting a school of young models. On the dance floor they circle closer and closer like reef sharks. Breffni's after a tall brunette with a fake tan and mechanical breasts. She seems familiar, but they always do. I've had plenty of girls like her, all forgotten. Crispen, tonight's designated pilot fish, will be happy with the leftovers.

I'm still looking for Rianne. I think I saw her by the pool tables. It's possible I bought her a passing rose and told her I'd like to put my finger in her pie. She may have slapped me.

Augustus leads a line dance. "Bring it back!" he shouts, twirling like a Four Top as eager secretaries and fresh divorcées shyly try to follow his Cabbage Patch, his Electric Slide, unsure of themselves, but having a ball, just happy to be retroactively learning the latest steps, thrilled to be tutored by a certified Master Negro. Augustus ignores the glares from the other dancers around them, from those too young to remember when Michael Jackson was still black. He's in a zone. He doesn't care as long as he's spinning and winning on the baseline. Scoring, for one. "The roof, the roof, the roof is on fire..."

And, giggling, one by one, his understudies join in, only mouthing the words at first, then, Long Islands and Blue Lagoons later, screaming out, "Burn, motherfucker, *buuuuuurn!*"

We're huddled on the couch for warmth like baby rats. The stereo's still on—"Single Life" stuck on repeat. "Single guys, clap your hands!" over and over. We're too tired to turn it off.

I prod Crispen, who's on my thigh, but he seems to have passed out. Breffni's still talking about the brunette and the fight her boyfriend picked with him outside the bar, quickly unpicked when Augustus walked their way. No one's listening.

"So where do I sleep?" I ask.

Augustus points to a thin mattress leaning against the wall. I notice he's wearing gardening gloves.

"Why the mitts?"

"Keeps 'em steamin' fresh," Crispen says, stirring at last. His chuckle turns to heaves. He grabs Breffni's bowl. Its new contents are indistinguishable from the old.

"Don't laugh, Pappa," Augustus says. He peels off a grey glove, exposes a ring. It looks as if it cost more than I do.

"Half an hour of turning faucets and flushing toilets. No stylists, no makeup. Fast and dirty. Easy money."

"You wear makeup?"

"On my hands?"

"On your face."

"Powder. Don't you?"

"No." I've never touched a spore of makeup in my life. I didn't even know powder came in brown. All of a sudden I'm nervous about tomorrow's go-see. I'm playing in the majors now. Can't afford a strikeout at my first at-bat. "What'll we have to do for that woman tomorrow?"

"Eva?" Augustus says. "The usual. She'll peek at your portfolio, make you do a couple of laps, then tell you there's not a big market for your type in Greece."

"Don't worry," Crispen slurs. "You'll be fine. You know how to walk, right?"

Suddenly I'm not so sure. In Nepean, cock of the walk. In Toronto, a shambling mound, lurching up and down the ramp to the tune of snickering models and simmering clients.

"Give me a professional demo," I say to Crispen. "Just for fun." But he's lapsed back into unconsciousness. "Augustus?"

"I don't do shows."

"Why not?"

"I'd break the clothes. Breff's the man."

"I've lost the use of my legs."

"Come on, Pappa," Augustus wheedles. "Show 'em how it's done."

Breffni slides off the couch. "You know the drill. Head straight. Stomach in. Pretend you have a tail and tuck it between your legs. And just walk."

He doesn't walk. He glides. As if he were a passenger on a moving sidewalk. Up and down the living room, looking side to side, while Cameo's single ladies clap their hands. Until he walks into the wall and collapses.

"Well, that's my cue for beddy-bye," Augustus says.

"Me, too," Crispen says, awake again.

Breffni hasn't moved. It doesn't look as if he will until morning.

I turn off the stereo, pull the mattress off the wall, lie down. It's like sleeping on a playing card. "Do you have a sleeping bag or some kind of foam to put under this thing?" I ask anyone.

"What are you? The princess and the pea?" Crispen growls, still on the couch. "Stop complaining and turn the lights off."

It's dark and cold and they're snoring in stereo. Breff is herking and jerking on the floor next to me, no doubt chasing women in his sleep. I'm still high as a weather balloon. My bed's spinning. Doubts and misgivings are pulled from the recesses of my mind by centrifugal force. From this mattress the life of a Toronto model appears as glamorous as laundry. I'd like to press Save at this point in my life, just in case things don't work out, in case this was all a big mistake. I'm messing with a fragile balance, I have to move carefully. Life itself is too good to be true, and if I were to think about that too hard, I'm afraid God would catch on and pull the plug. Good luck isn't always as simple as it seems. Payback's a mother. The mean happiness quotient takes care of that. That's the average level of happiness I'm allowed to maintain in my life. I'm a firm believer in the principle of Even Steven. Like a sitcom hero, after a few adventures, I always return to the status quo. Tomorrow, with Feyenoord, the chance to become a one-name model. Iman. Elle. Instantly recognizable. Stacey. Any more good luck will skew the quotient. Something's got to give. Things, if left to themselves, always even out in the long run.

THREE

I knew I was in trouble last winter when I first noticed the hairs growing out of my shoulders. The first strands, long and curly, were misplaced pubes. Now I have two fine epaulettes of black hair—a matching set to go with my legs and chest. I'm as hairy as a tarantula.

"You're the hairiest brother I've ever seen," Augustus says, accosting me on the way to the shower. "Turn around, Pappa. Come out here. Check him out." He pulls me with one arm into the living room where Breffni and Crispen are slurping cereal.

"Ugh," Breffni says. "Put him away. We're eating."

"Ever think of shaving?" Crispen asks.

"Cream's the ticket," Augustus says.

I saw a tube of Augustus's cream in the bathroom. Lye, thinly diluted with the promise of vitamin E. The warning, if it had one, would read: "Do not combine with skin. Not for internal or external use. If ingested, induce vomiting and call next of kin." No thanks. I'd live with my fur. All the models these days shave, pluck, or wax. But as we all know, fashion works in cycles. Hairiness used to be next to godliness, considered by many a sign of virility. At least it was in those old sitcoms and pornos. Surely the trend of making all male models as smooth as marshmallows must come to an end. And when it does, I'll be ready, my coat, glossy and neat, my puffs of shoulder hair, angel wings.

I slink back into the shower. To my surprise, yesterday's trickle of hot water is a monsoon. All of my anxieties about the morning's go-see swirl clockwise down the drain. My penis sings in the rain. Back out, covered in a T-shirt and sweater, I tell them about the wood lice in the bathroom.

"Wood lice?" Augustus asks, incredulous.

"Are they contagious?" Breffni is only half kidding.

"Only if you're made of wood," Crispen says.

"They don't actually eat wood. They live on rotting vegetable matter. They're attracted to moisture and dark corners. So let's try to leave the door open from now on."

"How come you know so much about bugs?" Crispen asks.

"My mother's a zoologist."

"That sounds serious. What happened to you?"

"I thought I wanted to follow in her footsteps when I was young, but I failed grade nine science for salting all the worms and I never recovered."

"So what'd you do in school?" Crispen asks.

"I took psych, concentrating on the biological basis of behaviour. But I started looking at myself like I was a stranger, so I dropped out. And here I am. Now can I get some food? We're going to be late."

I eye the bag of Lucky Charms, but Breffni warns me off with a look. I reach instead for the bag of desiccated generic flakes of corn on the top shelf, pour them into the only bowl left, a tea cup, then jump back in horror.

"Don't worry," Crispen says. "The black ones are lucky."

I dump the bowl into the sink and settle for some leftover bee spittle on toast.

"You look like you could use a caffeine suppository," Crispen says. "You'd best perk up. This is the big day. Your first cattle call. Your first taste of who's hot and who's snot. And you'll get to meet Chelsea Manson."

"Don't trust Manson," Breffni warns. "He'll steal the eye out of your head. But he's a good agent. At least the clients seem to like him. And that's really all that matters. As long as he gets the bookings. But he's gotta like you, or you're done."

It's only 8:30, and already I'm stressed. I pop some vitamin C for courage and some iron for good luck. "By the way, I took a message for Simien from Feyenoord while you guys were sleeping." I wave the pink piece of paper. "What do I do with it?"

Augustus smiles. "What do we do with messages for Simien, C.J.?"

"We put it in his in-box." Crispen takes the slip of paper, holds it aloft for a second, then lets it waft slowly into the bin by his side.

I frown. "That's the garbage can."

Crispen nods. "Indeed."

"Well, if he asks, what do I tell him?"

"Don't worry about him. Just concentrate on your audition. Are you going to wear that?"

"You don't like it?" I glance at my lucky sweater. It got me hired at Moore's and laid in Syracuse.

"You need something tighter, so they can see your body," Crispen says. "This isn't a flippin' Christmas pageant. They'd have us parading around naked if it were legal."

I check out what they're wearing. Breffni's baby blue T-shirt is almost transparent; Crispen's yellow one clings like a wetsuit.

"Remind me to take you shopping," Crispen says. "You can wear one of mine for now. Just try not to sweat, okay?"

I admire myself in the windowpane outside the agency. In this V-neck shirt even I have muscles. The only flaws are my chest hairs sprouting above the low-cut shirt like weeds.

"And there's the lovely and talented Crispen Jonson. You'll do our show, *n'est-ce pas?*"

The speaker and another man are coming out the door as we mount the steps. The one with the scarf grabs Crispen by the collar and teases him about the time he went on without his shoes. The other one, the guy wearing what appears to be a uniform from a Chinese prison, stares at me but says nothing. Breffni trails sullenly behind us, still annoyed at being woken up just for this.

"It's a zoo in there," the one with the scarf says, turning to the rest of us. "Chelsea didn't tell us he was holding a cattle call at the ranch, or we wouldn't have come. He didn't even offer us treats. Anyhow, have to go. See you." He points at Crispen. "Next week." And they're off down the stairs.

"Who are they?" I ask.

"The Zaks brothers," Crispen says. "Tom's a designer. His brother—I forget his name—is a stylist. They're good, and they put on great shows. I'd be surprised if they don't book you, the way Tom's brother was checking you out. They like to add a dash of pepper to their shows."

Breffni catches up to us. "They're not that good, their shows are weird, and they pay lousy."

"But they always hire the nicest-looking women," Crispen says. "And there's free booze."

The hall inside is wall-to-wall models. One of them bumps into Crispen and gives him a punch of recognition. "Are you doing the Felicity show this year?"

"Every year," Crispen tells him.

"Maybe this time we'll, like, actually be wearing clothes," the new-comer says, laughing. "See you there." He disappears into the crowd.

"You do a lot of shows," I say.

Crispen shrugs. "They like my walk. I don't know why. I never learned how to do it or anything. They just seem to like it."

"He usually walks with a toothpick in his mouth," Breffni says.

"With a toothpick?"

"It was one of my first shoots," Crispen says. "I was nervous and forgot to take it out. And they loved it. So I do it sometimes, so people know it's me. Kind of like a trademark."

"What else do you do?" I ask, hoping to glean some last-minute tips before it's my turn.

"I can't...there's no room in here. We have to check in first, anyway, tell them we're here. It's first come, first served unless you have a shoot today."

"Last time Eva was here I grew a beard waiting in line," Breffni says.

Thin flamingoes and burly Bobs are lined up in all directions. I grimace. "All these people are ahead of us? It's not even quarter past nine yet. Why can't we tell them we have to be somewhere?"

"There's no such thing as having to be somewhere unless you have a shoot," Breffni says. "And they'd know if you have a shoot. They book your shoots. Trust me. I've been through it a billion times. All you can do is wait your turn."

Rianne is at the foot of the stairs, clipboard in hand. She's not at her best. She looks about as good as she did at last call the previous night. We make our way over, and Rianne adds our names to the list. She doesn't look me in the eye.

"I'll tell you when to go in." She points to a set of large silver double doors. "In there. When I call you. Crispy, Breff, you know the drill."

We shuffle off, and I grin. "Crispy?"

"If you ever call me that, I'll rearrange your face like you were Mr. Potato Head. I take it from her 'cause I'm paid to."

Crispen herds us toward the wall near the doors where all the other models are loosely lined up. It's as if the cops put out an APB on anyone under twenty-five and over five foot eight. A summons served to all able-bodied models. An old-fashioned cattle call. And the cattle bear the same brand—we're all Feyenoord models. There are so many of us that I can't believe there's enough work to feed everyone, let alone the other models from the other agencies in the city. I pray for a model-borne plague and carnivorous runways. A model-eating lizard.

"Breff..."

Breffni turns. Rianne is on the stairs. She touches the corners of her lips and pulls them up in a smile. If she were any greener, she'd look like the Joker.

"Why am I even here?" Breffni mutters.

"Why are you here?"

"He's here," Crispen says, "because if he doesn't come, he knows they'll never put him up for any auditions he actually wants. Business is business, but they're petty like that. It looks bad for them if their best models are all no-shows. That's why I go through this crap every year."

"How come Augustus got out of it?"

"Biggs? He'd be here if he thought he had a chance. But every year, when the Europeans make their rounds, they always tell him the same thing. He's too big to fit the clothes. I keep telling him to bulk down, but he just keeps getting bigger. I think he's addicted to being huge."

"Maybe the muscles have actually grown over his brain," Breffni suggests. "They're slowly squeezing it into juice."

"I think he's like that creature from that cartoon. He absorbs all the rejection. All the negative energy just makes him bigger."

We stand shoulder to shoulder, surrounded by guys in their twenties and fifteen-year-old girls in cutoff T-shirts. Exposed navels. Illegal thoughts.

"How old are these girls, anyway?" I ask.

"Impossible to tell without carbon-dating," Breffni says.

"Young enough to need a permission slip from their parents." Crispen grabs my head and whispers in my ear. "See that guy?" He points into the crowd.

"The guy with the blond hair?"

"Yeah, he's garbage. Can't walk. About as much talent as a Japanese rock star. Don't trust him. Last time we were at a shoot he gave me a piece of gum that makes your breath smell like puke. All day everybody kept moving away from me, and I couldn't figure out why no one wanted to be on my side of the group shot. He said it was a joke, and we all laughed about it, but I heard him later in the change room talking to one of the ad guys about my stinking breath. But don't worry, pretty boy," he says in the general direction of the tall blond, "when you least expect it..."

"Watch your tongue, C.J.," Breffni says. "If people hear you and he happens to break his face, they'll be after you." To me, he adds, "Not only do the walls have ears, they have fists. It's a small world, modelling. Everybody knows everybody."

"Payback..." Crispen nods, still glaring at the blond. Then he peers at me. "How did you get into this crazy business, anyway?"

"It's a long story."

"We have forever."

"Well...the abridged text? This girl Melody got me into it."

"Girlfriend?"

"Ex-girlfriend. She told me I was good-looking enough to be a model. I wanted to find out if that was true. So I did."

"And how'd you end up here?"

"The Faces contest."

"You won Faces?"

The tone of incredulity whenever I mention Faces is beginning to grate. "No. Manson spotted me and told me I could work here. No guaranteed contract or anything." I look at Crispen. "What about you? How'd you get here?"

"Later. I think Rianne just called my name."

Crispen pushes through the throng and disappears into the room. I follow behind him to the silver doors. They aren't closed all the way, and through the crack I glimpse flashes of Crispen as he struts for his hidden audience. It's the strangest walk I've ever seen, in that he doesn't have one. He just walks the way he walks—lopsided, two full sneakers of attitude, and fully toothpicked.

"Chelsea spotted him in a bar in North Carolina." Breffni is beside me, peeking through the doors.

"What was Crispen doing in North Carolina? And what was Chelsea doing there?"

"Chelsea? I'm not sure. I think his lover at the time was a freshman at one of the universities. He used to fly to Raleigh every second weekend. Crispen was going to school there till he got kicked out."

"For what?"

"Not my place to tell. You'll have to ask him."

Breffni and I each get a door in the forehead as Crispen pushes against them from the inside.

"Already?" I ask. He couldn't have been in there more than three minutes.

"It only takes five seconds to say no and two minutes to explain why. I'll meet you guys outside."

"Stacey?" Rianne flaps her hand at me. My turn.

Eva is disappointingly plain. She's a tanned, greying woman, wrinkled like her green scarf. She smells of cigar, and her eyebrows are pulled taut like bows. "Hello, dear. Please sit," she says in an accent I assume is Greek. Her mouth moves, but her eyebrows don't. She motions to the stool in front of her.

I hand her my book. She flips through without lingering on any of the shots. The kiss of indifference. Hope evaporates like milk.

"Very nice, thank you. Would you walk for me, please?"

The room has its own mini-ramp, raised carpeted blocks that form a capital L. I do my best, but between Breffni's advice and Crispen's example, my confident walk becomes a limp. My hips are out of joint, my arms feel six feet long. They swish uselessly at my sides, and my smile at the top of the L catches her checking the clock on the wall. I would have done better to crawl along the ramp on all fours or wriggle up and down it like a snake. At least I would have arched those impossible eyebrows, earned a story over cocktails back in Greece. My shoulders slump, my feet are broken. I keep moving until she delivers the coup de grâce—a curt thank-you. Returning to my perch on the stool, I'm ready to be dismissed.

"You seemed much more relaxed at the end. That's good."

"I guess resignation can be a relaxing influence."

She smiles. "You have a nice look but not much experience. And, to be honest, there isn't a big market for blacks with us right now. But if you plan on coming to Greece, please give us a call."

She doesn't specify who "us" is, or give me any way of reaching them, but it's better than "Are you sure you want to be a model?"—the line one of my friends in Nepean was slapped with at his last go-see.

I slide off the stool, feeling as if I'm still on the ramp—eight inches off the ground, drunk on adrenaline. I'm more excited by this first failure in Toronto than I was by my first success in Nepean. I might have struck out, but at least I'm in the game. I push through the doors, too hard maybe, nailing a peeping model on my way out.

Chelsea Manson's goatee is gone and his hair is now silver, but he's still wearing black and laughing at everything. Like those sinister characters in black-and-white movies who find everything funny. Then he stops laughing. "But where's Simien? He hasn't checked in for a couple of days."

I shrug. "He...I haven't seen him yet. He doesn't really live with us anymore." I wonder if I've said too much.

"Well, where the hell is he then? He missed a shoot yesterday. Just didn't show up. He's never done that before. Did you give him the message?"

"I never got any message. I just got in yesterday."

"Right, right."

Manson laughs. "But listen," he says, scribbling a date, time, and name. "This is for Thursday. Make sure he gets it. His phone isn't working, his pager isn't working. I'm thinking about sending pigeons." He laughs again. "But enough of that. How did it go with Eva?"

"She told me to look her up if I ever get to Greece."

"Too bad. Well, don't worry. You're beautiful. We'll get you ready in time for Kameleon."

"What's that?"

"Kameleon? That's the day Kameleon Jeans comes to town."

"Who's that?"

"They're the hottest company around these days, ad-wise. You remember those spots with the blind albino guy?"

"No."

"They're huge."

"Where's Kameleon from?"

"Germany, I think."

"And when are they here?"

"In about two months. Plenty of time. You'll be the talk of the town by then. Now let's take a look at your book."

He studies every shot from every angle, chuckles at the last one—me knee-deep in snow. He slides it out of my portfolio and hands it to me. "We won't be needing this one. Give it to your mother. Hmm." He's looking at the shot of me, shirtless, on a deck, supposedly sunning myself. "The chest hair, eh? Yeah, that may have to go." He looks at me. I stare back. "Just a thought." After a moment, he says, "Oh, boy, that's a pretty serious scar on your shoulder. Have you ever thought of surgery?"

"The scar's from surgery."

"Oh, keep it then. Scars are sexy." He laughs once more, snaps the book shut. "Well, we'll have to do some testing. I know a few photographers looking to shoot a couple of creatives soon. But your look is catalogue. That's where you'll be the most marketable. I'll get Shawna to arrange some go-sees with The Bay, Sears, the other big ones, and we'll have to make a new comp card. These old DBMI paper flyers..."

He rips them out of the front pocket of my book. "More souvenirs for Mom. Tomorrow go to Copy Cat and they'll set you up with a new one. Until you get some new shots, you can use this one, this one, and this one." He plucks three shots from my book. "For the front." He grease-pencils an *F* on the top corner of one. "And these two." He marks a *B* on the others. "For the back. Highest quality laser copies. Colour on cardboard, of course. They'll be able to shrink them down to the right size because they have our comp-card format on computer file. It's all done digitally now. Are all these measurements right? And tell them just to use your first name. From now on you're Stacey. There can't be too many other guys around called Stacey.

"We'll want to put you on the next head sheet. Right here." He points to a spot at the top of the poster. All the models' heads are shrunken into little boxes, as in a high-school yearbook. The top row is prime real estate. Oceanfront property. "That'll be about $400, I think. Shawna will give you the exact amount."

Four hundred dollars is more than three times what I shelled out to be on the DBMI head sheet. But in Toronto a head-sheet shot pays for itself with one booking. Feyenoord sends the head sheet off to clients. Clients see the head sheet, ask to see your book. If they like your book, they ask to see you. And then they book you. At more than $100 an hour. The head sheet is a bargain at twice the price. It's like taking an ad out for yourself.

"And here's a voucher book." He hands me a small white loose-leaf volume with the Feyenoord F in black on the cover. "The white copy goes to the client, the yellow one goes to me, the pink you can keep. One of the models can show you how to fill it out. Your hourly rate is—let's make it $150 an hour to start. It's not much, but we'll top it up once clients get to know who you are. Then they'll be lining up all the way down Yonge Street to book you. Of course, twenty-five percent comes off for commission."

I'm still giddy about my rate—$150 an hour would buy a knapsack full of black-and-white film. Maybe even that digital Nikon I've been eyeing for months. I only made $80 an hour in Nepean. But as my elementary arithmetic finally kicks in, I realize that with a twenty-five percent commission I'll be left with about the same amount of cash.

"I'm just wondering. I only paid a fifteen percent commission at DBMI. Where—"

"We charge the standard fifteen percent. Another five goes to DBMI as the parent agency."

I forgot about Sherri Davis and Liz Barron. They didn't send me to Toronto for my health. But my calculator is still working.

"Now..."

"The other five percent? Contingency fee. To cover the cost of the courier service, sending your book off to clients, that sort of thing. If the cost of doing all that is less than the five percent we take off, we give you back the difference at the end of the fiscal year."

"Oh."

"But enough about money. Would you like some tea? Where are you staying?"

"With Crispen, Augustus, and Breffni."

"Is he smoking weed?"

I'm not sure which one he's referring to, but I shake my head, anyway.

"I can smell it on your shirt. Tell him to give it a rest. Listen, before you go, one thing. This city is the Bermuda Triangle of models. A lot of good ones get lost. Drugs, partying, women. Men. You're with Feyenoord now. You represent us. Promise me you're going to keep your ass so clean you fart bubbles." He snorts and slaps me on the back, then calls after me, "On your way out check with Shawna. I think she has something for you today."

The hallway is still bumper-to-bumper with models. I elbow through, going out of my way to step on the toes of Crispen's blond enemy, but he doesn't feel a thing. He's up next.

One might think being dunked on is the most humiliating experience in basketball. Not so. If someone crowns you by dunking on your head, as long as it doesn't look as if you tried too hard to stop him, you can wipe the eggshells from your forehead and jog back on offence. You can still shoot it in his eye—a jumper from the top of the key—then talk some trash. Two points by any other name are just as sweet. Being dunked on is easily forgotten. The shame of having your shot blocked, on the other hand, lasts until you win the next game. It's not only the shot that's being rejected, it's you, your best effort, erased, wiped away by a wave of the arm. The grunt when the basketball hits his hand, the look—is this the best you can do?—and the ball sails away out-of-bounds perhaps, or toward the other basket, the start of a fast break. A four-point turn-around. Return to sender.

I've used up all my moves trying to get past the other guy. My knees snap, crackle, and pop. No warm-up. I'm as flexible as a basketball. I stumble forward, lean backward, unable to gather my legs under me to elevate. I resort to the first move you ever learn, the one they teach you in school, the one you unlearn on the playground. The shot of the desperate and the white. The fadeaway. But I can't fade past him. I'm a flightless Bird. My opponent is bearded and dreaded, with conical calves. He doesn't even bother to swat my shot. Instead he grabs it out of the air with two hands and is on his way before I can call foul or feign a twisted ankle.

The clients, representing Punch Cola, make notes on their clipboards. A line is drawn left to right. A name, perhaps my own, is crossed out.

"Okay, boys, playtime's over. Line up, take off your shirts one at a time, then run some lay-ups or whatever. Show us what you've got."

I slink to the back of the line and peel. The only one skinnier than me is the man with the big black clipboard giving the orders. Each model takes his turn, launching himself at the rim, vaulting on unseen springboards. Dunks, double-clutches, three-sixties. Breffni goes for a reverse lay-up off the glass. Augustus frightens the rim with a tomahawk dunk. Crispen draws a murmur, throwing himself an alley-oop, tucking it neatly into the bottom of the net. He jogs back into line behind me.

"You should've put some cream on your legs," he whispers. "You're ashy like Vesuvius."

I nod. Right now I have bigger things to worry about than my dry legs. It's almost my turn.

"And thanks for the shoes." Crispen hands me back my sneakers. He forgot his.

I lace the sneakers slowly. Like a boxer desperately down on points, I'm reduced to swinging wildly, going for the bomb. On my rare Sunday-afternoon forays onto the basketball court I can usually convince the ball over the rim on the third or fourth attempted dunk, at least on the outdoor hoops bent by the weight of hard-core ballers and kids with chairs. But in recent years basketball rims have receded like my hairline. This elementary-school hoop is shrouded in clouds. Seagulls circle overhead. I think back to high-school days, track and field, sixth place in the class high-jump finals. I breathe. I measure. I run. But my approach is all wrong. More like a triple jump—unnatural, three-legged. The ball and I sail under the rim, through the mesh, and into the wall. Thankfully it's padded with a blue mat. I peel myself off, leave a vertical pond of sweat on the plastic. Lucky for me the poster Punch Cola hastily taped to the wall doesn't come down. Bruised, ashamed, I trot to the back of the line. If I weren't brown, I'd be red. I don't get another attempt.

"Schmidt, Battis, thank you very much. Everyone else I call, please grab a blue script from the table. The rest, take a white one."

Battis, the other first-round cut, is lanky and pale. He's the only model on whom my crossover move actually worked. It's a long walk out of the lineup to the wall with the watercolors where our bags are lying. The other models try not to look at us; some are already reading through the script and practising the line. It's at moments such as these that one wishes for the existence of transporter beams. Spontaneous combustion. I don't even bother to change. I stuff my bag and hoist it onto my shoulder. Behind me the man with the big clipboard shouts, "Please slate for the camera! Your name, agency, look left, look right. Then read the line. And keep your shirts off, please."

The wood lice are hiding, and the mushrooms under the bowl toilet have been harvested. I'm alone in the bathroom, waiting for the others to come home. The longer they're at the audition, the more aware I become that I'm not.

I haven't cried since the day my father gave us his new phone number, and I chuckle as the tears snail down my face. I didn't expect to land the role. After all, what are the chances of a rookie grabbing a speaking part in a national soft-drink commercial? A commercial worth hundreds up front, thousands in residuals. Why Shawna sent me out for an audition casting for basketball players is beyond me. It reminds me of my humbling high-school gym class, being picked by substitute teachers to demonstrate basketball drills. They always looked baffled when I said I couldn't play, as if I'd told them I couldn't walk. Being embarrassed on the basketball court this morning isn't the thing that hurts—I'm used to that by now. Nor is it being rejected for the role. What's bugging me is being denied the chance to say the line. I don't know what the line is. I don't even know if I'd have been any good. But they'll never know, because they didn't even give me a shot. I feel like a kid watching his helium balloon drift over rooftops and telephone poles. At the audition the rope slipped through my fingers, and right now it seems like the single biggest injustice in the world.

My razor's still lying in a puddle on the counter, covered in grains of black beard and drifts of shaving cream. I pick it up. I'm even lighter in this mirror. My pelt, even more noticeable than I thought. It would be so easy. I'd be reborn, hairless as a chick. Smooth as the top of my feet. A Samson in black-and-white negatives, empowered by the trimming of my hair. Lightly I pass the razor over my chest, millimetres from my skin, not close enough to cut. Over the nipples, the lubrasmooth strip angled low. I listen to the *snick, snick* of the blades catching each hair. Again and again the razor lowers, a scythe through a black veldt.

"If you're going to do it, at least use some shaving cream, brother."

I whirl, brandishing my blade. A tall man stands in the bathroom doorway, smiling. Either he's Simien or a helpful burglar.

"But I wouldn't do it if I were you. I did it once when I was starting out. It was fine for a couple of days till the hair began growing back. Ever had chicken pox?"

I nod, still holding the razor.

"This was worse. Man, the itch when it started to grow back. And the stubble rubbing against the shirt. It was like wearing a steel-wool vest. Like I said, it ain't worth it."

I drop the razor into the sink.

"You must be the new guy." He grins and leans against the door. "I've got to hand it to them. You're the one thing they were missing. Now they've covered the spectrum." He puts his hand to his mouth, holding an invisible microphone. "Black and bald? Big and black? You want 'em, we got 'em. Too dark? Don't worry, we got mocha. Fifty-one flavours of Negro." He laughs. "You know, they won't hire any other black models now that their collection's complete. Now that they've got their light-skinned brother, their mulatto, tragic or otherwise, they don't care, as long as you reflect those brown light waves, brother. Ever wonder what the world would be like if the word *light* were called *dark*? But that's another story."

I sense that he's stopped talking. I wasn't really listening. I've been looking at his eyes. They're green. He's black. He doesn't need them to be the most unusually beautiful man I've ever seen. His eyes are long and sad. His nose is narrow and hooked. You could rappel down his cheekbones. I've never seen a Moor before, but he's everything I've imagined one to be—tall, regal, Solomonic. Like those Spanish paintings of a black Jesus.

"So what's your story?" he asks.

"My story?"

I follow him into his bedroom—my bedroom—and tell him about the contest, my move, my first go-see, my first audition.

"Don't sweat it," he says, pitching clothes from the closet into a cardboard box. "You could have read that line like James Earl Jones and they still wouldn't have cast you because your nose is too long or your eyebrows are too dark. If there's one thing about this business, it's that you get used to rejection."

That's about as comforting as the thought of eventually getting used to a bad smell.

He grabs the cardboard box and tosses it into the living room. Snatches another and begins to empty drawers. "I can't believe you came here without a contract. You didn't even try the market first. The Ashanti have a saying—'You don't test the depth of a river with two feet.' But you're here now. Best to make the best of it."

Just then I hear the *chunk* of the elevator thumping shut, and seconds later Crispen is through the front door.

"Stace, man, my shoes! You took off with my shoes!"

I'm out of the bedroom. "Your shoes?"

"Well, the shoes we were sharing. Come on, man. I had to play African-style. You know how hard it is to jump barefoot?"

Breffni and Augustus troop into the apartment behind him.

"So did you get the part?" I ask Crispen.

"That's not the point. You can't just pull a Houdini like that and leave a brother swingin' in the breeze. Shoeless Joe and shit."

Simien steps out of the bedroom, carrying the last of his cardboard boxes. He looks through Breffni, Crispen, and Augustus as he heads for me. "I know none of these guys will give me any messages, but if you get one for me, call me at this number." He hands me a business card. *Simien* in black italics, and two phone numbers. "The second one's my pager. That's only for emergencies. Like the Bat Signal. Please call me if someone calls me. Because of these jealous, petty people I missed out on two shoots already."

"Why would we give you messages about Feyenoord shoots when you're switching to another agency?" Crispen asks. He doesn't move when Simien brushes past him with a box. If push came to fight, it would be hard to pick a winner. Crispen looks more like a fighter, but Simien seems more dangerous.

"I need my messages because I haven't officially left yet. I'm not telling Manson anything until it's official. I don't want to give him a chance to spread any more rumours about me before I make my move. Why give Feyenoord a running start?"

"But why are you switching?" I ask.

"Five percent, brother. Remember that contingency fee? Biggs, what happened when you wanted to buy your car and you asked Manson if you could have the difference between that five percent and the actual money you owed for the couriers and the other stuff right away instead of at the end of the year?"

"He told me he couldn't do it till the end of the year."

"Of course he couldn't. Because he has the money tied up in investments and mutual funds that only come due on a certain date. That's why it seems like the end of that fiscal year is always at a different time."

Augustus frowns. "So?"

"So that's five percent of my money paying for his second Mercedes, his apartment in Raleigh. So tomorrow, I'm going to tell him either I get my cash now or I'm gone. He'll hum and haw and promise to have it for me in a week or a month. But he won't have it. And I'll be working for

Maceo Power the next day."

"They any good?" Augustus asks. "Things are kind of slowing down with me at Feyenoord. I've been thinking of making a switch for a while now."

"Maceo doesn't do any hand modelling."

"That's right by me, Pappa. I'm tired of that stuff, anyway. I want to do some real modelling for a change. That's why I came to Toronto in the first place. How can I get any real shoots if all they keep sending me on is hand modelling?"

"What's wrong with that? You make great coin doing what you do, don't you? Like the Egyptians say, making money selling manure is better than losing money selling musk. It's all about selling yourself. How much you can get, how much of yourself you have to sell to get what you want in the end. That's why I'm making moves."

"For five percent?" I ask. "Isn't the extra five percent worth it to be with the biggest agency in the country?"

"You don't get it. Modelling is a means to an end. You have to know what you want in the end. Breffni wants to be in the movies. Augustus wants to be a real model. Crispen...I guess he wants to meet women. The problem with you guys is you think you know what you want, which is worse than not knowing at all. You're all obsessed with the means, not the end."

Somehow I feel compelled to answer the question he hasn't asked. "I want to work overseas."

"That's the means. What's the end?"

"Like I said, Europe, contracts, Hugo DiPalma, Brian Chin. Shoots in Tahiti. My own line of...anything."

"But that's the means. What's the end?"

"I don't follow."

"See what I mean? Another lost brother. Shame."

"You're the only one around here who's lost," Crispen growls. "At least he doesn't spread his cheeks to get shoots."

"I almost feel sorry for you, Crispen. You can't stand to see another black man succeed. But, of course, you're too green to be black, anyway.

Don't worry. When I'm gone, you'll be the man at Feyenoord. As they say in Ghana, if there were no elephants in the jungle, the buffalo would be a great animal."

"Well, like they say in North Carolina, fuck you. And get the hell out my house."

Simien smiles, picks up his last box, and closes the door behind him.

I hold my breath until I hear the elevator door slam. "Well, he seemed nice enough before you guys showed up. What's up?"

"With Soul Brother Number One?" Augustus says. "Two years ago when we met him he was cool."

"Great guy," Crispen says. "Loved him like a brother. Then he started getting big, with all the ad campaigns and contracts and whatnot. And slowly he turned into the back-to-Africa-preaching, ass-kissing fag you saw before you today. But on the positive side, at least you have your own room now."

"He's gay?"

"A friend of mine who went to Milan with him said he caught him and a photographer together in the washroom," Breffni says.

"Caught them doing what?"

"Put it this way. There were two pairs of shoes inside one stall."

"But how do you know that's true? People used to make stuff up about me all the time."

"It wouldn't surprise me with Simien," says Augustus. "All that weird-ass African shit. He's not African at all. He's from Victoria, B.C."

"That doesn't necessarily make him gay."

"Well, we've never seen him with a woman," Augustus says. "You got a woman, right?"

He seems to be eyeing me suspiciously.

"I told you last night. Ex-girlfriend." Then I remember. "I have to make a call. Is this the only phone?"

"Yep," Breffni says.

I scoop up the phone and take it as far away from them as the network of extension cords allows. Five rings later I get a flat recorded voice.

"Your call has been forwarded to an automated answering service."

Then a pause, and her own voice, "Melody Griffin," softly, ending on a high note, a question. Then the voice again: "Is not available. Please leave a message after the tone." The tone.

"Hi, it's me." I try to make whispering sound amorous. "Just wanted to let you know I'm thinking of you. Had my first audition today..." I'm not sure what to say to a girl who halfheartedly slashed a wrist because I left her for another city. The others are pretending they're not listening, but the television's on mute. "Well...bye. Call me when you get a chance." I leave my number.

I shuffle back with the phone, expecting to field questions.

Breffni's first. "Your ex?"

"Yep."

"White girl?" Crispen probes.

"How'd you know?"

"The way you talk to her."

"How's that?"

"The tone of your voice."

"And besides," Augustus adds, "a black woman would've already had your new phone number by now."

They all laugh.

"Don't tell me you guys have a problem with me dating a white woman."

"On the contrary," Crispen says. "I highly recommend it."

"It can be very beneficial," Augustus agrees.

Jerking his thumb at Augustus, Breffni says, "Angie paid his rent last month."

"And Christine lends me her credit card twice a week." Augustus shrugs, as if he had no choice.

I turn to Crispen. "You, too?"

"I've been known to accept a few campaign contributions from well-meaning donors," he says, smiling slyly.

"Man, you guys give dogs a bad name."

"Don't look so shocked. They're getting their money's worth," Augustus insists. Then, in a television sotto voce, he adds, "For as little as pennies a day, you, too, can make a difference in the life of a Negro. That's right. Guess who's coming to dinner?"

"And sleeping over in Jenny's room?" Breffni contributes.

"And keeping the spoons," Crispen adds. "Now, of course, some brothers—" Crispen glances at Augustus "—sway a little too far over to the light side. Remember Bobbi?"

Augustus groans.

"Biggs was living with this 200-pound woman. She paid the rent. She gave him a car..."

"The Mazda?" I ask.

"The same. Bobbi's doing. But when she caught him with all those other girls, she gave him the boot. And that's how he ended up here."

"It was only supposed to be for a couple of weeks," Breffni says. "That was last year."

"Speaking of white trash, me and Breff saw Bobbi at the Palace last week. With some short brother. Small-time player."

"No surprise," Augustus says. "Like they say, once you go black..."

They set off on a second round of Bobbi stories, but they're all variations on a theme. I gather my things from the corners of the living room and cart them into my room. It smells strongly of incense and slightly of naphthalene. I open the window and study the view of a brick wall. The fire-escape ladder is a ladder to nowhere. I dump socks into drawers, hang shirts in the closet, fold sweaters into milk crates.

Simien has kindly left his mattress. I lower myself onto it gingerly. If what they said about him is true, these stains could have come from two dudes.

As I become slowly sealed in the envelope of sleep, I wonder what Melody would have thought if she heard the boys talking about their white girlfriends. I suppose I should be outraged, but instead I feel strangely left out. Cheated, because I'm not getting anything out of my relationship except suicidal affection. I wonder if Melody would have been as willing to bleed in the bathtub for a white man. I wonder how long it'll be before she realizes she's being short-changed. I ride horses. I don't mind the Beach Boys. I think black people are better off here than they were in the jungle. When Melody's with me, does she really notice the difference? I'm not the genuine article. I come with no pedigree of negritude. These things never would have crossed my mind back in the days when I wore corduroy pants that went *zwee, zwee* with every step.

There was no black or white in my world until that day at camp when David Wiener asked me why I looked like poo. Since then I've realized the world isn't shot in colour film, where everyone's a different hue. It's shot in black-and-white. There are only different degrees of one or the other. We're black, or we're white. Or, like me, we're shades. Insubstantial images of something real. Reduced almost to nothing. The only thing worse than living in that black-and-white world is living in a grey one, in which race doesn't matter except to everyone else. In which nothing's black or white, and everything's both. The problem with living in grey is that one grows no natural defences. Growing up grey is like growing up weightless on the moon. To return to earth is to be crushed by the weight of one's own skin.

FOUR

"Look up. Look to the side. Wow, your eyes are, like, really scratched, man," the makeup man says. He gives me drops that make the world go around. "And you have an oil slick happening on your nose." He wheezes out the contents of a bottle, splurts it onto a cloth, and wipes my face. Then I'm frosted with brown powder.

"I...don't normally wear makeup."

"Then you don't normally work," he says, and continues dusting with his makeup brush. Craning his head back every so often, he holds me up to the light to make sure there aren't any patches of my true colour showing through.

"What's this for, anyway?" Crispen, already made up, is sipping water in the corner.

"I don't know. I wrote it down somewhere. Something for a software company, I think." I pull out my appointment book. My go-sees, appointments, and auditions are written in red. This, my first booking, is written in black. Our Feyenoord appointment books are the same ones used by all five Feyenoord agencies across the world—books obviously not manufactured by a Canadian printer. Every page is full of obscure holidays and questionable celebrations. Samoan Independence. Jeudi Noir. All-Cherubs' Day. And every day, the size of the moon: quarter, half, full, harvest. I can't figure out who would find that useful other than a werewolf.

"Let's see. All I wrote down was 'computer shoot.' Sorry." I probably should have paid more attention when Shawna explained it to me. I simply went into shock when she told me I was actually booked.

The photographer, Brian Bean, claps to get our attention. Next to him are a man and a woman, both short, both, it would seem, younger than I. "This is Darryle and Jeanie from Mycrotel. They'd like to go over the concept for this spot."

Darryle plucks out several sheaves of paper from his briefcase, sets them out in order on the large table by the window. "Hi, everyone," he says. Everyone is me, Crispen, one female and two male models from other agencies who I've seen at auditions but usually ignore, a young black boy, a young white girl, the stylist, his assistant, Brian Bean, and his assistant.

"This is the storyboard. We're going for a friendly, family fun-type thing. High-tech, but warm. Approachable. Big smiles and all that. Making learning fun." Jeanie nods. It doesn't look as if she ever approves of much.

"Does everybody have sunglasses? A white T-shirt?" The stylist takes over, issuing each of us bright silver jackets. "If you do, put them on. These jackets go on top of them."

"Shawna didn't tell me anything about bringing anything," I whisper to Crispen. He pulls out a white T-shirt and sunglasses from his bag. "You should always carry that stuff in your modelling bag, partner. Makeup, tape, a towel, lip balm, a white T-shirt, a black T-shirt, sunglasses…and a book, if you don't like waiting while you wait. I have an extra T-shirt in my bag, but you might not want it. It's sort of a backup backup. I call him Old Stinky."

The stylist spots me. "No shirt?" He turns to his assistant. "Do we have anything for him? Thank you." He tosses me a white tank top, and I sling it on.

Soon we're twirling and gyrating to trip-hop as multicoloured lights flash overhead. An intergalactic dance bar. I, as usual, am the family man. In tow, the young black boy—my six-year-old "son," whose mother is obviously several shades darker than I am. I'm to take the kid in my arms and hold him up to the lights.

"It'll all make sense in post-production, don't worry. There's all kinds of special effects and characters and things that the computer guys are going to cook up for the ad. But I need you to hold him up like you mean it. You're in love. Not...like that. You know what I mean. Like a son. He just won the pennant, or whatever. Yeah, like that."

The kid is as light as a Frisbee. I want to wave him around in the air, squeeze him just to hear him *wheep* like a dog toy.

As usual we spend the first half hour shooting Polaroids. Brian Bean and his assistant set our scene, tell us to freeze, the flash goes off, they empty the camera's magazine, flap the Polaroid in the air, then huddle together with Darryle and Jeanie in the corner, who tell them how much better it would look if I were Chinese, or if I were holding a puppy instead of a kid. Then Brian and his assistant come back, jiggle the lights a little to the left, and shoot another one. This goes on for an hour. A call-and-response with F-stops and shutter speeds. I'm getting paid to stand on an X made of tape. So I stand. My meter, running.

Eventually the lighting's just right, we're clothed in our shiny grey space jackets, and they're ready to shoot colour. I hold the boy aloft, pretend I've won a prize, and smile.

"Chin up. Eyes open. Don't try to look so sexy. Less smile. It looks like you're about to eat him. Less...less...okay, now you just look evil. More—that's it! Magic!"

It's not long before the boy's crying, and his mother, who's drinking something out of a thermos on the sidelines, is forced to waddle onto the set and placate him with promises of video games and Oreo cookies.

"Makeup!" Brian Bean shouts. "His makeup's running to hell. Where's Tanya? Why is she out having a butt now? No, I didn't tell her to. Shit." To the boy he says, "You're doing great, little man." To me, "Just perfect.

Keep smiling." He spins around. "Shit. Okay, let's take a lunch. Fifteen minutes, please." He turns to us. "Help yourselves to food. There's plenty."

I gouge out a piece of cheese, grab a handful of crackers.

Crispen walks up to me, eyes wide. "What are you doing?" he whispers. "You don't eat the food!"

"But he offered it to us."

"Well, you're not supposed to actually eat it, fool. Models don't eat."

"What are we supposed to live off then? Flash-bulb light and runway dust?" I glare as the crew gorge themselves on slivers of tandoori chicken and honeydew melon. I hope it's all off.

Crispen's scene is shot next. He's with an older model and a young girl. They're supposed to be moving up an escalator, pointing to objects on either side of the stairs, things that will be added in later digitally. The "escalator" is a five-foot stairway to nowhere.

"Hey, it's Ronald McDonald," Crispen says, pointing at the distant wall. The young girl looks and laughs. "And over there, it's your mom in her underwear." He indicates the other wall, where the child's mother is standing, definitely not in her underwear, but turning red just the same. The child laughs again.

"Magic! That's the stuff. More pointing... Well, you all have to point at the same thing. Yeah...no...just decide on a direction, and everybody point there. That's it. Magic! Out of film."

Five minutes later they're done and setting up for my final shot. "Do you always talk when you're shooting like that?" I ask Crispen.

"Yeah, it helps me get in the moment. Makes it real. As real as it gets with pancake makeup and a fake white daughter, anyway."

"Are you done?"

"Yep. You have two scenes. I have one. Don't look so happy. We both get paid the same."

They're ready to shoot the bar scene. An older male model with antennae is our waiter. He's supposed to serve me and my young protégé the software, a box on a plate. When we get our huge plate and open the box, we're to act surprised.

"More surprise, please. Like the box just spoke to you. That's what happens, right?" Brian Bean asks, turning to the clients.

"The box?" Darryle says. "Yes, in the software, it talks back."

"Right. So more surprise. Big eyes. Open mouth. Try again in five."

The waiter comes back and hands us the box. I suspect he stepped in front of me, but I continue, anyway.

"Hey, look at that. A box! That's not what I ordered," I say to my new son. He opens his eyes wide, mouth a big O. Nails it.

Brian Bean grins. "Brilliant. That's the good stuff. A couple more like that and it's a print. Keep going, guys. Three more."

Three more, and Brian Bean shows the clients our twelve-second scene. Backward, forward, slow motion, reverse angle. Darryle smiles. Jeanie asks if it's too late to make me Asian, digitally maybe.

"So now you're talking to the camera, too," Crispen says. Stealing my style, eh?"

We're hanging up our silver jackets, folding our silver pants. "Borrowing it," I say. "That's okay, right?"

Crispen thinks for a moment. "Sure. Anything to help out a brother. Did you bring your voucher book?"

"Yeah. But you'll have to show me how to fill it out. Our DBMI vouchers were tiny. This bastard's as big as a poster."

Crispen whips out a pen, starts filling in both of our vouchers. He presses hard—three copies. He writes our names, the client's name, address, the number of hours, our hourly rates.

"Mine's $150 an hour," I tell him. He writes "150" on my form, fills in "220" on his. I almost break my eyebrows. Under "usage fee" he adds $4,000 to the total, the bonus of being used for a national campaign. It looks as if I'll be able to afford meat for a change.

"Do you want me to take your voucher back with me?" he asks. "I'm going to Feyenoord this afternoon, anyway. Yellow copy's for the agency."

Brian Bean signs my voucher. I rip out the white copy, hand it to him. Rip out the yellow copy, hand it to Crispen. The pink copy, the only proof so far that I am, in fact, a real model, flutters alone in the field of blank forms. It can take up to six months to actually get paid. In six months I may no longer be a model. Or real.

The rest of the day, like most, is a blur of go-sees and auditions. Clients thumb through my portfolio, tell me how much potential I have, how much better I'd do in Munich or Miami or Cape Town. Most of them don't even bother to ask me to walk. When I leave, I have to remind them to take a comp card to remember me by. My new comps—four of my best shots copied onto a small cardboard card—cost $300, most of it borrowed from Crispen. He knows as well as I do that it may take me six months to pay him back.

I'm supposed to see Clive Thompson at 1:30. His studio is somewhere in the grey wasteland of North York, and it takes me an hour to find it, even with a map. The elevator opens into a hall that thumps with dance music. I check my appointment book. Fourth floor, turn left. But I hear something else and turn right.

There are some sounds that will always turn people's heads, no matter what they're doing. The sound of falling change. The word *nipple*. The sound of a young girl crying. She's in the corner at the other end of the hall, sitting on the floor, her hands clasped around her knees.

"What's wrong?" I ask.

"Nothing." Brown hair, decent body. I think she may have served me drinks somewhere before. She doesn't look up.

"Sure?"

"Yeah."

"Tough go-see?"

She glances at me. Now that most of her makeup has leaked off, I'm surprised to see she's only about sixteen.

"He told me I'm not really cut out for it."

"Modelling?"

She nods.

"Clive Thompson? That's terrible." I know he's right, though. The dance clubs of Toronto are filled with girls like her—young shooter girls who can only make it by on their tips. Because so many guys are always trying to sleep with them, they get the impression they're hot. By the time they discover they're not, they're usually too old or too married to care. This one made the mistake of believing her patrons. The only work she'd be able to get would be in a makeup commercial. They'd hire someone that looks a little like her for the "After."

"It's probably just that you're maybe a little too short."

"You think?" She lifts her head off her knees.

"Yeah. You know how they like those big, long girls. Why don't you try acting instead? They don't care how tall you are."

"I used to be in the drama club at Sir Leopold Carter, my old school. And my teacher always said I was pretty good. I had a guy come up to me once. From a talent agency, I think."

My head nods while I escape through the back door of my mind. I wonder if I did the right thing by lying to her. Maybe I should have been honest and told her she'd be better off going back to school. Better to know and accept this now than to have one's heart broken a thousand times before the age of nineteen. The ancient Greeks actually determined a mathematical equation for beauty. If I knew what it was, I could show this girl her face is a problem that can never be solved. I wonder if the formula still holds. Is math ever wrong?

She thanks me for listening, and I turn left down the corridor, toward Clive Thompson's studio, knowing that if things go bad, there will be no one out here willing to lie for me.

I'm in the bathroom at a McDonald's in the Annex, desperately trying to take off my makeup. But not even their industrial soap has any effect. If any man whistles at me, I'll cut two holes in my jacket and wear it as a mask.

I'm supposed to see an apartment at 2:30 near Avenue Road, but I forget to allow for wind resistance on Bloor Street, and no one's home by the time I get there. Yesterday I told the agency that I'd be moving out of Breffni, Augustus, and Crispen's model apartment, and they said a new model from out west would take my room next week. If I don't find a place soon, I'll be sleeping next to that guy.

I leave McDonald's and step around a bare-chested man playing a drum on a plastic barrel. Wearily I pull out my map and weigh my options. Every neighbourhood has a name: the Annex, Swansea, Rosedale, the Beaches, Cabbagetown. I've tried the first, following up on ads. The last sounds pleasant enough. Its name reminds me of Sunday-morning British cartoons. I can see Hedgehog and his friend, the talking tugboat, living there. I've noticed a lot of FOR RENT signs in other neighbourhoods, so I figure I might as well try my luck.

At Bay and Bloor secretaries and salesclerks are out on their second lunches. They'll exchange high heels for white sneakers at five. I avoid the streets with more homeless than homes. It's getting cold, days away from the first snowfall, but it's still a beautiful afternoon to walk. I'd hate to be driving in this circus—at every intersection accosted by street anemones with dirty squeegees and shiny nose chains who offer to defile your windshield for a dollar. I head down Bay, deciding to cut across town on College or Dundas. The megalopolis is a labyrinth of one-way streets and traffic-control signs, many of them contradictory. On one street a sign reads: 1 HOUR PARKING 9–3. Two feet away another sign warns: NO STOPPING. I have visions of earnest drivers hurling themselves out of their windows as their cars glide along in neutral.

Yonge Street is the hungriest street in the world. Hot-dog carts line up along the curb like taxis. I stop in front of one stand boasting BEST SAUSAGES IN TOWN. Its neighbour proclaims: BEST SAUSAGES IN THE CITY. Clearly one is lying. Either would be gastrointestinal suicide. I halt instead at a newspaper kiosk and buy a bar of happiness and a can of rotten teeth.

I'm still not sure where Cabbagetown begins and ends, so I check my map, stop a passerby, and ask, "Excuse me, is this the best way to Cabbagetown?" I trace my proposed route on the map.

"Yeah, that's right," the man says as I lean into his bad breath.

"Okay, thanks," I mumble as the guy ambles away. In my experience there's a fifty percent chance people will answer yes or no to any given question, regardless of what the truth actually is. You used to be able to ask directions from gas station attendants. But now that none of them are actually from Toronto, one might as well ask the pump.

I stroll into a restaurant to get detailed directions. It could be a diner off the highway. Small Formica tables. Yellow flycatchers. Everyone in baseball caps. There isn't a nonsmoking section. A bus driver, teasing the waitress about her new hairdo, is getting the usual. If I buy something, maybe they'll help me. I glance at the menu, which dangles over a long hot plate. Eggs and hamburgers are being fried together.

"What'll it be?" the cook asks. A greasy Band-Aid hangs from one finger.

"Thanks, I'm just looking." Even the carrot cake seems greasy. Now that I'm a working model, I guess I should listen to the boys and watch what I eat. "Could I just get some toast, brown, no butter, and a glass of water?"

He hands me a plate of cremated bread and a paper cup of warm, brown-smelling stuff from an open jug. I think I see plankton. I throw them both out and head outside, directionless.

On Carlton Street I meet more white trash in track suits and ill-fitting tattoos. The obese zip around in mechanized chariots. Construction workers operate heavy machinery in their underwear as I glide by a pawnshop. In the front window little black men with thick red lips and cheap red vests clutch lanterns and pool cues. Nigger art.

Eventually I reach Cabbagetown. The streets are lined with apartment buildings featuring pastel aluminum balconies. The better-looking ones have graffiti spray-painted on their lower walls. The worst are being decorated as I stride by. It seems to me that most of Cabbagetown's inhabitants must only be able to afford cabbage. One half-decent building has a BACHELOR FOR RENT sign in an upper-floor window. There's a basketball court nearby and a small restaurant downstairs. On the lawn by the main door a sign announces: IF YOU LIVED HERE YOU'D BE HOME BY NOW. Except somebody has changed HOME to DEAD. I'm not sure what that means, but it doesn't inspire confidence.

A grey man is doing tai chi in the parking lot. I recognize a few of the forms: White Crane Spreads Its Wings, Push the Boat with the Current,

Cloud Hands, Yellow Bee Returns to Nest. I took a couple of tai chi classes by mistake in college. By mistake because I confused tai chi with tae kwon do. When I didn't hit anybody by the third class, I dropped out and took karate until somebody chopped me. The man teaching our tai chi class always talked of being effortless and yielding, quoted the *Tao Te Ching*, taught us the proper way to embrace tigers and repulse monkeys, but he was only a master's student, no older than I was, had pimples, and was failing Introduction to Neurobiology and Behaviour. So what could he know of yellow bees and white cranes? In the class all our movements were rusty, jerky, as if we were breakdancing, popping and locking, doing the Robot. The man in the parking lot is a crane, actually possesses cloud hands. I don't want to interrupt him, but it's getting dark and I need a home.

"Sorry to disturb you, but do you live in this building?"

He doesn't answer. Golden Cock Stands on One Leg.

"Maybe you could tell me what this building's really like."

I watch him go through the forms: Wind Rolls the Lotus Leaves, Swallow Skims the Water. Maybe he doesn't speak English. Maybe he's one of those monks who's achieved the Tao and is no longer ruled by his senses. Maybe he's trying to answer my question another way. I look for hints, a hidden message disguised in the movements—Roaches Scuttle Along the Floors perhaps, or Faucets Drip Through the Night—but he's inscrutable.

I can't wait forever. I need a place to live, and this one looks as good as any I've seen. There are no police cars outside the building, no laundry strung from the balconies. The address is 555 Munchak Drive. In tai chi, five is a magic number. Five Repulse Monkeys. Five Cloud Hands. To me the magic number is $650 a month. That's my budget. It's not much, but I'll be lucky even to afford that. Bottom line: I'm desperate. As the *Tao Te Ching* says, "What is firmly established cannot be uprooted. What is firmly grasped cannot slip away."

The monk's now into Snake Creeps Down. He's a personification of the form, a philosopher in motion—yielding, supple, balanced, rooted. Soft, not hard. Always moving. According to the Taoists, stagnation is the cause of disease. Nature moves unceasingly. Movement prevents stagnation. The healthy always go with the flow. So I will, too. If a Chinese monk watching a fight between a bird and a snake led to the development of tai chi, in which symbolism is religion, who knows what my watching this monk performing could lead to? I move toward the door. Every step is slow, effortless, yielding. The symbolism isn't lost on me. I'm conscious of the delicate balance. Life is like pulling silk from a cocoon. Pull slowly and steadily, the strand unravels nicely. Pull too slow or too fast, it breaks.

FIVE

Humans are trusting creatures by nature. We throw car keys to guys dressed in red, hire children to look after ours, allow strangers near our throats with blades. Crispen has one hand on the razor, the other on my chin. I'm not sure if he's holding himself steady or preventing me from inching away. I wince every time he rasps the blade past my jugular. His touch is firm, his strokes bold. I wonder how long it would take an opened artery to pump me dry.

"Relax! Stop jumping around or I'll slice you. See, you gotta use long, straight strokes—even pressure. When you were doing it, it looked like you were chopping at your face with an ice pick, going over the same place fifty times and shit. Where'd you learn how to shave?"

"I didn't." I try to talk without moving my jaw. A ventriloquist.

"Didn't your dad ever teach you?"

"He left us when I started growing peach fuzz."

"That's hard. What about your mother?"

"She tried to teach me, but she had no clue. We spent hours in the bathroom trying to figure out how to work the electric razor. Eventually we gave up and used her depilatory cream. I went to school for three days with a rash on my upper lip."

Crispen shakes with laughter but doesn't stop shaving. Closing my eyes doesn't make it any better. "There. All done." He pats me dry. My face is so smooth it's sticky. Crispen strolls out of the bathroom.

"Hey, where are you going?" I call after him. "Aren't you going to fix my bikini line?"

"We're going to the gym. Coming?"

It's more of a statement than a question. Personally I can think of better things to do with a day off. Reluctantly I toss shorts, socks, and a T-shirt into a plastic shopping bag and follow the boys out the door.

We all fold into Augustus's Mazda and drive the couple of blocks to the Bally's downtown. Breffni signs me in as a guest. Inside it looks more like a dance club than a gym. Pumping beats, mirrors on every wall, skimpy outfits that seem to hinder rather than facilitate movement. Most of the men here wouldn't be able to scratch their own backs. Most of the women look as if they're just here to lift a man.

I spend the next hour and a half strung to pulleys, encumbered by weights of all sizes, pulling and pushing objects that would be far better left where they lay on the floor. Nearby Crispen and Breffni are a couple, shouting encouragement, grunting like warthogs, stooping over each other and occasionally stopping the weights from crashing down and crushing the other's windpipe. Augustus is as strong as tequila—by himself, heaving huge chunks of metal that, from here, look like ballast. I'm relegated to the Nautilus area, along with women, children, and the occasional rehab patient. I strap myself into bizarre machines that would have brought a tear to Franz Kafka's eye. These devices work muscles I didn't know I had but am distressed to find out I own. I learn that gravity even works sideways. Soon my arms become so heavy they have to be operated by remote control. Ligaments in my legs snap like turtles. Somehow I seem to become stronger when a woman walks by. I flush with embarrassment when one of them waits for me to finish, then climbs on and lowers the peg to an even heavier weight.

I corner Breffni at the water fountain and ask him if they're done.

"Almost. One more set."

He said the same thing after the rowing machine and the step master. I point to a short man working out on a nearby bench. "Isn't that that guy from *Forever Warrior*?"

"Paul-Claude Leloup? Yep. That's him."

I'm surprised and pleased to see he's doing biceps curls with the same-size dumbbells I was using. Only he hasn't put them down since I spotted him five minutes ago.

"They all work out here. Steve Davis, Volchenkov, Mark Ramsay, everyone who's in town making a movie."

"I know it's a cliché, but I've got to say it, anyway. I can't believe how short he is in person." Paul-Claude looks as if he could walk comfortably between the arch of my legs. "And who's the other guy?" The other man looks like Paul-Claude's doppelganger, only his features are slightly distorted. It's like peering at Paul-Claude in a rearview mirror.

"Probably his stunt double."

"Cool. So...can we go?"

"Just one more set."

When we finally do leave, my legs are petrified wood. I have to hold my swollen breasts as I go downstairs. From somewhere in the car Augustus has pulled out a bottle of thick, proteinaceous sludge. He tilts the bottle toward me, but I'd rather lick the sweat off his nose. Then I see the comforting red-and-white stripes of Kentucky Fried Chicken off to the right. "Can we get something to eat?"

"Are you mad?" Crispen almost shouts. "You can't eat that junk. You know the fat content of that stuff? There's enough fat in the skin to burn a candle for three months."

"I'll peel the skin off," I lie.

"Plus," Breffni says, "I hear their chickens are grown without brains. They genetically engineer them with tiny heads and huge bodies. Big fat eating machines with no brains."

"Isn't that a good thing? That way they don't think about the crappy conditions they're living in." I'm not upset that my meat is intellectually deficient. I'm not worried that my meat lacks moral fibre. But Augustus doesn't turn off at the red-and-white arrow, and I slouch back into the seat. "Freaking vegetarians."

"It's for your own good," Crispen says. "You looked a little soft in there, partner."

"A little?" Augustus snorts. "He had trouble lifting the bar, and it didn't even have plates on it yet."

"Now that you're doing this modelling thing full-time, you should start watching what you feed yourself," Breffni says. "And definitely join a gym."

"Right. How much is it?"

"About forty bucks a month."

"Forty a month? I can't afford that." In almost two weeks of professional modelling I've only landed one shoot.

"Don't worry," Crispen says. "We can top you up if you're short. You can pay us back when you hit it big." Breffni nods. Augustus looks less sure.

"Now can we eat?" I almost whine.

"No," Crispen says. "Let's go play a little basketball at St. Anthony's. It's 4:30. We'll be right on time for the after-school crowd. You have a ball in the trunk, Biggs, don't you?"

"Always, Pappa."

I groan. "You've got to be kidding. After working out? I can barely lift my arms to feed myself."

"It's good for you," Crispen says. "It'll get out some of that lactic acid."

That's the first time I've heard of more exercise being the cure for too much exercise. It sounds suspiciously like the dubious theory of drinking tequila to cure a hangover.

"Besides, Stace, you need a little practice," Crispen says. "Remember that Punch Cola audition a couple of weeks ago? You were an embarrassment to the race."

"Both races," Breffni adds.

"Fine," I say reluctantly. But then I'm suddenly buoyed by the thought of the Burger King across from the basketball court. If I can't sneak in while they play, at least I'll be able to nibble on the breeze and sniff discarded burger wrappers. Long live the King!

The court at St. Anthony's always seems hot, even in October. It's small, roughly paved, between the church parking lot and a small field where people from the apartment buildings surrounding the church walk their dogs when the weather's nice. Both basket rims are bent, and only the one by the parking lot has mesh. The steel mesh gleams like barbed wire if it's hot enough. Last week Willie, a tall Haitian, ripped two of his fingers badly and needed stitches after he tried to dunk.

The lines on the court might have been yellow once, and there's a free throw line at each end that no one can see anymore. The asphalt is pitted like an asteroid. Apparently one of the bigger craters snapped a boy's ankle the previous summer. The players complained to the people who run the church. They listened and nodded gravely, but the holes were never fixed. Recently they replaced the nylon mesh with steel and raised the rims an extra foot after the poor kids from the apartment buildings started playing there, fought with the Sunday School children, and ripped down the mesh and bent the rims. But the higher rims and the steel mesh don't seem to help. The kids who can jump and are tall enough still dunk, and one mesh is still missing and both rims are still bent. Augustus, who goes to St. Anthony's, says the church officials are always talking about tearing up the court and turning it into a parking lot, but they can never quite justify the cost of having the baskets taken out and the court repaved just to add ten parking spaces or so, though the vote's always close.

It's still early—the white kids are the only ones here, shooting jump shots and practising free throws at one end. They're always here first, despite strict warnings from their parents who usually live in the big houses with pools across from the Pavilion. The richer kids are very white, except when they get red, and always seem to wear Boston Celtics or Indiana Pacers or sometimes Detroit Pistons shirts and shorts, and are usually good shooters, and are always picked last. I still can't figure out why they come to St. Anthony's to play—they all have expensive metal hoops mounted in their driveways. Most of the poor kids around here have no choice.

"Yo, pass the pumpkin," Crispen says, swizzling a toothpick. Augustus tosses him the ball, and the three of them start knocking down shots on the one rim with mesh. It swishes like a metal skirt. I try a few halfhearted lay-ups, but after working out, lifting the ball is like lifting the sun.

Four Haitians are shooting at the far rim, which has no mesh at all. It's hard to tell if anyone's hitting a shot; the only giveaway is an occasional *"Merde!"* after an air ball.

Soon the Jamaicans trickle in, still yawning and talking about the night before. The Jamaicans own the court after school. They drift in from the apartments at about five o'clock and call, "I got gyeme!" Usually everyone eventually lets them have the first game, except other Jamaicans or some of the feistier Haitians, and sometimes there are fights. Most of the Jamaicans know one another and rarely scrap among themselves, except the short, stocky one, who battles everyone.

Now the Jamaicans have their track pants off, their beepers and cell phones stored in knapsacks or handed to girlfriends on the sidelines, and one of them shouts, "We got five. 'Oos runnin'?"

"We have four," Crispen says, counting us off. "Me, Breff, Biggs. Stace, you in?"

"You need me?"

"With you we have four." He turns to the Jamaicans. "We have four. Let's go four-on-four."

The tall one shakes his head. "We got five. We called game. Get one more."

Crispen turns to the four Haitians, who are changing on the sidelines by the picnic table. "Yo, we need one. We have four."

"We have four. You can run wit' us."

Crispen shakes his head, still chewing his toothpick, and walks back. "What about that guy?" he asks, pointing to a black teenager shooting by himself at the other end.

The teenager's black, but different from the rest of us: bushy hair, flat face, purplish lips. A Somalian—a distant cousin of the Africans I see every Sunday morning on the famine relief shows. He's wearing baggy knee-length shorts, and a wrinkled Chicago Bulls T-shirt that fits him like plastic wrap. It reminds me of the shirt that was always crumpled at the bottom of the lost-and-found box in elementary school, the shirt that never belonged to anyone.

"The Somalian?" Augustus asks, pronouncing the word *Smellian*. "You think he can play?"

I've seen Somalians play soccer before in the park, their black tent-pole legs thumping the ball to and fro with surprising force, while their families sit on brightly coloured blankets and feed pigeons. But I've never seen one play ball before.

"Doesn't matter," Crispen says. "He's here and we need one more. Stace, go ask."

He's playing with a blue-and-white rubber basketball, the type you see in old footage of Dr. J, the kind that comes free with a family pack of chicken nuggets. The Somalian misses a shot and chases after the ball with a strange shuffle-slide. He's wearing sandals. I didn't notice them earlier because they're camouflaged by a layer of grey dust. He vaguely reminds me of a doll I once saw on a school bus trip in Paris. The doll was smiling by itself in a small basket at a kiosk outside the Louvre. Black, with black cotton-ball hair, it featured baggy pants and a tight red-and-white-striped sailor's outfit. A handwritten card underneath the basket read: LE PETIT NÈGRE. On our way back from the airport a kid pulled something out of his bag and lobbed it toward me. "Say 'Hi' to your new friend," he cackled. The *petit nègre* landed on the empty seat beside me, grinning a lopsided smile. I melted into my seat while the bus swayed with laughter all the way to the airport.

"Yo, you want to play?" I ask.

"Sure," the Somalian replies, smiling. He grabs his ball, and we walk back to the others.

"Mogadishu!" Crispen says, covering up a fake sneeze.

"Bless you," Breffni says.

"Never mind them, Pappa," Augustus tells the newcomer. "I'm Biggs, he's C.J., he's Breff, he's Stace."

"Hamdi."

"All right, Hammy, two things," Augustus says. "If you get the ball, don't give it to those guys." He points at the Jamaicans. "And don't give it to him." He points to me. "Got it? And watch your step. The court's slippery and you've got sandals."

Crispen motions to the Jamaicans. "The only guy we have to respect is Latrelle. He's fast."

"As fast as you?" Augustus asks.

"The guy jogs over the speed limit, Biggs. You take Tuffy." He cocks a finger at the short, muscle-laden man covered in blue tattoos. The guy could bench-press a bus.

"Is he any good?"

"Not really. Just stay out of his face. He's dangerous. Keep away from children and open flames. He likes to fight. Can you handle him?"

"Are you kidding, C.J.?" Breffni says. "Biggs has muscles in his face."

"But watch your back," Crispen warns. "One of his buddies is liable to pull some cutlery on you. Air Messiah over here can guard the skinny dude with dreads. Stace, you take him."

"He's six-four!" I protest.

"No worries. Like my old coach used to say—if you can't beat 'em, beat 'em up. Put the hurt on him and he'll fold. Use your elbows. Go for the groin. We got your back."

It doesn't take long before I'm undressed and deflowered by my man. It's like playing a video game for the first time against the computer. I can't do anything to stop him. I guard him close, he blows by. I respect the drive and give him room, he shoots a jump shot in my face. I can jump like a bean, but I'm still trying to figure out what to do while I'm up there. Last week Crispen taught me to block shots with one hand instead of two the way I used to in volleyball. But when I jump to challenge this guy's shot,

I'm left waving at his chin. The only way to get a finger on the ball would be to extend my arms with a winch. He scores four of their five points.

The Somalian, even in his frictionless footwear, isn't good, but he's effective. His long arms and longer fingers erase shots, cling to rebounds, scoop up loose balls.

Crispen's doing his best to keep us in the game. He shakes and bakes his man out of his shoes, pulls up at will, takes the ball to the hole with impunity. A toothpick in his mouth all the while. At first I worry that someone might ram it down his throat, but he's so fast that nobody has time. The rest of us belong at Madame Tussaud's Wax Museum. Even the Jamaican spectators ooh Crispen appreciatively as he takes another one of theirs to the cleaners, leaves him starched and pressed on a hanger. But whenever I jog down to their end I hear the taunts from the extras sitting on the sidelines—"In his eye!" Every time my man shoots a jumper over my outstretched hand, I hear, "Ooh, broken ankles!" And sometimes I get the more oblique *Na gyeme, na nyeme, na fyeme* when they want to rub it in. Again he crosses me over, crosses me inside out, so that I'm left sniffing his wind, and the game's over.

"What? Game's to eleven, partner," Crispen says, holding on to the ball.

Latrelle laughs. "Game's to seven."

"What are you talking about? First game's always to eleven. Rules of the court."

"Not this court. Game's to seven. By one. So sit down, clown."

Crispen moves toward Latrelle but is spun around by Augustus. With his free hand Crispen pitches the ball at the Jamaican's head, but it misses and rolls into the bushes. One of the Haitians retrieves it and begins to organize his squad for the next game.

Breffni glances at me, then says to Crispen, "Relax, C.J. Payback next game. And wasn't that your ball, anyway?"

"Next time we play zone," Crispen mutters.

He might as well have thrown the ball at *me*. "Sorry, boys, I wasn't much help out there."

"No offence, Stace, but you couldn't guard a stick of celery," Crispen says.

"Sorry, man. I did my best. Next game you're probably better off playing without me four-on-five."

"Easy, C.J.," Breffni cautions. "Get him next game."

"And if he tries that shit again I'll debone him," Crispen snarls.

We sit on the sidelines and watch as the Jamaicans make short work of the Haitians.

"You were the man out there, Crispen," I say. "Did you play college hoops?"

"Yeah, for Shaw. Two years, anyway."

"Injury?"

"Kicked off the team."

"For what?"

But Crispen's lost in the flow of the game. After being down early, the Haitians start fouling the Jamaicans every time they get the ball. Now the score's tied. I'm happy to see the guy I was guarding shaming his man almost as easily as he did me. He scores another, from long range, and the Jamaicans are up one again.

Crispen turns to me. "I attacked the coach. Went after him on the sidelines during a game."

"Why?"

"It's a long story. I wanted to play point guard, he wanted me to be a shooting guard. I wanted to take architecture, he wanted me in phys ed. But what really gets me is that not two months after I was kicked off the team, a white football player tried to strangle his coach during practice. He was only suspended for five games."

"You think it was because you're black?"

"I don't know, man. The world's so fucked-up these days I don't know what to think."

"Amen," Augustus says. "Like yesterday I was trying to cross the street. I was waiting by the crosswalk, and this lady pulls up beside me, you know, at the intersection. She looks at me. I look at her. And then I hear *chunk-chunk*. She hits the automatic locks. I mean, what was I going to do? Get in with her?"

"Ignorance plain and simple," Breffni says.

"Ignorance can be good comedy sometimes, though," I say. "Back in elementary school, kids used to think my hair was made of Velcro. They'd take turns putting things in it—pens, erasers, rulers—just to see if they'd stick."

The others nod. Whether in sympathy or in agreement with the aim of the experiment, I can't tell.

The Haitians, through a combination of unfriendly fouls and friendly rims, are winning six to five. The Jamaicans try to lob it to Latrelle, but the pass is too low. It sails under the rim as he soars above it. The ball lands underneath the picnic table and rolls into the parking lot.

Simien is coming down the path, carrying his own ball, basketball shoes slung across his neck. He nods to us, ties his shoes. Crispen doesn't have to ask him if he wants to run. All is forgotten once the sneaks are on and the ball's in play. There's no question of who's sitting out. I complain loudly of a sore ankle to spare them the embarrassment of having to tell me that Hamdi's their fifth man.

The Haitians are tired; Simien and Crispen are on. They hit shot after shot. Anything they miss, Augustus puts back in. When Augustus crashes the boards, others tumble to the ground. When Augustus goes up to put back a rebound, he takes others up with him, until the third point of their third straight game when he screams and stumbles to the sidelines, holding his hand.

"I'm cut! Damn it! Quick! Does anyone have a Band-Aid? Some hand cream?"

I examine the cut. "Don't worry. It looks all right. Somebody must have scratched you. Just wash it when you get home." I might as well have told him he has two weeks to live.

"Scratched me? With nails? Man, I could get infected. Specially those nasty Haitians and their long-ass nails. I gotta go home and take care of it."

There's no arguing with him.

Breffni laughs. "If you want to mess with his mind, tell Biggs he's getting liver spots on his hands."

"Or hairy knuckles," Crispen adds.

The others have stopped their game long enough to make sure Augustus still has all his fingers. They ask me if I want to fill in. I decline, pointing vaguely to an ankle, and they pick up a white kid who was doing push-ups on the sideline.

I stretch out in the dying grass and try to keep warm as the teams flow back and forth from one basket rim to the other, like waves lapping the rocks. There doesn't seem to be much greenery in Toronto, even in the parks. I miss the wide-open spaces and leafy islets of green that make up Nepean.

There's a sparsely wooded field across from the court. It's late October, and there are only twigglings of green left. Fallen orange, yellow, and red leaves cover the grass like a bad carpet. I get up and walk down the path, over a sunken barbed wire fence, and into the field. A sign is tacked to a big tree: NO TRESPASSING. THIS MEANS YOU. I doubt they mean me. There's a thick, slow-moving river to the right. Floating in the water is a hubcap, a hockey stick, yogurt containers, pink Styrofoam blocks. One so rarely sees Styrofoam in everyday life that it's surprising how much of it ends up on the shoreline. The ground is soggy, spongy. Little ponds are cut off from the river by tall grass. In the spring they'll be muddy with tadpoles. Memories of spring nets and Mason jars, soakers, rain boots, squelching mud rise up. May days in the forest behind my house, searching for frogs to ignite, or lying in the yellow grass by the river, staring at the clouds, until the horseflies got too bad. I bend, swish the dark water with one hand, imagine myself here in seven months. The tadpoles will have already formed back legs but will still have tails and gills. At the cross-roads of maturity. Maybe one more week and they'd emerge from the pond as frogs. Unless the pond dries up. Death in the mud, only a few feet from the river.

Back at the court Augustus has returned. He's brandishing an unwieldy video camera, the old-fashioned sort, the kind that rests on your shoulder.

"Just act normal," he directs, waving the camera in my face. I shy away, pull my hood tight over my head, draw the strings. I don't want to be captured on video. I dread the moment weeks, months from now, when the tape will be held triumphantly aloft and smacked into the VCR, some rainy night when none of their girls are home and all the weed's been cultivated. Video reveals the banality of life. It sucks away the "could haves" and "what ifs," leaving only the "what is." It captures everything that's happened, everything that's happening and, in a moment, everything that will happen. A photograph, on the other hand, is full of possibilities. It only captures one instant, leaving what's come before and what will come after to the imagination. The future is possible, the past mysterious.

Augustus gives up on me, focuses on the game. I close an eye, make a round lens with one hand, imagine what Augustus sees through his monochrome viewfinder. He focuses on Crispen. Crispen pilfers the ball from a Haitian, dribbles behind his back at half-court, confounds the last defender with some sleight of hips, leaves him behind in favour of the rim, attacking it with gusto. He dunks so hard the rim gongs. The thin metal pole that holds up the rim is still shaking long after Crispen runs back the other way to play defence. Augustus lowers the video camera.

"Did you see that shit, Pappa? He was tap-dancing around those bitches. I think I got it all on tape." He aims the camera and resumes his visual play-by-play.

Augustus is right—it will be a good piece of video, worthy of the sports highlights at six and eleven. No doubt Crispen and Augustus will be replaying it later over beer and girls.

I turn my imaginary viewfinder to the rim. If I were following that sequence with my Canon, I would have taken a different shot. Black-and-white film. Shutter speed 1/125. F-stop at 8. In the foreground, Crispen in midair, the ball still cupped in one hand. From my shot you wouldn't be able to tell if he was still going up or coming back down. Using 100-speed film, he'd only be a blur. A rising comet. A falling star. And I'd be shooting him from behind. You wouldn't see his face, only the back of his bald head, his boxers billowing out from the top of his low-riding shorts. A 28-millimetre lens, and the real subject of my shot would be in focus. Hamdi, the Somalian, under the hoop, calling for the ball. Both hands spread palm-forward, long arms outstretched. With the film I'd use you'd feel every grain of sand on his sandals. From the look of sheer joy and abandon on his face, it would be hard to imagine Hamdi dragging dead American soldiers from his jeep through sandy streets. In my mind's eye shot, clearly Hamdi's open. The Jamaicans, all wearing shirts, are rooted, chess pieces. The only two moving in this frozen tableau are Crispen and the Somalian, both shirtless. In this picture you wouldn't be able to tell if it's autumn. Hamdi's black skin is polished with sweat. The last of the October sunlight glints dangerously off the metal mesh. The sun is my backlight, the Somalian fills my frame.

SIX

It's rush hour, usually my favourite time of day. My old apartment in Nepean faces west, and from three to five o'clock it's bathed in sunlight, even in the winter. Every afternoon I'd come home from school, pour myself a glass of water, slip on my shades, and stretch out on my couch, basking like a walrus in the sunlight. I'd lie there, reliving the summer Abbey and I saved up enough for a week at Cable Beach, every day spent squeezing the last ounce of juice from the sun, then a shower, a change of clothes, and down to the Sunrise Grill for snapper and peas, maybe some slots at the Hilton at eight.

But my degree's been abandoned, my old apartment's hollow. Abbey, last I heard, is dancing for money in Kingston, and I'm still trying to scrub makeup off my face. I dial the shower to Sandblast and scour my face with a sponge.

Towelling off, I look around my new apartment in Cabbagetown. Life has come together quite nicely: a television, a desk, a dented lamp, a real wood dresser, and a bedside table that sits beside my futon, quietly holding my life in its ochre Ikea drawers. My modelling portfolio sits atop of the bedside table, covered by the thin, dusty film of bachelorhood. I reach across my pile of clothes, which are still steaming fresh from the dryer, and pull open the drawer. It tilts and out roll pencils, condoms, cologne testers, sweets hoarded from Halloweens long past, and a large manila folder on which pens have been tested and lovers' names scrawled. It holds the debris of arguments, deceptions, teenage lusts, forgettable passions. I rummage randomly through the letters and smell the perfume of every girl I've dated, each striving jealously to reclaim a memory. The scents mingle into a tangy fragrance, reminding me of everyone and no one at all.

I sort through the memories, holding each up to the light from the window. A note from a grade nine locker. A napkin from a hotel at Cable Beach. Fourteen rose petals, precious shards of a long-forgotten romance. Some crumpled poems. Coupons entitling me to massages from girl-friends who would no longer remember my last name. A few insincere birthday cards. A small pink bow cut from a bra—Melody's.

To her credit, she was a great help with the move. I only had three hours and just enough room for the six small pieces of furniture I have now. The rest—the old couch, the mattress, the hibachi—all went off the balcony. I waited until midnight, then hauled them over the sixth-floor rail into the trees below. I wasn't the first: the branches sagged with futons, armchairs, plastic stools, patio chairs, all suspended in the trees until the next big storm, or until someone saw something they liked and poked it down with a broom.

Melody begged me to reconsider, to think of her for once. I told her what I always tell her: that Toronto was something I needed to do. And besides, I said, loading the last of my books into the van, technically we weren't even going out anymore. Luckily her aim was off and the lamp missed both me and the van, landing on the curb. She squealed off in her Honda, her face blurry with tears. I didn't hear from her again until yesterday.

When I first moved in, I kept a picture of Melody on my bedside table. Now I have my portfolio there instead. I like it near me when I dream. So far I've done testing shoots with three photographers, each one more expensive than the last. One day they'll be asking for the privilege of testing with me, and I won't have to pay a cent. They'll be doing it for the prestige, to add a handsome beauty shot to their professional portfolio. Right now, though, they're just doing it for the money. Cash, no chaser. An hour, two rolls of film, a few crazy angles, and I have two or three decent new shots for my book. It's coming along now. Here, in the middle, my first tear sheet, cut from the pages of PC Universe, the Canadian edition. Me in that Ziggy Stardust space jacket, holding up the little black boy, surrounded by aliens who offer us glowing boxes of software. I still haven't seen a dime from that shoot. Every day I make the routine call to Feyenoord between 4:00 and 5:00 p.m. "Any shoots for tomorrow?"

"No."

"Any checks come in?"

"No."

"Any idea when?"

"Check again tomorrow."

Making money used to be more fun when I was a kid on a paper route delivering the Ottawa Citizen to affluent doctors and weary housewives. There's nothing like the feeling of being able to collect a fistful of cash from strangers every week. Now I do a shoot with the knowledge that I won't see a cent for weeks or even months. And when I do get a cheque, it leaves me cold. I don't even remember what I'm being paid for. All my money goes to pay my bills. I'm being forced to make some tough choices—like whether to buy a toothbrush instead of toothpaste and brush my teeth without paste, or to buy the toothpaste instead of the toothbrush and smear the toothpaste onto my teeth with a finger. I can no longer afford the coin laundry. I wear my dirty clothes into the shower instead. Poverty is the mother of invention. Meal planning consists of deciding which days I'll eat. Lately it's only been every second day. At bars rounds are on others. On dates money is mysteriously forgotten. The subway is a limo.

Luckily I don't have to pay for electricity, water, or heat in this apartment. Unluckily, because I don't pay, I have no control over the elements of my biosphere. Now that it's November and the snow is starting to fall, the heat is being pumped in unmercifully. It's getting so warm in here that chocolate is a liquid, orange juice a gas.

Opening the window provides no relief. Thanks to a clever bit of engineering by the fellows who run the small restaurant downstairs, their kitchen fume hood exhaust is angled so that any breeze pumps the stink of their grease into my apartment. If I leave the window open, everything smells of bacon. When I eat dinner, even my salads taste fried. My two plants on a stool by the window become lacquered with oil. Leaves break off. Deep-fried.

On Munchak Drive most residents have no time for the law. Two blocks away, in Rosedale, they have no need for it. They guard their rose-coloured houses from us with fences, dogs, security guards. Their houses are so expensive, they're named after eras—Victorian, Georgian, Tudor. There are more basketball hoops in these driveways than there are in all of the city parks put together, but you know these boys can't play.

We have our own court across the street. The games usually start at four and sometimes end at the morgue. I've gone down there to shoot the ball around a few times. Often I'm turned back by police tape, a reminder of our precarious existence. In the days when our furry ancestors ruled the earth, the span of our years was determined by how fast we could run, swing the club, climb a tree to avoid mastodons or sabre-toothed tigers. Now our lives are in the hands of overworked airline pilots, newly licensed drivers, gang bangers looking to make a quick reputation. The other day the man I saw in the hall fixing the elevator looked suicidal.

I open the window wider, try not to breathe. On the street a phone rings. I know somebody from this apartment building always calls the pay phone outside whenever a cute girl walks by. I try to imagine what he has to say by the woman's response. Shock or laughter or anger. You can tell a lot about a woman by how long it takes her to hang up the phone.

A couple of blocks away, to the left, is a huge movie trailer full of American actors. It squats like a diplodocus on Bloor Street, blocking traffic. On the other side is Winchester Park where people of all colours stroll and play games. From here it looks like a fair. A man is frolicking with his German shepherd. The dog drags an old Frisbee around, its best friend. Not far away Indians play cricket. Near the grocery store young Filipinos slouch against a wall, whistling at shy Filipinas as they walk by, while Tamil women group together, plastic shopping bags hooked to strollers. There seems to be some kind of cultural festival going on down there, for whom and for what I can't see. There are more brown people outside than usual, many of them wearing yellow and orange. Dozens of people from the surrounding apartment buildings are out on their balconies, waiting for snow maybe, or for the fireworks many of them seem to have released. One by one the brown people in the park unleash their pyrotechnics into the darkening sky—small ones, corner-store explosives that pop and hiss.

At the corner a prostitute yells at a black man in a toque and a puffy yellow jacket. Perhaps her pimp or dealer. "You're nothin' but chump change! Chump change!" The black man says nothing, just stands there. "Chump change!" she screams again. With the sun descending between the buildings and the shadows of her long legs lengthening, this could be a decent shot. I grab my camera off the shelf, focus, snap a couple of pictures. When the pair look up, I duck and close the window.

Opening the window has only made me realize how nice and cool it is outside. Everything near the window is covered in powdered grease. I dust my plants, water myself.

Even the photos I've put up on my walls are becoming oily, curly, brown, like withered leaves. Soon these pictures may actually become oil paintings. I'm saddened because the photos are my own work. I haven't had time or cash to mount them or even have them properly developed.

The smell of the restaurant's double burgers and baby-back ribs is making me hungry. I stalk through the kitchen in search of prey. My bread-maker is in its usual corner and in its usual state—empty. I bought it from a pawnshop on Dundas Street, thinking it would be cheaper to buy ingredients and make my own than to buy bread from a grocery store. But there's a reason the bread-maker ended up in that pawnshop to begin with. Its bread is inedible. Flat like pita, spongy as a lung, gloopy like Play-Doh.

Whenever I bake a loaf, I'm always scared to open the lid, terrified of what I'll find when the steam clears. I root through the cupboards. The only things I have left are two Rice Krispies squares. For a model, Rice Krispies squares are the devil's food. So easy to make, so full of infernal calories. I tap the squares, but they're so hard I hear an echo. Slyly I look at the stack of dirty dishes and lick them clean. I spot another cockroach sprinting for cover. Before it can hide under the pans I spray it with Mace. I have a can in every room. I blow on the roach to see if it moves. It doesn't. But I happen to glance back at it five minutes later, and it's gone.

I wander around the empty apartment, wondering what to do, then flip on my stereo. It's small—only twelve watts of power—but it's loud enough to drown the one room of my apartment. I throw on some Grover Washington Jr., but soon he's busy playing another solo and has no time for me.

I'm supposed to be at the fashion show by 7:30 p.m. It's 4:30 now. There isn't much I can do for the next three hours. Even the television has forsaken me. At this time the tube is lousy with talk shows and soaps. A nap is out of the question. I can't afford curtains, and it's still too light out. Even at night, with the glare of the streetlamps, it's like trying to sleep on a fully lit football field. Usually I wear an airplane eye mask stolen from first class when the flight attendants weren't looking. But invariably, in the middle of the night, there will be a noise—gunfire outside or creaking inside—and I'll rip off the cloth like a catcher tearing off his mask to snag an errant foul ball. But it's always a car backfiring or someone creeping around upstairs, and I'll go back to sleep.

It seems I have no choice but to be patient and wait. These days it seems I'm always waiting for something—photographers, who are always late. Later, if they're not paying you to be there. Photo shoots are exercises in patience and are as boring as drum solos. Even here at home I'm always waiting—for a phone call from Feyenoord, for instance. Every ring is a possibility. Life as a bachelor is just as boring as it's cracked up to be. Occasionally I resort to playing card games or Monopoly with myself, but every card from Chance that reads "Pay each player..." is an embarrassing reminder of my solitude. Sometimes, just for fun, I try creating weather in my apartment, using the heat of the oven, the cool air of the window, and the water vapour from the shower. I've managed to introduce a cold front and a low-pressure system, but rain, as yet, has eluded me. I'm suddenly reminded of one of Simien's African sayings: "Work and you will be strong. Sit and you will stink."

I even hear, see things differently. Right now I can pick up the tinkle of freezer coolant, like the sound of melting icicles. Sensory isolation sharpens the mind. Everything slows down. The green neon numbers of the alarm clock on my dresser seem brighter. It's 4:44. No matter when I look at the clock, it always seems to be 4:44. My mind is fuzzy. I feel like a grandfather. The other day I discovered my oven mitt in the freezer. Yesterday I left the house again in slippers.

Now Grover's really grooving. Soon all the instruments will join hands and sing. My model bag is packed, my shoes shiny, soles taped. In two and a half hours I'll be floating down the runway, smiling at everything that moves. If I'm lucky, they'll feed me after the show. I pack the two Rice Krispies squares in my bag, anyway, just in case.

"I had the dream again last night," Breffni says, zipping up his pants. They're too long—they sweep the floor like a Zamboni when he walks.

I hand him the tape. "Which dream is that?" I practise undoing and doing up the clasps of my braces. If I don't get it right, the Zaks brothers will hang me by them after the show.

"I have this recurring dream that I'm having sex with a horse. But I always wake up just as I'm about to have my turn to be on top."

I laugh at the image of Breffni being mounted by a horse. That's what happens when you live alone.

"Where the hell's Biggs?" Breffni asks.

"Maybe he's still at the gym."

"No, he's probably getting his taste," Simien says. He arrived here half an hour earlier than everyone, has already tried on all of his clothes, is relaxing on a stool.

"Don't worry. He's just running on CPT," a brown model from another agency tells us.

"What's that?" I ask him.

"Coloured People's Time."

"No, I think Simien's right," Breffni says. "I'll bet you any money it's sex."

"Less talking, more modelling," says Darren, the younger Zaks brother. He always sounds as if he's joking, but rarely is. "Breffni, you look like shit. You're all puffy. You should get less sleep."

"Relax, man, I'm sick." He spits into the garbage. His phlegm is the colour of grass.

"Which charity is this show for exactly?" I ask. "AIDS? Breast cancer?"

"Children's rights," Breffni says.

"Weird place to have a fundraiser for children's rights."

"A bar? Yeah, I suppose it is."

For a city like Toronto the Acropolis is a relatively small bar. But it's still big enough to lose your friends in unless you're linked with rope mittens. It's only 7:00 p.m., but it's already filling up with favourite clients, fashion press, and the miscellaneously fashionable. The Zaks brothers' shows are always a must-see for those who must be seen. The brothers are Canadian, but the European fashion establishment is starting to accept them despite that, or at least is choosing not to hold it against them. Their winter line made *Glam*, *Revue de la Mode*, *Chic!*, and television's *Fashion Police*. Crispen has travelled with the brothers to Miami, New York, and Los Angeles to promote their new collection of hats. According to Crispen, Tom Zaks actually cried when Crispen told them he couldn't do this show. The agency put me up to replace him. Apparently they owed Chelsea enough favours to agree. And besides, it's only a charity show.

"How's the movie coming along, Simien?" one of the other models asks, then elbows Breffni.

"Written, did most of the casting, mailed off my grant proposals last month. Now all I have to do is wait."

"Well, if Trevor Hood and Jesmin Banks aren't available, you know where to find me." He laughs, and the others join in.

Augustus bursts through the hinged door, a black cowboy entering a gay saloon.

Breffni winks at me. "You're late, Biggs. What's up?"

"Hey, what can I say, Pappa? Time flies when you're having sex." He laughs.

"Right!" Breffni chortles. "Pay up, boys."

One of the other models gives Augustus an old-fashioned high-five. "What's the news, brother? We don't see you out on shoots anymore. I heard you moved back to the States."

"No, man, I just switched agencies a couple of weeks ago."

"Which one?" the model asks.

"Maceo Power."

This is news to me. I've been so busy moving that I haven't seen the boys in almost two weeks. I had no clue Augustus made the move to Maceo. First Simien, then Augustus.

"Why'd you switch, Biggs?" I ask.

"I got tired of that hand-modelling stuff. It's pretty hard to break in here to do anything else. When the clients hear my name, all they want me for is my hands. I knew I had to do something when I was at a shoot a couple of weeks ago, modelling shorts and stuff, and the photographer had me stick my hands up in front of me, right into the camera."

"In front of your face?" I laugh, only a joke, but by the expression on Augustus's face I know it's not.

"So what are we supposed to be doing out there, anyway?" Augustus missed the walk-through earlier this afternoon.

"There's no runway," I say. "We just walk through the bar, single file, go into the different rooms, do a little pose or whatever, and keep going. There'll be a model sent out every minute or so. Keep to the right-hand side, 'cause there's models coming back the other way. It's like a big loop."

"Sounds simple." He takes off his shirt.

"Man, you're something funky, son," Simien says, shifting to a more distant bench.

Augustus sniffs his armpits, shakes his head. "Sorry, Pappa. I ran all the way here from the subway. Does anybody have any deodorant?" He looks around the room.

All the male models are suddenly lost in their hats, swallowed up by their clothing racks. Nobody wants to get his stink on their stick. I sigh and hand him mine. He smears the gel over both of his fragrant forests, but that only seems to seal in the funk.

Twenty minutes to go until the Zaks brothers open the box and let us loose down the ramp. Most of us are still making sure everything is the right size. We were fitted yesterday at rehearsal, but shoes have been known to grow three sizes overnight. Collars that were snug yesterday are boa constrictors today. Everyone's in various stages of undress. Augustus's rack is next to mine. He's completely naked from the waist up and down. His penis is so long he has to coil it on the floor like a rope. I angle away, camouflage mine in the shadows of my hanging ties. For some reason I'm always a little shy to show it to other guys. My penis isn't imposing in its resting state. It's soft and wrinkled, like an old man. Not that it doesn't have my full confidence in the field. But around other guys, the ocular tape measures are unfurled and I can almost hear sighs of relief. In the first years of high school, after the Jennies and Suzies left us languishing on the sidelines of the dance floor, we'd walk home along the train tracks, still hammered, and the boys would compare. I'd always laugh and keep look-out. Scared, because I was black, and thought I'd disappoint. I'm surprised that, even now, it's okay if Augustus sees me, but not Breffni. Maybe it's because I don't want to be responsible for spoiling the myth, letting down the side.

Everyone's in their first outfits now. The girls are wearing big hats, old-fashioned, fluffy like poodles. Big puffy coats. I'm getting sneezy.

"I think your coat's full of birds," I say to the model next to me. She's from Quebec, she's fifteen, and she's engaged.

"How's that?"

"I'm allergic to feathers. Does anyone have any Kleenex?" She pulls one out of her bra. "Thanks." This isn't helping. I'm nervous enough as it is. It's humbling being surrounded by models who can afford to take their meals instead of just making them. They're all athletic, confident, and gorgeous. I dread the third outfit. It has only one piece—boxer shorts. Luckily I did some push-ups and arm curls before the show to pump up. I've come to learn that my arms are inflatable waterwings. But no amount of pumping will prepare me for parading around in my underwear in front of hundreds of strangers, many of them carrying cameras.

"What do you think of the boxer-short thing?" I whisper to Breffni.

"Don't worry there, Tweaky," he says. "It's a walk in the park."

"Yeah, but most parks around here are pretty dangerous."

"Pass me my shoes."

The two brothers are becoming more frantic now, scurrying among us to adjust hats and rearrange busts, peeking out into the crowd to see if the photographer from *Là* is here yet.

"You know what to do," Darren says. "Around the circuit once, stay to the right-hand side of the floor. Just have fun, for God's sake, nothing formal. You'll only be in each room for about twenty seconds, so you have to make your presence felt while you're there. Take your time, interact. It's a party. Whoop it up."

Darren catches a whiff of Augustus and whispers something to him. They both walk out the back door. Five minutes later Augustus is back, face dripping, smelling like lavender. I don't know which is worse.

The show, it seems, is being delayed another half hour. The crew from Citytv isn't here yet, nor is the reporter from *Fashion File*. I'm still starving. I follow my nose into one of the back rooms and discover a half-eaten buffet: tubs of cold beer, plates greasy with samosas, slivers of tandoori, hectares of green salad, things impaled by toothpicks. It's food probably meant for the after-party, though it seems some members of the crew have been helping themselves. There are beer caps and toothpicks piled neatly in a corner. I twist myself a beer and pick off a few delicacies. Twist myself another.

"Watch out for those samosas," I tell Tom, who wanders in and catches me taking a swig of my third beer. "They're hot enough to melt your mascara."

He chuckles. "It's nice to see a model eat for a change. I always spend a bloody fortune catering these things and nobody ever eats a damn thing. You have some sauce on your chin."

"Thanks." I raise the bottle to him, but he's already gone. Soon a few other models gather at the table, like zebras at a watering hole. Since I haven't been snatched by crocodiles or mauled by lions, they figure the coast is clear. My work here is done. I wander back, another beer in hand.

"Listen, Pappa, do me a solid?" Augustus asks, buttonholing me on my way to the washroom. He pulls his video camera out of a bag. "Take a couple of shots of me out there?"

"You can't be serious. I can't. I...I don't know how."

"You're a photographer, aren't you? It's easy. Just point it at me and focus."

"I'm a photographer, not a cameraman. And I won't even have time for that foolishness. I'll be lucky to get all my clothes on and off in the right order."

"Come on, man. My parents have never seen me do my shit."

"And by parents you mean girlfriends."

"This button's record. It's autofocus. No worries. Thanks, Pappa."

Soon we line up in order, hats cocked, smiles sharpened. One of the dressers is at the door and gives each of us the signal to go out. We're brightly coloured paratroopers invading Alphabet City. Breffni's first. He walks on air. One minute later a black-haired model sets off. He picks up his feet high and dainty when he walks, like a horse at a dressage show. In a minute I'm next.

The music out here is loud, the awful ululation of what's politely called "word music." My path is lit by candles. It's amazing how little I can see of these people who are so close to me. I'm confused, have nowhere to focus. Peeling off my cardigan slowly like an old man doing a striptease, I pirouette, and then I'm into the next room. This one is better lit. Everyone seems to be drinking and smiling. I'm not sure if they're smiling at me or at the clothes. There's a big collection box in the middle of the room. I have to pass by it on my way out. I look wistfully at the piles of tens and twenties lying in the clear donation box—enough to live on for at least a month. In the next room there's a three-story cake.

I follow the candle trail back up the stairs to our change room. It's taking longer than anyone expected. Unlike most shows, there's actually a line of models already changed and ready to go out. From here we can hear the hoots and hollers as different models enter different rooms. The volume of cheering depends on the model and how tight their clothes are, and if the room has its own bar. I have time to sneak another toothpicked treat and a sip of beer. When I come back, Augustus is about to head out. He spots me, cups his hand over an eye, and cranks a finger in circles by his ear. I pick up the video camera, part one of the curtains, peer through the viewfinder. It's dreadfully dark. The autofocus zooms hither and thither, can't keep up as Augustus walks and turns for the crowd. A real photographer never uses autofocus. I wish I could switch to manual, but I can't figure out how. Everything through the viewfinder is blurry. I give up and put the camera down. Everything's still blurry, and it's my turn again. I meant to leave the toothpick in my mouth accidentally—Crispen's not here and you can't copyright a toothpick, after all—but when I get a stern "Take that thing out of your mouth" from the dresser, I toss the wood into in the garbage and head down the stairs.

The crowd is noticeably looser. Polite claps have turned to whistles, and the music has switched to Celtic. My eyes are stuck on autofocus as I stray over the median into oncoming traffic and collide with the model coming the other way. I grab her, do a two-handed jig, spin her back on her walk. The audience in the room claps. They think it's part of the show. I wink at Simien and Breffni as they pass but have to move aside to make room for Augustus. He's striding in the middle of the room, oblivious to everyone else but himself. His walk is surprisingly graceful for a man whose head weighs more than I do. Encouraged by the hoots and hollers, he breaks into a moonwalk. The carpet recoils in horror, bursts into flame with the friction.

Back in the change room, it's time for the dreaded third outfit. The boxers are 3-D; they have knots of fabric, tufts. They're obviously underwear not meant to be worn underneath anything. I'm terrified. I need another drink. If I'm going to show my hairy self out there, the least I can do is apply local anesthetic to my ego. I imagine a horrified hush falling on the room as I enter, then see myself running from a hail of beer caps and cocktail umbrellas. The advice, "Just picture them in their underwear," comes to mind, though that probably wasn't intended to be used by anybody actually in their underwear. Just as I'm about to go out, the dresser grabs me.

"Your fly! Button up your fly!" I fumble with the buttons below, finding it suspicious that girls always seem to notice that our flies are undone.

The music has switched again—Cuban salsa now. *"Se revuelven...todo el mundo se revuelven..."*—"Everybody is spinning..." This song at least speaks to me, even if I only understand the chorus. I know enough Spanish to order a beer, but not enough to ask for it in a glass. Teaching me Spanish and taking me fishing were the only two good things my stepfather ever did for me without being asked to by my mother.

I'm skinny, hairy, and cold, but the crowd doesn't seem to mind. The waitresses are flowing freely now. One of the men at the back of the third room is holding up a number written on the back of a cocktail napkin. I think it's his. The salsa seems to be getting louder in every room. The tinny cowbells seize my limbs, the horns propel me into the crowd. I grab an older woman standing by the speaker. She's big, but it's obvious she knows how to move. We salsa by one of the Zaks brothers, who's nestled in the crowd. I think it's Tom. I can't tell if the expression on his face is one of delight or horror. I seem to have crossed the line between being a floor model and a demo model, but I don't care. Lines disappear and are redrawn. They don't know who I am; most will probably never see me again. My anonymity which, an hour ago, couldn't be shed fast enough, is now a protective shroud. Crank up the whirligig! "Everybody is spinning..." The crowd claps in unison as we cavort madly through the rooms. Some of the other models have stopped, line the walls, clap along. Augustus leaps out of our way. The cameras follow us down the candled trail.

SEVEN

His name is James and he's the best stylist east of Castro and north of the Village. Celebrities fly him across continents and underneath oceans to work with their favourite photographers. James and Alvaro, the photographer, are smoking a fatty and trying to decide which record goes best with my outfit. I'm wearing stubble, a heavy white shirt, and a thick tie half done up in a make-believe knot. Yesterday over the phone James convinced me to cut my hair close and let my beard grow out just for this shoot. I'm still slumped in a corner, told not to move, while they root through milk crates for some music.

"Models always need music," James says. Alvaro passes him the joint, he inhales, exhales, and continues. "Everybody has some kind of music inside them. Hearing music just brings it out. Good models don't need to hear it in their ears. They hear it from inside. You're not that good yet." He smiles at me, winks at Alvaro.

From my days studying English at university, I dimly remember a line from somewhere: "The man that hath no music in himself..." But I can't remember the rest, who wrote it, what happened to such a man, and if it was fatal. I hear nothing within me except the gurgling of my empty stomach.

"There's nothing here, *papito*," Alvaro says. "Where does that girl keep the good stuff?"

It isn't their apartment. It belongs to a lawyer friend of Alvaro's who's at a conference in Idaho.

"You know what?" James says. "I think I saw some more records in her bedroom."

About ten minutes later there's the *snick, snick* of James's elaborate Roman sandals, and they're back, holding two platters. It's possible James's top button was done up when he left.

"Okay, okay, it's like some old shit, okay, but it's good. James doesn't like it, but we'll give it a chance, no?"

If I were gay, I'd fall madly for Alvaro because of his voice. It's soft and round, full of delightfully Spanish jous and hokays. He's from Guyana, which means he could be just about anything. Alvaro loads the old-fashioned phonograph, which sits on an ebony table. It's old pimp. Every so often the record skips, and James and Alvaro take turns throwing makeup brushes at the turntable to make it hop.

Alvaro's arranging the lights around me; James is lying on the couch. The stylist is tall, California blond, and wears white pants and a white shirt. He's good-looking, but somehow looks hollow. He must have lost weight recently—his clothes billow around him like white robes. Unless, of course, that's the style these days, which is always possible. The couch is white, too. Earlier James was talking about his other home in Montego Bay, and how he wants to retire there in a month or two, teach the natives how to take good pictures. Now he seems tired, happy to let Alvaro do all the work.

Alvaro is short and has olive skin, deep brown eyes, and bouncy lips. For years he was an assistant to Clarendon, one of Toronto's better fashion photographers, now striking out on his own. James decided to help Alvaro as a lark after seeing me at the children's rights charity show, recommending that Alvaro use me for some testing to build up his thin portfolio. I jumped at the chance. James charges $400 an hour, Alvaro about $150. I'm getting both free. I only have to pay for prints of the shots I like.

Settling on the floor, I get as comfortable as I can. It's a nice place—a penthouse suite on Queen's Quay, overlooking the harbour. In the summer there would be sailboats. The shelves are heavy with bright pottery, clay bowls, glazed vases wildly coloured and striped, like Mexican blankets. Some of the smaller bowls hold green and grey grains that smell like flowers.

"Those are nice," I say, pointing at the bowls on the shelf. "I just moved into a new apartment and I'd like to add a bit of colour to the place. Do you know where I could get stuff like that around here on my salary, which is small?"

"Take it," Alvaro says. He picks up a small bowl and holds it out toward me.

"I can't do that, I mean—"

"Relax, *papito*. I made it. I make clay and ceramic pottery in my spare time. These are all mine. I gave them to Nina. She's got so many of them, she won't notice. I'll make her another one tomorrow. Take it."

He puts the little pot in my hand, closes his hand over mine, takes me over to my modelling bag, and opens my hand, operating me like a toy truck. The bowl drops into my bag.

"But don't tell James, okay?" James is still in the washroom. "He always wants me to give him all my pot. Pots. Oops." He giggles. "Freudian slip. You want some?" He offers me a toke.

I desperately hope he did, in fact, make the bowl and isn't randomly giving away other people's possessions. I'm not sure how many joints he smoked before he got here.

"No thanks," I say. "Not now."

"What are you trying to do, ruin his eyes?" James is back. "I spent all night matching all the clothes to those beautiful brown things in his head. Why do you want to go and make them all red for? Get out of my way. Go take some pictures or something."

"Okay, *papito*, don't get mad," Alvaro says. "I've got some crazy ideas for you, okay? Reflections. It's all about reflections. Everything we shoot. Reflections."

"Fine."

"Now, you, stand here in the corner," James tells me. "It's a sexy corner. Good angles. Don't look so happy. You look like a schnauzer. No matter what they ask you to do, no matter how happy the great ones look in the pictures, there's always that hint of suffering in their eyes. Happy, sad, it doesn't matter. Now move a little to your left. Alvaro has some sexy ideas today."

For the next forty-five minutes I dance to the castanets of the clicking shutter and the flashing flash. Alvaro is shooting me in the reflection of everyday objects. Reflected in the penthouse windows. Reflected in the shiny toaster. Reflected in a large soupspoon. The light bends, I'm Dalíesque, melted, like time. Every so often from the couch James calls out, "This is shit!"

Alvaro replies, "It is shit," or asks, "This is good, no?"

James just smiles and murmurs, "It's good."

Finally Alvaro stops to reload the camera. We've already gone through two rolls of black-and-white.

"It's great to do some crazy stuff like this," I tell James. "I'm pretty tired of doing those boring catalogue shoots. All I ever do is put my hand on my hips or stick my hands in my pockets or look off into the sunset or gaze into a girl's eyes or laugh with the boys. I want to do different types of shoots, show some personality, tell the camera who I really am, establish an identity."

"Do you have control of your life, or are you controlled by the slings and arrows of outrageous fortune?" James asks. He takes a long drag, comes up for air.

"The slings and arrows, I think."

"You have to learn to shape your look, reinvent yourself. All the top ones, that's how they stay there. Christy Budd? She used to have long black hair. Now she's a cherry blonde. Lana Polinski? She used to be ninety-eight pounds, straight as a stick. Now she has implants. They're always changing. The body is plastic. You have to shape yourself into whatever it is you want to be."

"Sort of gauge the trends, fit the fashion."

"No, you'll go nowhere if you do that. Don't ever try to do exactly what the public wants. You'll never be able to get it right. Give 'em something different. They'll either ignore it, or they'll love it."

"I think it all starts with getting the editorial shoots that give you the chance to do something different. I have enough trouble getting work now. If I tried to change my look, I'd never make a penny."

"I'll see what I can do," James says. "No promises. Sometimes it just takes a little word of mouth to get the ball rolling. And once it starts..."

"Okay, boys, I'm loaded and ready," Alvaro says. "I had an idea while I was in the can. See that mirror?" He indicates the bathroom mirror. "We can pull both sides out, get that effect, you know, where all the mirrors are reflecting each other."

"Like the hall of mirrors?" I suggest.

"Yes!"

"Done to death," James drawls.

"I know, I know, *tonto*, let me finish. Now if I were to get him in there, but only some of the mirrors had his reflection—you know, edit out the rest digitally—that would be sexy, no?"

James doesn't answer. He's fading away, fingering the potted palm tree by the couch. Reflections of Montego Bay in his eyes.

"Well, I think it's sexy," Alvaro says. "Let's go. And take your shirt off. Like you're about to take a shower."

Thanks to about a month of gym time and mouthfuls of creatine, my arms are almost al dente.

"Ooh, I love that scar." Alvaro traces the worm in my shoulder with his finger. "James, we have a sexy scar here. I think I'll work it in, okay?"

I'm impressed at his blatant disregard for perfection. I pose, grimace, flex, sulk. We finish off another roll in the bathroom.

"James, *niño*, I need to ask something, okay? *Madre de puta.* Are you listening to me? *Coño, hombre.*"

"That doesn't sound very nice," James says softly, still lying on the couch. I don't offer to translate. "He's just jealous." James takes a final puff, tosses the burning nib into the garbage. "Because I can get a prescription for this stuff."

"Are you coming?" Alvaro asks. "I want to talk to you about something in here." He's in the bedroom now.

James sighs and lifts himself off the couch. "Coming."

It's already five o'clock. Cold, I slip on my shirt, wait on the couch. After twenty minutes, it's obvious they won't be coming back for a while. I gather the rest of my clothes, stuff them into my model bag, and lift another bowl off the shelf. As Alvaro said, the woman probably won't notice. And if she does, the photographer can damn well make her another one tomorrow.

The good thing about having a girlfriend is that you learn something new about women every day. Unfortunately none of it ever helps. I told Melody I'd call her some time this week. I got in late from the testing shoot, treated myself to two greasy gyros at Mama Luke's, and picked up the phone to tell her I missed her. But instead of being grateful for the call, Melody is in tears again. Apparently Sunday is the start of the next week. I went a whole week without calling her, and it was our anniversary on Wednesday. I should have known better. That's the way she is. She's the type of girl who eats watermelon with utensils. It would be pointless to say the week begins on Monday, or that there's no real reason for us to go on celebrating anniversaries since we broke up over a month ago. I try a different tack instead.

"Why are you always so obsessed with time? Everything has to be on time, on your time, or there's hell to pay. I don't work that way. Haven't you ever heard of CPT?"

"What's that?"

"Coloured People's Time."

"What's that supposed to mean? You don't call me because you're black?"

"No, it's just that white people are so anal about time. 'Oh, my God, it's

5:15!'" I spout in my best white person's voice, which is basically my voice but higher. "'We were supposed to be there at five.'"

"That's not funny. If I made fun of black people the way you make fun of white people, you'd call me a racist."

"You do it all the time. You just don't know it."

"That's bullshit. Besides, you're half white, remember?"

She's fond of pointing that out lately whenever she thinks I'm becoming too black. She seems to take it upon herself to prove to me that white girls are okay, as though I never went out with any before. I suppose she forgets that my mother's white, and that I love her very much despite that.

Melody is about to let loose again, but I make a preemptive strike. "Let's not fight anymore. I called just to say I miss you." The sugar dissolves instantly.

"You do? Then when are you coming to see me?"

"Why don't you come down here? I have my own place now, remember?"

"I can't. I have exams." Melody is studying for her master in social work.

"I won't be able to get up there until after Kameleon comes."

"What's that?"

"I told you about that. Kameleon Day, when Kameleon Jeans comes to Toronto to look for fresh faces. For their ads and stuff. It's huge. It's my big chance."

"If they wanted you, that would mean you'd be working overseas, right?"

We're heading back down a slippery slope, so I pretend I didn't hear the question. "I have a few ideas about what we can do when I come to see you."

"Is that all you ever think about?"

"I didn't mean it like that," I say quickly, though now that I think about it, I am thinking about it. Truth is, sex has been on my mind a hell of a lot this past month. It's been so long I can't even remember what sex is really like. I'm sure that's part of nature's little plan. We're actually designed with sexual memory blocks to prevent our active imaginations from accurately reliving sex through fantasy, forcing us to seek out the real thing. Like women who have had children—their minds are wiped clean of the true extent of the pain of childbirth so the memory of the agony doesn't stop them from having more kids.

"I meant for your birthday present. While I'm there I'd like to take a picture of you. A sexy one. Tasteful, but with your top off. I have this idea. You know those venetian blinds? They're half-open. I'd shoot it in black-and-white, with you sprawled on the bed, a shaft of moonlight across your breasts. Your face wouldn't really be visible, just your body in the moonlight. And I'd frame it and everything."

"It sounds filthy," she says excitedly. "Did you do anything special on Wednesday?" she asks, changing the subject. A stumble here could prove costly. Luckily she doesn't give me time to answer. "I can't believe we've been together for three years."

"Well, we're not together anymore, right?"

"What are we then?"

"We're friends."

"But when you come here, will we...you know..."

Not to would be inconceivable. "We'll see."

"This is weird. Why couldn't we just stay together, try to make it work long-distance? It's not so far away."

"We've already been over this. I need to explore, discover who I am, and I can't do that if I'm stuck in the past." *Stuck* was the wrong word, but it's too late—Melody's already crying again.

She'd be in her bed by now, clutching Monk Monk, her ratty little monkey. That monkey always scared me. It has a maniacal expression on its face and a yellow banana in its hand, sewed tightly to its small fist. It looks like a machete. Whenever I'm in Melody's bed, I always toss it out, not altogether gently, and she always protests before snuggling up to me again.

I won the monkey for her at the Ottawa Exhibition three years ago last Wednesday. She saw me standing in front of the basketball booth and asked if I played, since I was tall and everything. When I lied and said yes, she asked me to win her something. I tossed ball after ball at the trick hoop. Most weren't even close. It cost me $8, about the same price as a real monkey, but it all seemed worth it when the vendor unpegged the nasty brown thing off the wall and handed it to her, tipping his hat. She squealed with delight, thanked me, and named it Monk Monk on the spot. That afternoon I found out she liked Miles Davis, feminist poetry, and being on top. That monkey's been with her for three years, survived every one of her vengeful roommates, every one of our breakups, including this one. If she had to choose between me and the monkey, I wouldn't give myself decent odds.

The only thing I've kept from our three years is the pink bow from her bra, a remnant from the weekends when we lived on sex and peanut butter. I open my bedside table and take it out as she begins to tell me again why we should stay together and what she'll do with herself if we don't.

The bow looks like a little rose. It has a tiny pearl in the middle, an artificial one I expect, though I don't know much about bras or their value. A woman could tell me they cost a quarter or $200 and I'd believe her either way. Judging from the bow, it looks as if the bra it was attached to could have been expensive. A designer bra, or a family heirloom.

Now Melody is talking about the drugs she's taking for her anxiety, and she wonders out loud what would happen if she swallowed them all at once. I know full well that the minute she thinks our relationship is really over she'll be back at the Palace or the Grotto with her friends, checking out the new boys from school. Her heart is a sieve. She wouldn't hold the hurt the way I did with Joanne and Elaine and Nikki and Alexandra. Three years from now she'll be with another brother, and I'll be thinking about her and whether, maybe, I should have stuck it out. But I play along with her tragic scenario, tell her I wouldn't be able to live with myself if she did something like that, tell her about the sexy pictures I'll take of her when I'm there… Then the timer I set goes off and I tell her my dinner in the oven is ready and I have to go. I wonder what Melody's having tonight, and how long it will be before she'll have someone else over to share it. And how much I'll care.

EIGHT

There is a cat that's always lost and found in my building. People are forever putting up ads on the lobby walls, inside the elevators, on the washing machines: BLACK CAT MISSING. ANSWERS TO THE NAME GATSBY. PLAYFUL, FOND OF STRING. CALL BEFORE 10:00 P.M. or FOUND—BLACK CAT. LIKES CHEESE. MEOWS A LOT. CALL STEVE.

Every once in a while a naive Samaritan will find the cat and go knocking door-to-door like a salesman, offering a cat instead of encyclopedias or high-school-band chocolate bars. I'm not surprised when I answer the door and see the black cat awkwardly cradled in the arms of a young woman. She's holding it as if it's a human baby.

"Excuse me, I just found her wandering around on this floor. She doesn't have a collar or anything. Do you know who she belongs to?"

I shrug. "She doesn't belong to me. I'm allergic to cats." Not to mention pollen and dust and horses and shrimp and grass. My mother used to tell me I was allergic to the planet, that my father, after he left, was an alien from beyond the stars.

The cat complains loudly, wriggles like a salmon in her arms. "I think she's hungry. Do you have any milk or something?"

"I'm all out," I say, not bothering to check. I don't have enough in my fridge to feed myself, let alone a stray cat. "You shouldn't really feed adult cats milk, anyway. It's bad for their stomachs. They don't have the right enzymes to digest it."

"I didn't know that," she says. "I've never had a cat. But in all those cartoons, you know, you always see the cat drinking out of a bowl of milk."

"You can't believe everything you see in cartoons," I say, smiling.

She laughs. "I guess not. So if you're allergic to cats, how come you know so much about them?"

"Actually, I think I heard it on TV. I watch a lot of documentaries and nature shows. 'What's new, pussycat...'" I sing, rubbing the cat's head, careful not to get too close. I can't tell if the cat's flattened ears are meant for me or the song.

Despite its owner's apparent disinterest, the black cat seems to be one of 555 Munchak Drive's healthier pets. This building, or the Shack as it's called by unfortunate neighbours and local police, isn't too kind to its pets. Every night through the thin walls I hear the shrieks of tortured animals. During the day, there's always a procession of disfigured pets— a three-legged dog, a cat with half an eye. They wheeze down the corridors, dragged along on leashes that are always too short, their owners acting as if nothing's wrong.

"All this time I never knew it was a her," I say, noticing the animal's nipples. "But she seems to get lost about once a month. Maybe it's a cyclical thing. No offence," I say to the cat.

The woman laughs. "You've seen this cat before?"

"Kind of. She's sort of an inside joke in this building. You must be new around here."

The woman's in her mid-twenties. Blond hair, blue eyes. Not beautiful, kind of stumpy, but close enough to my age that I would have noticed her if I saw her. I lean on the door, opening it wider.

"How did you know?" she asks. "I just moved in last weekend. But I'm on the fifth floor. You wouldn't have seen me around, anyway."

"Maybe not." Of course, I probably wouldn't have seen her even if she was my next-door neighbour. The residents keep pretty much to themselves in this building. I've only met three people on my floor—a Somali across from me, and two guys from Alberta down the hall. And I've already been here almost a full month.

This high-rise reminds me of a phenomenon I learned about a couple of years ago in social psychology class. Something called urban-withdrawal syndrome—how industrialized urbanization leads to people living in smaller and smaller units, isolated from one another. Friends scatter, households are broken up, intimate exchanges are few and far between. The emotional isolation of the individual leads to the eventual breakdown of society. I can't remember whose theory it was, but he or she could have conducted most of the research in this building.

Here we pass one another without saying hello. We stare at the elevator ceiling as we go up, look away as old people struggle with heavy parcels, ignore children crying for their mothers. Morning papers are stolen, doors aren't held, society breaks down. If she just moved in, she has a lot to learn.

"I figured you're new since you're carting that cat around. I wouldn't worry about that thing if I were you. Even if you find whoever owns it—if they admit it—it'd be back meowing in the halls tomorrow."

She looks disappointed. "Oh, well, I guess there isn't much point. I mean, if it's just going to run away again. Maybe she'll find her apartment by herself when she's hungry enough." She unhooks the cat from her sweater and puts it on the ground. "Off you go, girl."

The cat scrabbles down the hall's threadbare carpet, disappearing around the corner. The woman watches it go, then turns to me. "I know this will sound strange," she says, smiling hesitantly, "but do you have any ice cream? For me, I mean, not the cat. I'm dying to have some ice cream, but I'm defrosting the freezer. Whoever had the apartment before me left it the way it was. I think they must have been storing a body in there or something. There was, like, this dark red stuff frozen in the ice. Ugh." She shudders, and I laugh.

What a strange thing to ask a guy. Do I have ice cream? I've had girls show up at my door asking for a lighter or a bottle opener when it was perfectly obvious they didn't have any cigarettes to light or bottles to open. But those girls were all the same—they wore puffy jackets or caps of the latest football team and had makeup smeared on as thick as mortar. BMWS, Crispen calls them—Black Men's Women. But this girl's totally different. She's wearing blue jeans, a plain white T-shirt, and a pink sweater that could have been knitted by my grandmother. Innocent as a hot cross bun.

She knocks her boots against the wall outside my apartment before stepping inside.

"It's still snowing out?" I ask. It's a ridiculous question, implying I'm unable to turn my head slightly to the left to look out my two long windows. But I can't think of anything else to say.

"I think we're setting some kind of record. But it's still kind of hot in here, isn't it?"

"We could spontaneously combust," I say. It's late December. In this building the heat is now on full blast. My apartment has become a pyre.

She laughs. "You have a nice place, though."

"Thanks." I'm not sure if she's being sarcastic. "Have a seat," I offer, tossing pants, rolls of film, and the TV remote onto the floor. "I'll get some ice cream."

I open the freezer, not sure what I'll find. Thankfully I still have a couple of spoonfuls of ice cream that I've been saving for Christmas. I put it into a bowl, open the fridge, and root for something for myself. I'm nearly blind with hunger. There are some leftovers: a box with remnants of a TV dinner—a crunchy steak, soggy carrots, and a two-by-two-inch cup of pie. They're about as appetizing as the crumbs on the top of my range hood.

In the bottom cupboard there's some rum given to me by Simien after he returned from a shoot in Jamaica. Overproof. Kicks like a kangaroo. Normally I don't drink—alone, anyway. I have a horror of doing that. My stepfather drank alone. I've lived through enough nights of flying fists and mother's tears to scare me into sobriety when I'm alone. But loneliness does strange things to strange people.

For instance, Mahmoud, the guy who lives across from me. He left his family in Somalia last winter and moved into the Shack, apartment 234. One morning I was telling a small black boy not to drive his Tonka truck in the hall outside my door—I was trying to sleep one off—when Mahmoud opened his door.

"He must play here between our doors," he said, beer dripping off his breath. "He's our son. If he can't play here, where else?"

I couldn't argue with that, and he invited me in for a beer. As I said, Mahmoud and the Albertans are the only people in this building I've talked to, except the super, which is pretty much like talking to yourself. The Albertans threw a party a couple of weeks ago and invited everyone on the floor. Of course, I was the only one who showed up.

I remember Mahmoud's apartment: a mattress, a small black-and-white TV, a phone that blipped every couple of seconds as if it was trying to ring, and a fridge. The last was empty except for a case of beer. "Isn't drinking against your religion?" I asked.

"It's the cold," Mahmoud said. He had never touched alcohol in Somalia and only occasionally smoked something called khat, which made you high, but only a little. "I have to wear a winter jacket to bed," he said. And it wasn't just the weather that was cold. He told me about firecrackers through his window and spray paint on his door.

I know how he felt. Sometimes, on my way to the elevator, a little kid would run up and yell "Monkey!" only to be whisked away by an embarrassed parent. Every night I can hear what the cold has done to Mahmoud. At nights he walks around his bachelor apartment, clinking the night away. There are always empties rolling in the hall the next morning.

"Why don't you get a job?" I asked him. He shrugged and said you needed training. "Doesn't the government give some kind of training for immigrants?"

"Yes," he said. "I'm enrolled in computers." He turned to me. "Why computers? Why don't they give me training in something that will get me a job. A trade. Like electrician. I have skills. Why computers? Is anyone going to hire me to do computers?"

I couldn't answer him. I have half a degree and sit home all day watching the Learning Network.

I pour myself a glass of rum. "Do you want something to drink?" I ask the girl. "Juice? Rum?"

"Juice would be nice."

I have no glasses left. The only "juice" I have is Kool-Aid. It's been in my fridge so long it might have acquired hallucinogenic properties. I serve it to her in a shot glass. She's made herself comfortable on the couch, legs tucked at her sides like wings. It must be nice to be small. A couch becomes a bed. Knees fit.

"My name's Janesca, by the way."

"That's a strange name. East European?"

"Nice try. Actually, my dad made it up. He was in love with three different women at the time and couldn't decide between Janet, Vanessa, and Cathy. My mom didn't know about the other women, didn't care about the name, so they called me all three. Weird, eh?"

I down another shot of rum. "So how d'you like this dump?"

"Like I said, it's nice. Messy, lived-in nice. Reminds me of my grandfather's house."

"I meant the building."

"Oh. Sorry. I love it so far. I've only been here about a week, though."

She loves it? The hall carpets are orange, the mail boxes are labelled with the names of tenants long since deceased, the dryers are incinerators, the inside of the elevator is covered in mysterious phrases like SPICY CHIMP BOY and I LOOK LIKE YOU, ALI BABA. And phrases not so mysterious like NIGGERS GO HOME. And then there's the *roo-koo-doo* of pigeons on the balcony at five in the morning, and the cockroaches.

Because of the cockroaches, I have to keep my dirty dishes in the fridge and my garbage on the balcony. On the warmer days the bags writhe with maggots. The cockroaches are everywhere. In the kitchen. In the bathroom. In the unlikeliest places. In my slippers. In the fingers of gloves. Inside my stereo speakers. I've developed a predatory eye for them. I can spot small brown things from great distances, even camouflaged on the mottled hall carpet. But I don't smush them. Whenever they're in danger, cockroaches will release their eggs. A brilliant evolutionary adaptation, which is why the Shack is crawling with them.

Instead of whacking them I capture them alive in a jar or a plastic cup. I'm a kindly executioner. I give them a last meal—granola bar crumbs or a piece of stale toast. Then, in the morning, I spray a little Raid and the jar becomes a gas chamber. Periodically I rattle the jar to check the roach's vital signs. By midday it stops running. By four it looks decidedly unwell—antennae drooping and lifeless. By evening the cockroach is twitching on its back. Then it stops. Finally it's flushed down the toilet or flung off the balcony. Burial at sea or in space. But I'm far from happy at the thought of killing them. On the contrary, it makes me sad. It's an admission of mortality. That I could, at any time, be just as easily wiped out by the cosmic shoe of a car crash or a heavenly spray of brain cancer.

"You think this building's nice?" I say. "Where'd you grow up—Bosnia?"

"Halifax, actually. Is it really that bad?"

"Well, to tell you the truth, I dog this building every chance I get. I tell all my friends how I can't stand it and will move out next week, but I've been here almost a month already and it looks as if I'll be here a couple more. It's all I can afford on the salary of a crappy model."

"You're a model?"

"You sound surprised." I don't blame her. I'm wearing glasses and a track suit, and my hair is looking decidedly afrolicious.

"No, I didn't mean like that. It's just I've seen you around during the day and you're always well dressed. I thought you might be a drug dealer or something."

If I lived in any other building, she'd be licking the ice cream off her eyebrows and plucking the bowl from her forehead. But as a young black man living in the Shack, I just shrug and pour myself another shot. "My buddy Augustus is from Nova Scotia. It sounds like a cool place to live. Why'd you leave?"

"I shot my boyfriend," she says, mouth full of ice cream. "My ex-boyfriend, I mean. In the leg."

I'm not as surprised as I should be. I'm on my fourth shot of rum and I can't feel my teeth. Nothing will disturb this cool. "Mind if I ask why?" I say from the bathroom, screwing on my penile silencer by peeing on the inside of the toilet bowl.

"We were planning to start our own candle business. I make candles. He's good with money. I gave him my savings, he took off. I found him, but he spent my money on a Jeep. So I shot him."

"Why did you come to Toronto?"

"I wanted to get away, find a job, make a fresh start."

"Well, good luck," I say, leaving the bathroom. "Work around here's pretty hard to come by."

"I don't buy that. My ex-boyfriend used to say, 'If you seek, you shall find.' He'd say it in a real deep voice, like he was a preacher or an announcer or something. He was only joking, right, talking about finding the can opener or my car keys. But it's about the only useful thing he ever said in five years. I'm sure I'll find something. Eventually."

We're quiet for a couple of minutes. She scrapes the bottom of the bowl. I throw another rum down the well.

"What are we watching?" she asks, resting her spoon on her lip.

"The Learning Network."

"You like these animal documentaries?"

"Yeah. I find it helps me understand people a little better. Strip away all the bull, and that's all we are."

"Well, I don't know about you, but I'm not one of those," she says, pointing her spoon at the screen. It's a moray eel. "Ooh." She shivers. "That ice cream made me cold deep down inside." She pulls the blanket closer, draws me with it. Is she flirting with me? I catch the scent of her pheromones. Her mating feathers are on display. Her hair looks soft and manageable, as in those TV commercials. I don't know what split ends are, but I bet she doesn't have any. From this close I can see the little blond hairs on her upper lip, fine like cilia. Her eyes are half-closed. Is she asleep? Is she nervous? Is she praying? Janesca, I notice, has large hips and ample breasts—an important reproductive consideration when selecting a would-be mate. Her blond hair and blue eyes offer a distinct evolutionary advantage in this cold, white climate. Our progeny would be mulattos—able to roam both hemispheres at will. A new hybrid species that would compete with local populations, eventually choke them out and replace them, spread like zebra mussels.

I imagine us on an ice floe in the frozen tundra, huddled together for warmth like musk oxen. The camera zooms in, capturing the beauty of my tropical plumage. I court her, stamping my furry feet, beating the age-old rhythm, signifying my intent, warning off intruders. The western grebe collects seaweed and twines it around its beak to symbolize building a new home. I have no seaweed, but I offer her a shower instead. She refuses.

"I think I'd better go."

"I...I didn't mean with me," I stammer. "I just thought you might...to get warm..."

"It's getting late. I'd better go."

She laces up her boots. I stare, too numb to stop her.

"Thanks for the ice cream." And just like that she's gone.

The giant panda, when bamboo is scarce, will only select a male that's exactly the right size, shape, weight, even smell, thus ensuring the continued existence of the species. Why can't I find a girl? I'm clean-smelling, I give kind and thoughtful gifts, my feathers are bright, my horn is pointed and sharp. Joanne left me because I nagged her about her legs. Elaine didn't like the way I always had to have the last word. Nikki said I was too tender, not caring enough. Alexandra didn't even leave me a note. Monkeys, deprived of social contact, become asocial, incapable of mating. I'm alone again.

Of course, it was silly to offer Janesca a shower. For three weeks now the building's management has been turning the water off from nine at night until the next morning. They say they're repairing the risers, but I think it's a plan they drew up to save money. Every afternoon I'm forced to fill thermoses and measuring cups, rationing water like a shipwrecked sailor, a Bushman in the Kalahari. If I don't make the nine o'clock water curfew, I shower with a watering can, wash the dishes with club soda. The African elephant can collect enough dew off its back to make it through the dry season. Can't it?

I can sip the rum now. It goes down smooth, thawing my insides. I'm not really drinking alone—Janesca left her spoon here to keep me company. The bottle's almost empty. I toast Simien, my Africanadian benefactor, my friend. He's not really a friend. None of them are. They're just weekend friends—Augustus and Breffni and Crispen and Simien. We get together every Friday night, drink, try to pick up women, and tell one another stories about it the next weekend. I never see them during the week.

Last month we tried getting together every Wednesday night for poker. But Augustus took it too seriously, bought a poker hat, cigars, his own chips. Breffni didn't take it seriously enough and lost a lot of money. One night we all fought. Crispen punched a wall and broke a knuckle, and that was the end of Wednesday-night poker. It's loneliest in December when it gets dark by five o'clock. The days will keep getting shorter until there are none left. And then the cold sets in.

Every winter flies contract something known as fly mould. It grows inside them, slowly choking them to death. I find the flies coated in fine white fur, suck them from windowsills and baseboards with my little vacuum cleaner. Of course, when I die, the worm will have turned. The hunter will become the hunted. Flies will crawl over my carcass, sucking me up, completing nature's cycle. Who else would find me here but flies? I've read all the stories in the newspaper of old men, dead for months, bloated, privates buzzing with flies, bones gnawed by cockroaches. I never return messages until days later, I only see my friends once a week. The only person who'd miss me is the guy at Mama Luke's who delivers large gyros with extra tzatziki.

I'm lying on my couch, sweating like a boxer. I slide off and stagger out to the balcony to escape the heat.

The snow is still coming down hard like rice. Cars are buried in the parking lot. On the hill old toboggans lie abandoned like broken chariots. I don't have running water, but it's good to see that our tennis courts are still lit at 11:00 p.m., hidden under nine inches of snow.

A pigeon has left a circular trail on my balcony. I wonder what it was looking for. Once, a pair of pigeons tried to build a nest behind my garbage bags. Every morning I'd sweep the twigs and leaves off the balcony, and every evening the pair would fly back with more crap in their beaks. Finally I sprayed the birds with oven cleaner and they never returned.

I told Melody about that and she cried, but what can you do? After all, why did those two pigeons deserve nuptial bliss when I'm stuck here with a licence to model and no one to rub my head at night? I long to join them in their migration south, where game is plentiful and waterholes abundant. No mate will make the trip with me this season. My nest is empty. I forage on my own.

I can still hear the TV from out here. Another zebra's been caught by a lion. The zebra always struggles briefly, gives a pitiful honk and a wheeze, then lies still, resigned to its fate. How can it surrender so easily? I'd scratch, bite, kick, fight to the death, like those busy beavers that would rather gnaw off their own legs than be caught in a trap. But my trap is more subtle than a lion, colder than metal.

Every winter a mould grows inside me, threatening to choke me slowly. Perhaps this year I'll be spared—I see no outward signs of mould yet. But African violets flower even weeks after their roots are dead.

NINE

Jerome, the model from Montreal, is in the washroom rolling a joint the size of a didgeridoo. He knows he won't get caught. Most of the airport security guards have other things on their minds.

Robert from GK Models is window-shopping at the duty-free shops. I already did the tour half an hour earlier—stores the size of closets selling novelty jams, maple syrup, maple jelly, maple mustard; spoons of all kinds; cups that say DAD; Lilliputian SkyDomes and CN Towers.

Elaine from Grüe Advertising stares absently at the burly soldiers plucking their brown duffle bags off the nearby carousel. A girl stands next to her, dressed all in black, with five metal studs in one cheek. There's so much metal in her face, it looks as if she's been hit by shrapnel. The studs are aligned in the shape of a cross. Somewhere Jesus is shaking his head, or rocking with laughter. The girl is waiting for her bag. By the colour of her clothes and the glower on her face, I wouldn't be surprised to see her waiting for the arrival of her sarcophagus. But there's nothing to pick up. The middle carousel's still moving, but it's empty except for one bag. It's the last suitcase. Brown leather round and round the carousel. The bag has three different tags from three different airlines. One lock is missing. It could have been here since Lester B. Pearson was a prime minister and not an airport. It looks bored. All its mates have been grabbed by grubby hands and thrown onto trolleys. Now the empty trolleys line the walls. Soon most of them will be pressed back into action. The two conveyor belts on either side are both full—suitcases, mostly black, some brown, some red; rucksacks; garment bags stuffed so full they look like body bags; metal film cannisters, probably from San Francisco or Vancouver; a child's car seat; a pair of skis, badly scratched from scraping rocks or scraping the airport tarmac; a light pink suitcase, black with foreign footprints. Baggage hawks gather by the hole in the wall, ready to snatch luggage the second it appears. These people would crawl through the hole in the wall into the baggage room if it weren't for the sign warning not to. I notice Elaine is also staring at the lone suitcase. Round and round, down the conveyor belt, past me, past Elaine, past the girl in black, through the shredded black curtain, back to wherever it came from. Soon a heavily gloved luggage technician in steel-toed boots will pull it off and throw it onto the reject pile. I wish I were hidden inside it.

Next to the carousels teenagers and men in suits play video games. Every now and then happy-looking pilots stride by in smart uniforms. They obviously haven't eaten the airport chicken. Nearby the girls at the rental-car kiosks are trying to outsmile one another. Next to the kiosks is the money exchange. Beside the booths an Asian man hawks $5 shoe shines. Business is slow. Above him, on the overhead arrivals board, most of the flights are red thanks to the snowstorm.

We're all waiting for David, the photographer, and Angelus, his assistant. They're still at Terminal 1, moving the gear. The shoot was supposed to have been outside on one of the unused runways. I suppose there would have been something symbolic about modelling on a real runway, but it doesn't matter now. Nobody counted on last night's eight inches. The grounds manager had to explain three times, first to David, then to Angelus, and finally to Elaine, why the airport couldn't spare the crew to get runway 21 cleared in time for our shoot. For the past hour David and

Angelus, with the help of a spare baggage handler and a mechanical cart, have been ferrying lights, cameras, and action from Terminal 1 to the luggage carousels at Terminal 3. The two terminals are so far apart you have to take a flight to get from one to the other. So we wait. None of the models complain. Our call time was ten, and that's when we start getting paid, regardless of when we actually begin shooting.

I'm finishing the last of my donair. I know donairs are bad, but due to the artificial airport economy of $5 Cokes and $15 sandwiches, it's all I can afford. I'm hungry, eat it too quickly, dribble special sauce all over myself. Now I have gobs of white on my shirt—thankfully my own shirt and not the one I'm supposed to wear for the shoot. It looks as if some-body came all over my chest—a porno money shot in tzatziki.

Jerome's back. He's still wearing his Kente cloth sarong, which has become fashionable in Montreal. They flew him here because he's as short as models come. He's five foot ten, six feet in his special shoes. The size thing is all because of Ricky, the ex-Olympian. According to Elaine, Ricky told the Air Canada people he wouldn't do the shoot with anyone taller than he is. He's only five-seven. The ad people laughed and told him that would be impossible. Eventually they compromised at six feet. Crispen's six-one, Simien's six-two, Augustus is too tall sideways. All three of Feyenoord's top guns were out of the running. Shawna, our booker, desperate to land this shoot for one of the agency's models, convinced the clients that I'm only five-eleven, which I am if I duck.

Ricky's in the bar, comforting himself with a rum-and-orange. He brought photographs of himself and the rest of the relay team at the Olympics—gold medal held aloft to the crowd in triumph. In the pictures he looks even happier than the other four, the four who actually ran the race. Today Ricky even has a special felt pen to autograph the photos with. But so far no one has asked him, or even recognized him. So he's at the bar, sitting sullenly in the corner, muttering about how he doesn't have his own trailer, though Elaine patiently explained how trailers are only for supermodels and movie stars. I find myself almost feeling sorry for him. Being the fifth-fastest guy on the team, a hundredth of a second slower than the others, must be tough. I'm only here, after all, because I'm an inch shorter than the other black models. I'd join him for a drink, but I blew all my money on the donair. The bar is the sports kind and is across from the conveyor belts. Inside it's always noon. It has fifteen television screens. Somewhere in the world it's the playoffs.

A man in a big Russian hat picks up the brown suitcase, looks at the tag, puts it back, and walks away.

"I wonder whose it is," I say absently to Elaine, meaning the suitcase, but she doesn't understand, or care, and remains silent. She's only interested in one thing.

In five years of high school I learned two things: tequila shouldn't be mixed with anything, and never trust a woman named Elaine. That this Elaine isn't blond, isn't nineteen, and isn't also seeing Simon behind my back matters little. She's an Elaine, and she's not to be trusted.

"I know we didn't talk about it earlier, but we think it would really make the whole shot," she says, turning to me. "It would definitely be worth it in the long run."

"Did you ask the agency?"

"Yes, we did."

"And they said?"

"They said no. But we thought we'd ask you, see if you'd be cool with it."

"Cool with shaving my head?"

"Yes."

"For one shoot?"

"Yes."

"What would happen tomorrow? What do I do if someone wants to book me for a catalogue shoot this week? Tell them I'd love to, but they'll have to wait two weeks for my hair to grow back?"

"We're willing to pay extra."

"How much?"

"A thousand."

That's two shoots. For two weeks of baldness.

"Think of it," she says. "A shot in a major fitness magazine with an

Olympic gold-medal sprinter."

"He was an alternate, wasn't he? And won't I be in the magazine, anyway, even if I don't shave my head?"

"Yeah, but it won't be as good a shot. Robert's bald. Jerome's bald. Ricky's bald."

"What can I do? Even if I wanted to, I didn't bring my razor."

"Angelus has one. He'll take care of you."

"Does he even know how to cut hair?" Not that it matters. Cutting my hair with a razor is like mowing a lawn. Straight strokes, up and down, a little overlap. And if you miss a spot, all you have to do is go back and raze it again.

"It's up to you. But you'd better make up your mind soon. David should be here any minute."

Every ten seconds, somewhere near us, someone is saying hello or good-bye. A man in a suit and dark sunglasses holds up a sign for Mr. Vanderbeer. Nearby a middle-aged woman in a track suit clutches a card that says WELCOME HOME, NICK. I wonder how long Nick has been away that he needs a sign in order to recognize his mother. Overhead, Muzak plays Jimmy's "The Wind Cries Mary." Is nothing sacred? With all these distractions I find it hard to maintain my pose.

"A little to the left," David, the photographer, tells me. "That's it. Hold the baton higher. Higher. That's it. Hold it." I freeze, one foot off the ground, the other leg bent in half, one arm flexed crooked behind me. My other arm is stretched toward Ricky, proffering him the baton.

Even though I was one of the fastest kids in my high school, I never ran relay for the team because I could never master the exchange. The guy behind me would hand me the baton, and I'd juggle it, fumble it or, on the next exchange, shove it somewhere the runner didn't like. But this exchange, mute, frozen, is perfect. David clicks away gleefully until he runs out of film and Angelus hands him another roll.

All four of us, black and bald, are lined up in one of the hallways by the rows of Air Canada ticket counters. We're all wearing Lycra tube tops and short shorts with saucy red maple leafs on our behinds, almost but not exactly like the kind Ricky and the other four wore at the Olympics. We all have numbers on our backs. I'm number sixteen. Almost but not exactly my lucky number. Nobody has bothered to ask why all four of us are running at the same time.

The flow of tickets at the counter has slowed almost to a halt. Heads are turned. The "Next please, next please!" of the ticket agents is almost as loud as David's instructions.

"Okay, let's change the order a bit. Jerome, you switch with Stacey. No, Robert, you go to the back. Ricky, stay there in the front."

Apparently, though, Ricky isn't staying anywhere until he gets some fruit.

"But, sweetie," Elaine says with a big, thick smile, "we'll be taking lunch in half an hour."

Ricky shakes his head. "Ya don't unnastand," he says, accent thick as a couch. "I'm a professional runna. I 'ave to keep heatin'. An apple, a banana, whatever you got."

Elaine turns to Angelus, rolling her eyes. "Can we get him a piece of fruit? From the machine over there or something?" To us she says, "We'll take a five-minute break. Don't go anywhere."

I busy myself spinning the baton in the air, trying to catch it without rapping my knuckles or clattering it on the floor. A little girl with two pink barrettes in her hair watches me, fascinated, eyes big as ears. She's wearing a yellow turtleneck and a yellow tartan dress. The small pointed crest on her turtleneck makes her look like a young crewwoman on a spaceship. I stop twirling my baton, and the girl moves on, bored.

After Ricky finishes most of his revolving apple, we start up again. Every so often the crowd that's formed around us scatters to the *meep-meep* of the airport carts that carry the lame, the late, and the lazy.

We run three more stationary relay races, then David calls for lunch. The crowd suddenly surges forward. A young woman asks me for my autograph. An older man pushes past her, shoves a pen and paper into my hand, and says, "For Karl. No, wait, make it to Emily. Ah, what does she know about track? Make it to me. To Karl."

I search for Jerome and Robert, but they, too, have been overrun. I shrug and sign "To Karl. Nice to meet you, Stacey Schmidt." Karl thanks me, glances at the inscription, and walks off, even more confused than I am. A couple of feet away Ricky is smiling, signing pictures, pumping hands, laughing and shaking his head every time someone mentions the Americans, who came in second.

A young brunette steps up to me. "Which one are you, anyway?" she asks.

I think for a minute. "Floyd Stanley," I proclaim, and smile, expecting her to laugh at the joke. Instead she hands me a corner of her T-shirt and asks me to make it out to Christine.

Floyd Stanley. He ran the anchor leg. The man who gave Canada the lead for good. The world's fastest man until last month when someone else ran faster. Ugly as this terminal. Dark as my sneakers. But, I suppose, tall, black, and bald. I sign her T-shirt in his name.

"And him, by the way," I say, pointing to Jerome, "he's Jean Thermonville." Might as well go all the way.

She looks at Jerome. "Oh, yeah, I recognize him from those commercials. Frosted Milk or something, right?"

"Right. And that's Ricky...Ricky...you know, I win a gold medal with the guy, but for the life of me I can't remember his last name."

"I don't remember him."

I pull her close. "He was an alternate," I whisper. "Good guy, though. I'm sure he'd love to give you his autograph."

"Thanks. You know, you guys look much better in person."

I sign five more autographs, laughing to myself, wondering when someone will finally put an end to this inadvertent charade. Then a burly man steps up to me, grabs my hand, pumps it vigorously, one hand overlapping onto my wrist.

"I'm...I...I just wanted to say that you boys did us proud. You made us proud to be Canadian. I'm a police officer and...I just wanted to say that you did us proud..." He looks at me fiercely, lips pursed. There are tears in his eyes. After a moment, he asks, "Do you mind if I take a picture of you with my daughter?"

"Look...I'm..."

He thrusts her forward—the little girl with the pink barrettes. "She wanted to come and meet you."

I have three seconds in which to decide which is worse—letting them down now or playing along and making them happy until someday when Dad's proudly showing off this photo to his buddies at the station, one of them realizes I'm not Floyd Stanley. If there isn't one already, there should be a heaven just so I don't get in, and a hell to make sure I burn a little bit for this. The flash from the camera is blinding, but I'm a professional. Even while I'm lying, my eyes stay wide open. At least for a little while they'll be able to say Floyd gave them a great smile.

"No, you didn't," Crispen says around another mouthful of beer.

I shrug. "What could I do? I mean, really, I look about as much like Floyd Stanley as I look like Biggs."

"Isn't the agency going to freak when they see your new hairdo?" Crispen asks.

"You mean baldy over here," Augustus says, rasping his fingers over my stubble. Hairs sharp as ground glass. I think it hurt him more than it did me.

I grimace. "I saw Chelsea today when I went in to drop off the voucher slip from my shoot."

"How'd he take it?" Crispen asks.

"Not so well. That's why I dragged you boys out tonight. I'll have another beer." I do. I left a message for Simien to come, too, but he hasn't shown up.

"How does it feel, partner?" Crispen asks.

"Feels good."

"No fuss, right?" Breffni says. "Shower and go, bro."

"You got it," I say.

It's not what I mean at all, though. Physically my head is different, of course. Surprisingly cold. It feels like a knee—bumpy *and* smooth. But they have no idea what I've gone through. The white hairdressers who shook their heads, refused, and said they couldn't cut "that type" of hair, as though my head were covered in feathers or fur. Or the smiley barbers who tried, used scissors instead of clippers, who left me with a fuzzy mound. They'd look so pleased with themselves when they were done, as though something important had happened. "There," they'd say, "now you look just like Carl Lewis." Or Martin Luther King or some other black person famous or dead. You'd think going to a black hairdresser would be better. But it wasn't. I always felt naked, even before they started cutting, as if they knew I didn't belong, as if I had no right to be there in the first place. Conversations changed. Subtly, but I could feel it. They'd ask me how I wanted it, then ask again, with less of an accent, less slang, as though I'd just demanded their licence and registration. I'd drip with sweat under the plastic cape, like a boxer jogging in a garbage bag. They'd apologize for nicking my ear, instead of laughing and telling me to hold still. I'd nod without looking when they showed me the back of my head, then slink out, leaving a big tip. Was it them? Was it me? Who cares? It doesn't matter anymore. I can shave myself now.

"Speaking of hair," Crispen says, "what the hell are you doing with yours, Biggs? Are you growing it again? You look like Pele."

"Yeah, I'm growing it out. That's the style now, in case you haven't noticed."

"Where is it the style? In Brazil?"

"G'way." Augustus runs a manicured hand through the square puff on his head. His hairdo reminds me of high-school days, back when brothers cut their locks in geometric patterns. His hair looks like a rhombus. It hasn't grown in evenly. It's possible it never will.

"Check out that girl over there," Breffni says. "Doesn't she model for SMT or something?" He's on his fifth shot.

"The one with the big breasts?" Augustus asks. "Yeah, I think I saw her in a flyer somewhere modelling underwear."

"She wasn't always stacked like that," Breffni says.

Augustus leers. "She had a boob job?"

I wouldn't be surprised. Her breasts are geodesic domes, big enough to house several teams of scientists and their equipment. She's wearing a low-cut dress that's only staying up thanks to a wish and some gum. She pulls up a stool beside us and orders a Black Russian. I'm almost disappointed that Crispen doesn't slide next to her with the now-classic "You wanted a black Russian? I'm black. I'm Russian." He probably figures she isn't worth the effort. She may be a model, but the bar's lousy with them. Most are dressed down in their civvies—tight T-shirts with swirling logos, or muscle shirts with extra muscles. The majority smell of pot, and likely got into the Rum Runner the same way we did. A couple of hours ago I sent a fax to the bar with my name, my agency, and the names of my three guests. Most bars in Toronto love models, but the Rum Runner is mad for them. They weren't about to turn down a Feyenoord model, especially one called Stacey. At the door the bouncer couldn't conceal his disappointment. I had to produce two pieces of ID to prove I was Stacey, but there was nothing he could do. We were on the list.

"Hey, I was in the *Toronto Star* today," Crispen says.

"Really?" I say. What did you do?"

Crispen pulls out a tattered page and spreads it across the bar counter. I move my beer, pull the article over so I can read it. "Is this today's?" I ask.

"Wednesday's."

"Damn, you're in the headline and everything." The headline is CASUAL STYLE HIDES SERIOUS POTENTIAL. There's a picture, too—Crispen lounging against a wall, chewing his toothpick, with the caption "Crispen Johnson, with trademark toothpick, relaxes downtown."

I'm impressed. "Why no toothpick tonight to capitalize on your fifteen seconds of fame?"

"I wanted to be incognito."

"Seriously, though, this is big. Your own profile in the paper."

"Trust me, partner, it's not that big. They do one of these profiles of a local model every couple of weeks. Breffni's done two. Simien has the record. I think they did four on him. We're becoming old news. I'm sure they'll be showing up at your door any minute now."

"I don't think so."

"Why not?"

"It didn't go so well at the agency today."

"About your hair?" Augustus asks. "Did Chelsea see it?"

"Yeah."

Crispen leans forward. "So what did he say?"

"Well, after cursing me in Italian for five minutes—"

"Chelsea's Italian?" Breffni grins. "I didn't know that. Manson doesn't sound Italian."

"Apparently he is. Anyway, he kicked me out."

Mugs are lowered. Chairs swivel.

"For cutting your hair?" Breffni splutters.

"Among other things."

Crispen whistles. "Damn! That's no good for the league. What exactly did he say? And why'd you cut your hair off, anyway?"

"The money."

"How much did they give you to cut if off? Five hundred? A thousand?"

"About that."

"So you obviously didn't do it for the money."

"No."

"So why'd you do it?" Crispen asks. "To piss them off?"

"I got tired of being the Acme Mulatto—always clean-cut, nonthreatening. Whenever I see the pictures they take of me, I imagine them running a caption underneath like 'If your daughter had to bring home a black man, don't you hope it would be one like this?' I've told Chelsea a hundred times I want to change my look, take a few chances, develop a bit of personality, but he always says I'm fine the way I am, except for the hair on my chest. He won't rest about that. Every time I see him he tells me to shave it. He always says I look like an otter. So I figured if he wants me to shave so badly, I'd start with my head."

"Man, that was a dumb-ass thing to do, Pappa," Augustus says.

"Kameleon's in like four days."

My heart is punctured, my stomach deflates. I completely forgot about the Kameleon Jeans audition. With the big go-sees like Kameleon you only have one chance. It's not like you can train to become better-looking. You either have it or you don't. Those who are passed over aren't rediscovered. That's why most new modelling sensations are young. I can't vow to wow them next year. Once they've seen you, rejected you, your only hope is a new name or a new face.

"I'll have to find another agency in four days, I guess."

"Why don't you try Maceo Power?" Breffni suggests.

"I wouldn't bother, Pappa," Augustus disagrees. "They didn't do anything for me. That's why I switched back."

"You're with Feyenoord again?" I say, surprised.

"I wasn't getting good shoots with Maceo. At least with Feyenoord I had the hand-modelling gigs when things slowed down."

"But didn't you switch so you didn't have to do the hand-modelling thing anymore?"

"If you think about it, hand modelling isn't really that bad. I mean, if I have a gift, it seems foolish not to use it, right?"

"It's going to be hard to find another agency in four days, partner," Crispen says. "Why don't you talk to Chelsea? I'm sure he'll get over it. Hell, I'll talk to him for you."

"Thanks, but I don't think so. He said some things to me when I left..."

"Like what?"

"Well, for one, he said I was a talentless bastard."

"Maybe you heard wrong," Breffni says. "Maybe he said you were a talented bastard."

"Yeah. That's much better. And when I asked him about the couple of shoots I was booked for next week, he said he'd book someone else because us guys are a dime a dozen. I couldn't go back to working with someone who thought that."

Crispen scowls. "Us guys? What'd he mean by that? Us black guys? What exactly did he say?"

"He said, 'You guys are a dime a dozen.' I think he meant us models."

Crispen shakes his head. "I don't think so. He meant black models are a dime a dozen."

"Are you sure?"

"Breff?"

"Black models."

"See?"

"Why would he think that?" I ask. "There aren't that many black models around. You'd think we'd be exactly the opposite of a dime a dozen."

"I bet he meant one size fits all," Crispen says. "Think about it. Whenever Simien can't do a shoot, I get his shoot. And if I'm busy, they try to put you up for the shoot." He waves at me, spills his drink. A green slug trail of vodka-lime heads toward the edge of the table, drips onto his shoes. "As long as it's a brother, Manson doesn't care. I always figured that was the game he was playing. I just can't believe he had the nerve to say it."

"Let's not get carried away. He—" I try to say, but Crispen's unstoppable.

"Why else would he kick you out for such a dumb reason? I mean, it was stupid of you to cut your hair, but what about that time Breffni grew the goatee?"

"It wasn't a good goatee," Breffni protests. His eyes are shiny.

"No, it wasn't. It was a nasty goatee. But they didn't kick you out."

"I think you're making this into a bigger deal than it really is," I say.

"You think? Let me guess. The shoots you had for next week—was Cowboy one of them?"

"Cowboy Watches? Yeah."

"Got the call today. Cowboy. I'm booked for next week."

"No shit?"

"Shit."

"What about my Gordon Hill shoot?"

"I think I'm doing that one Wednesday," Augustus volunteers.

"Man, I can't believe this. We're disposable. Like razors."

"Well, we'll see how disposable we are," Crispen growls. "I'm disposing of myself. I'm out. I'm gone. Dime a dozen, my ass."

"You serious?"

"Watch this." Crispen marches unevenly toward the coat check. The bar's only phone is around the corner. Three minutes later he's back, smiling. "Done."

"Was anyone there?" I ask.

"Left a message. Damn good one, too."

"Are you nuts?" Augustus says.

Breffni jumps to his feet. "That's nothing. Watch this."

We order another round while we wait for him to come back. Ten minutes later he does. "Tape ran out," he says, and orders a matching set of Jack Daniel's.

"What happened to your shirt?" I ask.

Slowly he looks down, glances up again. It appears as though someone pissed on his chest. "Washroom," he says.

"You shouldn't have done that," I say.

"It wasn't the urinal, man. I leaned against the counter. It was wet."

"Not your shirt—quitting. You shouldn't have quit."

"Hey, you have to stand by your man, right?" Breffni can hardly stand, let alone by his man.

"You guys are crazy," Augustus says, shaking his head. "You can't quit like that. For all we know Stacey could have heard wrong. We don't know what Chelsea meant. It's easy for you guys to leave. I'd like to, you know, but I already left once, and I just left Maceo, so I can't go back there. I mean, I could, but you know I can't."

"Nobody's asking you to," I say.

"You know what I mean. I just can't." Augustus looks as miserable as I feel.

"Don't worry about it, partner," Crispen says. "Get your modelling shoes on. You're about to get all the negroid work in the land till we find an agency."

"Huh?" I say.

Crispen grins. "Let's find some ladies!"

We run into Simien at the downstairs bar, next to one of the three dance floors.

"Check that one out," Augustus says, pointing at a redhead with breasts the size of mangoes and an ass as big as a plum. She sways randomly back and forth to the music, like one of those mechanical flowers that swoons when you make noise.

"No thanks," Crispen says. "I like my booty shaken, not stirred. A girl's got to be able to move."

"Speaking of booty, Rianne's supposed to be coming out."

Augustus turns to me in amazement. "Why? Did you call her?"

"Well, we were at the agency the other day and she was talking about how she never gets to hear any good music or dance when she's with her white friends. Besides, she's nice."

"She's nigrified," Crispen says.

"And why you going around bringing sand to the beach?" Augustus complains. "There's plenty of women here without bringing your own."

"Yeah, but a bush in the hand is worth more than a bird in the bush."

"You Negroes are sad," Simien says. "Chasing after white girls like mongrels."

Augustus barks like a dog.

"Nothing wrong with white women," Crispen assures Simien. "Our ancestors died for the right to screw them. Are we supposed to stand by and let all they fought for go for naught? Not only is it our right, it's our duty."

"That's right," Augustus says. "We're like mosquitoes, Pappa. We don't care if they're black or white."

"You can't tell me you never wanted one," I say to Simien. "White girls are like all those things black guys say they hate but deep down can't get enough of. Like Michael Jackson."

"It's not my type of look," Simien says.

Breffni jabs Simien in the arm. "Come on, look at that one. Tell me she's not your type. Hell, she'd be the pope's type." The girl's breasts mock gravity.

"Beauty standards differ from culture to culture," Simien says. "Dark skin, wide noses—that's my standard."

"What d'you think would happen if we digitally combined the facial profiles of the Miss Universes of each country in the world?" I ask.

"We'd get some ugly-ass creature," Crispen says. "With fangs and shit."

"Probably," I agree, and we all order another round.

Soon we settle into our weekend routine. Men haven't changed much since the days we gathered to prepare for the hunt. We consume our ceremonial liquids, boast of our exploits, plan our strategies, adjust our special costumes, dance the ritual dances.

Crispen wears a shimmering purple shirt that breaks light into prisms. He's chewing the plastic sword from someone's drink. Breffni sports a bright-yellow-and-green Arsenal soccer shirt and even brighter Puma sneakers. According to Breffni, Arsenal lost the premiership this afternoon by one point to Liverpool. He'll halfheartedly whisper "Go Gunners!" to anyone within range. Augustus features jeans and a vest with nothing underneath. He has too much relaxer in his hair. Too much for this decade, anyway. Simien is decked out in a shirt with more holes in it than thread—a piece of black netting. I shouldn't be able to notice that his nipples are erect. I, on the other hand, look innocent in a white turtleneck and beige slacks. As innocent as a bald black man can appear. Breffni, the only one of us who's ever shaved off all his hair, showed me how to wax my scalp. My polished dome reflects the strobe light like a dirty mirror.

Tonight DJ Tightee Whitee is manning the turntables. He's spinning something we've never heard before, but the beat's good, so we separate into hunters and gatherers. Breffni, Augustus, and Crispen head off to try their luck on the dance floor. Simien and I settle in at the bar to see what we can cultivate, though in Simien's case the jury's still out as to what he's hoping to gather.

"How's the new place?" I ask to break the ice. Whenever I'm alone with Simien, I feel as if I'm on a first date.

"Not so good. The place was kind of big for just me, so I decided to sublet the basement apartment to a student."

"I'm surprised a student would be able to afford something in that area." Simien rented a three-bedroom house in the Lawrence/Yonge neighbourhood.

"That's the thing. When I asked him how he was going to pay the rent, he told me his student loan would cover it. I didn't think anything of it till he parked his Lexus in my driveway. He neglected to tell me he was supplementing his student loan income with pharmaceutical money. There were all these characters over at the house constantly. Sometimes I'd find them on the lawn or in the bushes early the next morning. It was embarrassing."

"Did you call the cops?"

"Think about it. A black man telling the cops about a drug ring operating out of his house and blaming it on a white university freshman? Not an option."

"So what'd you do?"

"I took his door off."

"What?"

"While he was at school I removed the door to his room."

"What'd he say?"

"He was pissed. I told him I was repairing the door, and I never put it back on. What was he going to do? Call the cops? So he moved out."

"Well done. Gandhi would have been proud."

"Thanks. Speaking of moving out, Breff tells me you were given the heave-ho at Feyenoord. Best thing that could've happened to you. You'll like Maceo Power."

"Well, I haven't decided where I'm going yet. Everything happened so fast."

"Don't worry about it. I'll talk to Amiris tomorrow."

"Who's Amiris?"

"She's Maceo Power."

"What about Maceo?"

"There is no Maceo. Not since the nineties. He moved back to San

Diego. Amiris took over and kept the name because it's a good one. Better than Amiris Alvarez. She thinks so, anyway, though I keep telling her to change it. You can't really own anything until you own the name, including yourself."

"Thanks, man, I appreciate it. But I think C.J. and Breff might need a hand relocating, as well. They quit, too."

"I heard. No problem. I'm sure Amiris will be thrilled."

"After all those guys did to you, with your messages and everything? Pretty cool of you to help them out, especially since we'll all be competing for the same jobs."

He smiles. "Competition? I don't really think of you guys as competition. Besides, you'll have the town to yourselves pretty soon. I won't be around much longer."

"Why not?"

"I'll tell you later. Rianne's coming over here."

Rianne pulls up a stool. Crispen and Breffni aren't far behind.

"So why'd you do it?" she asks.

"Man, I don't want to talk about it anymore. Can't we just hang out without talking about business?"

"Fair enough. So I guess this means you won't be my client anymore."

"I guess not. What does that mean?"

"Whatever you want it to," she says.

"Are you still going out with that girl from Nepean?" Simien asks. Breffni and Crispen each give Simien a kick under the bar, but he must have asked on purpose.

"Not really," I say.

"You don't sound convinced," he says. "Why are you still seeing her if you don't really like her?"

"Because she's a repository of pussy," Breffni says. This earns a laugh from the guys and a cuff from Rianne.

"Check that one out," Crispen says, pointing to a dreadlocked sister with telescopic breasts.

"Are you guys always this horny?" Rianne asks.

"Apparently you've never heard of guys," I say. "I'll be back."

The washroom is a dismal affair, full of yellow puddles and brown smears. None of the stalls have toilet paper, and there are no paper towels. I pee gingerly, careful to avoid any splashback from the elderly urinal puck. It smells worse than the urine. I'm rocked by a pee shiver and accidentally nudge the man next to me. He tells me it's no problem and wants to know if I saw the game, but I shrug and tell him in Spanish that the coffee is almost done. Never trust a man who's willing to talk to you with his penis in his hand. I wash mine, but there are no paper towels, only a rusty blower. I press the button. It puffs lukewarm air for thirty seconds, then stops, hoping I won't push the button again. I don't. I could dry my hands faster by blowing on them. My slacks will have to do.

I'm drunk enough to throw a quarter into the love meter and a loonie into the Breathalyzer for fun. I put my palm on the first, blow into the second. Neither result is surprising. Apparently I'm very much in love, and very, very drunk. According to the Breathalyzer, my blood is mostly composed of booze. The other machine on the wall caters to the desperate. If asked, it would happily dispense a comb, cologne, or a condom, depending on how close you are to getting laid. I'm tempted to buy a flavoured condom, just in case, but then I remember I'm already packing. When Rianne called to say she was coming out tonight, I put two in my wallet. Sex is something I usually have to try at least twice before I get it right.

Back at the table I order a drink for everyone except Augustus and Rianne, who are nowhere to be found. "Where's Augustus?"

"Still on the dance floor, I think," Breffni says.

Crispen takes a sip of his drink. "I hope so. We'll have to keep an eye on that Houdini bastard."

Augustus's expertise as a disappearance artist has been well documented. It seems to happen almost every night we go out. We dance ourselves out, look for our ride, and discover he left an hour earlier with the first girl who said she loved rhythm and blues. Since then we've learned that if Augustus is driving, we'd best either watch him carefully, pick up a girl who's brought her own car, or else be ready to cab it.

I spot him on the floor, below the stage, right in front of the stack of speakers. He's got three beers in two hands. Two older Asian women seem to be with him, though from here I can't tell whether they're studying him out of romantic interest or morbid curiosity. Tightee Whitee mixes it up, switches to some old-school Biz Markie. Augustus hands one of the women a beer and sets the other two bottles on the speaker. They both topple over and smash on the ground, but Biggs doesn't seem to care. He begins slowly, shuffling backward and forward.

I tap Crispen's shoulder. "Oh-oh, I think Augustus is about to break."

"Damn! Should we go out there and stop him?" But it's too late. The circle has already formed.

Augustus calls out each move as he goes—the Wave, the Flare. Then he's into his third move, but he already seems tired. His Electric Bugaloo has lost most of its voltage, his Robot's in desperate need of oil. He drops to the ground onto his back and shoulder and shouts, "Windmill!" It's a backspin of some sort. Augustus appears oblivious to all the broken glass. He'll feel that tomorrow.

"Biggs is so drunk he probably thinks he's spinning a hundred miles an hour," I say. "That guy's a figment of his own imagination." But Crispen isn't listening. He's a few feet away, dripping with women. It becomes depressingly clear to me that I'm not going to get any action with Crispen at the top of his game. There's a species of bird that lives in the rainforest whose mating ritual is so complex it actually takes two males acting in concert to attract a female. They perform an intricate aerial dance: one flies below the other, then both quickly switch positions until the female is suitably impressed. The catch is that only the senior bird actually gets to mate. The younger bird has to wait until he reaches maturity and finds an apprentice of his own.

"There's nothing here," I complain to Breffni and Simien. "I need something tonight. Anything."

"What about Rianne?" Breffni asks. "She's easy as me."

I frown. "Yeah..." But it's too late for that now. She left with another guy twice as big and twice as black.

"Let's get out of here," Simien says. "I'll take you to a real club. Finish up your drinks." He still hasn't finished his first, so I do it for him. Breffni downs his own drink. Twice.

"What about Crispen?" I ask.

"Forget about him," Simien replies. "We don't have time." He's right. Crispen's the kind of guy who takes an hour to leave a club—slapping backs, kissing hands, hugs all around. Last I saw him he was edging toward the back door, a nifty young blonde clinging to him like a limpet. I'm glad I don't live with the boys anymore. The only thing worse than going home alone is going home alone to a home in which everyone else isn't.

Outside, a lurch of drunks stumbles through the streets singing "Roxanne." On nearby corners girls are lined up for guys.

"At least they look like hookers," I say brightly. "In Nepean our hookers wear track pants and sneakers. On a completely unrelated subject, I need to get some money."

The inside of the bank machine kiosk smells like a science lab. It's full of unidentifiable odours, all of them unpleasant. While I wait for my money Breffni urinates in the slot labelled WASTE. Judging from the smell, I don't think he's the first.

When the money finally comes, I throw away the printout without checking my balance. In the past couple of weeks I've been making some decent money. But now that I don't have an agency I'll be back to checking pay telephones for change.

"Brother, can you spare a million dollars?" The bum outside the door has a sound marketing plan, only asking for cash when we come out.

"Now why do they always call us brother?" Simien asks. "And why are they always white? Have you ever seen a black bum in Toronto?"

Come to think of it, I haven't.

"Ah, fuck yourselves," the bum snarls, rolling over.

After the others walk by, I toss the bum a loonie. There, but for the grace of God and strong cheekbones, go I.

"Can we get something to eat first?" Breffni asks, shivering. A sobering breeze blows from the south.

"There's nothing around here except House of Patty," Simien says.

Breffni snorts. "I thought those fake Irish pubs went out with the virtual café."

"It's Jamaican."

I can see the red, yellow, and green curtains from here.

Breffni wrinkles his nose. "Ugh. Curry goat ears? Salt toes? No thanks. Why do black people still eat that slave food? You're free. Go grocery shopping or something. Buy a steak."

"I've been in there before," I say. "They even serve something called cow mouth."

"What's that?" Breffni asks.

Simien smiles. "I believe it's the mouth of a cow. Not all Africans eat that nonsense. I can't stomach Jamaican food, either. I've never understood why they love to eat offal."

"Americans aren't any better," Breffni says. "Crispen cooks up some crazy stuff, like collard greens and pig's feet."

"What are collard greens, anyway?" I ask.

"Weeds, basically," Simien says.

It is odd, come to think of it, how much of black culture is made of scraps. Odds and ends. The stuff everyone threw out or that no one ever wanted. Fish heads and hooves and washboard blues. No wonder we're all so fucked up. It's tough surviving on a culture founded on castoffs and hand-me-downs. I buy a patty, anyway. It's hard as a puck, hot like kerosene. I grimace.

Breffni laughs. "As far as I can tell, Jamaica's only contributions to society are Bob Marley and jerk sauce. Possibly ganja. There's the hot-dog man. I think I'll have some fries. You guys hungry?"

"Are you kidding?" I say. "You shouldn't eat anything off the street. Don't you watch those news magazine shows?"

Breffni ignores me, buys a $3 carton of greasy sticks, and anoints them carefully with ketchup and vinegar.

Simien shivers. "Damn, it's cold!" He's wearing short sleeves, and we've all been sweating.

"What's wrong?" Breffni says, mouth stuffed with fries. "Can't stand the great outdoors?"

Simien stamps his feet, trying to get warm. "I love the outdoors, just not in Canada."

"You wouldn't survive in Nepean," I say. "Speaking of survival, I'm still starving."

"What happened to your patty?" Simien asks.

I point to the garbage can.

"What about Faroush's Pizza Donair over there?" Breffni asks. "It must be all right. There's already a lineup, and it's only 2:00 a.m."

"At 2:00 a.m. people will line up to eat hamsters if they're wrapped in pita," Simien says. "They don't know any better. How else can you explain donairs?"

"Donairs are the anal sex of fast food," Breffni says.

"Hey, back off," I say. "The donair's our national food back home. Nepean's the capital of donair pizza. Our grocery stores even sell make-your-own donair kits"

"Here in Toronto we firmly believe donairs are best left to the professionals," Simien says

"I bet you don't have anything in Nepean like Pizza Korner's donairs," Breffni says. "Three for five bucks."

"That's too much donair for any man," Simien says.

"We have something better," I say. "At Maison Kebab you can order something called the Superdonair. It's like they take all the donairs ever made and glue them together. I think they slide the big revolving donair from the spit and wrap it in a pita. The last one I had was so big it lasted three days. I had to throw it out because of the flies."

It's louder in Faroush's Pizza than it was at the Rum Runner. The Arabic music is so loud the bottles of pickled beets on the shelves quiver and shake like belly dancers. Faroush works alone, whirling between the slabs of donair, the triangles of pizza, and the cash register. I wonder how it's possible to be so hairy and yet so bald.

"Faroush is the man!" the guy at the front of the line screams. "He's the only man." The guy's being held up by two of his buddies.

"What would you like, my friend?" Faroush asks the drunk.

"Pizza with gravy."

"One pizza with gravy," Faroush says, and dances off to the heat lamp with a ladle.

"It's the best," the drunk tells us. "The fucking best pizza in the world. Is he the man or what?" The guy turns to the rest of the congregation. "Is he the man?"

The lineup roars its approval. Nobody in here should be driving. Some won't even make it home in a cab. The girl in front of me orders a donair.

"You like full service?" Faroush shouts. The girl nods. Faroush does a little dance, then with one brisk motion rips off the first half of the aluminum foil wrapped around the donair and hands the fast food to her.

"Up and at 'em, Stace, you're next," Breffni says.

"Large donair, hot peppers, extra sauce to go," I say.

Faroush cleaves and ladles. "Full service?"

"Sure. Why not?"

He dances and rips.

I grab the donair, suddenly happier than I've been all night. If you can't get laid, get a donair.

"Fa-roush...Fa-roush...Fa-roush is on *fi-yer*," I sing.

Breffni and Simien join in. "We don't need no water, let the mother-fucker burn... Burn, motherfucker, *buuuuurn*!"

Faroush doesn't get the joke. Moments later neither do we.

"I have AIDS," the waiter says, smiling, by way of introduction. "Can I get you a drink?" His makeup is caked on so thick each pore has a face of its own.

"I'll have a shot of Captain Morgan's rum if you have it," I say.

Breffni shakes his head. Simien's in the washroom.

I survey the club. "So this is the Mercury Olive?"

"Is this Simien's idea of a joke?" Breffni asks.

It's hard to make anything out through the darkness and the thick smoke. The overhead smoke suckers do their best, but they might as well be straws. My shirt has become asthmatic. The only light comes from the hundreds of candles stuck onto the tables, hanging from chandeliers, violating every fire safety code. I'm pretty sure the men in the corner are violating every other code. Rain boots are the latest craze. Everyone salutes one another with an elaborate handshake I've yet to master.

"If you go to the washroom," Simien warns when he returns, "watch out for the bastard in red. The guy kept trying to grab my ass while I was taking a piss." He dries his hands on my shirt.

"Hell of a place you brought us to, man," Breffni says.

"Funky, isn't it? It was decorated by Karie Nishimoto. I think she won an award. All the art's hers, too."

Most of the artwork on the walls involves naughty puppets doing wicked things to each other. The walls themselves are the colour of blood. All the drinks are named after planets.

Breffni shudders. "This place is creeping me out. I bumped into a girl I went out on a date with once. I'm not sure if she's become a lesbian or began as a man."

"Come on, get into the mood," Simien says. "It's just for jokes. Let's go dance. DJ Mouse is spinning tonight."

Mouse is a short man in an oversize white suit. He's wearing a huge explorer's hat. The brim's so big I'm amazed he can see what he's doing. He's hunched over his turntables, which are balanced on a stack of car tires to minimize the vibrations from the dancers. On the floor dancing men wave lit cigarettes like wands. Others move their hands, conducting invisible orchestras. The brief infatuation with the 1970s has passed. The 1980s is the decade of the moment. Some of the men wear fluorescent leggings, others sport upturned collars and polo shirts. Two fellows are dressed in cricket whites. They take turns paddling each other to the delight of the crowd.

"No thanks," Breffni says. "I'll pass." He seems to have resigned himself to the fact that most of the women here are only interested in one another, so he vanishes to the bar.

I'm intrigued by it all. "Isn't that the designer...what's his name?" I say to Simien.

"Greg Cowpland."

"Yeah. He's with another guy."

"So?"

"But isn't he married to that model?"

"She's purely decorative."

"Oh." I'm impressed with the pair. It takes courage and conviction to do the fox trot to techno.

We join them on the dance floor. Simien points to a woman whose drink is leaking slowly onto the ground, but I can't make out what he's saying. We're surrounded by speakers, dozens of them, aimed at us from all directions like guns. In the corner a guy pounds forlornly on a pair of bongos. We have plenty of room to dance. Almost everyone's on the second floor, watching the drag show. Simien dances as if he's been poured out of a glass—fluid like treacle. We jive silently together for what seems like an hour, then head to the bar for a glass of water.

"You said you weren't going to be with Maceo Power for much longer," I say. "Why not? Aren't they any good?"

"They're excellent. Amiris is one of the best I've dealt with. She's not big here, but they all know her in Europe. She used to work for Napolitani. Came here with her girlfriend four years ago. Her girlfriend hated it and went back to Milan. Amiris stayed."

"I'll have to get new comp cards and everything, won't I?"

Simien nods.

"Damn." I foresee several more months of brandless foods and no-name clothes. "At least I'll be able to change up my pictures a little. Will she help me do something with my image? I'm not getting anywhere with this catalogue crap."

"What do you mean?"

"At Feyenoord all they did was send me out on department-store go-sees.

That's the kind of shit I was doing in Nepean. What about the editorial stuff? The magazines? How can you make an image for yourself if all you're doing is modelling clothes that are on sale?"

"Well, first of all, forget about creating an image. Once you start working, the image will find you."

"But you have to have an image. The one I have obviously isn't working. I'm hoping Amiris can make a new one for me. New pictures, new look, new image."

"Never let them create your image for you. I don't have to tell you what happens when they do. Why do you think black people are so messed up? Our image has been repackaged and sold off to the highest bidder. Soul is for sale. Our own souls are disposable, like gloves. Don't worry. Your image will come out on its own. Relax and make money. You can't carry two faces under one hat."

"That doesn't even make sense," I say.

Simien frowns. "It's a proverb. It's not supposed to make sense. Why do I bother talking to you?"

"I wish you wouldn't. All you do is spout those stupid proverbs. You sound like an African fortune cookie."

"Proverbs are the daughter—"

"Fuck off!" I snap, and move down the bar away from Simien.

It's been a bad day. In fact, it's been a pretty awful year. If I thought about it hard enough, I could probably trace my string of rotten luck to puberty. Life sucks from the moment your balls drop. There's probably a proverb warning against the lining up of several shots of rum on a growling stomach, but luckily Simien's too far away to remind me. I need the kind of comfort only rum can provide. A model without an agency is like a prisoner without connections: lost, vulnerable, and easily screwed. If Maceo Power isn't the perfect chance for a fresh start, then I don't know what is. I'll even shave my chest if I have to. Let Amiris reinvent me. I'll be putty in her hands. Screw Simien. Who's he kidding? It's modelling, for Christ's sake. By the very nature of our profession, our characters are untrue, subject to question, flimsy as a nightgown. I'm willing to give my body for the team. Success is but a phone call away. All I have to do is seize the opportunity. First things first, though. I knock back the first of my four new shots.

Simien sits down on the stool next to me, two vodka-limes in hand. He's trying to broker a peace deal. I take one of the vodka-limes and nod. The show from the second floor has unofficially moved up here. The drag queen is blond and big as a linebacker. She's doing a song I've never heard but which the crowd seems to know. Everyone sings along. We watch in silence. After a while, the beat changes from Africountry to disco. DJ Mouse throws on "Got to Be Real" by somebody. We look at each other.

"I think he's playing our song," I say.

We stow our drinks and prance onto the floor, joining an impromptu conga line. Friends once again.

A cheer rises from the mob. The drag queen has taken her hair off. She's a balding man with stubbly hair. It looks red, but it's hard to tell if it's her hair or the spotlight. She twirls the blond wig over her head to the beat. Everyone laughs as if it's part of the show, but I don't think it's something she planned in her dressing room. I think she did it for the hell of it. The way a kid will kick down a sandcastle it took him hours to make. The drag queen pirouettes and flings the wig into the crowd. Another roar. Her smile isn't just for them, I can tell.

TEN

"Yes. Yes. Yes. No. Yes. Tomorrow. The fifteenth. That's tomorrow. Yes." Amiris puts one hand over the receiver, rolls her eyes at me, and mouths "Sorry."

I make myself more comfortable on her round couch, sigh, cast about the office. It's a tiny agency. From the outside it looks like a convenience store, one of those abandoned grocery shops that never sells anything except bus tokens and gum. In a previous incarnation it was the campaign headquarters of a defeated provincial Conservative Party incumbent. A few blue banners still straggle in the higher corners, out of reach of anybody without a ladder. Amiris hasn't even gotten around to removing some of the election signs from the window.

Her office is just as messy. Pictures and comp cards are scattered around the room, two or three thick in some places. There isn't much in the way of decor except a couple of paintings that must have been gifts, and a poster on the ceiling, the kind you usually see at the dentist's office, full of humorous pictograms.

Amiris has shorter hair than I have, and her biceps are bigger than mine. She's plump like a pigeon and dresses like a mechanic. There's a tattoo on one shoulder, melting slightly with age, and wind-catcher earrings adorn her head. She's not a looker, but she's good at her job. In twelve days she's managed to line up more shoots for me than Feyenoord did in three months. If Chelsea Manson has his finger on the pulse of the fashion industry, Amiris has her finger up its ass.

"So are you going to be in my acre of the woods?" she says into the receiver. "That's right. Queen West. Why don't you drop by? It's just across from that. On the other side. Yeah, any time between eight and six. That's it. Right. *Ciao*." Amiris hangs up, jots something down, then smiles at me. "Sorry about that. How long do we have—about an hour? When did they tell you to show up?"

"Eleven."

"So about an hour. That was Chad Lanoue on the phone. He's thinking of stopping by tomorrow. Chad's one of the heaviest hitters around. Too bad I couldn't have signed him in time for the Kameleon audition, but never mind. Where were we. Where's your book?" She speed-reads, eliminating, rearranging. "I like you better the way you are now. Bald is beautiful. Unless you have no choice. What about a goatee? Can you grow one?"

"I've never tried, but I'm probably hairy enough."

"I don't suppose you could grow one by eleven?" She snaps the book shut. "It's too bad what Feyenoord did with you. Wrong approach. They're trying to make you beautiful. You're not beautiful. You have to try to be different."

Simien warned me. She's as blunt as a telephone pole.

"I have a shoot for you this afternoon, by the way. Good one. But don't worry about that now. Worry about Kameleon. We don't have much time. Did you bring your makeup? Clarice went home, so I'll have to do it. Lie on the couch. Let's see what I can do about that pimple. My God you have long eyelashes. Like a pig."

"So how does this work exactly?"

"No different than the thousands of other go-sees you've been through, except this is a little bigger. Actually I lie. It's a lot different. The first part's normal. They'll look at your book, talk to you and whatnot. The second part's the trick. Usually they do something...a little odd."

"Like what?"

"Last year they set up a couch and a bed and had the models seduce each other."

"And the point was?"

"You'd have to ask Dat Win. He's the brains behind it all. And I use the terms *brains* loosely. It's all very eccentric, even for the fashion world. But it works. All of Hollywood's makeup and hair people are buying Kameleons, which means the stars are only one fashion cycle away from wearing them."

"And if they take me?" I know the answer but, like a child at bedtime, I want to hear it again.

"Big money. Large money."

"And fifteen percent for you."

"You got it."

"And if they don't choose me?"

"Not the end of the world. Don't worry. I have plans for you. Europe's only part of the picture. Have you ever thought of South Africa?"

"No." I hadn't, and it's not what I want to hear. I'd rather talk about Ashford Bing, a model from Nowhere, British Columbia, who got a contract with Kameleon two years ago. Now he owns planes, trains, and automobiles. "Do you think I'd have a better chance if I shaved my chest?"

"Are you kidding? Chest hair is a natural resource. Like...corn. It's huge these days."

"Where is it huge? I never see any models with chest hair."

"Not here you don't. It's big in Brazil. Massive."

"So?"

Amiris sighs. "Brazil is fashion's Petri dish. Whatever survives there shows up on our runways and magazines six months later."

"And this has nothing to do with the fact that you're from Rio?"

"Not a thing. Remember those wigs all the kids were wearing last year? Started off in São Paulo. And felt shirts? Those were all over the fashionable ends of Brasilia a couple of months ago. Now they're everywhere."

"So chest hair's in?"

"The next big thing."

I laugh. Soon models will be getting chest-hair grafts. Comb-overs. Amiris tamps the sponge in my eye, and I jerk away.

"Hold still! You need a bit of colour. More so. Just look up at the ceiling. See how many of those picture things you can solve by the time I'm done. The record is six."

I try, but with someone smearing me with makeup I'm just as likely to solve the riddle of the pyramids. I give up, close my eyes so she can do my eyelids, and imagine what life would be like with a contract from Kameleon. No different perhaps, except I'd be rich and happy.

You only get an idea of how big a city is when you walk through it. In Toronto there are the flower boxes and brick sidewalks of Bloor Street West; the mansions and private schools of Forest Hill; Yorkville, where even gum is designer; the drugs of Regent Park. This city's so big you can walk by two murders and three Chinatowns. Nepean's so small you know where all the cops are hiding.

There's a big car race in town and some of the wider streets are closed. I can't see the cars, but I can hear them—like the whine of 2,000-pound mosquitoes. The streets are littered with people dangling on overpasses and bunched on rooftops, trying to get a glimpse of the racers as they go around. I can't understand their fascination. It's like watching traffic. I ignore them and press on.

The Kameleon audition is being held, appropriately enough, in the fashion district. Walking through that neighbourhood is like strolling through a museum exhibit of an old trading post: ancient warehouses storing pelts of animals long extinct, stores with racks of petrified furs in the windows. Then I arrive at the audition—a warehouse packed with petrified models.

Inside it smells of losing. Everyone's just a little too hot. There aren't as many models as I expected. But those who are here have brought their cleats and are ready to play. One model is going up and down the line, yacking it up with agents, clients, other models, but he's got nothing. All the male models are white except me, Crispen, Augustus, and two others. One of them reminds me of an African dictator—black as my shoes, receding hairline, nervous smile, invisible profits stashed in suitcases. He's got the shortest shorts I've seen outside of a pool and has an impressive bulge the size of a tuber. But I'm not scared of him. The other dude is the one to watch. He's a mulatto, so light I'm not sure he's black enough to pass the paper bag test. He's called Mellow Cornell, his real name. Mellow collects thick sheaves of bills at every shoot. He has big, big hair and a Vandyke. His skin looks so soft you want to touch it. He shocked the modelling world at the last big show by wearing a thick moustache and a yarmulke. He can dance, too, has already served his apprenticeship in several music videos, and has graduated into the world of film. I saw the last one he was in. They even let him talk.

"What's wrong?" Crispen asks. "You know, rocking back and forth like that is the first sign of insanity."

"What's Cornell doing here?" I ask "What does he want a Kameleon contract for?"

"Keeping his options open, I suppose. In case his next movie bombs."

Most of the other models are jockeying for space in front of the warehouse's only mirror. Crispen and I hang back, Crispen because he already knows he looks good, me because I know I don't. Unfortunately stress makes me break out. Now I have an enormous zit in the middle of my forehead. It could be an insect that's burrowed into my skull. The makeup Amiris caulked it with does nothing. She warned me against squeezing the pimple, but I already knew better. If I squeezed, it would erupt and I'd scar badly—the mulatto's curse, among others. So I have to suffer on the biggest day of my life with a termite mound protruding from my forehead.

"You realize we're all going to have to go on a diet again," Breffni says.

"Why?" I ask.

"Look at these guys. They're all 130 pounds. Biggs's arms weigh more than that."

"You mean these?" Augustus flexes, kisses each bicep fondly.

"That's right. Muscle's out. Thin's in. Abs are key. Like him." Breffni points.

The model shoving his way to the front looks a little like Jesus—skin the colour of burnished brass, hair like lamb's wool. He wears a T-shirt that's cut off below his nipples. They're all doing everything they can to stand out. Geza features a fur boa. Construction vests are making a comeback. There are two or three felt shirts. Mark Ross struts around in a bra.

"Where's Simien?" Augustus asks.

"You haven't talked to him?" Crispen says. "He's out."

Augustus grins. "Out of the closet?"

"Out of modelling."

"What?" I blurt. Then it clicks—what Simien was trying to tell me the other night. When he said he was leaving, he didn't mean the agency. "Why?"

"To make his film in Africa," Crispen says.

"Africa?"

"He left two days ago."

"Damn!" Africa? I guess that's what Simien meant by a means to an end. "So it's just you and me. And Biggs."

"Has anyone warned you about these auditions?" Crispen asks. "I went to the one last fall. They rented out a club and watched everybody."

"Do what?"

"Nothing. Everything. They hired a DJ, cranked up the music, served drinks and whatnot, and watched them talk to each other, dance, drink, pick each other up. Whatever."

"Yeah, Amiris told me. And they just picked a winner?"

"Apparently."

"That sounds easy."

"Or hard. You wouldn't know what to do."

"I don't really know what I'm doing, anyway. I might as well be having fun doing it."

"That's the spirit."

"Garrick Ross!" They're calling out the first models, and I realize I've forgotten to sign in. The list is five pages long. I'm tempted to scratch out Mellow Cornell's name, but someone's already beaten me to it.

I've only been up for two minutes and already I'm running out of things to say about jeans. "I also have a lot of fresh ideas. Kameleon is an innovative company, and I'd love to be involved in the creative process. For instance..." I didn't actually prepare any ideas. I probably should have thought it through first.

"Interactive ads...uh...for instance. Viewers could vote on-line as to which colour jeans would be in the ads. So while the commercial's on my jeans would change colour, depending on how many people were voting for each one. Changing colours. Like a chameleon. Though I guess the ad would have to be broadcast live from each station running the ad, with staff dedicated to changing the colour of the jeans every time the spot was on. So it probably wouldn't work. But...you get the idea. Is this thing recording?"

The klieg lights in front of me are blinding. I have no idea if the video camera has even started recording my pitch. A man in a short pink sweater told me to begin talking once the little red light went on, and to stop when it went off, but I don't see a red light of any kind. I'm alone in the room. What to do but keep going?

"Or you could try a different approach. Interactive in another kind of way. Get real people involved. Real jeans for real people. Actually that's not a bad slogan. You could take really bad-looking people and throw the jeans on them. I can hear it now. 'If *he* looks good in Kameleons, just think how good *you'd* look. Of course, that would defeat the purpose of hiring a model."

I'm exhausted, more by the futility of my arguments than the effort I've expended explaining them. I realize I've been standing the whole time. There's a chair by my knees, so I sit, shake my head, laugh. "Here I am trying to tell you how to do your job when I don't even know how to do mine."

I can see the light now from the corner of my eye. When I try to peer at it directly, it disappears. I open my mouth but can't think of anything to fill it with. Time to take a moment, marshall my strength for one last salvo. But all I can think of is Simien and what he's up to right now—making last-minute revisions to his script in Africa, checking out locations, holed up somewhere doing a casting call. Only he's the caster, not the castee. I'm starting to envy him. Being a model is so much more stress and so much less reward than I ever imagined. I dread go-sees like a piano exam. I hate cattle calls, tramping the ramp in the occasional show, auditions, like these, armed with my portfolio, my biceps, and my stock of well-worn jokes. Like Willie Loman with a tan on a shoeshine and a fat-ass smile.

I smile. "It's almost comical how ill-prepared I am for this interview. I spent hours studying the history of denim. I can tell you ten unusual things about Levi Strauss. I can quote from a leading analyst's report on the long-term viability of jeans and cords, but I wasn't ready to talk about me. I can't even remember the question. Was there one?"

A breath. What have I got to lose?

"You want to know about me? My name's Stacey Schmidt. I'm six feet tall, not six-one. My interests include amateur psychology and photography. I like to play the cello. I have skinny arms and weak wrists. And this bump on my forehead? It's a zit. And one of my nipples is slightly wider than the other. You can see it if you like."

I stand and unbutton my shirt. "I have a scar on my shoulder, a mole on my neck, a faint discolouration of some kind here on my back, and I refuse to shave my chest no matter how much you pay me." I fold my trousers, slip off my boxers. "I'm an innie, not an outie, a helmet, not a hood and, like eighty-seven percent of adult males, my left testicle hangs lower than my right. Anything else?"

The camera doesn't answer. I'm gripped by the sudden urge to put my fist through the lens.

"You like this?" I turn around. "You like this?" I spread my cheeks. "You like this?" I ride myself like a pony, slapping my bare ass all the way to the finishing post. "I don't play basketball. I hate rap music. I like easy blondes. I like to imagine girls in bed with themselves and one of my pictures, and I pretend I like to talk to cameras. To tell you the truth, I hate talking to cameras, especially when there's no one behind them."

I spread my toes, arch my back, reach for the ceiling. "You like this?" I hold my pose, stare into the lens, feeling neither the breeze from the half-open door, nor the look of the man in the pink sweater who's holding it open. I'm captured by the miniature upside-down me reflected in the lens of a camera which, for the first time I can remember, seems on the verge of talking back.

The office is cold and quiet. "Don't worry about it," Amiris says. "They wouldn't know a good model if one kicked the shit out of them. Did they tell you anything else?"

"Not really." My chest is tight. "Just that they look forward to seeing me next year. Is that good?"

"No, they always say that. That's their way of saying they don't expect you to go anywhere between now and then."

Perfect. Modelling's kiss of death. I don't feel well. Opportunity has once again slipped through my fingers. I've fumbled on the five. "I really shit the bed on this one, didn't I?"

"Listen, it wasn't that big a deal. Besides, there's still a chance. The people who blew you off were just Kameleon's underlings. Dat Win looks at all the tapes personally."

"Is there any way I can prevent that from happening?"

She laughs. "People always think they did worse than they did. Relax. I'm sure it wasn't that bad."

I didn't tell her about the nudity, nor the mooning. I'm sure she'll find out soon enough when she's called as a witness at my trial.

"And if you did really blow it, no problem. All that TV stuff's not that important, anyway. There's a lot of action on the Web these days. I just hired a girl, Natalya, as the head of our Internet Opportunities division. She's the only one right now, but I expect big things."

The Internet—real modelling's poorest cousin. Is this what I have to look forward to? Exiled to the farthest reaches of cyberspace?

"That's the future," Amiris says. "In about two hours you have a shoot at the Scarborough Fair. A real shoot. An editorial for *Venue*. It's one of the most prestigious fashion magazines in Toronto. The only fashion magazine in Toronto really. If I'm right, and I think I am, their editor is just about to get a job offer from *Lashes* in New York. They loved the stuff you did in the Inertia ads. And they told me Simien put in a good word for you. That reminds me." She pulls out a thick brown envelope from somewhere on her desk. "He left this for you."

"Thanks." The envelope isn't addressed to anyone. It's pregnant with meaning, so I tuck it into my portfolio for later.

"By the way, I hear from some of the clients that you like to talk to the camera."

"Is that bad?"

"No. Use it. Whatever. The clients think it's great. *Venue* loves that kind of stuff. The weirder, the better. *Venue*'s pretty artsy, but everyone in the industry reads it. Don't worry. You'll be fine." She sounds as if she's trying to convince herself.

The fair smells of straw and cigarettes. Carnies are everywhere, putting up tents, assembling booths, testing weighted balls and crooked hoops, mounting unwinable stuffed animals. I wander around the bumper cars, the Tilt-a-Whirl, the Viking Ship, the Gravitron, lost like one of the hundreds of children who will be tomorrow. Most of the rides are still being put together. The Ferris wheel isn't moving and won't be without a couple of more bolts. Everything is emblazoned with the crest of a manic clown with crosses for eyes. An odd logo. In traditional cartoon lingo that would mean the clown is either dead or drunk.

I peer into one tent, hoping to find my shoot, but it's the wrong one. Clowns swear. The magician can't find his scarves.

Most of the carnies are sitting in the bingo tent. They're largely silent, waiting for tomorrow and the flow of adolescent cash. The carnies actually look like carnies. Women are missing teeth. Men have third-generation tattoos. I ask one of them if he knows where the shoot is. He grunts and motions over his shoulder. Behind his booth three men hammer the last pipes that will propel screaming children down and into a tank filled with brownish water. Beside it is a sign—THE CHUTE. Beside that, another sign: YOU MUST BE THIS HIGH TO RIDE. An arrow points at my groin.

"No, I mean a fashion shoot." I pantomime a camera, gently press the shutter.

He shrugs. "Ask at the food court. Someone there might know." He draws me a map in the straw.

I pass rows of booths selling candied things, turn left at the Whack-a-Mole, left at the roulette wheel. The International Food Court is a hastily constructed village of plywood replica restaurants that seems as if it cost more to assemble than it would have to bring the restaurants themselves. There's nobody around. The yellow lemon stands are still shut. I notice the few carnies who are around aren't eating their own food. They may have criminal records, but they aren't dumb. I tap a little kid's shoulder, but when he turns around I see he's on a cell phone. He raises his finger in an "I'll be with you shortly" gesture. "I need four. Four. Don't you know how long that's going to take? At least...at least twenty minutes. I don't care. Well, you can tell him to fuck right off. You can tell him I said that..."

I try to find the entrance to the fair again, but I don't remember seeing the Mystery Mansion on my way in. I would have noticed the drawings, which could be spiders or werewolves. A woman is writing poems on the front in blood-red paint. She's only finished one: HERE LIES HUGH. INSTEAD OF

GRAVY, SHE SERVED HIM GLUE. I wonder if the children will find that as funny as I do.

An older man stacks beer bottles onto little shelves inside his booth.

"Do you know where the fashion shoot is being held?"

"Wanna try one? Free?" He tosses me a grey baseball.

"What do I do?"

"It's the Beer Smash. Try and smash 'em with the ball. He indicates the rows of empty bottles. By the smell of his breath, he probably drank them all himself, possibly in the past half hour.

"No thanks."

A nearby sign promises elephants and horses that do math. I don't see any horses, but you can't miss the elephants or their trails of dung. Three elephants are chained to pickup trucks. They have dark circles under their eyes and look as if they haven't slept in weeks. The pachyderms sway back and forth, listlessly sweeping straw with their trunks. One of them spots me, leans over, whispers, "Kill me now. I have riches..." I pretend not to hear and keep walking past the video arcade, past two tents too nasty to house models, under an arch, back to the main rides.

Nearby some carnies try out their games while others test their portable headsets and five-watt speakers. "Come on over, Smiley. Hey, there, you look lucky! One-two-one-two. Sibilance, ssibilance..." One carnie has recruited a half-dozen others to try out his water gun horse race.

"And they're off!" The six carnies, with deadly concentration, one eye closed, tongues wagging, try to spur their water-powered mounts toward the winning post. "Okay, guys, that's fine." One by one they stop squirting, put down their guns, and amble off to man their own rides. The guy who was shooting at the yellow horse seems disappointed. His horse was in the lead.

To my left there's a row of shiny port-a-potties waiting to be defiled. To my right, a row of phones. I pick up a receiver and call the agency.

"Maceo Power, can I help you?"

"Is Amiris there? It's Stacey."

"Shit, shouldn't you be shooting something by now?"

"The shoot's in about twenty minutes, but I can't find it."

"I told you, it's at the fair!"

"I know that. I'm here. But did they say where?"

"Where? I don't know where. They didn't say. Just ask around."

"I did. No one knows."

"Well, keep asking. You can't miss this shoot."

"Right." I hang up, lift the receiver again, punch Melody's number. The phone rings. Her voice mail answers.

"Melody, it's me. I don't know how much longer I can take this. This is the worst day ever. I went to the most important audition in my life and got laughed at. Then I get a good shoot for a good magazine, and now I can't find it. I'm getting hot, my makeup's melting...I...I just want to come home and see you. Would that be okay? But I don't have any money. I don't know if—well, we'll talk about it. I've got to go."

There's only one man nearby. He's cleaning his booth, which is adorned with faded watercolour Dolly Partons and Elvis Presleys in different poses, most of them drunken. It's a game—throw a ball into a basket. If the ball stays in the basket, you win a prize. The prizes are brightly coloured plastic bats kids can smash one another with.

"There's a fashion shoot being held somewhere at the fair," I say to the man. "Do you know where?"

"Hmm?"

I notice a small sign tacked to the counter: TO INCREASE THE DEGREE OF SKILL REQUIRED TO WIN, THE BASE OF THE TUB HAS BEEN REINFORCED WITH A RUBBER INSERT. So there truly is honour among thieves.

"Listen, do you know where the—"

"Try over there." He points to nowhere.

"Thanks."

I take the road less travelled. It leads to what must be the carnies' living area: rows of trailers with satellites, pup tents with graffiti, Coleman-powered lives. There are padlocks on all the doors. Some of the carnies are relaxing in hammocks, others are fixing their trailers. Everywhere there's the sign of the manic clown. I feel as if I'm the hero in a cartoon adventure book. Tintin. The Hardy Boys.

There's a girl sitting on the steps of a smallish trailer. She is almost exactly unlike Melody in every way except one. She has the same indescribable aura of sexuality about her that draws me like a moth.

"Excuse me, I'm looking for a fashion shoot. Do you know where it is?"

"Why? Are you a model?" I'm disappointed she had to ask.

"I'm supposed to be shooting something for a magazine."

"I saw them setting up some lights and stuff in the big red tent. There were some skinny-looking girls walking around."

"The big red tent with the swirly top? Isn't that for the animals?"

"Tomorrow it's for the animals. Today it's for the models."

"Thanks."

"Do you want me to tell your future?"

"I'd love to, but if I don't get to this shoot in five minutes, I won't have any future."

"Well, you're walking the wrong way. It's over there."

The roller coaster needs some vitamins and a good meal. With its bony frame it could have been built out of matchsticks. The support beams are bowlegged, each resting on four small blocks of wood. I almost expect to find a coaster under one leg. A sign reads: THIS RIDE IS NOT RECOMMENDED FOR GUESTS WITH HIGH BLOOD PRESSURE, NECK AND BACK INJURIES, PREGNANCY. Someone forgot to add COMMON SENSE to the list. A smaller sign beside it says: DO NOT FORCE CHILDREN TO RIDE IF THEY ARE FRIGHTENED. Does it happen so often they had to make a sign?

The photographer gives the signal. A pimply teen in a black heavy metal T-shirt puts his weight behind the lever, and the roller coaster groans. Our carriage clacks up the wooden slats, climbing slowly like an old man up the stairs. I glance at the crowd below. I'd give anything to be down there. I test the safety bar, stifle the urge to scream, "Stop the ride!"

The roller coaster halts, anyway. For a second I'm afraid that it's broken and I'll be stuck up here until they can build an even bigger roller coaster to get me down. But the stop's all part of the plan.

"Okay, hands in the air!" the photographer below shouts through a megaphone. All six of us—two other men, three women, all beautiful, all forgettable—dutifully put our hands in the air and do our best to look bored.

"That's the idea. More blasé. You're going fast, but you don't care." The photographer's whispering into the megaphone now, trying not to cause a scene, but some of the carnies have already gathered. I open my mouth a crack, pretend I'm stifling a yawn.

"Good, Stacey, I like it," the photographer says. I can only assume he's clicking away. He said later he'd digitally blur the background to make it seem as if we're travelling incredibly fast while we remain stationary. I have to admit I'm looking forward to seeing the finished product. I wish I thought of the shot myself. It's a fitting metaphor for those of us who belong to the Generation of Ennui.

The photographer seems to have stopped shooting. He, his assistant, and the art director huddle together. The photographer picks up the megaphone. Apparently we're too high and they're too low. They can't quite get the clothes from there. The clothes were designed by students at one of the local art colleges. *Venue* runs a tight joint. Its clothes and models are always free. The entire operation is based on the premise that the students will do anything to promote their lines and the models will do anything to get good editorial shots for their books. It works out great for everyone. Especially *Venue*.

"What if you guys stand up in the roller coaster?" the photographer asks. "Is that safe?"

I'm not a big fan of that.

"It's kind of high," yells the girl to my right, my date for the next hour. Right on, sister.

The photographer turns to his assistant. "Is it that high?" The megaphone's still on. His assistant nods.

One of the models in front of me wriggles out from behind his safety bar and stands. "How's this?"

The photographer peers through his viewfinder. "No, no, that doesn't work. No, no, never mind. We're bringing you down."

The model barely has enough time to sit. Our cart jolts forward and creaks back toward the start. I pray there aren't any loops.

They're jigging and rejigging the lights, toying with exposures and filters. One of the carnies has been recruited to hold up a reflector board to give us more light, but there still isn't enough.

"Can we open up the top of the tent a bit to let in some more sun?" the photographer asks.

The carnie shakes his head.

"Can we take down one of the sides?"

Again no.

The photographer sighs. "All right." He turns to us. "Five-minute break. We'll get this thing figured out eventually."

I've worked with most of these models enough to know they have nothing to say. Two of them are playing hacki-sack with a ball of tape. The girls are talking about boys. I pull out Simien's envelope from my bag, open it in a corner. Most of the letter is "to thine own self be true" variations on a theme. The bulk of the envelope is actually a creased pamphlet entitled *Modelling Made Easy*. It seems to have been written by a model of some kind, a super one by the sound of it. I'm intrigued. Inside the cover is an inscription from Simien: "It may be hard to believe, but this thing got me through six years of the business. Whenever I lost sight of the end and got caught up in the means, I flipped through this. It always put everything in perspective. All the best. P.S.: If you want to know why I left, turn to page 21." I do so after stealing a scone from the food tray when no one's looking.

Page 21: "There are three types of models. (1) Those who are happy modelling and want to do it forever. (2) Those who talk all day of doing something else but never make the move. (3) Those who make a specific decision and move." I wonder what Simien is trying to tell me.

The photographer, his assistant, and the carnie are still trying to figure out if they can add another light without blowing the generator. I figure I have time for a quick flip through the pamphlet.

Page 2: "The modelling profession is here to stay. Robots alone will never sell shampoo or lipstick or aftershave lotion. Models are hired every day. One of them could be you."

Page 4: "Nails are sturdy, but they are not tools, and if you use them for opening containers and the like, they will suffer. They are not to be used as substitutes for wooden or metal implements."

Page 8: "Even people blessed with perfect skin get an occasional pimple."

With indispensable advice like this at his disposal it's no wonder Simien rose so quickly to the top of his profession. Perhaps the author's saving the best stuff for last.

Page 16: "Always remember, the best shots are simply extracts of one long, continuous, gracious movement. Keep moving. Above all avoid carefully contrived 'poses.' These lack style, emotion, and impact. Almost always they look artificial and awkward."

Not bad.

Page 18: "Skin falls into oily, dry, and normal categories, too. Test yourself to see what your type is. Clean your face with your normal cleanser and use a mild astringent such as witch hazel afterward. Wait one hour, then wipe a piece of tissue paper (the type you wrap gifts with, not paper tissues) over your face."

Less so.

Page 27: "Hirsutism is not highly regarded in our society on men or women. For a model it is an absolute negative. Body hair must be removed. This does not mean covered with makeup or bleach creams. It must be removed completely."

That's no good. Then again, what does she know? It's obvious she never had to contend with chest hair. I mean, it's not like trimming a bikini line. Chest hair has tough, firm roots like crabgrass. The very fact that she thinks you could even try to cover up it up with makeup or bleach creams proves she has no clue what she's talking about. I close the pamphlet in disgust, then check the publication date. If it was published recently, it would prove that Amiris's theory about the rebirth of chest hair was bollocks. But it was printed in 1984 when models still looked like people and $1,000 was a lot of money.

"All right, I think we've almost got it down," the photographer finally says. "You can go ahead and put your clothes on."

We didn't put clothes on earlier because there were hardly any to put on, and they didn't want us to get cold. A cold model is a bad model, especially in these outfits. Mine is simple—a black skintight bathing suit with three little yellow, blue, and green lines on the side. I squirm into it. Aside from the presence of a hem and the absence of a frontal aperture, it looks like a pair of shiny boxer shorts.

For this shot we're supposed to be a team of lion tamers. The lions, of course, will be added later. I'm not sure how these outfits relate to the concept of lion-taming, but I'm confident all will be revealed by the photographer. He's a slim, short, orange-brown sort of man, the first photographer I've seen with a wedding ring or a tan.

"Okay, back to your marks, everyone. Petr, here's your whip." Petr has graphite abs and a geometrical chin. Most of the photographers I've talked to think he's the best thing since the last thing. I think he's too much like a cartoon—all squares and boxes. Next to him I'm a stick figure.

"Steve, here's yours. Stacey..." He looks me up and down, eyes lingering on my chest.

The art director walks over to him. "This isn't quite what we're going for. This isn't going to work." He shakes his head.

"That's why you should always check their books first instead of hiring them by their comp cards," the photographer says. In my case it wouldn't have helped. Amiris pulled what few body shots I had out of my book.

"It's okay," the photographer says. "We can still make this work." He glances at the makeup man. "Don't go anywhere. I have a plan."

After a few minutes, the plan becomes clear. I'm not thrilled, but who am I to question a man with a $2,000 suntan? I've never worn this much makeup in my life. Even on Halloween. I feel as if I'm starring in a Barnum and Bailey production of *Cats*. The makeup artist has led me over to the edge of the tent near the flap where there's more light. From here I can see the other animals—the poodles, the arithmetic horse, the elephants. One of the elephants looks right at me. I almost envy him.

The makeup artist smears some more paint on his glass palette, takes a knife, spreads it. Takes another triangular sponge, dips it in the makeup, and rubs me with it. My pores are being sealed, perhaps for good.

"I think I have some in my mouth."

"Of course you're going to get it in your mouth if you talk. The only good model's a quiet model. There's a good lad."

I go back to gazing out the flap. I can almost see the carnies' trailers from here. After I'm done, I think I'll ask out that cute little fortuneteller. I wonder if she already knows that and has fled. But if the carnies caught me walking around with this much makeup on, they'd laugh, then bash me. To console myself I try to think of all the men for whom makeup is a daily part of their lives—news anchors, female impersonators, makeup artists, morticians. I read in a magazine once that Egyptian men used to wear makeup every day, applied it as liberally as women. And they'd anoint their gods with the stuff, too. Along with offerings of food, makeup was used to keep their gods alive. Egyptians would even take makeup with them to the grave. Wealthier Egyptians were buried with servants and makeup. Makeup was their ticket to eternal life. Of course, their makeup was lead-based, which helped get them there quicker.

"Hold still and open your eyes. Almost done."

He's attached nails to my fingers, fur to my feet. With all the makeup my head weighs five pounds more. I have trouble straightening it. Keep cool, I tell myself. Just pretend you're an ancient Egyptian. This makeup might well be your passport to the cosmos. I wonder if models existed in the days of Cheops and Tutankhamen and whether they were buried alive with their pharaohs. And if those ancient models knew their lead makeup was slowly killing them, would they have cared?

ELEVEN

It happens to be pouring, but it doesn't always rain when dreams go bad. Sometimes there isn't a cloud in the sky, and then you wish it would rain, so you wouldn't have to explain to anyone why your face is wet. Sometimes there's snow, and each crunchy footstep is slow motion, as in those dreams where you're running full speed from the vampires or the lizards but your feet are stuck.

I take the magazine out again to make sure. I'm not afraid to get it wet. I need a good look. It's even worse than I thought. The caption reads: "The Beast." The picture features Petr and me in a cage, Petr with a whip, me on a stool growling at the camera, my hands and feet covered in fur, my face slathered in brown makeup and bristling with whiskers. Even Amiris had the sense not to say anything to me at the agency other than "You'll do better next time," though we both knew there wouldn't be one.

Around me people pass by in raincoats, hoods pulled down as if they're astronauts or scientists from one of those dumb plague flicks. The air smells of boiled hot dogs.

I thumb through Simien's pamphlet, searching for advice. But in thirty pages there's only one paragraph about screwing up: "Rejection is the hardest part of modelling. No matter how well you may think you're pre-pared, it's still going to be a problem. However, depression must be avoided at all costs. It's self-defeating. Every job has its ups and downs."

Only one paragraph, and she's still got it all wrong. Rejection isn't the hardest part of modelling. The hardest part is humiliation. When you're rejected, at least no one else knows you failed. Because of the Beast, Toronto's fashionables are looking and laughing. Who's going to hire a beast to launch their new lines? This isn't the way I drew it up. What are my choices? Steal all the copies before they hit the streets? Pack away my face and put away my smile? I'm skinny, I look like a goat, and in five years I won't have any hair on top of my head. My window of opportunity is being sealed. I only have Melody to look forward to and she hasn't spoken to me in two weeks. It scares me to say it, think it even, but right now she's the only thing I have left, and I don't even really have her.

I'm a character caught in a half-assed love song, and it's maddening because I can't make it stop. The way Melody's lips prune when she pouts. The way she hugs herself, or kisses her own hand when you aren't looking. I wonder if Melody still looks as good now as when I left her. I don't have the money for a ticket. Things have been so tight these days I've had to steal envelopes from the instant teller just to write Melody letters, most of which have been returned unopened. The boys aren't around, or I'd hit them up for money. I know Amiris would give me an advance, but right now I can't go back to the agency. I have no choice but to call Melody, hope she has pity and a major credit card.

Why is it that pain inspires art? Why couldn't it be something else? Like contentment. Or pleasure. Everything I see is a photograph. The blue-and-white flicker of distant TV screens, like the flare of far-off lightning. Rows of flashing red car alarms blinking like Christmas tree lights.

Melody said she had to sell the car to make her rent. She offered to meet me, but I think the walk will do me good.

I pause, wondering which way to go. In this area some roads end in an accent—Tassé or Épée. Others, like Costello, end in a river. I follow Costello to the end, stroll along the bank. A school of fishlets follows me, expecting alms. I pick up the husk of a sunflower seed and toss it to them. They swarm, each taking turns tasting it, spitting it out, disgusted. I feel guilty for wasting their time. There should be a sign saying DO NOT TEASE THE FISH. Farther down the river I can see a duck caught in the rapids. It's zimming through the water like a motorboat. It's impossible to tell from the duck's implacable expression whether it's shitting its pants or having the time of its life. To the left of the river is the hill where I learned to roller-skate. Back then it seemed so steep. Now I realize a ball wouldn't roll down it without being pushed. Even farther there's a grove of trees. I know each one individually. The pine tree with the wasps' nest, for instance. I remember a wasp landing on my hand but not stinging me. Ever since I've fished wasps out of pools and left them on my food. The birch tree was known as the chicken tree because, Melissa convinced me, if you peeled off the bark, the white wood inside tasted like chicken. Melissa was the first girl I loved, the first one not to love me back, the only girl I've ever eaten a tree for.

The pile of boulders is still there. When the sun blazed, we'd bake mud pies on them and watch Brad Taylor eat them. His brother got me back by tricking me into drinking a cup of his urine. By the boulders is a grassy hill where I set up my tent. From which, I'm still convinced, Tom Sidey stole my purse. It was as natural for me to carry a purse as it was for Tom Sidey to steal it. It was simply in our natures. Neither of us gave a damn about anything except my having my purse stolen and his getting caught. I can still smell apple juice and Arrowroot cookies.

The town houses are across the field. They're paper buildings with paper doors, bunched together like cells in a paper wasps' nest. It's strange being back in a city where the roads change their names three times, a town in which the cabs are blue and everyone's last name is Roy. It's even weirder being back in my old housing complex. Everything's still almost the same. There's a tree where a fence used to be, a post where a tree once was, a fence where there was none before. Nothing has really changed, and I'm not yet old enough for that to be comforting. When I look at one of my old neighbourhood trees, all I can think of is that it was there before me, it's there now, and it'll be there long after I'm gone. I kind of hoped that once I left, the neighbourhood would decay, fall instantly into ruin. Things are no better, no worse, no different. Maybe some houses smell more of curry than apple pie. Maybe fewer kids leave their bikes outside at night. But if I were to ring the bell of 43 Monterey, I almost expect Johnny Franklin to answer the door, ready with his plastic soldiers and his grandfather's revolver. We were a great team. I'd always play the Indian, he the cowboy. Children, if left to themselves, always figure everything out for themselves.

I never noticed the number of bird feeders and the amount of patio furniture. Strange, since there are few birds and no patios. Every yard is concrete, every lawn four feet wide. But with their feeders, gnomes, and deck chairs, residents can convince themselves, at least for a while, that they live a little better than they do.

The other side of the street is as mysterious to me now as it was then. The Schultzes and the Wieners lived there, and that was good enough for me. I've come full circle. It's getting dark and there's nothing more to see. I wonder why I've never been back here since the day my family moved out of this neighbourhood twelve years ago, especially since Melody lives four blocks away, across from the public pool. She isn't home yet, and the pool is closed, so there's nothing to do but wait.

"You're bald," Melody says.

"I needed a change. Like it?"

"I like you no matter what. Do you like the flowers?"

"I love them." Actually I hate them. They're flagrant flowers. Garish reds and yellows. Spiky things that could only have been intended to prick or to snare. I'm not crazy about flowers at the best of times. I can't stand to watch them wither slowly and die—a grim reminder that I, too, will crinkle, crease, dry up, blow away. Flowers are mortality in a box, and even the box reminds me of a coffin.

"I got you something else, too," she says, handing me a small yellow box wrapped in tissue paper. "Open it."

It's a bottle of cologne. It feels expensive. A great gift, especially since, due to recent cutbacks, I've been reduced to daubing my pulse points with mouthwash. "Wow! You really shouldn't have..." I mean it. Not only is it extravagant, but it's obviously fraught with romantic intentions. My only gift is my presence.

"You like it? It's new. Well, it used to be new. I bought it before...we stopped seeing each other. I was going to throw it out, but I kept it just in case."

She's about to cry. I move in with a hug. "I'm glad to be back. I really needed to see you. Everything's been going so..." I give her a kiss, long, lingering, slightly wet.

Melody draws away. "Stacey, are you horny?" She has the subtlety of pepper spray.

"No, why?" I am, of course, but it's hard to get away with the lie. A man's penis is like a dog's tail. I draw her close again. Another kiss. This time she doesn't pull back. I unbutton her shirt, fumble with her bra, take one of Melody's long nipples in my mouth. It's like sucking on a straw. Slowly I unbutton her pants, but they won't come off without a fight. "Why do you always wear such tight jeans?"

"I know you'd like all my clothes to have drawstrings, but that isn't practical."

"You're right." I tug again.

"Let me," she says.

I cover her chest with kisses, wind my way down. Belly. Button. Around the bend. Downtown. Her pubic hair is dirty blond, the colour of dry grass. Her smell is as familiar as my own.

"My turn," she says.

I've never been so turned on in my life, but I say that every time we're together. She has a good body, 135 pounds, not too soft. Sexy legs, short but shapely. Gymnastic calves. I'm always excited by our contrast—hot chocolate and *guimauve.* And she knows how to move. She's a good Catholic girl. Blushing when the lights are on. Fucking on the first date.

Melody is strangely quiet. Normally she's always begging me to do something kinky—to take her against the wall, on the table, in the shower. I stopped wanting to do stuff like that since the first time we tried it years ago when we thought we were the first ones to have sex in a change room or in a stairwell. Since then I've learned that kinky sex usually means getting cold, dirty, and sore.

"Slowly," she says, and I obey.

The elemental joys are these. The smell of my skin in the sun. Playing a long A on a cello. The first fifty yards of a run. The moment of penetration. She winces in pain, then sighs with pleasure. Dimly I wonder if she's been as faithful as she sounds. It's hard to trust a beautiful woman whose pillows smell of smoke.

Usually I don't have trouble making it last, but tonight I'm ready, like a teenager about to explode. "Wait," I gasp, and she freezes, a fawn dropping for cover, sensing danger, until it's safe to move again. "Okay."

I gaze down the length of our bodies. For some reason I'm reminded of a documentary I saw recently, the last thing I watched before my cable was cut off. I thought one of the things that distinguished humans from other creatures was the fact that we were the only species to have sex for fun, and the only mammals to do it face-to-face. But I learned that day the rare pigmy chimpanzee in central Congo does both. Their sex organs, unlike those of almost all other animals, are always swollen. They're always ready to mate. In fact, sex is their social glue. They do it to greet, appease, reassure, reconcile. They do it morning, noon, and night. When they're excited, nervous, happy. They do it with friends, mothers, sisters and brothers, babies. Even males with males, females with females. They do it on the ground, on all fours, even swinging from the trees.

"What's wrong?" she asks.

"Nothing, nothing. Don't stop."

Afterward we lie together, cuddled, silent for at least ten minutes.

"Can I see the picture?" she asks.

"The Beast? No."

"Is it that bad?"

"Yes." I pitched it out the window somewhere between Nepean and Tweed.

"It's probably not as bad as you think."

"It is."

"You can't share it with me?"

"No."

"If this is going to work, you're going to have to start sharing more. Everything, not just the good stuff, but the bad stuff, too."

"I didn't come here to share the bad stuff. I came to get away from it."

"So I'm you're little Fantasy Island? Forget about all your troubles for an hour, then on your way again?"

"I'm not on my way again." Right now the last thing I want to do is leave. It's warm, I'm safe, and everything in my life seems like someone else's nightmare. I realize I've forgotten to book out at Maceo Power. Amiris will probably figure it out. I'll call her in the morning. Melody's still talking.

"Too much for you? What is it exactly that you want? You said it was because of the distance. That's not going to change now, is it?"

She chronicles the past two years of our relationship, complete with footnotes and bibliography. I blink at her stupidly, not willing to give up, but I can't fight sleep. I go down hard, tranquillized like an elephant.

After some makeup sex and leftover pie, I look around the small apartment. Not much has changed since I was last here almost a year ago. There isn't a lot of furniture, but what little Melody has is all beige. She bought it at the same time, after her Florida aunt died. There are several pictures of children dressed as bees and an old photo of Martin Luther

King, torn carefully from *Time* and taped to a wall. The door to her bedroom is open. Her bed's big and nondescript. It has no headboard. There are two dishes by the door for her cat, Ziggy Stardust. I can't see the kitchen from here, but I know what's in it. Two sets of cheap china, one with flowers, one with bees. A toaster, a toaster oven, a can opener, a can sealer, a sandwich maker, a rice steamer, a waffle iron, and two blenders, one for ice and one for fruit. In the fridge there are some unpronounceable vegetables, mustard, pie, and a bottle of wine. White. The apartment is almost perfectly clean. She has someone come in every two weeks to vacuum. I sneeze loudly.

"It's Ziggy Stardust, isn't it?" Melody always insists on using the cat's full name, the way she does with me when she's mad. "I didn't have time to bring him to my mother's this time. You should have given me more warning you were coming."

"Sorry, it was just a spur-of-the-moment kind of thing." If I thought about it, I probably wouldn't have come. Another loud sneeze. Soon the neighbours will be banging on the wall.

I nudge her playfully. "Why don't we go out?"

"Now? Stacey, it's almost eleven. Nothing's open."

"Damn. I forgot where we were. In Toronto you can buy a record or file for divorce till four in the morning."

"There's that new movie place. It's open twenty-four hours."

"Where?"

"Where the old drive-in used to be. They built a huge movie cavern. I've been dying to go, but I haven't had anyone to go with except Jesmine, and she doesn't like scary movies. Let's go see a scary movie."

The streets are surprisingly busy for a Wednesday night. Girls, scantily clad and heavily perfumed, are heading to the bars, following each other by smell, like ants. I wish I could join them. Perhaps not surprisingly there's been a corresponding rise in the level of black men out and about.

In fact, there seems to be more of us around here than I remember seeing growing up. Back then they could fit us all in a movie theatre, with room to prop up our feet. Now there are enough of us on this street alone to demand our own radio station.

"Since when don't you like holding hands?" Melody asks.

I didn't realize I wasn't. I extend my hand. Her grip is tight and dry.

The theatre is in the east end. In Nepean the east and west ends are only separated by a couple of blocks, a bridge, and socioeconomics. But we decide to take the bus, anyway, for old time's sake.

The bus must be on its last run. It rumbles through empty downtown streets, stopping only for red lights. Melody, two young black men, and I are the only ones on board. We're up front; the other two are on the bench at the back. The taller one wears a yellow, black, and green leather outfit. The short one sports a Philadelphia 76ers shirt, basketball shoes, and baggy Kameleon jeans. They talk loudly in Jamaican. I sniff to inhale their negrosity, then glance down at my Boston College sweatshirt, Levi jeans, and New Balance tennis shoes, vowing to find something a bit more exotic tomorrow, even though I can't afford it.

The bus stops at Gervais and St. Germain to let on an old lady. By the sound of her voice and the look of her hat, she's clearly mad. She only has $1.45, but the bus driver lets her on, anyway, with a smile. Suddenly the guy in the Kameleon jeans points out the rear window and laughs. The other follows his friend's finger and joins in. Fifty yards away another black guy is running toward the bus.

"De bway na gwayne mek it. Raja! Go, Raja! Cho! De rasclat bway na gwayne mek it. Run, Raja!"

Roger gets there just as the doors close. His friends laugh as he pounds away at the back of the bus. All three of us know the driver won't stop.

"If Raja ever fine mistah bus driva, him fe buss him up sometin' good!" More laughter.

Melody leans over and whispers fiercely, "I'm glad you're not like them." She squeezes my hand, her blue eyes glistening strangely in the orange bus light.

As we get off the bus and walk toward the theatre, she asks me why I released her hand as the two black guys passed us, but I don't remember letting go.

It's just after one and neither of us is tired, but we can't think of anything else to do. Less than twenty-four hours in her company and I'm already bored. We try to play Monopoly, but Ziggy Stardust seems to have eaten most of the hotels. Melody offers to give me a massage, but without essential oils every hair would be teased, pulled, plucked. It's hard to relax when you feel as if you're being waxed.

Melody shows me photos of her and the girls in Cancún, her and an occasional famous movie star at the Hard Rock Café in Orlando. She tries on all her new hats for me. Melody loves hats. She sings "Can't Get Enough of Your Love" in a funny voice.

"Why don't you put on some of that sexy stuff I gave you last Christmas?" I ask.

"That was two Christmases ago."

"Whatever."

"All right."

She snaps on garters, transparent bras, underwear with relevant holes. When she's harnessed up, she struts across the floor in an exaggerated runway swagger. I'm jealous. It seems to come so naturally to women. It took me two months to learn how to walk on a runway. I still haven't got it down, and I'm a professional.

Melody leans against the lamp and leers at me in her best impression of a $100 whore. "You like?"

She's crisscrossed with pink marks where the straps cut off circulation. Bits and pieces are falling out. The white frilly lace clashes with her sour-cream skin. I'm less turned on than morbidly excited.

Melody reaches into my robes. My penis is already cocked. I push her down onto the ground, don't bother to unstrap her, brush aside her underwear. She hasn't showered after the second time. She tastes like rust.

"Let's do it here," she says. The hardwood, I know from experience, is gritty and carpeted with cat hair, but I'm too tired to put up a fight.

I feel a curious sense of detachment, as if I'm not really here. I watch as her hand grabs my penis, guides it toward her. My head swells, waxy like a mushroom. My apparatus is poised. Carefully I lower and insert it.

This third time she feels surprisingly soft. Tenderized. A lump of dough ready to be shaped. I've never noticed how pale her skin is. It's white like toilet paper. I go through the motions, groping and grunting on cue. Sex is as emotionally fulfilling as a sneeze.

She gazes into my eyes. "What's wrong?"

I look away. "Nothing. Nothing at all."

"Stacey, is this relationship only about sex?"

"No," I answer, too slowly.

She pulls away. "Is that why you came back?"

"I told you. I wanted to see you."

"So does this mean we're back together?"

"Does this have to mean anything? I mean, does it have to...do we have to talk about it now?"

"No, you're right." She smiles. "What are you thinking?"

"Nothing."

"Are you bored?"

"No."

"Do you want to sleep?"

"No."

"Do you want to watch TV?"

"No."

"Why don't you take some pictures?"

"Of what?"

"Of me, silly. You said you would. Remember? On the phone?"

"I'm not in the mood."

"You've been in a bad mood since the movies. Come on, it would be fun. You promised. You can take some naughty ones if you want."

Now that she's gotten this in her head, it would take more out of me to dissuade her than it would to take pictures. "Fine. I need some music, though. And some more wine."

I stumble over to the stereo, still naked, root around. Nothing but old seventies albums. Songs that last the whole side of the record. Double-necked guitars and twenty-minute drum solos. I guess anything sounds good if you listen to it long enough. Thankfully she still has the Miles Davis CD I sent her a couple of months ago to make up for something. As Wordsworth said, jazz urges tranquillity of the soul. He'd actually been talking about tea, but if they had jazz back then, I'm sure he would have agreed.

Melody changes while I set up the camera and a light, load a roll of film. "On the couch," I tell her. It's a pullout. We pull it out. She hops up dutifully. Naked.

"Lie beneath the window. There's some nice light coming in from outside."

"I hate that light."

"Well, it's great for shooting. Lie flat, maybe draw up one leg."

Her face is hidden in the darkness. Rays of light from the streetlamp outside illuminate slices of her shoulder, chest, and stomach. A shaft of shadow halves her breasts. I'm beginning to get a little excited. With this light, a little luck, and a roll of my best black-and-white film, this could actually turn out to be a decent shot.

"A little more to the left. Yeah. More sexy. No, that's just trashy. Just...lie there."

It's fun to be taking the pictures for once. I needed the break—modelling can be hazardous to your mental health. Some primitive tribespeople believe a photographer steals their souls when he takes their pictures. The longer I model the more I realize those tribespeople might be onto something. Actors, it's said, are given the chance with every role to bury parts of themselves they don't like, explore parts they do. Models, though, are condemned to explore and exploit sex and vanity, everything that's most narcissistic, superficial, and unsavoury. Forced to stew in our own neuroses.

Melody has closed her eyes. She's at peace. In this dreamy half-light everything is neither black nor white—the bed, Melody, my face reflected in the window. It occurs to me that this is the only time we've been the same colour. But she wouldn't know that or care. It must be nice to be in her pale world, blissfully unaware of the missed taxis, the money up front, the hateful white stares of those desperate to reclaim their fallen princess, the mocking black snickers of the jealous guys who have all had their own white bitches at one time or another, the sucked teeth of the bell-haired Jamaicans who are too good for you, anyway. Melody has never had a truck whiz by, splashing her with cruel words, leaving her to walk home, drenched and furious, "Hey, nigger!" dripping into her shoes. She's under the impression that I have the best of both worlds—dark enough to be exotic, light enough to be immune from it all. She doesn't realize you can't have the best of both worlds when you belong to neither. Just look at the mule deer. It's a cross between a species of deer that hides from its enemies and another species that runs away from them. When it smells a wolf or a mountain lion, the mule deer doesn't know whether to run or hide, and it's always eaten first.

Stepping out of the light and into the shadows, I can hardly see my hands. I'm black like me. Even if Melody opened her eyes, I doubt she'd be able to see me. She told me on our first date that she liked me because I wasn't too dark. I took that as a compliment then. Now I know better. I'm not like "them."

I load another roll of film, thinking I'll change things up a little. Melody becomes my freeze model, my mannequin. I arrange her body, her limbs, in positions, each more suggestive than the last. It's someone else's turn to be the beast. She doesn't seem to mind. It occurs to me that *mannequin* is French for *model*.

Taking her hands, I move them into her lap. I'm intrigued by her hands. They're long for her body. She'd make a good piano player. Or pickpocket. Like one person in a hundred, she has pioneer palms—the insides of her hands are tough, leathery, like a saddle.

I place her hands lower, into her hair, spread her fingers, retreat behind the camera. "Okay, now move your fingers."

"You want me to touch myself?"

I want to see how far she'll go. "Yeah, it's a great shot."

"I can't do that."

"Why not?"

"I...can't."

"Just pretend I'm not here. Close your eyes. Lose yourself in the moment. Listen to the music."

The music is loud, frantic—Miles Davis diddling on his trumpet. She closes her eyes. Her hand disappears in the shadows. I'll feel nothing until I'm back in my makeshift darkroom, bathing the film lovingly in brown sauce, admiring the prints as I hang them up to dry. Until then I watch her coolly as she degrades herself for the camera. And why should I feel anything? I'm just doing my job. Is that what photographers experience when they shoot me, made-up and stripped-down, selling myself in order to peddle a T-shirt or a bar of soap? But this is no catalogue shoot. This is an editorial. Melody's not hawking a product, she's selling an idea. An ideal. Vulnerability. Shame. Contempt. My ideas are expressed through her. She's both the medium and the message. And I, as the photographer, am an integral part of the scene. Like a behavioural scientist conducting an experiment, you have to factor in how much your presence affects its outcome.

Suddenly she opens her eyes, sits up. "I can't do it. Let's forget about this. This is stupid."

I keep shooting, lost in the moment.

"Stacey, stop. I'm serious."

The clicking of the shutter is music, the camera an instrument. Melody joins in, up and down the scales. Angry, scared, vulnerable, defenceless, pathetic. The uncontrived, unalloyed states a photographer searches for, almost never finds. I'm getting it all. Yeah, baby, yeah... The way her hair falls over her face, the way the makeup is smudged. Her eyes are ringed with black, like a linebacker's. The way she holds out her hands—a disgraced movie star trying to block the camera with her palms, her pioneer palms.

The way she tries to cover herself with a pillow, then throws it at me instead. I duck but keep shooting. "That's it! Don't stop."

Through the pupil of my camera I can see hers—wide, black, glistening.

"*Stop stop stop stop stop stop stop!*" she cries, jumping off the bed. She runs past me into the bedroom, still naked, sobbing louder now as she slams the door. Which is just as well, because I'm out of film.

Miles smiles at me from the two brown speakers, his bleak, muted trumpet spiralling through the window and out into the cold February night. Melody snores quietly, a counterpoint to bass, horn, and drum. The apartment is dark except for the incandescent moonlight of the street-lamp streaming through the window. All is in perfect harmony. Only I'm out of key.

In the light from the window Melody's face is pale, like the bottom of my feet. Slowly I tiptoe through the doorway, careful not to wake her, float past the bed toward the window, drawn like a fly to the light. The blinds of the apartment facing me are closed, but they're sheer enough so that I can see a man moving behind them. He parades across his room, an actor veiled in gauze, playing out an eerie pantomime. It's strange to think that everybody else is doing something at this very moment. Sometimes I wish I could be them all.

A woman stands on her balcony, looking toward the bay. She must have a better view than I, because all I can see is the parking lot, her building, and the new church. The neon cross on top of the unfinished church beckons, its warm red light offering salvation across the dark skies of this cold, wintry night. Christ finally got fed up with the sepulchral Vatican and packed his bags for Vegas.

I came back to say I was sorry, but Melody's still asleep. By the time she wakes up, I'll probably be long gone—up the road, past the pool, through my old neighbourhood, along the river, to the bus station. Hopefully there will be room on the six o'clock bus. There usually is. I take one last look. I know I'll never see her again unless I bump into her and Ziggy Stardust in the park or, years from now, get a call from the coroner.

Melody shifts, murmurs, disturbing the peace that has accumulated around me like thick black cloth. She rolls onto her side, and all is well. Quietly I undo the latch, push out the window, and step onto the fire escape. The wind swishes through the trees below, invisible waves caressing a green shore.

Miles has stopped smiling, and the apartment is deathly still. Instead of dropping my horn, I lift it and howl at the sky. It's a full moon, baby. Hallelujah time. The cold February wind lashes my naked body. My negritude is invisible to everyone but myself. Across from me the woman is still on the balcony, bathed in the neon shadows of the church cross as she gazes at the bay. The rustling leaves sound like rain. Inside, Melody's breathing grows louder then, gradually, softer. I hope she's not dreaming of me.

TWELVE

Animal costumes, bright feathers, shiny pants, sequin tuxedos—Caribana revellers wind their way down Lakeshore Boulevard to the sound of soca. It's a procession of bad taste. Half-naked black women wave to the crowd with their booties. Costumes have been exhumed from carnivals of years past. Tits flap in the breeze. Streets are blocked off. A city already perplexed by one-ways and no-turns has shrugged and given up. Massive sound systems mounted on flatbed trucks snake their way through the city. Speakers are sore with distortion, blaring the hottest calypso hits of the day. Songs begging to be put out of their misery are sung by people who can't carry a tune. The air oscillates with noise. Everyone's moving to the left, everyone's putting their hands in the air. I've never seen so many black people and the girls who like them. Grownups blowing whistles.

Luckily I'm on foot. My shoot's over with and I have some time to kill before the modelling workshop at three. I'm surprised Maceo Power decided to hold it the same day as Caribana. The day should be designated a holiday, if only because of the traffic. As far as I know, the stylist is still on his way to this morning's shoot. There's a convoy of disoriented cars behind me, waiting to turn around. They'll be there until this tropical breeze blows past. I don't know how many more songs about donkeys I can take.

The parade has stalled on Oak Street. It moves like a caterpillar, expanding and contracting. Who can tell what's holding it up now? An unclaimed child on the parade route. A flat tire. A shooting.

I accept one of the proffered detours and end up downtown. Here you wouldn't know that ten minutes away almost a million people are shaking their bam-bams. On Yonge Street a man on a skateboard with a cell phone nearly runs me off the sidewalk. His wavy black hair writhes behind him in the wind. A Chinese man offers to write my name on a grain of rice. Nearby another man juggles, fumbles. Now that the sun's out the street vendors are sprouting, selling sunglasses that claim to block harmful ultraviolet but offer little protection against ridicule.

I'm thirsty, so I duck into a small shop. Inside, all the writing's in Arabic. The walls are covered with posters of blow-dried Middle Eastern movie stars promoting movies that were released fifteen years ago. The shelves are stocked in miscellaneous order. Most of the stuff is still in the original shipping cartons or gunny sacks. The store carries seven different types of beans, spices from around the world, fruits I've never heard of, tubers of every description. And there are flies. Everything's a little sticky. The only fruit juice is mango, manufactured by the East India Mango Company. It looks less like juice and more like a mango jammed into a bottle. The puree seems to have separated into its elements. I shake it, but I may still need a spoon. I think I heard it rattle. The cashier—the owner's wife—doesn't seem to know what to do. She charges me a dollar, though the homemade price tag on the bottom of the bottle reads $1.79. She doesn't open the cash register. There's no receipt.

Back on the street the shopping cart men are out again, slowly salvaging scrap metal from the garbage cans. One of them totes a balding German shepherd. It offers to lick me. I decline. Each cart is heaped with cans—pop, beer, soup.

It's almost three and I still have a way to go. I splurge and hop on a streetcar named Christie. The workshop's somewhere in Christie Pits, a big bowl of green, like an abandoned quarry grown over with grass and sports fields. On the soccer pitch are the Latinos. Each player has five or six fans who whoop it up every time he nods the ball or hits a good cross. ¡Olé! by all whenever anyone makes a clever play. On the baseball diamond the Toronto Blue Jays, not the real ones, take on another team from somewhere else.

I can't see anything that looks like a modelling workshop. I do find a red, white, and blue rubber ball, the kind I used to play with as a kid, the kind I didn't think they made anymore. It's lying in the grass by my feet. A little girl on the balcony of a nearby building looks down at me. I pick up the ball and hold it aloft questioningly. She stretches her hands over the balcony railing. I wind up and throw the ball. I used to play catcher for the Nepean Peewee Titans, but I surprise us both by nailing the toss. She disappears. It probably went into the house. I hope I didn't break anything.

The workshop is behind a copse of trees at the edge of the field. There are about a hundred children between the ages of rambunctious and ungainly. Their parents are more nervous than the kids. Everyone's brought their best daughter. Some are so cute their faces belong on cereal boxes. Others have mugs that belong inside the box. Most have brought high heels. A few wear miniskirts. I wonder if it's possible to be sexy at eleven. One or two are in wheelchairs. Not to be dismissed. A good-looking kid in a wheelchair can go far on the diversity ticket these days.

"Nice to see you, Stacey. You'll be with the yellows, I think." One of Maceo Power's part-time models is here with the master list. She scans it, checking off which kids will go with which models.

All the ones with yellow buttons are mine. I have thirteen. I gather my brood around me under a beech tree. "Hi, my name's Stacey Schmidt. I'm a model."

One of the girls puts up her hand.

"Yes?"

"Do you wear makeup?"

"Yes."

"Really?"

"Yes."

"Makeup?"

"Yes."

"Gross!"

"Right. There will be time at the end to ask questions. The reason I'm here today is to tell you a bit about the career of modelling."

The real reason I'm here is because Amiris asked me to go last week. At first I wondered why she chose me of all people to be among the five models representing the agency. Surely I wasn't Maceo Power's best model of success. Now I realize it's because all the successful models were booked for shoots. I don't mind. I like kids. Besides, it's my chance to give something back to the modelling community that I'm hoping will one day be good to me.

As I gaze out at the baker's dozen of eager faces, I want to yell, "Run, children! Stay in school! Say no to modelling! Join a choir!" Instead I tell them the history of the profession, the options for young models, the do's and don'ts, the dedication and perseverance it takes to make it in the business.

"Do you all want to be models when you grow up?"

I scan my little crowd to see if they're listening. Most aren't. Clearly the girls wanted a girl model to talk to them. Some are playing in the dirt. Others are braiding each other's hair. Most of the young guys look miserable. There are only three. At this age asking a guy if he wants to be a model when he grows up is like asking him if he wants to be a hairdresser or a ballerina. I have to kick two of the guys out because they can't stop laughing after I demonstrate the best way to apply powder. They don't care. They're here because their parents made them come. The rich parents want to get their kids out of the house for the summer. The poor parents hope their kids are a lottery ticket. The parents of stupid kids know their children will never earn a living with what's inside their heads. Each parent paid $50 for the course, most of which is going to the United Way.

At a glance it would seem I have a fairly good-looking bunch of kids. Some of them may even make Maceo's farm team. Three of the kids are brown. I don't have the heart to tell them that only one of them need apply. One girl, a brunette with mahogany skin and clairvoyant eyes, could start working today if she wanted to. It's hard to tell at this age if she'll be tall enough. Later I may be required to measure her parents. The only boy left is a serious-looking fellow. He seems older than twelve, and he's tall enough to be sixteen. With that bright, slightly confused smile he reminds me of me. The boy smiles a lot but never laughs. I'm willing to bet he's already seen one of his parents kick the other out. If he's ready to release all that repressed resentment on the runway, he could have a future.

I go over the proper use of pumice stones and other exfoliants, cover the pros and cons of salicylic acid, and then I'm out of material. I've got nothing more to teach them, and there's still at least a half hour to go. Luckily hands go up.

"How much money do you make?"

"Not enough."

"Why did you decide to become a model?"

"To meet girls."

"What happens if you're too short?"

"Try acting."

"Is it harder for guys than for girls?" It's the young boy, as earnest as a tax collector. I'm not sure how to answer. We pop pills to keep us thin, take pills to help us get bigger. Not as many people try to get us in bed every day, but I'm sure that's not the answer his mom, who's listening by the trees, wants to hear.

"Would you recommend it as a career?" he asks when I don't answer.

"No," I say cheerfully, trying to make it sound like a joke. But I look the kid dead in the eye and hope he hears me.

"No more questions? All right, line up." The individual assessment is next. We're to meet with all of them, ask them questions, take Polaroids, in order to weed out the weeds.

"Why do you want to be a model?" I ask each kid. Whoever designed the questionnaire only left me enough room for three or four words. I'm forced to reduce each answer to its basic elements.

The first girl pauses. "I always wanted to be a model ever since I was small." Her mother nods approvingly.

I write "parents made her."

The second girl answers, "I want to learn how to use makeup and hair like those girls in the magazines."

I write "issues."

When I ask the next thirteen-year-old where she's from, her beaming father tells me he drove her all the way from Nepean. "You really didn't have to," I say. "They do have a couple of agencies there, you know."

"Yeah, but none of them are any good. If you want your kids to go anywhere in the business, this is the place to be."

I nod wisely, jot down "desperate," take her picture, anyway.

Soon I notice I'm talking to kids with green, blue, orange, and red buttons. My lineup has grown from thirteen to more than forty. I call over the coordinator and point to the assembled throng.

"Do you mind, Stacey?" she asks. "Allison and Karina had to leave."

"Fine, I'll do it, but only because my afternoon happens to be pretty clear. And it's for charity. But I have to be out of here by five." If I wait any later, I'll be fighting with the Caribana crowd for a spot on the subway.

After twenty minutes all the children start to resemble one another. I'm beginning to suspect some of the mothers are putting their children through twice. Most of them have no chance, but a few, only a handful, are so stunning that even in the moist glare of the peel-away Polaroid you know they could be stars. They're the ones that worry me the most. I'm tempted to use all the tricks of my craft to save them from a life of poverty, indecision, inadequacy, and doubt. I can inflict on them a plague of shadows to make them look as if they steal change from fountains. I can shoot them in the sun to make it seem as if they live underground. I can shoot them while they blink, so they look as dumb as Dalmatians. I can tell them to smile wide, wider, wider, to make it appear they love to burn things. I can underexpose them, so it looks as if they have worms. It's amazing how easy it is to give an eleven-year-old a five o'clock shadow. Ten years from now they could end up in a park taking pictures of people they don't know because they have nowhere better to go. But I do nothing. What right have I to perform an abortion on their modelling dreams? They deserve the chance to try, to fail, to learn firsthand that not every door can be opened with a smile.

The pictures are done, my notes are complete. A couple of the kids and parents hang back, hoping to get some extra free tips, but I have nothing left. Sorry, guys, show's over. The agency will be in touch. And they will. Like everything else in the world that's free, this workshop was designed to interest people in things that aren't free. Modelling courses, like rust-proofing and extended warranties, are the most lucrative corners. No matter how their current flange of models is performing, they can always count on a steady supply of vain delusions and magazine dreams to get them through a slow season.

Jenna, one of the other models, is trying to make her way to the bus, but she's being followed down the dirt trail by a group of eager young girls. It's a shame we don't get commission for signing up new recruits. Uncle Maceo Wants You! If you're tall, slim, and have clear skin. Three of the girls behind Jenna have yellow wristbands.

The first drops of rain are kicking up dust on the infield. The Latinos on the soccer field play on. Near one sideline a child is kicking a small ball. It looks a lot like the blue-and-white rubber ball I found earlier. It seems unlikely the girl on the balcony would have dropped the ball again by accident. I'm beginning to think it wasn't hers to begin with. I scan the second-floor balconies but can't see her anywhere. I hope she's not in the group of girls following Jenna down the path like rats behind the Pied Piper. There's an ice-cream truck under a tree to their left. Maybe they're going for Popsicles. But I doubt it. Jenna works even less than I do. Maybe the children are treating her.

Amiris told me to meet her at Norway, but with this huge drunken crowd milling around, I have about as much chance of finding her as I would in the actual country. Tonight the arena is so full you have to line up to leave. They've packed away the hockey ice and put away the basketball floorboards for the annual Wines of the World trade show. I ask one of the men at the Norwegian booth if he's seen a short, bald woman. He smiles and pours me a glass of wine instead.

My wine-tasting glass is tiny, souvenir-size. The merchants pour so little into the glass it would take me the whole weekend to get drunk. But somehow many people here seem to manage it. One guy walks by wearing his jacket inside out. Another man slumped on a couch talks to a fern. The women, giggly, touch your arm to apologize for bumping into you. Scoring would be almost guaranteed, as long as you didn't mind your women a little wrinkly. I'm tempted, but I have to at least make a symbolic effort to find Amiris. She said she had something enormous to tell me. I leave Norway and head for Spain.

Most of the attendees are dressed smartly. Wines of the World is Oktoberfest for the rich, a cultured way to get smashed like a pumpkin. At $70 a ticket the price tag ensures that the people who love wine the most are kept outside begging for change. I didn't have to pay, otherwise I wouldn't have come. Free tickets were courtesy of Amiris, by way of a client no doubt. I think I recognized one of our models on the poster outside.

I skip the usual suspects: France, Italy, Germany. I'm interested in the lesser-known wine producers, countries that owe people money, nations with state-controlled vineyards, booths with homemade signs. Moldova's first. The man in the booth bears a disturbing resemblance to Vlad the Impaler.

"You've heard of us?" he asks hopefully, holding up a bottle, label forward, for me to inspect. It looks as if he printed the label on a computer.

I shake my head. I've never heard of the brand or the appellation. I'm not sure I've even heard of the country.

"Try?" He pours generously. It's surprisingly smooth. I shuffle on.

At the Portuguese booth a man insists I sniff the wine before tasting it.

I refuse. To me all wine smells like the juice I left in my thermos over school holidays. I'm not interested in inhaling it unless someone can prove to me it's possible to get high from the fumes. I down my sample like a shooter and smack my lips just to annoy him. I move on.

The number of countries represented is astounding. I didn't know Sudan made wine. I didn't even know it had trees. Even Trinidad and Tobago each have their own booths.

I travel across three continents and two peninsulas. Nearby in the corner a man with a handlebar moustache gives a lecture on the art of enology. He talks passionately about wine ratings, how to tell if a wine is dry. It occurs to me that whoever came up with the word *dry* to describe wine didn't really put all that much thought into it. I venture on.

A large banner boasts WINES OF AFRICA. I wonder if anyone here realizes that Africa isn't a country. South Africa has the largest booth on the continent. The people in it seem slightly embarrassed—big white men with stiff, starched collars. They look too rich, too well dressed, to be selling wine. They're displaying an impressive array. I ask one of the men if he has any vintages that predate the end of apartheid. He ducks behind the counter, doesn't come back up.

Mozambique is next door. Two nervous-looking black men in dashikis smile as I approach their booth. The bottles of the Mozambicans are still full, their tablecloth, unlike most, is still clean, but if I were them I wouldn't worry. Later tonight alcohol, the great leveller, will provide them with a steady stream of customers who won't care what country their booze comes from.

"*Oye, niño.* There's a girl for you." Amiris has snuck up behind me. She's pointing at a thin blonde with tourmaline eyes.

"Where the hell were you? I was at the Norway booth, but I couldn't see you anywhere."

"I'm sorry. I was talking to Mohammed." She indicates one of the two guys from Mozambique. They look like brothers. "Most of his family was killed in the wars. I thought you'd end up wandering this way eventually. Besides, I wanted to give you a chance to get some booze in you to prepare you for what I've got."

"What do you have?"

"Let's get a glass first. Mohammed?" The man pours us thick wine from an earthen jar. "You're not going to believe this," she says. "Well, maybe you will. But I doubt it. Remember Kameleon Jeans?"

"Yes..." I say warily.

"They want you. Soon. Can you get to Germany by next week?"

"If this is a joke..."

"I'm serious."

"Just like that?" It sounds too good to be true.

"Yeah, well, they're not exactly a normal company. You're probably too young to remember the scandal six years ago when they hired a young blind guy to front their campaign. I think the boy was twelve, and he had, like, white eyes. He was spooky."

"Really? No eyes." I'm only half listening, still in shock. All I can think of is *why me?*

"Don't act so stunned. You're hot." She can see I don't buy it. "They liked your look—hairy chest, scar on the shoulder, character. They told me they were looking for a model who didn't look like a model, but they didn't want one of those freaky ones who look as if they're a freaky model."

"They were after the guy next door sort of thing?"

"More the guy down the street. The guy on the bus. I don't know what you did, but apparently your audition tape blew Dat Win away." Amiris is looking at me strangely. I'm not sure how much she knows, or if she's made copies of the audition tape.

"Cheers, by the way," Amiris says, and we lift our glasses. Mohammed smiles.

"How much?" I ask.

"We haven't talked numbers yet. Nothing huge but decent, I imagine. Great exposure. They're looking at a worldwide campaign, mostly in movie theatres. You know, those previews? You'd be in those."

"Cool." The idea of a forty-foot me has its appeal.

"Hey, over there, the guy with the kooky hat, that's Fernando from

International Talent Management. Two years ago he wanted to buy me out. Now he wants a job. Do you mind if I go over there and gloat for a while? You'll be here?"

"Yep."

"Promise? I don't want to lose you."

"I won't move."

Mohammed holds up the jug. "More?"

"Why not, Mohammed?" Another thick glass of sour wine to celebrate, though I feel less exuberant, more relieved. It's taken me six months to land something decent, but I'm finally on the road to making bullion—selling jeans, the symbol of macho rebellion and social commentary. I wonder what type I'll be peddling. When I was growing up, there was only one kind of jeans, back when newspapers were delivered by boys, not men, back when I wore a shower cap to bed. Now every culture has its own jeans, from the tight and white trailer-style to the baggy-saggy of the hip-hoppers. Luckily big, wide jeans have bell-bottomed off the scene. Now everyone's wearing them rolled up at the bottom the way farmers do. I can only wish that whatever campaign I'm fronting won't be too far-out. They'd better not be pink. I hope I'll actually be wearing jeans in the ad. I'm leery of promoting allegorical clothing. Will I be serious, mysterious? Will I be happy in the lap of a Corvette, a gum-chewing girl at my side? I can only assume they'll fill me in, give me a character and a part to play, though I wonder what they want with a homemade dude like me. Amiris said they like the fact I don't look like a model without looking as if I couldn't be one. But I can't quite believe that. Very few things in life work the way they're supposed to, so I'm genuinely astounded when something does. Take spiderwebs, for instance. Until I saw for myself, I couldn't believe spiders actually caught flies with silk. I mean, I can see the web myself and I'm no fly, a thousand eyes and all. But, of course, the farther you're standing from the web, the easier it is to see.

"How are you doing tonight?" The girl says *you* as if she knows who I am. She's young and is wearing a short black dress that has several port-holes offering views of her naked white skin.

"Good. You?" She looks familiar but is too short to be anyone from modelling, too young to have been anyone I met at Rum Runner or the Pound.

"This is *sooo* the best." Her breath is vinegary. She leans closer. I move away. "But I lost my date. I was here." She points vaguely over there. "And then he was over there." She indicates the same spot. "Then he was like, I'll be back, and then he was gone. My parents are *sooo* going to kill me." Her eyes are wide.

"Why's that?" I don't like where this is going. I need a drink.

"Mohammed?" He smiles, pours me another glass. Looks at the girl, looks at me. Looks away. Even Mohammed wants no part of this.

"I was supposed to stay with Brad, and now I can't find him. I can't go home like this. I've got wine on my dress." She's practically dripping booze. Her sleeves are so wet she's flammable. She looks up at me, seems to expect an answer.

"Why don't you call your mom? I'm sure she'll understand. Moms always do."

"Not my mom."

"No? Why not?"

"'Cause she's a bitch."

"I'm sure she's not."

"You met her today. She yelled at you. She's *sooo* a bitch."

I remember now. "Too short" was what I wrote this morning next to her name at the audition. She's one of the girls. Not one of my yellow-wristband girls, one of Jenna's, I think. I took her picture. When I told her about the height minimum, five-nine, for most models, her mother threatened to complain to my manager.

"If you can't go home," I tell her, "why don't you go to the courtesy counter and make an announcement?"

"That I'm lost?"

"No...for Brad. Tell them to ask him to meet you at the courtesy counter."

"Are you ill? Then everyone would think he ditched me. And he didn't. He got lost." She starts crying.

Where's Amiris when you need her? I'm sure she'd know what to say.

"I can't go home. I have to stay somewhere else. I'll have to find a hotel. That's the only way. But Brad has my purse. I don't have any money. Do you have any money? Come with me." She tugs my hand. "Let's go find somewhere."

A nova of late-night fantasies explodes in my head. "That's...not a great idea for me right now. I've got to stay here tonight. But I have a friend you can stay with. This way." Brad would kill me if he knew I was sending his drunk girl home without him, unless he's already found someone better.

I guide her to the door, hand around her waist for support. I try to avoid the portholes in her dress without success. Her skin is as smooth as her dress. I'm tempted to put her in a cab, pin a note to her addressed to Crispen and Breff. They'd know what to do with her. But that would be wrong on so many levels, most of them federal.

A reluctant cabbie pulls up. The driver looks a little put off as she stumbles. I bet he knows at least ten ways to get vomit out of a Crown Victoria.

"Can you take her to 2576 Rosewood?" I ask the driver. I turn to the girl. "Those are the Feyenoord apartments. Ask for Trina in apartment 12. She'll take care of you. Here's $40. That'll be plenty. It's not too far. I'll call Trina in twenty minutes to see if you got there okay." I won't, but the cab-driver doesn't know that.

"You were really nice today at the thing. The other girl left, but you stayed till the end. That was really nice." She's lying in the back seat, legs slightly open. I avert my eyes. Momentarily.

"Thanks. Well..."

"Can I have your autograph?"

"My autograph?"

"Here." She tugs on the neck of her dress, baring her breast and the beginning of a nipple.

"Hah. Funny."

"I'm serious. Right here."

"I...better not."

"Give him a pen," she tells the cab driver.

He glances at me. I shrug. My first autograph. It isn't exactly how I planned it—signing a drunk girl's tit in the back of a taxi—but then again, nothing ever ends up exactly how you plan it. Besides, every model's got to start somewhere. Three years ago Tyree was washing eggs for a living. Now, according to *People*, he owns a duvet stuffed with shredded hundred-dollar bills.

The driver's marker writes surprisingly well on bare skin. I sign my name slowly across the top of her breast.

"Let me see!" She reaches across the front seat to the driver's rearview mirror, adjusts it to get a better view, admires her bosom. I admire my handiwork.

"Solid!" she says, turning this way and that. It's backward, of course, but the quality of the autograph is undeniable. I've been practising at home for months. Thanks to a lot of spare time and a leftover psychology textbook, my signature has changed six times in as many weeks. But now I think I have one worthy of Kameleon's new man. I critique my work in the mirror.

The *S*, with high form and regular pressure, indicating intelligence. The *t*, loopless, the sign of an independent thinker without regard for the norm. The *a*, no wasted movement, thrifty, pragmatic. The *c*, a rounded, modest. The *e*, medium-size, characteristic of the introspective. The *y*, the large lower loop of a great lover.

Bold but not extravagant. No ostentatious strokes to signal a desire for attention or a need to be noticed. Still a couple of graphological neuroses to iron out. My *y* has a pervert's loop, my *t* the low bar of desperation. But it's a one-word name now. Stacey. And that's a start.

"Tell me the truth," she says. "Am I too short to be a model?"

"Don't worry about it. Even if you are, there are always other things beside modelling."

"Modelling's nice..." I close the door and wave. The cab speeds off into the night, ignoring the first stop sign. A race against wine.

So she wants to be a model? I wonder where she'll end up. I can still see the cab, stopped at a distant light. She's probably already passed out.

Her name suddenly comes to me—Amy. Is Amy modelling material? She likes booze, she's easy, she likes older men—she's a natural. Tomorrow I'll put her on the callback list. Or I'll rip up her photo and shred her application. It's curiously satisfying to hold someone else's career in my hands. The light turns green and the cab rolls off into black. A model is born, or lies stillborn in a back seat.

I pick up my little glass, thank the doorman holding the door open for me. From inside there's the sound of raucous ten o'clock laughter. Wine drips from the ceiling, wine runs from the faucets. The caring has stopped, the fun has swollen, and Amiris must be wondering where I am. I straighten my belt, comb my tie, ready to join the party.

THIRTEEN

"Dude, there's gotta be something better than this," I say, looking around in despair. Breffni just laughs.

The hostel is only five minutes from Kameleon's offices, so it has proximity going for it but little else. It's populated by an international assortment of characters with a taste for eyebrow rings, leather pants, and prescription drugs. One young German has FUCK YOU! tattooed in broken English on his right arm. The rooms are less rooms than barracks. There are twelve to a room, fifty to a floor, ten floors. Bunk beds. The mattresses have the load-bearing capacity of a towel. The bathrooms are so nasty I'm overcome with the urge to have myself laminated. In the sink there are sprinklings of beard. A rat of long hair sticks out of the drain, and I'll be damned if I'm going to pull it out. There are brown stains in the shower. The urinal is a trough. Breffni and I are side by side, pissing gingerly in separate directions, trying not to spray each other, but the drain's backing up and waves of urine are threatening to wash gently over our toes.

"It's just for two nights," Breffni says. "Till we can find something a little better for you in the long term."

"Right now something better would include the alley outside the hostel. Did you see the floor? I think those were bloodstains."

"Did you pack sandals?" Breffni asks. "The last person I know who walked barefoot on a hostel bathroom floor contracted trench foot."

"What if I just stay in my socks?"

Breffni shrugs. "Take your chances."

We shower with our eyes closed. Afterward I lay my wet socks out on the radiator like strips of bacon. Crispen's talking to a man lying on a bed, the only one who's still here. Everyone else is downstairs having whatever meal is dictated by their time zone.

"He used to be a model, too," Crispen says to us. "Back in the day. Damn."

"Thomas," the man says, offering a hand from his bed. But Breffni and I aren't close enough to take it and it's withdrawn under the covers.

"He's from Sweden," Crispen says.

"Who did you model for?" I ask.

"Everyone," he says, waving a thin arm.

I'm not convinced. The man's tall enough—his feet flop over the far side of the bed at the knees—but with his vague good looks, blond moustache, and gestating stomach, he looks more like an ex-porn star than an ex-model.

"And now?" Breffni asks.

"Now I travel. I meet people. I live for free in the hostels. I clean their bathrooms and they give me bed and food."

"You clean the bathrooms?" I ask. "Didn't you make any money modelling?"

"That was a long time ago," Thomas says, pulling the blanket up a little farther. "There was a lot of money. And a lot to buy."

"We're here modelling, too," I tell him.

"Really?" Thomas sits up. "Who for?"

"I'm here to do some jeans ads for Kameleon."

"You're the new Kameleon Man?" Thomas smiles. "Good for you. What happened to the last one, that albino fellow? Didn't he die shooting the ads? That's what I heard."

"Is that true?" I ask.

"No, it's not," Breffni says. "It wasn't the albino. The last Kameleon Man was that Native guy. He's the one who died."

I frown.

"All three of you are models then?" Thomas asks.

"We're here for a week or so to get our partner here on his feet," Crispen says, slapping my back. "Nervous yet?"

"A little." Who wouldn't be nervous about spending the next six months in a country where you have to pay extra for a shower in your room and carbonation in your beer.

"Well, I wish you more luck than I had," Thomas says. He offers his hand. His handshake is surprisingly firm for a man in leggings. "The modelling business is a lake of leeches, boys. Leeches sticking to your face, dropping off the second you're not hot anymore, or the second the next hot thing steps into the pond. I used to be hot." He raises his hands, lets them fall into his lap. "Now I'm not. Does anybody have a cigarette?" He reaches into his bag. "I have matches but no cigarette."

"Sorry, no," I mumble, wondering if he was telling the truth about being a model. In this industry anything's possible. A month ago Tyree had to sell his jet, house, and pets just to pay his debts. Who knows? Maybe Thomas was once a Kameleon Man. Back when jeans were tight and only came in blue. I notice a bag wadded with cloths, a bottle of blue liquid, and a plunger hanging from his bedpost. It's still wet.

Crispen, Breffni, and I walk in silence down the cobbled streets. Munich so far is just a big, drab city indistinguishable from any other save by an occasional eagle crest or sandblasted swastika. German artists, it seems, were a sexually repressed lot. Most of their fountain statues are naked. Water comes out of penile fountains and nipular springs. In an alcove not far from an enormous Gothic tower there's a public scale. A grey-haired gent with a huge suit and a black briefcase steps into the alcove, puts down his briefcase, and steps onto the scale. He looks dissatisfied, steps off the scale, glances around, then takes his suit jacket off and steps back on.

"So what's it like being in the Fatherland?" Breffni asks me.

"I don't know what to make of it. Germany smells like my grandfather, but I'm not exactly sure why."

"Can we stop somewhere for a sec?" Crispen asks. "I promised I'd send my mother a postcard."

"Aren't we in a rush?" I ask.

"No," Breffni says. "If this Hostage Clothing thing is like any other cattle call, every model in the European Union will be there. We'll have plenty of time."

"Can I still do this when I'm supposed to be doing the Kameleon thing?"

Breffni looks at me. "You haven't signed anything yet, right?"

"No, that's next week."

"So? Hostage is doing an ad, they need some beautiful people quickly, why not make some quick gorgonzola? Christ, I just noticed C.J. actually has a bit of a beard."

"Yeah, every so often I let my cheeks germinate. Good for the skin. What I want to know is how you get that three-day-stubble look every day, Breff."

"I can't tell you. Trade secret."

"But I'm in the trade."

"That's why it's a secret."

"That makes no sense."

"Sorry, brother, can't help you. You wanted postcards? In there."

Germans are exact like change. Everything is painstakingly labelled. Lineups form spontaneously. No one jaywalks. No one speaks out of turn. Randomly I grab a postcard for Melody off a revolving rack.

The man at the counter picks it up, weighs it carefully. "Two euros."

"How come it says one euro on the sign?" I ask.

"This postcard is long. The others are square. Two euros."

"But it doesn't say anything about long ones being twice as expensive."

I'm not sure if he understands. He shrugs, picks up a pair of scissors, neatly lops off the right third, places the postcard on the scale. "One euro."

There you go.

"Everyone's so thin!" Crispen whispers to Breffni. "These guys look like they have rickets. Eat, my friends, eat! A meal a day keeps the mortician away. Is the messianic look back in again?"

"No, thank God," Breffni says. "This year it's refugee fashion—emaciated, beaten up, East European, Bosnian survivor type thing. We'll have to take a knee, sit this one out."

I survey the room. The guys are skeletons, so are the girls. Everyone's faded, sickly, washed-out, pale like marzipan.

"At least the giant-man thing is over," Crispen says. "Six months ago all the men on the runways were six-six, 250 pounds. The only people who could get work were Norwegians and lumberjacks. At least with this we're in the running. Stacey is, anyway. Skinny bastard. What do you do to keep so thin?"

"A lot of standing. Some sitting."

"You should make a video," Breffni suggests. "How to exercise without doing any."

"Like they say, training too much can be as bad as training too little."

"Who says that?" Breffni asks.

"No one. Just this modelling book I've been reading."

"Well, don't," Crispen says. "It's nonsense. You can't learn anything about modelling from a book."

"Well..." That's easy for him to say. I never went to a fancy modelling school. I learned and unlearned everything on my own. It's nice to have some guidance for once, even if it's only thirty pages, ten of which are about hair.

"That guy's a shoo-in." I point to a tall man sitting by himself in the corner. He's wearing a skintight black mock turtleneck, cut off at the apex of each bicep bulge. The guy is flipping through his own portfolio. It's as thick as four of mine. And that's probably his spare copy.

"Don't worry about him." Breffni says. "I remember him from Tokyo. Christophe or something. He's not a player. He's about as powerful as the peso. Pretty, but he can't move."

"He got a deal with Plastercine," a nearby model whispers.

"Really? So?" another whispers, not as quietly. "My agent told me to turn Plastercine down. Who's that guy?" He points at a short, ugly man sitting in a chair by the window, looking at books.

"Antonino Pino," Breffni says. "He's one of the clients. Be nice to him. Speak only if spoken to."

"Damn, he's ugly," I say. His hair is intermittent, patchy, but there's hair protruding from his shirt cuffs. He's a diseased squirrel.

"Be that as it may," Breffni says, "he's the second-in-command here." Breffni turns to me. "Why are we here again?"

"To make some drinking money," I say. "I spent all my cash on that Eurail pass. Are you sure it's a good idea? I mean, if I'm working in Germany, do I really need a rail pass for Europe?"

"First of all," Breffni says, "that pass lets you travel free in Germany. And you can even use it on the subways. Second, you'll have plenty of days and weekends free. Europe's not like Canada, dude. It's, like, an hour on either side and you're in another country. Seriously, you can take weekend trips to France, Spain, whatever. It's sweet. Eurail's the ticket. Hey, I think they're posting the picks."

Earlier Antonino Pino took our books and Polaroids and huddled with one of the other clients—a lanky man with a moustache that brings out his chins. Now he's taping to the wall the pictures of the models who made the cut.

"If you're here," Antonino says, pointing at the wall, "go through these doors please. We need you for half an hour only. If you're not with Powerhaus or Netwerks, pick up your money when you go out. Everyone else, thank you. This way please." Crispen's grinning mug is up, so, to my surprise, is mine. I can't see Breffni anywhere.

"I think I'll wait outside," Breffni says, seemingly cool. "Beers on you two tonight. And don't waste your time afterward chatting up the models. I think they're all married to David Bowie."

The models are marshalled and herded through the doors, down two flights of stairs, and into a basement decorated like a fifties-style diner.

"Why didn't they use a real diner?" I whisper to Crispen.

"Maybe a real one wouldn't look realistic enough. In movies they use milk instead of water in the rain sprinklers because water doesn't show up well on camera."

We're given clothes, tight and wild, then we're given our marks. Each of us has a spot on the floor and a person to hug. My partner's a young white girl with pyrotechnic red hair. She's as old as they come. She could get into a bar with her own driver's licence. Some couples sit on whirly bar stools. Others, like us, lean against the make-believe bar. It's made of Styrofoam.

"Don't lean too close," the lanky client says, "or the whole thing will fall down."

He's right. I think I weigh as much as it does.

"Okay, we're ready, everybody. Let's go..."

The photographer is a woman. I'm surprised only because every other photographer I've worked with was a man. She's carrying one of the latest digital cameras, the kind that will eventually replace her. And possibly me.

On the cue I reach over and give my new girlfriend a hug, firm and professional. I detect in hers an extra squeeze, the hint of a rub. I'm not sure if she's method-acting, simply improvising, or subtly inviting. I don't get a chance to find out because we're switched almost immediately. My new partner is a tan-coloured girl of indeterminate age and ethnicity. Judging from her smell—spicy—and from her English—choppy—I can only guess she comes from a country that didn't exist on my high-school map.

We repeat the hug, once, twice, then it's onto the next girl. I go through three more girls before the client and the photographer look at each other and nod. The money's waiting at the door. Less, much less, than Christophe would get, but enough to keep me warm, fed, and buzzed for at least three days. Four, if I stay at the hostel. Five, if I drink Turkish wine.

"Do you know what that was for?" I ask Crispen.

"No idea," he says.

I was way off. I always thought a youth hostel would be the young traveller's version of a college dorm. The life of the town. Fun concentrate. Instead this hostel is a hospital ward for the tired, the sick, the hung-over. Silent but for the tossing, coughing, whispering until around 8:00 p.m. when the night people slowly groan and rise, throw on clothes that are slung over beds and, at first, one by one, then in twos, fives, tens, exit into the night like bats from a cave.

Across the street a drunk man is being ravaged by another guy in the park. We pass by quietly. Who knows? They could be lovers. They certainly are now.

"What about there?" I point to the club on the corner. "There's no lineup."

"That's probably because everyone's already been killed," Breffni says.

"What about the next one? There's a poster. Apparently DJ Norman J is playing. Featuring special guest DJ Scum."

"Cool."

The bouncer pats us down with a smile. On the other side of the curtain the temperature is ten degrees hotter. There's more pot in the air than air. Kids wander around holding bottles of water, their eyes askew. Pupils the size of hubcaps. Nobody here has yawned since they woke up.

"Man, it's so loud you can't hear your ears," Breffni says. He screws a piece of tissue in each ear, then grins. "That's better."

The dance floor is littered with women. There's only one other guy. The way he's jumping around, it makes you wonder what he's under. We drop down the stairs onto the dance floor. I'm wearing a white cutoff T-shirt under my black shirt. In the treacherous black light my undershirt glows. I seem to be wearing a bra. We move dutifully to the music, aware neither of each other nor ourselves. We're mechano men, dancing quietly in all directions, each for our own reasons, to the senseless rhythm of invented music. Somewhere, sitting in his factory or lab, someone is laughing at his creations, these dance-club puppets, artificially Ecstatic, moving with pharmaceutical smiles. As I glance around, it's oddly comforting to know that Europe is still the centre of decadence, the real heart of darkness. It's where everyone under thirty is content to dance through the opening kickoff of this century's Jazz Age. But our jazz is mechanical, industrial, the antithesis of improvisation, soul's opposite pole. There's a reason our generation doesn't have any of those where-were-you-whens, like JFK or the Man on the Moon. It's not that nothing of significance has happened in our lifetimes. It's just that we don't care enough about any of it to remember. So we dance under the strobe light. Our moves are staccato, unreal, faster than life, an old newsreel. We can't stop dancing. Like the man in the fairy tale prancing to the tune of the witch's flute, dancing until there was nothing left but bones.

The women are all wearing too much makeup and too few clothes. They're looking around impatiently, as if they're waiting for a train.

"Sometimes I get so horny it's painful," Breffni announces. "Physically painful."

"It's kind of like male elephants," I say. "During mating season, when they're in must, they have stuff coming out of their eyes, they're irritable, mad with the pain of lust. No one gets in their way when they're chasing females. Even other males."

"I think we're in must," Breffni says. "I mean, look at those two over there." He points at two brightly coloured girls. Judging by the surface area of their makeup and the length of their miniskirts, they're girls with permanent drafts between their legs.

Their names are Tuli and Muli. They're Turks who have lived in Germany for six years. They don't speak English, but they make their intentions plain. The taller one caresses my starched penis through rumpled jeans. Breffni's got the short stick. His girl weighs almost as much as he does. It's as if you took a pretty girl, encased her in gelatine, then dressed her like a stripper.

Crispen walks up to Breffni, leans over, and whispers in his ear. "You're a model, for Christ's sake," he says, and jerks his head at the girl. "You can do better."

Breffni shrugs. "Everybody can always do better." I reach over and caress my girl's curly hair. I know what he means. The urge to settle is as normal as the urge to hold out.

"You're drunk," Crispen mutters.

Breffni bursts out laughing. "My head feels like it's in an oven." He's barely clinging to the wall.

"Just remember," Crispen says, wagging a finger. "Familiarity breeds disease." He stalks off.

"Which one is yours?" Breffni asks a little too loudly. "Tuli or Muli?" Both girls turn their heads.

I can't remember. "I miss Melody." My pronouncement surprises us both.

"Sssh," Breffni says.

"I doesn't matter. They don't understand English." The two girls are watching us expectantly, like dogs at a door.

"Melody? Your girlfriend? Man, don't even think about her." Breffni waves his hand unsteadily in my face. "You think she's been faithful while you've been away?" He laughs scornfully. "Hell, no!"

I'm not so sure. Men are simple. We're congenitally unfaithful. Women are unpredictable. Just when you think love's in the bag, they carve their initials in your back. I don't know what to believe. Melody has an easy heart and automatic thighs.

Ten minutes later Crispen's back. He points to his watch.

"Gentlemen. Curfew."

"What?" I drop my girl's hand.

"The hostel closes in like—" he checks his watch "—twenty minutes."

"How long does it take to get back?" I ask.

"About forty minutes. Half an hour if we leave the girls behind. Twenty minutes if we leave Breffni behind."

Breffni's lying on a couch. His feet are somehow still on the floor, twisting his spine sideways and up oddly. In the morning he'll need traction.

The fat Turkish girl has draped her coat over his lap. Her hands are nowhere to be seen.

"Has he passed out?" I ask.

"I'd say so," Crispen says.

"It's for the best. Let's boogie."

As we sprint through foggy Munich streets, I utter a prayer for Breffni. He'll be all right in the end. I'm running faster than Crispen, who's starting to feel everything he shot.

"Cramp!" he says, clutching his side. I'm just reaching my stride. I was a long-distance runner in high school before I realized black people sprinted or jumped. For me, unlike walking—standing even—running comes easy. Equilibrium ensues when everything revolves at the right speed.

I was surprised to learn that Simien's modelling guide devotes an entire page to the art of standing. To stand properly, it says, you have to imagine a thread stretching from the centre of the top of your head to the ceiling. You have to visualize it pulling you up very, very slowly onto your toes. You have to stretch up, keep your shoulders down, pull your stomach in, lift your heels, then stay on your toes to the count of five and very, very slowly lower yourself back onto the soles of you feet. As you do this, you have to hold your body in the same position as it was when you were on your toes. That's the ideal standing position.

Walking is like standing, only you're moving. At our modelling class they taught us that walking is like swinging a bucket of water over your head. The faster you swing, the less water you spill. To walk you have to balance imaginary objects on your head, weigh yourself down, centre yourself artificially, or the jug tips and balance is lost. To run all you have to do is run. The running takes care of itself. You don't think of how you look or what others think of you as you run. All that's on your mind is how to put one foot in front of the other even faster, and when you should stop running and start standing.

FOURTEEN

I'm meeting Dat Win at a club called Integrity. He threw me on the list, so I manoeuvre around the lineup and make my way down three sets of stairs into the basement.

I'm dizzied by the lights. Kaleidoscopic projections hit the wall. Twenty-five disco balls revolve in unison. Letters, seemingly at random, flash on a white screen. To those who have been here too long, they form words, sentences.

Anyone walking toward the dance floor has to step around a thin white teen breakdancing on the floor. On the floor itself some patrons have already begun taking off their shirts. I fear what's next, but so far they're keeping it clean. An odd sideways dance is becoming popular, though I'm not sure if it's something new that was started here, or the vestiges of a failed dance that wasn't picked up back home. Many are dancing with themselves. Few are drinking. Three or four kids have brought fluorescent skipping ropes and are skipping on the stage. Those who have popped pills stare in wonder, fascinated, thanks to their newly induced appreciation of colours and contrasts.

There are plenty of couches for resting and, if the need arises, petting. I take a seat at a table. It's near the washroom. I have to pee, but I'm scared to leave in case Dat Win arrives. I have a great seat. From here I can see most of the bar until the fog machine strikes.

It's by far the youngest club I've been to in Europe. Breasts are still under construction. Most of the girls can't, in good conscience, be hit upon. They're drinking shooters and things with cream.

All over the bar men wonder how they got stuck with the ugly one, and hatch plans to switch with their mates. Women go to and return from the bathroom in pods. There are only a few stools full of black people. They seem to know one another. We all nod to the beat. The bass is like ultrasound. Healing scar tissue. Interfering with pacemakers. There are baldheaded bouncers manning every post. Potted plants thrive in the corners, thanks to a healthy combination of dry ice and cigarette smoke. Two girls give each other massages in the corner. Watching them makes me sleepy. Resting my head on the wall, I can feel the bass in my brain. I can't tell if I'm becoming smarter or dumber, but I lift my head off the wall just in case.

Eyeglasses, I note, are big again. All the kids wear them. Mostly metal, some plastic. Plaid is both out and in. Sashes abound. Nobody's wearing shorts except me.

A teen comes up to me and asks for a smoke. I shake my head. Even if I had one I'd no more likely hand it over than I would its equivalent in cash.

Everyone around me seems happy except a short blond girl who looks as if she's been crying.

"Are you okay?" I ask.

"I'm fine," she says, sniffing. The mascara has already formed two lanes down her face.

"Are you sure? You look like you just broke up with your boyfriend or something."

"My boyfriend? He's right over there," she says, pointing into the crowd. "I'm just allergic to carrots, that's all."

"Ah."

A tall teen with a floss-thin goatee walks up to the girl and puts his arm around her. He's wearing the largest crucifix I've seen outside of Calvary.

"I see." I nod to them both and walk away, comforting myself with the knowledge they won't last.

Dat Win arrives an hour late and dressed in yellow. He's still as gorgeous as the old posters. Dat was the first Kameleon Man. Now he represents the company at home and abroad.

"Sorry I'm late, babe, but it's impossible to find a cab this time of night in my neighbourhood. What are you drinking?"

He fetches me a vodka-lime. He's drinking Perrier.

I point out the latest brunette I've been tracking, try to interest him in her friend, but he points to his ring, thick and gold. It's just as well. My brunette was kind of heavy, and her friend was wearing too much lacquer. She's the kind of girl who wears makeup to the beach.

"I'm glad to finally meet you," Dat Win says, fanning himself with an enormous hand. "In person, that is, not on video." He laughs.

I stare at my drink, not sure whether to join in or apologize.

"I liked your video. You know the jeans. Kameleon's got attitude coming out of both pockets. That's what it's all about in the jeans biz—selling attitude. Since the beginning, they've been about attitude. And sex. Attitude and sex. And camouflage. Mainly camouflage."

"How's that?"

"Jeans can make you into anything you want. Class and culture disappear. Like communism, only it works. Labourers and the proletariat wearing the same clothes. It's kind of ironic that America's uniform is Marxism's only living legacy. Did you know the first jeans were created for coal miners in California?"

I shake my head.

"Then they were worn by convicts as uniforms. Now they're a billion-dollar industry. Our jeans are one of Germany's top cultural exports, right behind strudel and porn."

"You know a hell of a lot about jeans."

"That's my job. They're my life now."

"Then why don't you model them anymore?"

"I did my time. I got out of the modelling end because I'm an artist. And there's no art in modelling."

"But you're in advertising now, right?"

"That's what I always wanted to do. I majored in advertising in school. It's an art. Like I said, there's no art in modelling."

"What are you talking about? Modelling's full of creativity."

"Creativity? You take directions, you act out other people's fantasies, there's almost no chance to express your own. That's why models get so messed up. That and the drugs, of course. Anyway, I shouldn't be saying anything bad about modelling to our model, right, babe?" He punches me softly on the shoulder. "This," he says with a wry smile, "is our dream." He lays it out.

We'll be shooting in a sewer. A real one with rats. We'll be shooting on a firing range. A real one with bullets. Forget motorcycles and leather, we're doing mopeds on ice or sand—they haven't decided yet. Scuba with jeans has already been done, so I'll be zipping down a guy wire, a paratrooper behind enemy lines. Do I mind lying in a casket? With jeans on?

"That's why I'm being paid the big bucks," I tell him, unthrilled.

"Kameleons were the first jeans in space. We want you to be the first model on the moon."

"The moon?"

"We're working on that." He takes a sip of Perrier. "You've heard of spontaneous combustion? Your jeans will spontaneously combust with the help of gasoline or something. The whole thing'll be speeded up so the ad will only take a couple of seconds. Almost subliminal. It's pretty safe, and it'll look super sexy."

"What happens when the jeans burn up? Am I wearing something underneath? It sounds kind of dangerous."

"There's an element of danger in everything we do. Even wearing jeans."

"Right. But didn't the last Kameleon Man die on a shoot?"

"Not true. He was shot."

"But didn't he break his neck falling off a roof?"

"After he was shot."

"I see. Presumably not by the company."

"By his girlfriend."

"There you go."

"So have you tried Germany on for size?"

"It's all right. Nothing to write home about." Which I haven't. "The women are beautiful but not very friendly. And I'm living in a craphole."

"Where, babe?"

"The youth hostel."

"Which one?"

"The crappy one."

"You're out of there. I'll take care of you. Anything else you need?"

"I'm a little tight for cash..."

"Not for long."

Dat Win pulls a wad of paper from his breast pocket, unfolds it, smiles, and places it on the table. The table's lit from the inside. It illuminates the paper like an X-ray, so I can see both sides without being able to read either. I pick up the pile. The contract's five pages long, full of spots to initial, date, and sign.

"Can I ask you a question?"

"Shoot, babe."

"Why me?"

He studies me for a moment. "What exactly are you racewise?"

"Half white."

"And?"

"Half black."

"Who's who? Your parents, I mean."

"My mother's white, my father was black."

"See, when I look at you, it's kind of hard to tell what you are exactly. I mean, you could be part Indian, part Asian. You could pretty much pass for whatever, right?"

"I guess."

"Don't give me that look. That's a good thing. It's something we can use. A couple of years ago everyone was caught up celebrating the exotic. The blacker the better. They searched under every rock for anyone who looked the part. I was one of them. My name used to be Peter." He smiles.

"Peter Win?"

"The agency made me use my Vietnamese name. It was the thing to do back then. But times have changed. Now if I had a Vietnamese model, I'd make him go by the name Tom Jones or Steve Smith."

"Why?"

"Things are different. We're done with the idea of legitimacy, pureness. The essential African, the essential Asian. All of that's done. Our ideas about race are changing. Gradually the world is swallowing the idea that we're all the same. And I don't mean that we're all the same inside. One day we'll all be the same outside. If we stir the pot long enough, you're what's left at the bottom. Kameleon isn't just about jeans anymore, it's about us. It's about humanity. It's about the net result, and you're it."

I nod, not really buying any of it.

"On your application form you said your mother's from Germany."

"Originally."

"And your father—you didn't know him, right?"

"He's from Providence, Rhode Island."

"But you didn't know him long, right? You don't know where his family was from?"

"Not really."

"You see? They could have been from anywhere. You just don't know."

"I guess not."

"You can't assume anything these days. You're fairly light-skinned, your eyes aren't perfect almonds. Who's to say you don't have some Guyanese or Sri Lankan in you? All I'm saying is why not go with the mystery."

"You want me to say I'm not black?"

"Don't get me wrong. Some of my best models are black. But you're a mix, which is true. No one's asking you to lie. If anyone asks, tell the truth about your other half. You just don't know."

We take a sip. I'm not sure my mother will be happy if I tell the world

I didn't know who Daddy was, but I suppose she'll get over it.

Dat Win winks. "Super, babe. So let's get it on." He hands me a plastic pen.

I sign with a flourish. My new signature's coming along nicely. The Schmidt is a gangrenous limb amputated for the good of the whole. It seems I'll be making twenty or thirty times more than I've accumulated in four years of real work. My father would be proud, if I knew who he was. That's worth a toast. I order another round.

"Sometimes you hear models say their lives were better before the big contract and all the money," Dat Win says. "That's crap. Your life's about to get a thousand times better. There's no downside to hitting it big. It's only a problem for people who can't handle success. Those people always try to return to the state where they feel happiest, even if that's being unhappy. Right, babe?"

"Right."

"You're friends with Breffni Beehan, aren't you? Good guy. Decent guy. He got a fairly big deal with Iceberg about three years ago. Good money, but two months into his contract he disappears. Can't find him anywhere. Three months later they spot him in Amsterdam, high as a kite, broke as a priest. Couldn't handle it. That's why he's stuck in a rut. None of the big boys will touch him now. Shame. He has a great look."

This I didn't know.

"Your life's about to change," Dat Win says. He looks serious. "You ready?"

I lift my glass.

"To success," he says, and we clink.

"Success." There's a smudge of lipstick on my glass, not mine. This contract isn't Hugo Boss or Polo, but it's a good beginning. Almost everything in life is better in small doses, anyway, including success. That's why Chinese tea tastes so good in those little cups. "So did you like any of my ideas?"

"Ideas?"

"On the videotape. The ideas about, you know, having people vote to change the colour of the jeans?"

"That's a winner. We were tossing around a similar idea a while ago.

Interactive ads. Design-your-own commercial type of thing. A contest within a contest. Solid."

"And what about my idea to use real people in the ads?"

"God, no. No one's ever been able to sell anything with real people. You're as close to real as they come. Flawed yet pleasing to the eye." He smiles and throws back the last of his Perrier. "Listen, babe, I gotta go. We'll be in touch."

"Next week?"

"Two weeks tops."

Dat Win offers to pick up the tab, but I wave him off. I tip the waitress for the drinks, tip the coat-check girl for getting my coat, tip the bouncer, too. What the hell.

FIFTEEN

It's only 8:30 in the morning, and already I feel as if I've been put through a garlic press. My mattress was an illusion. The bunk bed is a single jammed against the wall. Normally I sleep spread out. Like a starfish. Like a chalk outline. Last night I had no room to manoeuvre. My limbs were restless. My thoughts confused.

"What's for breakfast?" Crispen asks, appearing from under his blankets.

"It's a Continental breakfast," Breffni says.

Crispen grunts. "Damn! A Continental breakfast is just another word for a shitty breakfast." He leaps from his bed into some homemade slippers.

Downstairs there's also porridge, but it looks like a stool sample.

"Did you see the eggs?" Crispen asks.

"Those are eggs?"

"Yeah, but don't touch them. They look like they've hatched."

"I think I'll stick with the croissants."

"If you dig deep enough in the bin, there might still be a couple of chocolate ones," Breffni says.

"Chocolate? For breakfast?"

"Yeah. They're an excellent source of sugar."

I take a croissant, greasy with goodness. Breffni steals a handful of oranges from the kitchen. I unwrap two, eat them with gusto. The vitamins might come in handy.

Our room is almost empty when we return. The only one left is Thomas. He usually doesn't start cleaning till eleven, sometimes noon.

"Where is everybody?"

"All the Americans are on the train to Dachau," Thomas says from his bed. "Then later they're visiting the castle that inspired Disneyland. The Australians slept somewhere else last night. And that man who never talks, the one with the dirty hair, he left this morning. I don't think he's coming back."

"So what should we do today?" Breffni asks.

"Let's go to the park," I suggest.

"And do what?" Crispen asks.

"I don't know...just go see it?"

"Pass."

"We could go to a museum," I say.

Breffni raises an eyebrow. "Museum? No, thanks."

We all sit silently, dreading another day of nothing. Unless we work we've got nothing to do during the day except talk, nothing to do at night except club. Modelling keeps us off the streets. Lately there hasn't been much work, apart from the odd sniff. Dat Win said he'd call this week for three weeks now. Apparently the family of the last Kameleon Man is suing. Breffni's been doing okay, sometimes turning down shoots if they're too small or too far away. Crispen and I are in about as much demand as Guinea worm. They all want us for shows, but the show season is still months away. We have to content ourselves with gathering dew from upturned leaves, foraging for insects rich in moisture.

"I need to get out of here," Breffni says, swinging his arms like a petulant child.

"How about a run?" Crispen suggests.

Breffni and I look at each other and shrug. Neither of us has a better idea, so we lace up and head out. We jog in single file, Crispen in front, me in the middle, Breffni bringing up the rear.

A man is driving slowly down the street outside the hostel in a red convertible, a leash protruding from the window. A small terrier trots placidly beside it. Usually there's a bum on the bench running out of air. He wheezes and coughs, his chest rattles and hums. Whenever anyone walks by, he croaks at them in German. I don't know what he says. Normally he has a bike beside him next to the bench, a full bag of beer within arm's reach in the grass. Yesterday I saw a bouquet of red flowers in his bike basket and wondered who they were for. Sometimes I take his picture. He doesn't seem to mind. But today he's not there. All that's left of him are the six or seven aluminum cans in the grass. They'll be gone by lunch.

On our way downtown we stop at Hakim's for our morning *döner*. Hakim shears the cone of meat with his electric knife, heaping almost a dozen strips into each pita, with lettuce, onions, pickled beets, and plenty of paprika. He wraps them in foil and hands them to us, smiling. We all agree they're just compressed lamb shavings bathed in sauce, but at three euros apiece, they're the only warm food we can afford.

"You hear that?" Breffni asks.

We jog toward the music, Crispen still leading the way. He seems to have picked up the pace. The street opens into a large courtyard where a crowd cheers intermittently. The music's coming from speakers stacked two-people-high. There are six hoops and six teams of threes playing on the cobblestones. On the backboards there's a red M, probably for Martini, the new sneakers all the kids are wearing. They still owe me money. On either end of the yard there are booths selling shoes. Someone's giving away T-shirts, all of them extra-large.

"Damn!" Crispen says. "Ball? In Germany? How do we get in? It's a three-on-three tournament. We have three."

"I don't think so," I say. "It looks organized." There are teams waiting on the chalk-painted sidelines. "And we don't have our shoes or anything."

"We came out to get some exercise, right? What better way to do it than throw the ball around? Relax. It'll be fun." Crispen disappears into the crowd.

I look at Breffni. "Do you feel like playing?"

He shrugs. "I'm easy. I don't care what we do. At least it's nice and sunny."

Breffni's right. It's the first real sun we've seen in Germany. Breffni glances around, takes his shirt off, and lies on the cobblestones, arms spread wide.

"What are you doing?"

"I'm taking a sun bath."

"Good idea." Stripping off my shirt, I lie down and stare up at the blue sky, puffed with powder clouds. God's stucco ceiling. I close my eyes and imagine myself in my old apartment in Nepean before go-sees and runways, when all I worried about was paying off my student loan and getting laid. I sigh. Sunshine is, indeed, lube for the soul. "Man, if you people hadn't stolen us from Africa, I'd be lying in the sun like this every day drinking piña coladas."

"First of all, you immigrated to Canada," Breffni says. "And second, you should thank us. You were in the jungle being eaten by lions and shit. Now you have cars and air-conditioning. If it weren't for us, you'd still be eating caterpillars and making houses out of hay."

I suppose he's right.

The sun suddenly goes out. It's Crispen, standing over me. I'm in the umbra of his ass. "Don't listen to this cracker," he says. "We discovered mathematics, invented astronomy, established the first university... If they hadn't stolen us from Africa, who knows what marvels we would have created? We'd probably be living in domes under the sea, riding dolphins to work and shit. Now get off your asses. We got next."

It turns out we've stumbled onto a nomadic street-ball tournament. It drifts from street to street, city to city, giving gear to anyone who's got game.

"You think we can win?" I ask Crispen.

"I don't know who these guys are, and I've never seen any of them play but, yes, I guarantee we'll win. How good can they be? Germans may be great at taking over the world, but they stink at basketball."

Too soon the man in the Martini sweatshirt and pants whistles us over. The other team is waiting, white guys, all of them taller. The man says a few words, then looks at us.

"You understand?" Crispen asks me.

"No. Just keep playing till someone stops us, I guess."

"Cool."

Crispen takes a few tentative dribbles on the cobblestones. The ball bounces randomly.

"All right, Stace, you take him, and Breff can take that guy." He points as he talks. "I'll take the one with the ponytail. They're tall, but they're skinny, and I've seen them dribble. They have no handle. Let them shoot. Nothing easy. What's our motto?"

"No lay-ups," Breffni and I say in unison.

"All right. Go team."

They get first ball. Our opponents are tall, angular, with pool-stick elbows. They pass well, shoot poorly, drive rarely and, when they do, throw themselves at the hoop and fall backward, hoping the referee will bail them out with a foul. But the ref understands that calling a foul would only delay the inevitable. It's not even close. Even I get into the act. The guys we're playing seem overcome by gravity. I feel as if I'm playing on the moon.

"What's the score?" I ask, not even huffing.

"Many to few," Crispen says.

Crispen blocks a tentative shot, grabs the loose ball, and sails the other way, avoiding the drain at half-court to score. A toothpick, as always, dangles loosely in his lips. He doesn't even have to open his mouth to breathe. I still can't seem to control the ball on the rough stones. I concentrate on boxing out, rebounding, making the outlet pass. I leave the dribbling to Breffni, who's able to anticipate the uneven bounces, and to Crispen, who's too fast to care which way the ball goes.

We dispatch the first two teams with ease. The crowd cheers industriously as the *Auslanders* slaughter their boys on the court. After each game, they line up and shake our hands with earnest nods and serious smiles. Most Germans are friendly enough as long as they know you're not here to stay. It didn't take me long to notice that everyone who looks like me carries a shovel or a broom.

The third team is a little taller, a little tougher, and actually manages to score a few points, mostly on Breffni, who's too busy checking out the short blondie who cheers a little louder every time he touches the ball. Crispen glares at Breffni.

"Fine," Breffni says. "Let's stop messing around. Give me the ball on the wing."

Breffni scores the winning hoop on a long shot from the corner. The ball does a victory lap before going down.

"That's better," Crispen says, patting Breffni's ass. "Keep it up, partner. These next guys are players."

"I'm getting some water," I say.

There is no water, only pop at a stand manned by two quiet blond boys who refuse to keep the change. I snap open the bottle, take a sip, a breather, and glance around. A bum recovers a bagful of fries from the garbage bin. A woman at a nearby table moulds purple Silly Putty into small animal shapes and mutters something to herself or to her creations. I wish I had my camera.

A young girl is watching one of the other games. She has a brush fire of red hair, with two ponytails sprouting on each side of her head. A constellation of freckles. She looks sixteen, though I know she's much older. I'm awash with a chemical pang that starts in my chest and ends in my shoes. She claps at her boyfriend, one of the six guys playing on court three. None of them are worthy. I gaze at her forlornly, wondering why a model who's about to launch an international clothing campaign has so much trouble scoring. Being a model seems to offer few advantages. The girls we model with date moguls, soccer players, or one another. No one invites mediocre models to floating harbour parties. We aren't on any lists, or asked to be there when something opens. What good is being a model if no one knows you're a model? Or cares?

My redhead has run onto the court to hug her man. He's the tallest, with a ponytail and stubble. He has an arrogant smile. I hope we play them next.

"Crispen, did you tell those guys we were going to kick their asses?" Breffni asks. "'Cause they look like they want to kill us."

"I don't remember doing it, but it sounds like something I'd do," Crispen says. "Don't worry. Those guys were mad to begin with. They're just navy boys from the base."

"Yeah, well, they look like they just came back from four months in a submarine and are looking for some ass to kick."

The navy men are wearing grey T-shirts, matching funeral-black shorts, shaved heads, and expensive sneakers with the latest stealth technology. One black guy, two white guys. The black player is at least six-four in both directions—a huge Southern-fried Negro with a mountain range of muscles. He sports several chunky rings, none of which, I hope, were earned from basketball. One of the white guys is almost as tall, and thick like nougat. His nose is slightly askew, suggesting it was broken and then forgotten. He looks and sounds as if he was grown in Georgia soil, the kind of guy who has commemorative plates, a coon dawg, and kinfolk. The other white man is shorter, though still taller than I am. Wiry. His muscles, if they were uncoiled, would encircle the planet three times. His arms are as long as paddles and are covered in tattoos: Chinese symbols, a flaming skull, barbed wire, a menagerie of animals. His head is shaved so close I can see his brain. He talks to the black guy in an A-Train accent. "Who you want?"

"Take who takes you," the black guy grunts.

I glance at Crispen. "How are we going to stop the big guy? He's got at least fifty pounds on any of us. He'll be invincible inside."

"Oh, he's vincible," Crispen says. "I'll take him and front him."

"I'll give you weak-side help," Breffni says.

"No help."

"What if they lob it over you?"

"Have you ever seen anyone lob the ball over me?"

Silence.

"I'll take the big white guy," Breffni says.

"I guess I'll take the shorter fellow."

They brought their own ball, which they insist on using. "I'd like to get the game on before my visa expires," Crispen says. "Let's go, punks."

The black guy posts up, discards Crispen with a forearm, dunks the ball on Breffni's exposed head. Breffni's man has a deceptively sweet outside shot and hits two straight threes. My man is too fast, blows by me three times for lay-ups. Crispen, toothpick in mouth, spins for another two. He's our only real scorer. It's 9–9, win by two. I get an elbow in the eye, go down hard. The ref calls time-out. Quick water break.

"Shoot, I never thought I'd say this, but we could use Biggs right now," Breffni says. "He's the only person I know who could box out that orangutan."

"That's because Biggs stank so bad no one wanted to get close to him," Crispen says. He takes another huge gulp of air, looks tired. "Let's try to jam up the passing lanes a bit, make it harder for them to get it inside. Stace, play off your man a little bit. Make him shoot. Take away the drive. I'm going to turn my man to the baseline, then come and double."

The big man gets the ball, drives, Crispen turns him to the baseline, I abandon my man and try to stand in his way, but I don't think he notices. He jump-stops, splits our double team, goes over and through—10–9.

"Come on, ref!" Crispen screams. "He's hopping around like the Easter bunny! He's a travelling salesman! Call it, man!" The ref puts his hands up and shrugs.

"Shut up and play," the black guy says, throwing the ball at Crispen. It rockets off his shoulder.

"These clowns are getting mouthy," Crispen whispers as he inbounds the ball. "I may have to put them in their place. You got my back?"

"I don't have your back," Breffni says. "I don't have any part of you. You're on your own."

Crispen takes us all by surprise, penetrates, puts up a floater over out-stretched arms, up and in. We're tied.

They counter by pounding the ball inside. Breffni gets clubbed with an elbow, falls to draw the foul, but none is called. A lay-up, and they're up one. I pass the ball dutifully to Crispen, run a pick for him, they switch up. I've got the black guy on me now; Crispen's got the white guy on him. I clear out, hoping to draw my man away, but he doesn't respect my shot enough to follow and stands at the foul line, ready for Crispen. Crispen waves me away, banishing me to the far side, where I wait with Breffni. Isolating his man, Crispen fakes a shot. The man jumps and flails as Crispen sails by him. An arm, meaty and brown, stops Crispen's face as he's about to finger-roll us into another tie. Crispen screams and goes down, holding his mouth.

"You all right?" Breffni asks.

I give Crispen a hand to his feet. "Let's see."

He takes his hand away. Blood drips from his lip.

"I think that's from your toothpick, man," Breffni says. "I don't know why you play with a sharp piece of wood in your mouth."

"This is from the guy's hand. Bitch did it on purpose." Crispen whirls away, steps up into the black man's face. "What the fuck?"

"Going for the ball," he mutters, turning away.

"Bullshit!" Crispen shoves him in the back.

I don't like the look of this. I have no idea what Golden Gloves are, but I bet the black guy has a pair. He turns, and without a word hammers Crispen's face. Crispen dissolves to the ground, as though his skeleton has turned to water. Breffni and I rush the man. Breffni gets there first, dodges, and kicks the man in the chest with little result. The big white guy grabs me, hurls me aside, goes after Breffni.

The crowd cheers, as though we've won the game. I turn to meet the third guy. I'm surprised to find him right behind me. He swings. There's something in his hand. It feels warm, though not painful, and blood spatters onto his grey shirt. I'm down, holding my face. The guy looms over me, clutching the top of a broken pop bottle. The sharp end is red. We stare at each other. Suddenly there are sirens, and I see the boots and shoes of the fleeing.

I roll onto my back. It's still sunny, almost unbearably. The clouds are ribbons, slashed and rent, keloid scars. I squint. The sunlight hurts my eyes, but I'm afraid to close them, scared that if I do I'll never open them again. I'm tired and wonder why I still feel no pain. If a dinosaur stepped on a thorn, it would take about ten seconds for the nerve impulses to travel from its foot to its brain. I wonder how long it would take if it were stabbed in the face. There's a strong wind. Street vendors flutter overhead, flitting from spot to spot, trying to find the best location to capitalize on the afternoon trade. Businessmen hurry back from lunch. They check their watches, jump out into the wind, hands outstretched, and float off into the warm squalls. In a moment I'll get up and fly with them toward the hospital, or away from the cops. But for now I'm content to lie here, my face warm and wet, as if with tears.

A man who calls himself Alfred Tube laces up my face. One hand holds my jaw, the other the needle. His clothes smell of air freshener. He's close enough to kiss.

"Steady," he says. "It won't hurt if you don't move."

"It doesn't hurt, anyway." I don't feel a thing. I'm dizzy, thanks to whatever we smoked a half hour ago.

Breffni says he met Tube at a show in Amsterdam three years ago. If what Dat Win said was true, that's about the same time Breffni disappeared. Breffni swears Tube went to medical school before he was expelled for dealing drugs. I'd trust the man more if we hadn't shared the joint before he began stitching me up. Breffni, Crispen, a man who calls himself Zilzil Tibbs, and a woman named Sativa are all lying on the couch.

"Stay still," Tube says.

"Are you sure I shouldn't go to a hospital?"

"I'll take your no-insurance ass to the hospital if you want," Crispen says. "I'll even drive the getaway car after you rob the bank to pay for it. But who's going to explain to the cops why a couple of foreign Negroes were brawling on German soil? Think of your career."

"My career?" I touch the gash on my face, still warm. It feels a little tingly, a little dead, as if my cheek has fallen asleep.

Tube slaps my hand away. "Don't touch."

The apartment is a basement, dark in the corners, red everywhere else with lava light. There are a couple of handmade paintings on the wall, and dresser drawers of various shapes and sizes line the walls. On the floor are bales of marijuana, a flurry of smoking papers, a jam-jar bong. There are enough bricks of hash to build a house. Even the cat looks stoned.

Though I'm the worst off by far, Crispen and Breffni are also less pretty than they were two hours ago. Crispen's chin is cut from when his head hit the pavement. His nose has grown like Pinocchio's, and only one eye is open for business. Breffni's become a cartoon character. A hill grows out of his forehead. He still can't tie his own shoes.

"All done," Tube says.

I touch my face gingerly.

"Stop touching it. You'll be fine in a couple of days. Weeks."

"Let's see?" Crispen takes my face in his hands, twists me into the light, inspects me with his good eye. "It's not that bad, partner. But I hope it doesn't scar. Black people scar funny. Some brothers go through plate glass and don't get marked, others get scratched by a cat and it looks like their skin was professionally shredded. Vitamin E's the key."

I turn to Tube. "Do I need to do anything?"

"Other than eat, sleep, and shit? No. The stitches are catgut, not nylon, so I won't have to take them out. Eventually your body will absorb them."

"Catgut?" I don't know which is more disturbing—having cat innards on my face, or strings melting into my skin. I don't remember seeing Tube wash his hands.

"The stitches might smell a bit, but that's natural."

A smelly face will be the least of my worries. I trace the stitches with my finger.

Tube slaps my hand away. "I told you not to touch it. You don't want it to get infected, do you?"

"Listen to Tube," Breffni says. "He's a doctor. Was a doctor. Will be a doctor." I'm surprised to hear Breffni, having thought him incapable of speech for a good half hour now. Crispen's debating with the cat. It yawns as if it's just returning from a rave. Its name is Rock and Roll. Zilzil's kissing Sativa's arm.

"Steady as a rock," Tube says, raising his hands. Either his hands are shaking, or I am.

"You've still got it man. Yeah," Breffni says. He drops off the couch, crawls toward the bathroom. The cat follows, batting at his feet from behind.

"Let's roll," Tube says, clapping his hands. Everyone gathers behind him to watch. He gums two papers together, crushes up the pot evenly, tucks the lip, rolls the skin gently into a perfect tube.

"No origami today?" Zilzil Tibbs asks. To me he says, "Sometimes he makes animals. Birds and fish and shit. Last time I think we smoked Noah's entire ark."

"Not today," Tube says. "The operation took it out of me."

He twists and lights, then passes the pot around. Sativa, Zilzil, Crispen, then me. I hit it with gusto. My high was starting to fade. My stitches are a trail of fire ants. I cough, of course, and there are tears. The pot tastes sweet, maliciously strong. I start the countdown, hand off to Tube. He takes the roach, inspects it. I hope I didn't dribble on it too much. Tube draws, deep and hard, every alveolus working in unison. He grins and starts the joint on its second and, perhaps, final trip.

Crispen, who's been holding his smoke the whole time, finally breathes. "Time bomb," he croaks.

When the pot arrives for the third time, I wave it off. I'm already blunted beyond recognition. We sit in silence. Gradually my stricken face gains independence, seceding slowly from my body.

"I'm sorry, partner," Crispen says.

"Don't worry about it."

"It was all my fault."

"Forget it."

"I should've waited till after. The fucking guy shanked you, man. You didn't even see it coming."

"It's over. What can we do?"

"Don't worry, partner. We'll find the bitch-ass bastard and make him pay."

I shake my head and take a drag. "Do you think I'll need plastic surgery?"

Crispen peers at me, brows creased. "Yeah. Probably."

"Lovely. And how am I going to pay for that? I can't even afford to get stitched up properly."

"We'll find a way, partner."

"Maybe Tube can help." The bell on the cat's collar is made of solid gold.

"Forget about these guys. If you mess with them, they'll cut you up worse than those navy bastards. We'll find a way, right, B?" Breffni's back from the washroom. "Are you totally stoned? You're so quiet."

"I'm good. I feel like I've been wrapped in a tortilla."

"He's stoned," I say.

"You're one to talk," Crispen says. "You've been staring at that wall like you're related."

He's right. I thought I was okay until the cat started addressing me by name. "Anyone hungry?" I ask hopefully.

"There's food in the kitchen," Breffni says. "Bring back something for me, too."

On the kitchen counter I find a plate of sandwiches containing aromatic meats. I grab the coldest one and pour myself a glass of water. There are crumbs in the ice cubes. My feet stick to the floor.

In the living room Zilzil's talking at the top of his voice to no one in particular, making metaphysical expectorations about the Netherlands' national soccer team. Crispen's crawling around on all fours. Sativa's sitting shirtless on top of him, shouting, "Hya, mule, hya!" Her old, naughty breasts swing from side to side.

Tube watches with an amused smile. I'm not sure if he's gay, straight, or undecided.

"Why don't we do these?" Zilzil Tibbs asks, holding out a palm of desiccated brown mushrooms. They look like dried apple cores. Shrunken heads.

"Those things will take a decade off your life," Tube says. "Now why don't we all forget our troubles with a nice bong?" He waves the device at us expectantly.

Everyone passes except me. I take it, examine myself in its smoky glass. My face has been incised from cheek to jaw. I can't help but chuckle. My great-grandfather would be proud. Such scars were a mark of distinction among the young students of Heidelberg. He'd often tell me about the duels between freshmen over girls or over nothing in particular, resolved with swords at dawn to the satisfaction of both. The duellers, much like walruses, would only seek to mark, not kill. The loser would still win, proudly bearing a scar boasting of his willingness to take a slash for his lady or his honour. My great-grandfather once killed a man over my great-grandmother. I forget why. So does he. He sent a flower to the man's mother, a bouquet to his widow. So the story goes. If only he could see me now.

SIXTEEN

Page 23, *Modelling Made Easy*: "Stand in front of a bathroom mirror. With the edge of a bar of soap, trace the outline of your face. Then step back. Is your face wider at the forehead or wider at your jaw? If your face is a perfect oval, you have a perfect face for modelling."

I trace my face with a corner of green soap and stand back. My face was once a perfect oval, without mole, nick, or pock. From back here, without my glasses, I can still pretend. My face looks as smooth as a mirror, as soft as soap. Then I step forward, framing my face back inside the soapy bubble. Everything always looks slightly off in someone else's bathroom mirror, but there's only so much I can blame on hundred-watt lighting and toothpaste spatter. I've tried everything—vitamin E, topical and ingested; foul-smelling zinc; exfoliants; unguents; ointments; gels; salves; balms. But, if anything, the scar's become puffier, raised. A check mark turning from red to purple, and no matter what I do, no matter what I put on it or scrub it with, I can't erase it. The world of traditional medicine has failed me. Now I'm down to faith.

I consult my modelling Bible again. I've taken the liberty of studying it, have most of it committed to memory. Frankly I don't know how I've survived as long as I have without it. It's full of good advice. Page 17: "Whenever possible, wear sensible shoes." Or page 3: "If you are considering any type of cosmetic surgery, ask yourself—will the operation change who I am or will it simply improve my existing beauty?"

Perhaps, not surprisingly, my stitches have turned septic. I tried alcohol, iodine, Polysporin, Dettol. They just made it worse, killed my skin. My face has become deciduous; pieces of it peel off in postage-stamp-size flakes. Now all I can do is try to hide behind a veil of makeup. Page 10: "The first step—foundation. It is the base, the pedestal, upon which your appearance stands or from which it falls." I smear a thin layer of paste onto the Plexiglas palette, mix it around with a pâté knife, and daub at it with a foam triangle. On my face beige is yellow, brown looks red. I'm a white man with a neon tan. I try browner, browner. Now I look like a tree. Too brown. I give up, read on.

The secret, on page 11, the little-known technique of "building up" by slowly adding colour. No matter what I apply, no matter how thinly I add or what I take away, the results always end up impossibly garish. My face is a Halloween mask. A shredded garment no longer suitable for the job it was intended. A ripped tuxedo. Page 29 offers little comfort: "Some models have made imperfect physical characteristics work for them. A gap between the two front teeth or a prominent nose can be a mark of character." Nowhere in its thirty pages does the manual say anything about cuts, gashes, scars, or incisions. Nothing about basement surgery with needles of uncertain origin.

"You're running out of time," Tube says from the living room. "You have to choose and get out of here by 6:30."

It's decision time. Crispen was against the whole thing. Breffni was against the whole thing but told me not to get caught. I told him not to say anything to Crispen. He probably would have done anything to stop me. He might have even called the cops.

"I'm coming."

I'll make three runs, enough to pay for my face. Three runs and I'm out. It would be funny if it weren't so sad. I rinse my face, daub it carefully with a towel. It turns brown like mud.

"If it's so easy, why don't you do it anymore?" I ask Tube.

"I don't have to. I have people do it for me."

"Do they get caught?"

"Yes."

I don't say anything.

"It's an envelope, a bag, and some tubes. Easy as pie."

I nod.

"Then we're all set." Tube opens one of the dresser drawers, pulls out a small envelope, and hands it to me. Then he grabs two aluminum-coated bricks from the drawer and stuffs them into a backpack.

"Is that hash?"

Tube doesn't answer. He opens another drawer and begins filling the bag with various items—makeup, books, bras, and a hair dryer as big as a radar gun. A scrapbook tumbles onto the floor and erupts with pictures of a blond girl in various locations with various men, none of them me.

"Who's the chick?" I ask.

"I don't know. I got the bag at the train station. If the police find the bag, they won't think it's yours, right?" He hands me the bag.

"Why would a bald black guy be travelling with a hair dryer and tampons?"

"You got it."

"Good idea. Does it work?"

"Only if you don't have the bag on you."

"If I do?"

"If you do, you can always fall back on the old 'I was holding this for a girl I met' routine."

"Does that work?"

"Sometimes. Now I told you how this goes, didn't I?" He points to the small plastic tubes I'm to swallow.

"Swallow now, shit two days later," I recite. Tube nods. It sounds easy. "One question. What if I have to go between now and then?"

"You won't." He opens a top drawer, pulls out two plastic bottles of what look like medicine. "These are your faucets. This is off." He holds up one bottle. Kaopectate. "This is on." The other bottle is Dulcalax. "Take two swigs of this now and it'll tie you up till you're ready to deliver the goods." He hands me the Kaopectate. "Then take some of this." He gives me the Dulcalax. "And that should get the tap running again. Simple." It sounds like a drugged-out movie version of *Alice in Wonderland* starring Alfred Tube as the Caterpillar.

I'm not convinced. Turning my gastrointestinal tract into a key player in any plan, much less one that could net me a dozen years in jail, seems like a bad idea. "Do I really have to do it...this way? In my bum, I mean? Isn't there an easier way?"

"If there is one, I haven't heard it, and I've been in the business for ten years. I did toy with the idea of taping small quantities of dope to my cat so that if a sniffer dog went nuts the cops would figure it was after the cat, but I don't think Rock and Roll's up to it." On cue the cat climbs out of one of the dresser drawers and drops heavily to the floor. It meows at us, then curls up at Tube's feet. By the look in its eyes, it might have helped itself to his stash.

"Now when you come back I won't be here, but Breffni knows how to find me. Contact me and I'll get you the money."

"Fine."

"And I know I don't have to tell you this—it's really a standard disclaimer. If you show up and the stuff doesn't, I'll have you killed. If neither of you show up, I'll have you found, then killed. So stick to the plan, okay? The stuff's really not worth all that much, anyway. This is more of a trial run. If this goes well, bigger and better. Ready?"

There's a bowl of strawberry ice cream on the coffee table, a small bowl of plastic tubes sitting next to it.

"Just pretend they're chocolate chips." He checks his watch. "We've got to get you on that train."

Tube watches approvingly as I pick up the spoon and dip. The first plastic tube goes down as smoothly as a plastic tube. And I don't even like strawberry.

"A free one for the road?" He holds up a small white tablet.

"Thanks, no, I don't do...that stuff." I'm aware of the irony. I've only heard about Hi-C in the newspapers. It's the new designer drug that has parents checking their children's schoolbags. According to all the reports, prolonged usage of the stuff destroys nerve terminals, at least in rat brains. Only three more tubes to go. Rats might not drive cars, but even they're smart enough to stay away from drugs unless they're force-fed to them by scientists. It's kind of funny: despite all the rumours flying around back in Nepean, this is the first time in my career I've been forced to use my ass to make money. Two more to go and I'm getting dangerously low on ice cream.

This I guarantee: I'm the only motherfucker in this club packing a tube of Anusol in his pocket. It was a parting gift from Breffni, who came to see me off. He slapped my back, told me I'd need it. I suppose I can add that to the list of things I'm not looking forward to.

A stripper has just finished giving me ten minutes of hell for asking if she was a stripper. Which she is. But not the one I'm searching for. The club's almost empty, which is natural for seven o'clock. Near the other bar a group of gorgeous lesbians feel one another's breasts. Two of them are a couple. They seem extremely self-satisfied. And who can blame them? They're both sleeping with beautiful women. I know better than to approach them. No one around here matches even remotely the description of the girl I was sent to meet.

I take another sip of my vodka-lime to rinse out the taste of pink chalk. To seal myself tight I drank a quarter bottle of Kaopectate before I left.

A short woman with breasts as big as heads scans the bar from the doorway. If she's wearing a blue skirt, she's my gal. She steps into a shard of strobe light. I get off my stool, walk toward her. I'm not subtle, but Tube didn't say I had to be. In and out, he said, and I mean to do exactly that. She sees me, smiles, and meets me at the bar. The clicking of her straw-thin heels is audible above the music. Like all strippers, she's chewing gum and wears too much makeup. From up close her breasts are even larger than I thought, unnaturally big, filled with a mixture of silicon and helium, defying both gravity and decency. Her ass is lumpy like gruel. She looks dirty. A lap dance might prove fatal without an inoculation. I assume she's not at her best. I hand her the envelope. From its weight I can't tell if it's full of drugs, money, or both. But she seems relieved. She tucks it into her folds and strides away. I wait five minutes, then make my exit, praying the man with the hat isn't a cop. I have twenty minutes to make the train. The U-bahn's closer, but the S-bahn's free, thanks to my Eurail pass.

Fifteen minutes later I'm at the station. The city tourist office is closed, under construction. The office roof has collapsed, possibly under the weight of its own name—Fremdenverkehrsamt. The arrivals and departures board is in German. I can't tell which is which. Barcelona is on both. I take a random poll of three strangers. Two out of three say it's gate 24, with a margin of error of one. I check the map. It tells me YOU ARE HERE. Only I can't tell where that is. The train is leaving as I pull up.

I stifle a scream, but several waiting passengers turn around, anyway. An African man selling wooden birds smiles at me, holds up a bird. The next train leaves in nine hours. There's no choice. I slump onto a bench and settle in for the wait. A man lies across from me. Bugs circle him like flies around a cartoon bum. He doesn't smell strongly enough for me to tell, but somehow the insects sense his heady decay and, overjoyed, congregate.

I lounge horizontally, pull my hood over my head, contemplate my rear entry into the world of small-time crime. If asked two months ago, I would have said drug dealers were a slur against the human race. Now I'm peddling cookie-jar psychedelics. It could be worse, I suppose. I'm not trafficking heroin, after all, or crack. Hi-C is an empathagen, a hug drug. Its only effect is happiness. Its only hangover, dry mouth and slight fatigue. No one ever got hooked on Hi-C. No one ever died of an overdose. Tube told me more people croak swallowing ballpoint pens than from gulping Hi-C. But I'd be an idiot if I actually thought my cargo wasn't heading straight for the playground. I hope the stuff is at least pure. These days you never know. I wonder how much caffeine's in these pills, how much rat poison. This is going nowhere. I can't afford to give any more thought to the passengers travelling first class inside me, nor to the stuff in my bag, the hash that will make its way to the older dopesters, the earnest users, the hookah crowd.

Before I shoved off I phoned Dat Win at Kameleon and left him a message. Nothing about my injury, nothing about my new career. I just told him I couldn't do the campaign right now, I had lost a dear friend, and that I hoped to be back before we started shooting. I don't expect him to understand. Crispen wouldn't. He thought I should tough it out. Breffni said he understood, that he'd been there. I know I'm not alone. My modelling Bible says so on page 15. It's all there in faded black-and-white: "Self-doubt and depression are inevitable. If things get really bad, get away from it all. Finish your shoots and book out. Take a trip. See a friend. Recharge your batteries. Escape."

Lying on a train station bench at one in the morning with an ass full of dope isn't exactly what the author recommended, but losers can't be choosers. The midnight security guard has been eyeing me since his shift started. He marches over and demonstrates with his nightstick that lying down is *verboten*. I'm too tired to argue, too tired even to close the top of my backpack, which has fallen open. The hair dryer is too heavy and slides out, taking with it a bra and the scrapbook. The pictures once again are flung all over the floor. The security guard stoops and helps me gather them. He examines one, holds it up to the light. The blond girl with two girlfriends in bikinis. He smiles knowingly at me. "*Freundin?* Girlfriend?" he asks.

"*Nein,*" I answer. "My ex. Ex-girlfriend."

The guard nods at the picture again, whistles approvingly. I offer him a picture. He laughs, shakes his head, picks up his nightstick, and continues on his rounds. It's going to be a long night.

I'm somewhere between Munich and Barcelona, thinking of ways to get the old man's arm off my side of the armrest. At the back, beside the washroom, the smell of shit, perfume, and menstrual pads wafts toward me when the train slows. The guy in front of me is reclined all the way. I can smell his corn chips. The man across the aisle is alone.

The old man's asleep, head lolling sideways almost onto my shoulder. During the past two hours, he's managed to expand, spread like an oil slick, limbs oozing into my territory. He's impossibly tall for a man his age. I nudge him, but his arm is lighter than I expect and slips off the armrest.

"*Verzeihung,*" he says, turning to me. His breath smells sour, as if his mouth has gone off. His eyes are still half-shut. Trying not to breathe in when he breaks out, I edge away, hoping he isn't one of those old men who holds up bank tellers and grocery clerks with pictures of grandchildren who look just like them. I pull my hood over my head gangster-style. He pulls out a bag, begins cracking sunflower seeds and blowing out the shells with the ease of a parakeet.

The compartment door zips open, and a uniformed man turns to the passengers in the first row. "*Fahrkarten, bitte,*" he asks, waiting patiently while they search for their tickets. He takes them, examines them briefly, and punches a hole in them with the puncher chained to his belt.

I pluck my Eurail pass from my pouch and stare at it in disbelief. All the dates are already filled in. There are no more empty spaces. It would be possible to turn the 28 into 03 if I had a blue pen and a degree in graphology, but I have neither the right tool nor the appropriate experience in petty forgery.

The conductor is in the third row, stalled over some students who are trying to find tickets they never bought. I rise quickly and head toward the back without a plan. The washroom's free. I duck in, latching the door firmly behind me.

The washroom hasn't been cleaned since the days of Kaiser Wilhelm. There are ossified stains on the seat, puddles of piss on the ground. I construct a crude blanket with a latticework of toilet paper, spread it on top of the toilet seat cover. I place my feet all the way across on the sink to avoid the rivulets of urine below, which flow side to side with the tide, and settle in for the balance of the ten-hour trip. I wonder where the excrement actually goes.

Three hours later I assume we're in France from the sound of the cursing on the other side of the door. A man has been trying the handle for at least five minutes. Sorry, mate. What can I do? I hope he can tough it out until we reach Spain.

I slip in and out of consciousness, dream of food mainly and sometimes Melody. Announcements over the public-address system are unheard. Occasionally I glance out the window. The clouds make monuments, the land is burnt, a Marsscape. Things seem less clean as we move south. In the towns graffiti covers buildings, trains, trucks, houses. The train appears to be making good time. We've only stopped twice. We rocket over hot tracks on which forests of raccoons and squirrels have left behind their feet and tails. It gets warmer in the bathroom, so I open the small triangle of window, which is no bigger than the sail of a child's bathtub boat. The new air is a tonic. I greedily swallow cupfuls of breeze, sniff delightedly, but am disappointed. Because of its very freshness, the air gives new life to the smell I've become accustomed to since the south of France. I return to my uneasy half-sleep, ignoring the knocks of protest and cries of desperation from the passengers outside.

Hours later, Spain, a land of reds and browns, two-house towns. In every village we pass there's a farmer with a hat and a dog who waits in the field, watching the train. My ass is already itchy, perhaps in anticipation of its call to arms. I fish out the tube of hemorrhoid cream Breffni gave me. I don't even know how to use it. Do I finger and smear? Do I stick the tube up my ass and squeeze? Plenty of time to figure it out when I get there. I wonder how my hash is doing. I stored it safely in a baggage rack four cars away, so that even if the police do find it, there's no way they can trace it back to me. If my stash is discovered by fellow travellers and not the authorities, being unwittingly canonized as the patron saint of the biggest caboose party the continent has ever seen would be small comfort. Now might be a good time to check on the hash. Even if the conductor collars me, I'm surely within thumb-range of Barcelona by now.

I slip the latch. Everyone in the nearby seats is sleeping in various poses of discomfort. Sideways. Knees to chin. Heads lolling forward. Necks at chiropractic angles. I ease by aisle legs, trying not to disturb, and lurch toward the next car. A stout woman tries to coax her child to sleep. Two bearded students are having a discussion about the death penalty, pro and con, in Australian. Everyone who's awake glances at me briefly as I pass, longer if they're not French, who are used to seeing tall black men in nice clothes. Blacks, it seems, don't normally travel on trains in this part of the world. Unless as porters maybe. Or stowaways.

I reach the end of the car. There's a door, but no more train. I'm either confused or mistaken, yet I can see the rails flash by on the other side of the sliding door. The door is locked. I'm surprisingly calm. Did I store my bag at the other end of the train, a few cars up instead of down? But, no, I remember the heavy woman and her child, both of whom were screaming when I made my first trip.

I ask the passengers around me in a variety of broken languages what happened to the rest of the train. None of the answers, French, Spanish, or German, make sense. I hurry up the aisle to the Australians, who are quiet now. "Excuse me, do you know where the rest of the train went?"

"The rest of the train?" The Aussie's *train* rhymes with *Rhine*.

"The other cars behind us. There were more."

"The rest of the train separated a long way back, mate."

I shake my head. I didn't even know trains did that. Since when do trains break off into components? This can't be happening. "Do you know where exactly they came off?"

The two look at each other.

"I dunno," one of them says. "Lyon maybe. Somewhere in the south of France, I think."

"Don't be stupid," the other says. "Lyon isn't even near the south of France. Maybe Montpellier. I think we stopped there for a bit. Right?"

The first Aussie shrugs. "Ask him. He'd know." He points to the conductor walking toward us.

"Excuse me," one of the Aussies says, waving at the conductor.

"Don't worry about it," I tell him, and walk down the aisle toward the conductor, keeping my head low. We pass each other, and I breathe again.

The washroom's occupied, and I have to wait three minutes before a big bald man wipes, flushes, and emerges. The smell inside is almost visible, but I snap the door shut with relief, go over the facts. Several grand worth of premium-grade hash is in a bag. The bag is in another car of another train. The train is somewhere in the south of France. And I'm somewhere in Spain, south of Barcelona. The only solution? Get off as soon as possible, call the rail company and find out where the other train is, then ask them to hold my bag until I get there. And what if they peek in the bag? A street urchin of some kind is recruited for the rendezvous. Like in the movies. I'd be nearby, watching from a phone booth. If the pickup goes according to plan, I snatch the bag and try to get back on course, a little late but alive. Practical, feasible, and the makings of a kick-ass story if it comes off. All is not lost. The thing to do now is wait for the train to stop, and hope it does before I find myself irreparably south.

I feel hotter and sweatier than I should, more than a little dizzy. Not surprising, I suppose, for someone who's spent the past seven hours holed up in a moving lavatory. A change of clothes seems in order. I dip into what is now my only remaining piece of luggage—a plastic shopping bag containing Anusol, Kaopectate, Dulcalax, Tylenol, Listerine, boxer shorts, real shorts, and two shirts. I forgot to pack socks. I change into my favourite shirt. I'm secure enough in my masculinity to wear pink with pride.

The train jiggles and jacks for at least another hour. I'm getting dizzier. It's still surprisingly hot for a sun that's on its way down. Hot flashes. The onset of menopause. Patience. I pass the time counting disgruntled passengers with weak bladders. I wonder if, when I get off, I should call Breffni and ask him to tell Tube of my mishap. Tough call. Tube could just as easily send assassins as help. My intestines interrupt. Suddenly I realize my digestive system is still operating on a schedule that hasn't been reset for my delay. I was supposed to be excreting my cargo safely in a Barcelona bathroom. Now my ass is a time bomb, a grenade with a pulled pin. I rummage desperately through my bag, swallow some more chalky Kaopectate, but I know it's too late. The contractions are only five minutes apart. I have no choice. I have to poo.

I give birth, without the aid of spinal anesthetics or midwifery, to three huge, steaming piles. My sphincter has been split, my anus violated. I gaze longingly at the tube of cream in my bag, but relief will have to wait. Now the unenviable task of rooting through my own dung. The plastic tubes are surprisingly easy to find. Using a pair of pencils as chopsticks, I isolate the tubes in a corner, then hoist them into the sink for processing. There's something small and white in the last heap. It's too delicate for my makeshift tools, so I have to grab it with my fingers. It squirts away, and I'm forced to go after it again. Up close, held toward the dying light of that now impossibly hot sun, it looks like half a tube. I scoop up the last of my fecal remains and sift like a prospector, using tap water as my sieve, but still can't find the other half. I start to laugh. Do I have minutes to live? Hours? Days? And will I die with a smile?

I struggle to remember the stories I heard from other models. The average high for Hi-C seemed to last about six hours. One of the models— a girl with the improbable name of Heaven—told me she once took four pills and lived. From the look of the half-empty tube, I've probably ingested at least twice that. Soon I'll be getting happy and huggy. I realize with a start that I'm already half there. The train feels as if it's going sideways, and the armpits of my favourite shirt droop with sweat.

The last time I felt this messed up was the first and only time I smoked up with Melody. It was a huge joint—as big as a felt marker. It was clearly more than either of us could handle. Melody began rocking back and forth, combing her hair over and over with her hand. "Turn the music off!" she screamed, and I did. We knew neither of us should go into the kitchen because there were knives there. So we sat together on the couch, flipping through porn and eating cereal from the box. It seemed like the best meal we ever had. Everything was fine until she told me how beautiful I was. I pushed her face away, declared I had a lot of sadness, then burst into tears. I cried for nearly an hour while Melody watched, raking her hands through her hair. I don't think she had any idea what to do. Usually all the tears were hers. Sometimes she would even cry while we made love, and I would hold her, rocking her back and forth. It says something about both of us that those wet nights were some of the happiest moments we ever had, though I suspect neither of us could figure out what exactly that meant.

The train is slowing down. We seem to be arriving somewhere. Suitcases are being hauled off racks and strangers are saying goodbye. We click to a halt. The doors open, and no one will wait for anyone else to get off or get on. I wish this were my stop. I don't feel so well.

SEVENTEEN

Not long ago I found myself lying on the balcony, naked from the waist down. I've only been conscious for a couple of minutes, and somehow I'm already tired of my view of the beach and the smell of rotting meat. I haven't left the room for three days. My bones ache as if I'm not wearing them properly. At some point in the night I must have shit myself repeatedly. I think my ass is broken. I feel as if I've swallowed the sun. I spend the next hour wishing someone would roll me over.

Gulls fight over a store-bought chicken mysteriously abandoned on the pier. The beach isn't busy despite the sun. Most of the young tourists seem to prefer the five-minute taxi ride to the private beach where, according to the brochures, the sand is softer and the waves are gentler, and they can rent boats or parasail if they have the money. This beach is for tourists with fixed incomes and bad travel agents, or students and families who can only afford the all-inclusive. The beach is littered with black seaweed, coiled in mounds like spools of audiotape. The old tourists don't mind. They waddle like penguins in swimming caps toward the surf. Few are actually swimming, though. The water's solid with medusas. The children, far from being disappointed at not being able to swim, delight in taking sticks, walking into the water, and smacking the creatures into pieces, or impaling them whole.

A little boy in a green bathing suit hooks a medusa with a stick, launches it onto the sand with a flick of the wrist. It heaves there for a minute, melting in the early-afternoon sunlight, gives one more pump, then stops. The boy lifts it carefully with his stick and places it tenderly into the water, hoping it will propel itself back to sea. But the jellyfish doesn't move, and after a few waves, it's washed up again and is eventually stepped on by a young girl who cries.

An old man in a red jacket walks along the water's edge, yelling, "¡Miercoles, Miercoles!" to anyone who will listen. Occasionally he stops when someone beckons, and rips off a lottery ticket from a long sheet. He seems friendly. I wave to him, but he doesn't notice me.

From the esplanade adolescent Spaniards gawk at the tourists and their coconut bodies, practising their whistles and catcalls. Old men, pregnant in tight bathing suits, shoo them away, afraid their daughters will see something they like and beg to stay another week.

Vendors sell baskets and popcorn amid the palm trees on the esplanade. Parallel to the palms are rows of chairs, jealously guarded by old men with shrunken heads and enormous ears. They drag the chairs up and down the esplanade like hermit crabs toting their shells. The old men look ridiculous squatting earnestly in the rickety blue-and-yellow chairs—adults trying to debate on rocking horses. The men move in tight patterns, like the hundreds of pigeons that flock to the esplanade, forming, reforming, over bread crumbs. The old men don't flinch when the pigeons, filthy from the sand, fly inches overhead. The tourists duck, flailing cameras and umbrellas, afraid the birds will become entangled in their hair.

The pigeons spend most of their time chasing one another. The males, neck feathers ruffled, tail feathers fanned, pursue the females tirelessly, following them everywhere—land, water, or sky. The females avoid the males as long as they can, but the males win in the end. There's never a lack of pigeons, after all.

A boy runs into the flock of pigeons, arms wide, fear and delight in his eyes at seeing the birds scatter like cigarette wrappers in the wind, revelling in the joy of producing an effect on the world. Not far away another child kicks and chases a soccer ball by himself. One of the popcorn vendors, cigarette in his mouth, cries *"¡Mira, mira!"* and gestures to the kid to kick him the ball. The child screams, runs away, and resumes his game farther down the esplanade, leaving the popcorn vendor standing, arms held out, smiling.

I look back inside the hotel room and pity the maid who will have to clean up after I'm gone. The place is a mess. There's glass on the floor, and the wooden back of a broken mirror juts from underneath my bed. A small piece of chorizo sausage lies uneaten on the dresser. It's bathed in mustard. I dimly recall ordering it from room service the day before. Or was it the day before that? A sticky bun lies beside it. It was stolen from the train. Or was it the restaurant downstairs? Little tufts of a hotel napkin dot the bun like mould. Or is it mould? There's a Bible on the floor, with something written on it in red ink. Or is it blood? The handwriting is familiar, as if I made a clumsy attempt to trace my own writing. I can't read what it says.

I scan the room for more clues. Taped to the television set are a few incoherent reminders: EMPTY THE ICE, TURN IT DOWN, THERE'S MORE IN THE FRIDGE, CALL KARL. Karl might have been the reason I stumbled off the train where and when I did. Karl's my uncle, who retired from robbing investors in Germany and settled in Alicante four years ago. This note is crossed off with several bold pen strokes. Is that because I accomplished the task, or because I didn't? I don't remember making the call, or what his response was, if any. I assume he offered little help because I'm still here, broke and sore. I seem to have run out of Anusol. There's a small empty plate on the floor on which lies a croissant, on which a single word is written in jam—FUCK.

I'm beginning to feel better. I'm hungry and can crawl. I plan a flat menu—bacon, eggs, pancakes—that will fit under the door. Maybe a shower would do me good.

The mirror's cracked and bruised, as if something were thrown at it. It occurs to me that I haven't seen my own face in days. I know better than to look, but do.

When I was too young to read but old enough to work a tape recorder, I remember a story my grandmother read to me called "The Boy with No Face." I don't recall what the story was about, only that it terrified me beyond all reason. The boy's face, as I listened from deep under my yellow blanket, was blank. Blank white. I was more frightened of that face than I was of the dark. I don't know what scared me most—its inhuman form, its unnatural pallor, or simply the awful infinity of the thing. A face with boundless possibilities, capable of nothing. I punch at the mirror, and it falls off its hook, smashing into pieces on the floor. If the only luck I own is bad, will breaking a mirror reverse the polarity of my fortune and bring me good luck instead? I think I have to lie down again.

There are two cockroaches on the wall. They approach, eyeing me warily. They seem much bigger than cockroaches back home. From my vantage point on the floor they're as big as squirrels. One of them drinks my milk straight from the carton. The milk is on the counter, next to a pot of coffee, which has likely been there for three days. I get to my feet and help myself to a cold cupful. I drink it all, though it tastes like rubbing alcohol. For the caffeine.

I really should start looking for the rest of the drugs. At least ten pills, of course, never made it out of the tunnel. What happened to the excreted tubes is a mystery. The last thing I remember is being on the train, staring at them in disbelief. I'm glad I don't recall anything else. I overturn pillows and rake under furniture, but I know before I finish that I won't find a single tube. The room has already been torn up, as if I've been searching on and off for the past three days and found nothing. But I go through the motions, fully conscious this time, in order to fully quantify the degree to which I'm screwed. Nothing.

When I open my eyes again, it's almost dark. I can hear the bells and chimes of the casino downstairs. I'm lying down, and the cockroaches are on the sausage. I struggle to my feet, tiptoe to the dresser, pick up the chorizo, and shake it softly but firmly. Both cockroaches fall to the floor. One recovers and runs under the bed. The other lies stunned on the floor where it landed. I grab an empty plastic water bottle and nudge the fallen roach into it. As an afterthought, I scrape up the piece of chorizo and stuff it inside the bottle, as well.

Stepping onto the balcony, I raise the bottle and inspect the insect. It's given up trying to scale the slippery bottle wall and is standing on top of the sausage, waving its antennae from side to side.

"Unlucky, mate."

I've lost my friends, my career, and my drugs. The cockroach is trapped in a bottle that's about to be tossed from three stories into the sea.

I can still smell my room from the balcony. It stinks of old sausages. On the ground pieces of broken mirror wink like little puddles. In a few minutes I'll go back inside and flip the sign on the door handle from DO NOT DISTURB to ROOM REQUIRES SERVICE. It's taken me three days to accept that I can't hide here forever. In the distance the lottery man is still yelling *"¡Miercoles!"* Maybe I'll try my luck at the tables.

The bings and clinks of success. The silence of suckers. Men straddling two machines. Women wearing glasses and cigarettes. Two hands on the machines, as if they're playing pianos. Couples. One puts in the money, the other jacks the crank. Some keep their winnings in the tray for all to see. Others carry their buckets of coins the way a running back cradles a football. The regulars don't use coins. They have strings around their necks attached to credit cards plugged into the machines. Umbilical cords. Their play is cold and clinical, without pause. Men in wrinkled clothes. They've been here since Monday. Teeth as yellow as their chips. There are few pretty people in here. Nobody looks as if they're having fun.

I follow the soft carpets into the bowels of the casino. Dealers with hypnotic bow ties flip cards, stack and collect chips. Floating bartenders with bars on wheels minister to the thirsty. Every so often I see a man in a dark suit, an earpiece, and sunglasses. I know others are studying me upstairs from a ceiling ball. There are bank machines in every corner. No windows.

At the blackjack tables a row of Japanese gets lucky. The dealer smiles gracefully and pays out. Seven pai gow tables, green like golf courses, a few players run their chips through nervous fingers, poker faces left carelessly on their hotel pillows. People who always hold at sixteen, they stick to the yellow chips—the ones even I can afford. A few, men in suits or women with cigars, wield chips with holograms. Each chip is worth more than I am. Almost nobody plays keno. Those who do perch on the edges of their seats, using crayons to chart their losses. The roulette wheel's spinning makes me sick, and there's baccarat in another room, but it's for players only, and I'm not a player.

I wander. An automatic bingo machine wishes me a hearty "Good luck." I notice for the first time how cold it is in here. Enormous air conditioners from above pipe down icy blasts, cryogenically freezing gamblers on their stools. I wish I'd brought a cardigan.

There's a tiny racetrack by the waterfall. Ten people, mostly men, are seated around it. Grown men watch tiny plastic horses run around a plastic track. The jockey with the blue jersey wins, and a man at the back is happy. He collects his winnings and puts it all on green. Each horse is listed in the tabletop computers with its name, its odds, and a brief description. I study the field. Uncle Tom is the favourite at three to one. I pick Generation Z. Odds are sixty-six to one, but I like the look in his eye. The comments beside this horse are: "Unlikely to run good." If its prediction is as accurate as its grammar, I stand a decent chance. A sweet mechanical voice tells us we have ten seconds to place our bets. I shove two tokens into the slot and hope my horse doesn't prefer to run in the slop. "And they're off..." A few of the young bettors begin to cheer. Others quietly follow the action on the video screen or, unconcerned, plan their next bet and order their next drink. The horses roll on tiny wheels, though from afar their legs look as if they're moving. Generation Z starts well, but as the horses near the bend, most try to hug the rail, while Generation Z stays inexplicably on the outside. He has to run several extra inches, and no horse can make up that kind of distance. Everyone cleans up on Uncle Tom, the blue horse, who wins again. I curse Generation Z, my stupidity, the loss of two tokens. That was food money. I move on.

More machines. The one-token slots. King of Hearts. Joker. Grand Slam. Gold Rush. Double Diamond. Triple Diamond. Triple Double Jackpot. Now the names aren't even making sense. A sign above each machine announces how much it has paid out tonight. What's the strategy? Do you play the one that's paid out the most, figuring it's lucky, or do you go for the one that's paid out the least, thinking it's due for a big one. There's almost nobody here, only leftovers—half-drunk drinks, cigarette ash, and sticky swizzle sticks. Greasy fingerprints on shiny aluminum machines. An old woman has hit. She plunges her bucket into the flow of coins, praying it'll never end.

I tire of the bars and cherries, head upstairs to the second level. There are a bunch of locked private rooms, and a small art exhibit, which I ignore. It's even colder up here than down there. A glass walkway spans the casino. I stop midway across and glance beneath my feet at the sea of neon slots below. Like a glass-bottom boat in the Caribbean. I study the colourful reef below. From here I can still hear the little horses as they win and lose.

There's a small bar off to the side. They're playing music, some of it good. The joint reminds me of an airport bar. Awkward, out of place. The people inside not certain if they're allowed to dance or make noise. The bar's theme is Hawaiian. All the staff wear only grass and makeup. It's so cold, the bartender shivers quietly in the corner. Nipples are thumbtacks. The waitresses flirt to stay warm.

Most of the patrons are women, which bodes well for me. I'm optimistically horny. I know enough Spanish to get by.

A man dances alone in the middle of the floor without moving his legs, waving his arms from side to side in incredibly quick yet incremental gestures. It's almost impossible to describe, equally impossible not to laugh.

I'm hungry, have a martini instead, and another. I must be doing better.

Surprisingly calm. Resignation? Still in shock? I examine myself in the concave martini glass. My life right now looks bent, prismatic. *Rien ne va plus.* Crispen was right. Crime, it seems, doesn't pay, not unless you're a real criminal. Now I can't go back, not unless I pay Tube. And I can't pay him unless I model. I can't model until my face is fixed. And I can't fix my face until I can pay for medical care. I don't even have enough money to fly home, even if I wanted to. It seems like years ago that a generous Dat Win promised me Kameleon would do anything to help its new man. Right outside the bar next to a row of blinking video lottery machines is a row of phones. Why not? The worst he can do is say no. Or call Interpol.

Seven rings, and a hazy Dat Win picks up.

"Hello?" He always sounds as if he's talking a foot away from the phone.

"Dat?"

"I'm sorry. Can you hold a second?"

I say yes, but he's already clicked away. I'm a little surprised he has other callers on his business line at 10:30 at night. Maybe this wasn't a good idea. Then he's back on before I have a chance to hang up.

"Hello?"

"It's Stacey."

"Stacey Schmidt? Where are you? What happened to you?"

"Did you get my message?"

"I got your message. It made no sense. What's up, babe? Where are you?"

"In Spain."

"What the hell are you doing there? Toby get off me. Get off! Go play with something." His cat? His lover?

"I'm in a bit of trouble. I was hoping you could help."

"Trouble? With the law?"

"Not yet."

"That doesn't sound good, babe."

"It isn't."

I explain things to him—the fight, my cut, Tube, the drugs. When I finish, there's the hiss of static, the boom of the bar next door and, faintly, the happy dinging of a distant payout. Someone got lucky. After about ten seconds, Win finally speaks. All business, cold as the casino air, terse and exact, as though he suspects his phone is tapped.

"Well, Stacey, that's certainly a situation." I'm no longer his babe. "I'm sure you understand that Kameleon can't endorse anything illegal. It wouldn't be a good idea for us to involve ourselves in a…a situation. It wouldn't be a good idea for the company right now."

"I'm not asking you to endorse anything. I just need some help."

"I mean, personally, not from the company, I'll give you whatever help you need. Whatever I can do, you know?"

"I need money."

"I can't send you money. It would implicate…I just can't get involved in it like that. Money-wise, I mean."

"I just want to go home."

Silence.

"So what help can you give me?"

A deep breath.

"Go to the police. Tell them what happened. Maybe you can get a deal. I have a lawyer in Berlin. He's expensive, but he's excellent."

"I don't think that's an option."

"It's up to you. Where are you now, anyway?"

"Alicante."

"Alicante's nice. Too many tourists, though. Have you tried their *turrón*?"

"No, I haven't."

"Do you know what it is?"

"No. What is it?" I ask wearily.

"It's like peanut brittle, only it's made with almonds. It's too hard to explain. Just ask someone. Alicante is famous for *turrón*. Where are you staying?"

"The Hotel Paradiso."

"I've been there. For the casino. There's not much else to do in Alicante. You know what's nice? Valencia. By the way, some of your friends have been asking about you."

Breffni and Crispen? Or Tube? This phone call might have been a mistake.

The last thing I need is for Tube to find out where I am.

I hold on to the phone box to steady myself, suddenly exhausted. I can barely stand. "I know why you picked me," I say, as quiet as a puff of flour. I'm hardly moving my lips.

"What?"

"For the Kameleon Man. I know why you picked me."

"This isn't really the time—"

"Remember that idea of mine you were thinking of using, the one where people could vote on their choice of colour and style of the jeans?"

"Yeah?"

"To you I'm the pair of jeans, right? That's why you picked me."

"That doesn't even make sense. Listen—"

"I have to go now. Thanks for your help. See you around."

"Stacey—"

I hang up with one hand, still holding the receiver in the other. Of course, I should have known better. Simien used to quote an old African proverb: "The words of the night are coated with butter. As soon as the sun shines, they melt away." The binging has stopped, the winner is probably scraping coins into his bucket. I hope he turns around, cashes in, and heads off with something to show. I have nothing, not even an empty bucket. The only thing I haven't lost is money. I suppose you can't lose what you don't have. My hope, though, has melted like butter in the sunlight.

The only thing at this point that would make me feel better would be a woman. It's been so long, my insurance policy would require her to wear safety goggles. I walk slowly back into the bar, order another martini. There's a tall girl in a halter top who, I'm confident, could turn my luck around. I put down my drink, stroll over, and ask her to dance. I return to my drink, smoking, riddled with holes. What was I thinking? It finally dawns on me that these women are doing a double take for a different reason now. I'm Hephaestus in Apollo's clothing. The Beast, for real this time. At parties, burning ears, as well-wishing matchmakers condemn me with "He has a great personality..." I'm the one girls hope will hit on their friends.

I begin trolling for trolls. Near the bar there's a goose-faced girl with ripped blue jeans. Her red underwear deliberately balloons out of the slashed pants. I wonder if she's ever seen a picture of a rhesus monkey but approach her, anyway. She has low, ponderous breasts and strident perfume. Acne at age thirty. Her T-shirt says: GO DOWN OR GO HOME. I'm willing to call her bluff.

She's with five other girls, all smiles and giggles. Separating her from the flock proves easier than expected. I tell her I'm a wide receiver for an imaginary football team and that I have a room upstairs. She surprises me by saying yes. I'm surprised that it surprises me. That, in and of itself, is sad. But from now on nothing can be taken for granted.

On our way out young men in riverboat vests hand us moist toilettes. To cleanse our hands of sin, I suppose. We kiss on the elevator. Her lips smell like gravy.

There are more mosquitoes in my room than there are outside. I forgot to close the balcony door. Luckily the maid has turned down the room. There are mints on the table, and the corner of the toilet paper has been folded. The sheets are soft and new, the pillows hard and clean. I pull her close. She has thin, flapping folds of underarm skin, transparent bat wings. She caresses me eagerly enough, but I'm not into it. Even her huge, pointed nipples, conical like paper cups, fail to arouse me. I wish I were drunk. I don't need to drink to have a good time, but it sure makes screwing ugly girls a lot easier. She slings off her panties. Not too far, I hope, because she'll have to find them again soon.

"Do you want to?"

"Yes, but..." She reaches to the ground, fishes in her jacket pocket. "Use this." She brought her own condom. My Spidey sense is tingling. Beware of girls who know the bouncers. Girls with toothbrushes in their purses. During the past couple of months, I've learned it's always really strange for them and that they never do this kind of thing. This girl at least is honest.

I turn off the lights. Making love to a woman I can't see. A girl without a face. I wonder who she is. There's a ray of light from the pool outside. I notice a herd of ants walking down the wall. I wonder where they're going. Are they scouting, or did I drop something tasty under the bed? When they reach the headboard, they turn right and continue down the wall. The bed trembles with the woman's spasms. She's on top and getting louder and louder. I think she's scaring the ants. She comes once with little help from me and keeps going. I take it in stride. Pleasing women, like most things, is hit or miss. I find it hard to concentrate. What, really, is the point? So why am I in bed with this ugly woman, soaking freshly turned-down sheets? I wish I could have my penis locked, sealed with wax. Her volcanic breasts sway perilously close to my ruined face.

Soon it's over and I hand her the clothes that have fallen on my side of the bed. She doesn't ask if she can see me again. I almost ask her if I can borrow a couple of the holographic chips she won at blackjack. She closes the door, and I go back to bed. The ants are still streaming down the wall. I spread out, arms, feet, and head akimbo, an anatomical man. There's still plenty of room on all four margins. The bed's king-size, more empty now than when I left it four hours ago. I almost wish she stayed.

EIGHTEEN

There are twenty ways to look like an artist without wearing a monkey. Ponytails. Home-sewn clothes. Nails painted with real paint. Piercings and cigarette burns. Antique jackets. Yard-long sideburns. Tattooed ears. Souls for eyes. None of these artists look anything like that. They're middle-aged men mostly, a few pimpled students from the university, a pregnant woman. They smell not of pot or whiskey, but coffee and aftershave. There's only one who even remotely looks like an artist, a man with a corkscrew moustache and a steady stroke, but even he's a barrister by day who changes into ripped clothes after work.

The five-minute warm-up poses are over, and I'm ten minutes into a position that's only comfortable for twenty but which will have to last forty. I'm better at it than I thought I'd be, considering it's only my third time. This is almost exactly like freeze-modelling, only no one ever moves you. And you're naked.

There are about five people to the right of my head, three to the left, and at least two or three more on either side who I can't see from the angle my face has been set at. All beginners. The usual mix: mostly regulars, a few drop-ins who came to peek at some skin and who, after spotting me, make a few token scribbles and leave with a sigh and without their deposit. Those who stare are always escorted out. It's a free class, so no one's any good, including the instructor. He's younger than I am, possibly from a local community college or work-release program. He sports creaky sandals and velour pants. His hair is the colour of grenadine. I track him as he paces back and forth, trying to keep him in my line of sight without moving my head. He's been studying my naked body closer than any of the artists.

This week the class has been moved from the community centre to an elementary school. There's a big plastic castle for kids to crawl in, a stack of mats for naps, and plenty of corners for punishment. All the walls are yellow, and the beams in the middle of the room are padded.

To the class I'm known as "the guy with the scar." The only person who actually knows my name is the man who pays me, Arthuro, the instructor's boss and father, who always gives me cash and a piece of his sticky homemade *turrón*. I seem to be one of their favourite models, in part because I'm one of only three males, but mostly because I find clever poses and never shield myself with shadows.

A young student has a T-shirt emblazoned with Superman's S on his tiny chest. It looks as if he painted it himself. Not bad for a ten-year-old. I'm a little surprised. I thought all the superheroes these days were made of metal.

Today's class is mainly about eyes. *Ojos*. I'm not sure why there's even a need for me to be naked, but there you go. The building's air-conditioned, and they've explained to me time and time again that there's no way to turn it off. There's a breeze. I think I can see my breath. My balls are the size of rabbit droppings. My penis suddenly emaciated. I hope their drawings will compensate for shrinkage.

Several of them have brought their own easels. Others wield clipboards. A few of the hardier ones stand. Some draw on printer paper stolen from work. One man has a protractor. He picks up his drawing and takes a position behind me. I hope his intentions are honourable.

There's a mirror on the wall to my left. In its reflection I glimpse some of the works-in-progress. One artist has drawn me as an Indian woman. Another has left out my ears. In one modernist interpretation all of my appendages are stretched and flattened, as if with a rolling pin. My arms are hoses, my member touches the floor.

"Los ojos son la ventana del alma." The eyes are the window to the soul. The instructor lulls himself asleep with his own clichés. He trails off and picks up, words or sentences later, leaving phrases blank and students confused. I'm in danger of nodding off myself. I take a deep breath and try some rapid-eye movements to stay awake, but the instructor tells me to be still and stop making faces. The class creeps on. Mercifully the clock is behind me, so I can't check how little time has gone by. If hell exists, it would be a little like this. Just sitting there, doing nothing for eternity, while life goes on around you. Pretty soon you'd wish for the pricks and barbs of the pitchforks, the excitement of being chased by horned devils, the thrill of pushing a rock ceaselessly up and down a hill.

Now they're talking brushes. The instructor shows off a brand-new goat's hair brush, which the students are encouraged to buy after class. I wonder how many baby goats will have to die for art's sake.

The door jingles opens, there's someone new, but I can't turn my head. Apologies, the scrape of a chair on linoleum. She, whoever she is, asks her neighbour for more leg room. Laughs. Her voice is rough but whimsical. It holds the promise of fun. I'm overcome with curiosity. I search for her in the window to my right, in the mirror to my left, hoping for a reflection, but she's too far. I try to cheat, twisting my head incrementally, one degree per minute, but all I succeed in doing is straining an eyeball and earning a remonstration from the instructor, who tells me not to move after the ten-year-old complains. Thanks for nothing, Superman.

The class settles into silence, quiet except for the squeak of pencils, the scratch of sketchers. Those who use watercolours are silent as ninjas. Only a few in the class will finish me. Most will leave me empty, an outline, a ghost. Discarded versions of me, inferior because my nose is too long or my ears are too short, are strewn about the classroom. I've been buried in the wastebasket, crumpled beyond recognition, ripped into fragments, died a hundred deaths in less than an hour. My corpses litter the floor. This class is called Life Drawing. I wonder what I'm teaching them about life.

The class goes into stoppage time. I enter into a state of diapause. The fluorescent bulbs overhead bathe me in heavenly light. I feel as if I'm floating slowly toward them. I don't remember the next twenty minutes. My extremities go from numb to molten, back to numb. I wish I hadn't leaned so far to the right, leaving my left arm hanging out to dry. If this class doesn't end soon, I may need to amputate. But finally a chime goes off, congratulations all around, and it's over. I stretch myself back into circulation, shake a few hands, and turn to get a look at the latecomer.

Though I've moved off my mark, she's still sketching quickly with firm, confident strokes, using something that looks like a lump of charcoal. She seems not to breathe as she works. Her hand is the only thing that moves. In my mind we exchange places. She sitting on my stool; I painting her. Her hair as sea grass, swaying to invisible currents. Her eyes as disco balls, manipulating light to their own end. Her breasts as buoys, rising and falling with each breath. I can even paint her voice. Why not? It's my painting. I'd have to invent a paint to capture the colour of her skin, mix indigo and mango bark and pewter and then throw it away because all I've done is make a mess. I wish I could paint myself painting her. My brush is limp in my hands, my canvas blank as I stare, able only to render her with metaphors and similes, which are easier to use than paint but almost always the wrong shade. It's all academic, of course. I can't draw to save my life, or the lives of others. Even my stick figures are arthritic. The only suitable home for my art is on my mother's fridge.

She glances up and meets my eyes, and there passes between us that unmistakable flash that happens between two black people who find themselves outnumbered. The invisible nod, acknowledgement of the past.

The rest of the class folds papers and packs up boards. A few give the instructor money for the goat's hair brushes, which he promises to bring next week. No one shows me what I look like. They never do.

"Do you speak English?" she asks.

"Yeah."

"I hate to ask, but do you mind staying? Just for five, ten minutes. It's for a bigger piece I'm doing. Five minutes?"

"I guess so. Sure."

The instructor buckles on his motorcycle helmet, tells the woman to lock up after we're done, and we're alone. Strangely, for the first time since I took off my clothes, I feel self-conscious. As if the whole world is watching, only it's just her, sketching rapidly with charcoal, as if I'm already there in the paper and she's brushing off the dust. I'm impelled to talk, though I have absolutely nothing to say.

"That's a strange thing for a girl to wear in this day and age," I say, pointing at her T-shirt. It says: POWER NIGGER.

"They sell these on the street," she says, smiling. "Isn't it wild?" Fishing in her purse—a large cloth bag that looks more like a potato sack than a handbag—she pulls out a small brown doll. "It's a Negrito. It holds candy."

The doll is a black man of some sort holding a spear. Its lips are rouge-red, thick as caterpillars. Its eyes are coconut-white. The Negrito looks like a turn-of-the-century cartoon.

"See," she says, opening the bottom. "Little chocolates." She shakes out a few black pebbles, pops one into her mouth, offers me one. I decline.

"They sell those?"

"Yeah. It's like a candy dispenser designed by the Ku Klux Klan. Neat, huh? I collect stuff like this. Racist and sexist leftovers from the last century. In twenty or thirty years, when people come to their senses, this stuff will disappear. And I'll make it into a show of some kind. I'm B, by the way."

She gets up and extends her hand. I take it, and she shakes it two, three, four seconds. So long that we're into a second handshake.

"Bea? Like Beatrice?"

"Like the letter B."

From this close I can see that B strains the boundary between being beautiful and being plain. Whatever man she's with would constantly be trying to convince himself of the former. When I look at this girl, her clothes remain intact.

"So what do models think about when they're sitting for hours?" she asks, sitting down to resume sketching.

"Your mind wanders. Today I was contemplating the nature of hell."

"You believe in hell?"

"Of course."

"Heaven *and* hell?"

"Sure."

"And God?"

"He's the man."

"So you believe all of this—" she waves the charcoal in the air "—was created by one guy?"

"Sure. If God didn't exist, how did we get here?"

"We evolved from monkeys for a start," B says.

"But who made the monkeys?"

"They came from whatever came before the monkeys. The little monkeys. And the tadpoles. And the Big Bang and all that."

"You think we came from a ball of gas?" I ask incredulously.

"I find that easier to believe than a super being who can create it."

"But where did the gas come from?"

"I don't know," B says, frowning. "It just existed."

"But someone had to create it, right?"

"So who created God then?"

"He's just...there."

"But if God can exist without being created, why can't the monkeys?" she asks, brandishing the charcoal triumphantly.

"I...I don't know," I say sadly. "I'm sure there's an answer for that, but that's as far as I got in my theological development. My dad was the religious one, and he left my mother for a waitress."

"Well, I don't believe in anything," B states. Softly, though, as if she were a little afraid God might hear.

I don't blame her. She may be an atheist, but she's not stupid. "So you don't believe in heaven, either?"

"Nope." Her strokes are getting broader and slower. She seems to be waving at the page.

"If you did believe in heaven, what would it look like?"

B pauses for a moment. "I'm not sure. I guess in my world heaven and hell are the same place. It depends on whether you're happy when you're there 'cause, brother, you're there for a long time." She takes a step back and smiles. "I'm done, by the way."

"I'd love to see it."

She laughs and shields it from me. "Actually, it's not really done yet. I'm doing sketches of a dozen or so nude models, then I'm combining them into one man, to see what he'll look like. You know, like those studies of universal beauty. I don't know how it's going to turn out, but you're welcome to have a look when it's finished. Give me a call."

She goes back into her sack, extracts a wrinkled piece of cloth. I unroll it. Her name, phone number, and ARTIST are printed in simple black letters on a strip of Kente cloth. We leave the classroom together, and B locks the door behind us.

"Well...bye," she says, waving at me from the street. She has an achieving gait, walks as if she wants to get the most from every step. I watch her as she moves down the esplanade past the old men on chairs and the flocks of brown pigeons. The old men are too busy playing their own kind of games to notice her as she clicks by them on wobbly heels.

I cruise along El Barrio, handing club flyers to tourists. The leaflets tell them which DJs are playing tonight at La Playa and La Caverna, who's taking their shirt off and where. But it's a Sunday night and there isn't anyone on the streets, so I toss the flyers into the garbage, buy a bag of nonsense from a fast-food joint, and wander with the comfortable taste of fried onions in my mouth.

A British comic is doing a set on the patio of a small hotel. I lean against the rail to listen but move along once he spots me and starts incorporating me into his act. For sale on the corner are *gelado* and women, but I don't have money for either. Alicante is a town of rich retirees, condo owners who share time, and tourists who have brought their own golf clubs. Around here money doesn't talk; it whispers, suggests. Even in this small seaside town anyone can quietly arrange for almost anything to happen.

Nearby there's a late-night disco, one of the few I don't work for, but I'm too old. Down the street, workers mantle and dismantle the lights for the upcoming fiesta. They roll a creaky ladder through the streets, one man on the ladder, two men pushing him, one trailing, holding the lights. I walk with them for a while, but they turn toward the disco, and I can't go any farther.

The black woman's out again, wearing red eyes and her hair tied back. I'm not sure if she's out for sex, drugs, or rock and roll. I check into a pay phone and leave Amiris a short message to let her know I'm okay. But even on a plastic answering machine, with hundreds of miles of static between us, I'm almost certain she'll hear the lie.

I amble through town in a fog of my own fancy. I haven't stopped thinking about B since she disappeared into the cab four hours ago. I can't quite put my finger on why, or explain it further than that she seems to know something I don't, and that's enough to make me want to see her again. I dug around and found out what little I could about her from my friends at La Playa. It turns out she's quite famous, as much as artists get in a small Spanish city. She did a series of Africanized classics that hit it big recently. In particular her version of Rodin's *Le Penseur* as a black woman with an Afro has apparently inspired a whole series of posters and postcards.

Surprisingly her address is in the phone book. She lives on a street not far from the clubs. After I pick up my pay, one hundred euros in crumpled cash, I ring her bell, hoping I'm on the right side of the line between sweet and creepy, ardent and obsessed.

B lives in a melted house with a languid roof and drooping eaves. She comes to the door in a gown and slippers. From inside, candle glow, the sound of classical guitar, and the smell of burning plastic.

"Hi." I suddenly regret the lack of planning that's gone into my opening. "You said I could come over and see your work, remember?"

"Tonight?"

I think she's onto me. "I read somewhere that's the best time to see art."

She smiles, more out of pity than anything else but invites me in. "Sorry about the smell," she says as I take off my boots. "I was experimenting."

"Pottery?"

"With a recipe. I'm on the road a lot, I don't get a chance to cook much. And when I do..." She sniffs and her face goes sideways. "You get the idea. Why don't you put your camera over there?" She points to a couch. "Are you planning a shoot I should know about?"

"I don't trust the people where I'm staying. This is a nice place."

The ceilings are high and swirled. There are little statuettes everywhere—marble, limestone, alabaster—standing on small wooden tables. Some are animals with people faces. Some are people with swollen heads and genitals. "Do you live alone?"

"Yeah. It used to be me and three other girls."

"In here? What is this, a two-bedroom?"

"Yeah. Too many women too close together. We were able to run most of the household appliances on estrogen. Where do you live?"

"In a hotel. The Paradiso."

"The one with the casino? You might have already seen my stuff then. I have a little exhibit there on the second floor."

"I think I passed it by. Sorry."

"Don't worry about it. I told them it was a stupid place to put it but, hey, I'm just an artist. So what do you do?"

"Nothing really. I used to be a model."

"That sounds like fun."

I shrug. "I don't know about that. They give you clothes, you put them on, they take pictures, you get paid. It's like being a stripper, only in reverse."

"You said you *used* to be a model."

"Once upon a time. Now I'm...unemployed."

"I didn't think there was such a thing."

"An unemployed model? Of course. I can't get work anywhere right now."

"Are you kidding? Everyone wants a model."

"To do what?"

"I don't know. Beautiful people are always in demand. Like decent golf players. Companies find stuff for them to do afterward."

"Like ringers?"

"Exactly." B snaps her fingers. "They're ringers on the corporate soirée circuit. Executives need someone to invite to the cottage, right? I'm sure every firm has got at least two or three models tucked away someplace."

"You're crazy."

"Maybe." She smiles. "So why aren't you modelling anymore?"

I point to my gash.

"Bah." She waves her hand as though my problems were a smell. "All you need is a doctor and some minor adjustments. A nip here, a tuck there, and you'd be back to beautiful."

"I wish I could, but it costs too much." I'm already swimming in a sewer of debt. I could hardly afford to pay for plastic surgery unless it were drive-through or self-serve.

"Can't your family help you out?"

"My family doesn't know I'm here. They still think I'm working in Toronto. I showed up at my uncle's doorstep, but he called the police."

"If you're so broke, why don't you sell your camera?" She picks it up, turns it over. "You could probably get a good price for it."

"My camera?" I thought about it before, the day I tore the escort service want ad from the newspaper, the night I slept with a girl hoping she'd pay for breakfast. "I can't give up my camera. All I have in this world is my camera and my shots." The pictures are stowed safely under my mattress back at the Paradiso, where they'd lie undiscovered by casual thieves and ignored by serious ones.

"I'd love to see them," B says.

"Someday maybe. Say, what's up with the graffiti?"

The living room looks like a bus terminal. A washroom stall. A basketball court. All the walls are covered in graffiti. The original paint has been spray-painted over, here and there artistically, three-dimensionally, with shadows and highlights; in others, haphazardly, as if by children, or malevolently, as if by vandals. It's as oppressive as a parking garage.

B gives me an embarrassed smile. "After a while, I just got bored of my own taste."

"You didn't paint all this?"

"Are you kidding?" She points to the ceiling. It's a sloppily painted woman with pneumatic breasts and an amphibious mouth.

"So who did?"

"Whoever felt like it. I have spray cans all over the house. Whoever feels the urge can tag away. Sometimes my friends who have the key come in while I'm not here and paint me a little something to surprise me."

"Interesting." If their art is any reflection of their personalities, B has some odd mates. There are animals, both natural and mythic. Geometric shapes. Spirographic swirls. Mathematical formulas. Names followed by "wuz here" followed by the date. Some images have been sprayed over with black, then tagged with another colour. One "artist" has painted a disturbingly accurate portrait of the entire cast of *Three's Company*, including Priscilla Barnes. Carnal acts of all kinds.

"What about that one?" I ask. Down the hall there's a giant cartoon that bears a striking similarity to B. A flaming noose is tied around the figure's neck, it's being defiled by a number of winged beings, and it has an assortment of sharp implements sticking out of its sides. Its legs are also missing.

"My ex-boyfriend's magnum opus. I've been meaning to paint over that for a while, but it's a little too high to reach without a ladder." She looks me up and down. Her eyes are tape measures. "You're tall enough. Maybe you can help me."

She disappears into another room, returns, hands me cans of black and white spray, gazes at me expectantly.

"You want me to paint?"

"Spray over it with the black and paint something nice with the white."

"What do you want me to paint? Keeping in mind I can't."

She smiles. "Neither could my ex. Would you believe that's supposed to be me?"

"Really? I don't see the resemblance."

"I hope you paint better than you lie. Come on."

I shake the black can and spray, then switch to the white. It doesn't take me long. I step back.

"Is it finished?" B asks.

"Yep."

"Hmm. What is it?"

"What does it look like?"

"It looks like a white face with no eyes or nose. Or mouth. What does it mean?"

"Nothing really. He's just a character from a story my grandmother used to tell me when I was small. It's the only thing I know how to draw. Like it?"

B strokes an invisible beard. "It's kind of creepy, actually."

"Should I paint over it?"

"No. It's perfect." She looks as if she's waiting for something, but I have no idea what it is.

"Well, I guess I'd better be going." I move toward the door.

"Why?" she asks, grabbing my arm. "It's still early. Let's do something. Or go somewhere."

"It'll have to be something free." I pull my empty pockets into rabbit ears.

"Why don't we go to the beach?"

"At night?"

"That's the best time."

"Is it close?"

"It's five minutes away. Smell—" she inhales deeply "—the waves."

The beach is abandoned by all except lovers and crabs. A young man reads poetry to his girlfriend. As we get closer, the girlfriend turns out to be a guy. Then a very hairy girl. B has packed a bag. I carry the shovel, a long-handled affair with a small scoop. As we pass, couples peer at us suspiciously. Armed with a late-night shovel, we're obviously up to no good.

B drops to her knees. "This is far enough. Any closer and it'll get washed away." She empties the bag's contents: an old kitchen knife, a paint scraper, a garden spade, a plastic fork, a melon baller. She takes the spade and points to my shovel. "Start digging."

We dig. The hole grows deeper and deeper. I glance at her questioningly, wondering if the hole is meant for me.

"We have to dig pretty much to the water table," she says. "Water is the glue that holds the sand together."

"You seem to know a lot about digging sand."

"A friend of mine is a master carver."

"What's that?"

"Nothing really. That's what he calls himself. He travels around the world making sandcastles."

"That's his job?"

"He enters competitions sponsored by the hotel chains. The pay isn't great, but they pay his food and hotel. And when he isn't competing he teaches tourists how to build castles. Fifty bucks a family, one family every two hours or so. During the tourist season, that adds up. And it's always tourist season somewhere."

She grips my hands, dips them in the wet sand. "Pull the sand toward you quickly, so you don't lose the water. Build it up outside the hole. Slap it together into patties. Not so hard. You don't have to hurt the sand. Just form it softly like this." She jiggles the sand between flattened hands.

Our castle begins to take shape. We stack the brick, fashion towers. We weld the patties with water, erect walls. We cleave the sand into ramps, create staircases. We scoop with the melon baller, carve arches, windows. Pretty soon we've built a seaside Xanadu, complete with a moat and floating crocodiles.

"Come see my shining palace built upon the sand," B says, eyes closed. She's curled around the castle, twinkling her toes in the moat.

"Did you know that sand isn't just powdered rock?" I ask. "It's made of coral and shells and limestone and all sorts of things. And thousands of little creatures, too. Did you know there's about one million grains in a litre of sand?" I wonder how many grains we wasted on this thing. "What should we call it?"

"Does it need a name?" B asks sleepily. "I never name any of my pieces when I paint or sculpt. I figure that's up to whoever buys the thing. After all, we don't come into this world with a name. It's left to those who take care of us. Or to ourselves."

"Fair enough. I wish I had my camera, though. What a great shot. With some really slow film and a good light. And the right lens."

"You don't need that stuff," B says. She yawns with her eyes closed, like a cat. "Come over here. Hold your hands like this." She creates a pinhole with two cupped hands. "Look through and whatever you see— that's it. That's your picture. A moment in time. Yours to cherish, never to fold or fade."

"You don't take pictures?"

"It's all up here." She points to her eyes. In the reflected light of moon and wave they look bioluminescent. "Now let's tear it down."

What would have taken the wind days to blow away, the ocean an hour to melt, takes us seconds to kick down. Chaos theory can predict, with some certainty, which way a sand tower will fall if you dribble more sand on top of it a grain at a time. What theory can predict the tower's fall if stomped by feet, pummelled by hands? The ornate spires collapse into our meticulous moat. The drawbridge crumbles. Our house lies in ruins. B carved her initials onto the west wall. I engraved my name, Stacey Schmidt in miniature longhand, below hers. Now mortar, brick, and graffiti are grains once again, to be reborn as plaster in a crab's hole, or an itch in a woman's bathing suit.

The destruction complete, we lie on the beach, waiting for the sun. Soon B is breathing loud enough for two. I suspect she's fallen asleep. It occurs to me that she never showed me the portrait she was working on. No matter. The last thing I need now is to see myself through the veil of someone else's eyes. I curl up close, my head near her breasts. B's skin is warm and moist, like sand. Over the receding roar of the waves I can hear her inner workings. The gurgling of her stomach, the clicks and whirs of her heart.

NINETEEN

A limousine, stretched and black, pulls up to the art gallery. The driver opens the door, and two tall, well-dressed people emerge, flanked by a pair of beefy bodyguards. The man's wearing an expensive yellow suit. The woman's nubilous dress swirls in the mountain breeze. The couple wave to a nonexistent crowd, giggle, and stagger toward the front door. The young woman still clutches the champagne bottle. The man holds on to her for support. Both are thrilled to be alive. I'm happy to be one of them. The bodyguards escort us to the door, then hop back into the limo. B hired them for our morning soirée because I once wondered out loud what it would be like to be a star. I blow a kiss to a photographer who, impressed, thinks I might be somebody and snaps a picture, just in case.

To the serious art votaries, this is the only gallery in Granada. It's housed in an old bus depot abandoned years ago after a disgruntled driver came to work one morning with a chip on his shoulder and a shotgun. Because of the tragedy, the gallery has acquired almost mystic cachet. Some like to pretend they can see bloodstains. Others swear they can still hear the screams.

They haven't done much with the place since buses rolled and mechanics cursed up and down these concrete floors. It's been wired for light and sound, but there are still wooden skids piled up in corners. Feet crunch on screws, lugs, and nuts in the old maintenance bays. Overhead are enormous industrial fans that, if turned on, would suck dozens of little bohemian hats, their wearers, and their samosas up to the ceiling at an industrial rate. Some of the old buttons still work.

This show will be like all the shows: streamers, champagne, silver plates of caviar for the guests and, hopefully in a back room somewhere, a carpet of pizza for me. All the artists will be here, the kind who dress in dashikis and blame everything on globalization.

Tonight the waitresses are all dressed as flappers. The garters make some girls sexier, others less so. There's a jazz band, composed of spare musicians from surrounding towns. It's no secret that Granada is home to some of the world's worst jazz. I lead B through the entrance, down the hallway, and toward the first exhibit, and immediately things improve. Bad jazz is one of those things that's much better when it's happening in another room.

"There's Ali Shahan," B says. A tall brown-skinned man is blinking madly at one of the waiters.

"Should I know him?"

"He wrote *Every Good Boy Deserves Fudge*. This is the first time I've seen him without his surgeon's mask. I'm impressed. That guy's so obsessed with germs he only eats astronaut food and builds his own water out of hydrogen and oxygen. See that man to his left? He's a poet."

"What's his claim to fame?"

B shrugs. "None really. He's one of the last dub poets."

I shudder. I think *dub* is just a synonym for *bad*.

"Do you know how he met his wife? He was giving a reading one night at El Mariachi. He was there with a date, a different girl. But he walked up to the woman after the show and gave her his phone number with a poem attached. I think it went something like this." B scribbles on a napkin, hands it to me.

all poetry

sucks

you

i like

"She was his within days," B says. "Isn't that romantic?"

The dub poet is laughing heartily with a young Asian woman who's clinging to a steel pipe. He has his hand on her leg.

"Who's the girl?" I ask.

"She's a movie producer."

"Done anything I'd know?"

"Probably not. Her last film was *Das Booty*. Experimental porn."

"Sounds sophisticated."

"Don't laugh. She's already earned a couple of lifetime-achievement awards. And she's only twenty-six."

I look around. "So where's your stuff?"

"In the back somewhere, I think. This way."

I can't wait to see it. B's been unusually secretive. The basement door was locked for weeks, and every so often there was midnight welding and the smell of naphthalene. As I understand it, all the pieces in her exhibition, *Flux*, are made from unstable plastics, substances that fall apart at room temperature, structures that decompose at a molecular level due to vibrations in the air. Apparently the more people who see the exhibit, the faster it decays. Temporary art, which exists in time, not space. No journalists, no photographs.

"Your art is pretty much the exact opposite of what I do."

"Modelling?"

"Photography. Photographs capture images and preserve moments. They don't change. Your art is always changing and evolving."

"Pictures don't change? Have you seen old photographs? They yellow and fade when the chemicals break down. I'd say what you do is exactly like what I do, only it happens a little slower." She points to a room on the left. "Over there."

The door is locked. "Is your art that dangerous?"

"It's not dangerous. It's interactive. You go into the room and you have to figure out the first part of it in order to get to the stuff in the other room."

"That sounds like fun," I say, tugging at her arm, pulling her forward. "Let's go!"

B pulls back. "Not yet. Let's see the others first. I think you're going to like mine, though. And I have a surprise for you."

"Where?"

"In there." She points at the room. "Look at this one. It's nice."

We wander, B interpreting for me as I struggle to understand. She tells me about colours I've never heard of, themes I've never noticed, pictures that, to my eye, would make just as much sense displayed sideways or backward.

"This guy's onto something." B says. It seems the young artist, Knut Flo, has made a name for himself in artistic circles for his inspiring use of red.

She's intrigued by a series of sketches. They look magical to her, unfinished to me. The biggest one portrays a turret full of Moors at the Alhambra.

"Why is it that drawing a face with lines on it means the person's black?"

"If you don't have anything smart to say, tell him." She indicates the waiter.

I snag two glasses of champagne, but B waves off her glass.

"I'm trying to sober up. I have to make some announcements a little later."

I pour her drink down my throat.

"Hey, here comes Peebles," B says.

A tall man strides toward us with the determined air of someone who's about to miss his train. Unlike all the other artists here, he's not white, but I can't figure out if he actually has any black in him.

"Who is he?" I ask.

"I'm sure you've heard of him. He was the first photographer to incorporate human remains in his exhibitions."

"Is he the guy they put in jail?"

"Say what you will about his photos, you've got to admire his balls."

Peebles greets B with three kisses on her cheeks. He has a fluty voice and a thick caterpillar of hair on his upper lip. The man seems like one of those big-landmark-on-a-small-map kind of guys. His glasses, I notice, are filthy. Like a buggy windshield. To his credit, he does smell real nice. Woody, with a hint of citrus and something that reminds me of cumin.

He's arguing with B about whether someone's idea is original if it's simply a byproduct of mishearing another idea. He says his latest exhibition was inspired by something he read in *Shutter*, the photography magazine. His idea was to have a family go about its business as usual, then he'd yell freeze and everyone would have to stay in a tableau. He'd wait an hour, then photograph them to capture the decay of their poses. Trembling arms, fake smiles, a caricature of a scene: the family at dinner or the son playing with toys, or the wife on the can, grotesques of reality. Great stuff.

The article he read said: "Have your subjects maintain their poses for a short period so they don't start moving." Peebles thought it read: "until they start moving." The error inspired his exhibition, which opened last week to great critical acclaim. He maintains that because he didn't actually see the idea in print but imagined it for himself, the idea was his in all its brilliance. B argues there's no difference between perception and reality. The world only exists as we see it.

"You were acting according to your imaginary picture of the world," B says. "It doesn't matter what the article actually said, you stole the idea as long as you believed what it said was real."

Personally I think they're both full of shit. I feel like an extra appendage dangling at B's side. I mumble my apologies and stalk off in search of something to eat.

The buffet is as long as a bus. Crustaceans, mostly, on ice. The shrimps are huge, curried, and haven't been relieved of their heads. The lobsters are still snapping. I shiver. I can't imagine how people can eat those things. They're cockroaches with armour. Next to the shellfish are thin slices of greyish-white meat in a bubbling brown reduction. I believe it's fillet of weasel. I stop a passing waitress, but all that's left are water chestnut sandwiches. I nibble reluctantly. It's like eating tiddlywinks. I stop the next waitress, a tiny little redhead who's bearing booze. That's better.

I make my way back to B, who's still talking to Peebles.

"I hear you play the cello," he says. He arches an eyebrow, as if I were claiming I was constructed entirely out of wood. "What kind of music do you play?"

"Classical, mostly, a bit of jazz."

"Then you *must* have heard of Joachim Udaskin."

I confess I haven't and settle down for another lecture, praying the overhead fans will suck me away. Udaskin, apparently, is an American pianist who's rocking the world of classical music by taking well-known pieces and misplaying certain sections on purpose, in some brilliant post-modern way that represents the angst of the new millennium. That's Peebles's take, anyway.

"One note, just one note," he says, clasping his hands in supplication, "and flat becomes sharp, harmony becomes discord. Certainty, knowledge, the expected, all vanish, giving way to uncertainty, chaos. He questions, with that one note, what is harmony, what is music, what, really, is for sure in this world. It's musical metafiction." Peebles sighs, eyes glistening with genuine tears.

"I have to go to the washroom," I say, unable to stand it any longer. I leave them again and wander aimlessly, glancing occasionally at the works on the walls, paintings of geometrical shapes of various colours. Many of them remind me of the art we used to produce at Valleydale, my old preschool. I wouldn't be surprised to encounter a piece smeared in chocolate pudding. None of this so-called creativity speaks to me. Most modern art is just a conversation between the artist and himself.

A group of young artists, probably students, are huddled in a corner, debating the false genius of Salvador Dalí. I dismiss their arguments with a wave of my hand, call them all boobs, and leave them in my intellectual dust. I join a conversation already in progress about the importance of real art in the age of uncertainty, but I have to pluck my nose hairs to stay awake. All this talk is tapping on my nerves. For people obsessed with translating life into art, expressing universal truths, boiling reality down to its essential elements, no one here actually seems real. I'm surrounded by watercoloured painters and potters made of clay. Everyone's a print or a forgery.

The author of *Every Good Boy Deserves Fudge* is drinking alone at the cash bar. I lean close and tell him I'm a good boy and deserve fudge. He gives me the evil eye and stalks off. His drink's still on the bar. Untouched and already paid for.

I twist listlessly, wondering why I'm here, though I already know the answer. I don't come across women like B very often, unlike Breffni, who can find them by echolocation, or Crispen, who can follow their scent for days. She's not like the guys. She's not always looking for something else. For now I'm willing to follow her wherever her breath blows us. I don't care where we go as long as we keep moving. She's taken me on without a word of complaint or thought of reward. If my face wasn't spoiled, I would have understood it all.

The party is getting louder. I keep myself amused by ambushing the champagne boy, who's been trying to avoid me ever since I asked him to sing me a song. Happily blurred, I totter between groups of chatting artists, making occasional contributions, some of them in verse.

B and Peebles are still talking about something or other when I return. "So what are you, anyway?" I ask, interrupting him in mid-sentence.

"What's that?" he asks. Somewhere next to me a champagne cork pops and a woman giggles as the bubbly erupts onto shoes.

"Are you black or white?"

"What?" he asks, flinching.

"If someone yells, 'Nigger,' do you turn around?"

He almost drops his glass. B grabs my arm and tries to lead me away.

"Just a minute," I say. "Let him answer."

"That's a fucked-up question, man," Peebles says in a low voice.

It's the first time I've heard him sound like a real person. Everyone's watching. Suddenly I can't remember why I asked him, or why it even matters. I feel very small, and very sick. "It's only fucked up if you can't answer," I mutter, and let B drag me off.

"Wait here," she hisses, propping me in a corner. "I'll come back for you. I'm going back to apologize."

The room is swinging. The dub poet is dancing by himself, revolving slowly like a disco ball. Someone has brought his dog. It's wearing a bell on its collar, as if it's on the way to rescue skiers. I hit halfheartedly on a couple of waitresses, but my face precedes me. I look around for the Asian movie producer. I spot her lying facedown in a corner. I doubt she'll move again without the help of a necromancer.

A short man nudges my elbow. "Pardon me," he says in a Cockney accent. "I like your stuff. Very interesting."

"Sorry?"

"Your pictures. In there." He points to B's room. The man's either drunk or on something.

"I have no idea what you're talking about."

"You're Stacey Schmidt, right? The photographer?"

How would he know my name unless he's a friend of B's? But this man doesn't look as if he has friends of any kind. Even though he has all his teeth and doesn't boast any scars or tattoos, he gives the impression he's been ordered not to leave the country. Did Tube send him? I may be drunk, but I'm not stupid. I'm pretty sure this fellow didn't come for my autograph. My mind cycles through grim snapshots. Garroted in the corner. Shot in the back. Knifed in the ribs. I'm no martyr. I'm not ready to die for my art. I want to grow old enough to have back hair and one good ear. Old enough to have a midlife crisis. Sophistry is my first and only plan.

"Stacey Schmidt? You want that brother over there, the one talking to all those people. He's your man." Discretion is the better part of valour, though in a pinch cowardice will do just as nicely.

"Thanks, mate." He claps a hand on my shoulder. His fingers are thickly ringed with gold, all except his trigger finger, which feels crooked.

Peebles, innocently fragrant, is inducing laughs from his followers, unaware his life is about to change, probably for the shorter. The English bloke follows Peebles into the washroom. It's possible only one will come out. Unless the truth does first. I have to get out of here.

B's not by the statues, she's not near the paintings. I borrow a pen from a wandering art critic and scribble a makeshift will, allocating my assets to my mother, my debts to my father, not certain if a napkin is legally binding. I hand it to a waiter and instruct him to find B. The Brit has emerged from the washroom, without Peebles. I use a passing woman as a shield, hide in her wide shadow, stay with her as far as I can. She lets me off near the door to B's exhibit. I have no choice. I open it, and the door whir-clicks behind me.

The room isn't so much dark as unlit. Through a sun roof cut into the middle of the ceiling, fake moonlight bathes the room in an eerie blue glow. Two rows of little tea lights form a path to the other side of the room. Slowly I inch forward, careful not to step on or fall into anything. I follow the candles to the door, which starts where the candles end. No matter which way I turn the knob, push or pull on the handle, I can't open the door. I'm locked in. Then I hear a cello from hidden speakers, soft and far away, swathed in a distant hiss, as if coming from inside a shell.

Lights slap on, two of them, one from the ceiling, one from the floor, revealing a huge tableau, covered in what looks like headless cartoons. This seems odd, even for B. As I get closer, I see the cartoons aren't headless at all. Their bodies are painted, their heads are photographs. The photographs are mine. Just the heads, black-and-whites, from the collection I junked in a fit of despondency at B's flat weeks ago. I recognize the faces. The bum on the bench. The hooker on my old street. Simien in drag. The black man who sold birds. Melody.

Each of them has now become someone else. Which takes precedence? The figure or the face? I smile at B's statement, ask myself the question she wanted me to ask. Am I a man who's been beheaded? Or a body with someone else's features? It occurs to me that this is exactly how I've been feeling for some time now. A corpse walking around with someone else's mug pasted to my stump. There's a plaque illuminated with its own miniature light: PHOTOGRAPHY BY STACEY SCHMIDT. God love her. I study the tableau.

It depicts a beach. It could be in Benidorm or Barcelona or any number of sand traps in Spain or anywhere for that matter. There's no landscape except sand and water, beige and blue. It's painted in bright and hasty pastels, like one of those postcards you find in a revolving seaside postcard rack. The people are caricatures with distorted features that are meant to be funny, but never are. Everyone's doing something. There's volleyball and there's drinking. Women in stringy bikinis. Naked children building sandcastles. A father with his back to the sea takes a picture of his wife and children on the beach. Behind him, a monstrous wave. On the ocean, water-skiers. The driver turns to admire a half-naked sunbather, the rope is slack, the pyramid of acrobatic water-skiers totters behind him, about to collapse. A scuba diver has a bird perched on his blowhole, a swimmer sports a shark fin on his head. The latter is swimming just below the surface. Behind him, another shark's fin, a larger one. A second joker? A real shark? Two jet-skiers appear on the verge of colliding. A lifeguard in a tower is watching. He gazes to the left, while in the water, below him to the right, a hand protrudes from the waves, grasping for air, signalling for help. Overhead are parasailers in toothpick rigs. A gull dumps on an unsuspecting head. And higher, even higher, are those rain clouds? On the beach two people toss a Frisbee about to be seized by a leaping dog. A woman sunbathes, a crab heads toward her. Its intentions aren't clear. Nearby there's a man with a metal detector. His arms flail in excitement. Underneath the sand is a Russian submarine. A man on the beach sells lottery tickets. A little boy flies a bright model airplane that, if it's lucky, will miss the power lines. Who isn't in some state of flux? Something's happening to everyone. Advance the film by a frame, one-thirtieth of a second, and the picture changes. Water-skiers tumble, a camera's ruined, sunbathers are shat upon, jet-skiers lose their lives, a swimmer drowns. How quickly things can change. From status to quo.

In the corner, alone, surrounded by dozens of others, I find myself. It takes me longer than I would have thought to recognize me. It's a picture of my old face; I don't know when it was taken. I had hair. It's the only colour shot in the tableau, though it's faded enough to blend in with the blacks and whites around me. The photo's probably been ripped from a catalogue. I might have been selling underwear—packs of briefs, not boxers—or plastic footballs, or patio furniture, or another magazine run by the same chain. I'm trying to smile, but my heart's not in it. The result is fateful, tragic, a yearbook portrait of someone... I'm alone with a broom in my hand, sweeping the sand. I look sad. Why am I sweeping the beach? It seems a rather futile thing to do. If this is meant to reflect my current state of affairs, then I resent it.

Someone has been testing the doorknob for the past two minutes. A patron or a henchman? They can't get in and I can't get out. How long will I be forced to sit here and gaze at myself before the locked doors open? Unlike the people in the picture, my life isn't a tableau. Time hasn't been painted shut. If I know B, there's a hidden meaning to the collage before me, but I'm too drunk to figure it out. Perhaps the message is concealed in the face that stares blindly across the moonlit room. I follow my gaze, but I'm looking at a wall. To the right, however, I notice a small window near the ceiling covered in black crepe. It looks just big enough. I put my elbow through old glass, which comes apart in sections, like ice on a pond. If there's an alarm, it's silent. I waggle out of the window into the sunlight and take a last look at myself through the broken window. I hope the critics will be kind. My eyes do not follow me wherever I go.

When the bus driver shakes his head and whispers *"Loco,"* I almost turn back, convinced for a moment that, yes, maybe I am a little crazy. But he's stopped the bus now, the door's open, and I'll just look stupid if I sit back down.

The door snaps shut, and I'm darkened momentarily by a blast of hot diesel exhaust. I'm alone by the side of the road, a mile past the town of Pinos Gentil. I'm surrounded by furry mountains and the smell of pine trees roasting in the sun. It'll take me at least three hours to get to the top, maybe more. At the top there's a little bed-and-breakfast, my new hideout. I could have taken the bus, but by going on foot I'll be harder to track. No one can find me if they don't know where I'm going.

I begin climbing. I stay off the road, choose to use the labyrinth of worn trails carved into the dust by ancient muleteers. There's a dead dog by the side of the road. I have to leap over pink intestines that stretch across my path like skipping ropes. Occasionally cars pass by—old cars with things tied to their roofs, or with people trying not to fall out. The footing on the paths is unstable. Sand and stone shift under my feet. I feel as if I'm wearing heels. It's cooler than it was in the bus, which was sticky with labourers, but it's still hot enough outside to melt my ice cream before I have a chance to unwrap the cone. It seems as if the sun is shining just for me. Even the breeze is hot. I'm told you can ski these mountains yearlong, and I don't believe a word. I take a small bottle of water out of my pocket and twiddle off the cap. I'm glad I brought water but sad that I didn't bring enough. My wool hat is starting to chafe. I bought it from an African man in Pinos Gentil who promised me it would keep my head cool, but he lied. My head's basting in its own sweat. The hat itches and scrapes, as though it's knit out of nettles. So I toss it, watch it float over the side of the cliff like a Frisbee until the wind dies and it drops.

Below and off to the sides are whitewashed villages, orange groves. Almond and olive plantations. Still lives and stiller landscapes. The kind of scenes B used to paint before she found vitreous enamels and welding torches. I'll miss B, of course. I'm a little surprised that, even now as I flee for my life, I'm more worried about losing her than I am about being found. I just hope she can forgive me. The only thing I look for in anyone these days is someone who understands, and she did. I don't even have her picture. She never let me take one. The only reminder I have of her is the business card, indigo on Kente cloth, that I've kept in my pocket since we met.

I'm huffing uncomfortably now. Nothing like thin ozone and ultraviolet rays to cleanse the mind and purify the soul. I'm exuding booze. My sweat is overproof.

Spain squats below me, looking up. Somewhere near here people still live in caves. Every so often they come out to sing to the tourists. Today I hope they stay in their caves. From up here you get a great view of the city. Stone-white or clay-red houses, a honeycomb of alleys and blind walls, interior patios, mosques. If it weren't for the architecture, it would be hard to believe that my distant cousins, the Moors, ruled this country for 700 years.

If I could pick a time and place to live in, I would chose here in the days of Tarik, when a black guy became the master of Spain and Africa began at the Pyrenees. Palaces of quicksilver and gold. While Europe was dark, life here was lit with outdoor lamps. In London they walked on mud. Here they strolled over paved streets. In Paris monks were illiterate and baths were illegal. Here both libraries and baths were public. Nowadays the only evidence the country was once owned by brothers is that sometimes you'll come across a Jesus painted in black.

I drag my feet in the dirt, raising clouds of dust behind me. From far away a dog barks at a church bell. Birds circle in the sky. They're high enough that I can't tell if they're pigeons or vultures. The sun beams like a schoolgirl. I've sweat my weight in water. This region sees 250 days of sun, all of them today. I still remember bits of wisdom from *Modelling Made Easy*. Page 6: "Avoid the sun at all costs, for although it may feel good, it will age you." This from the book that advised me on page 8: "Don't look into the camera or talk during the filming unless asked to do so." Page 34 says: "You may be given but a single opportunity in your life-time that will make the difference between success and failure." Page 7: "Always carry a pen."

Today, or yesterday, or tomorrow I was supposed to launch the Kameleon campaign. In the end, of course, Simien's book is right. "You may be given but a single opportunity in your lifetime that will make the difference between success and failure." My time-limited offer has expired. Operators are no longer standing by. From the moment I began putting on clothes for a living, I've suffered exactly sixty-nine inches of disappointment and seventeen joules of angst. I'm tired of being a golem, pursued by the fashionable phantasms of fashion. I'm tired of eating tissues soaked in water just to feel full. I'm tired of being black, Brazilian, Cuban, Indian, Mexican, Pakistani, Portuguese, Lebanese, depending on who's signing my voucher book. I know everyone has their cross to bear, but mine feels as if it's burning. My punishment is hereditary. I belong to a half-race of traitors. I've learned my lesson. Being brown is exhausting.

A cloud, the only one I've seen in the sky, rubs against the sun. In its shadow I come to life. I pull the book out of my satchel and begin with page 1, "Never give up on your dream," and work my way to page 30, "A career as a booking agent or fashion coordinator can be just as rewarding," tearing out pant turns, cattle calls, callbacks, powder puffs, blush brushes, cover sticks, cotton balls, lip gloss, lip pencils, pencil sharpeners, clothes pins, safety pins, diet pills, water pills, weigh-ins, and launch them one by one into the breeze. The sheets flutter into the trees below, leaves returning home. A few flap along the ground to be collected one day by nesting birds or prisoners. I feel better than I have in months. I've been liberated by my broken face. I only wish I could get my hands on my portfolio. I'd have ripped out each test shot, each tear sheet, spreading bodies and heads across the burning Sierra Nevada.

Despite the heat, I'm rocked with chills. I've stopped sweating. My skin is as dry as the sand. From overhead the UVA rays swing wildly for my head, while the UVB go downstairs to the kidneys. A tiny brown dog is sniffing my feet. I ask him how much higher I have to climb to get to the top, but he doesn't know, or won't say. I feel dizzy and a little nauseous.

It's at moments like these that I'm convinced the sole purpose of my life is to make a statement about life itself. I'm the real exhibit here. Temporary art that falls apart before your eyes. I'm both the genius and the masterpiece. I sit down, unable to walk any farther.

Overhead a flock of stylists howls insults from above. Melody offers to do my makeup. I tell her as loudly as I can that I won't be needing make-up anymore, but she doesn't hear or doesn't listen and cakes my face with powder. Of course, she doesn't have my shade. I'll be the fly in your soup, she mouths. I'll blow you a sweet loopy grain of a kiss. I brush the makeup off with my hand, find my face is coated in white sand.

My heart pounds astonishingly loud in my ears, as if I'm listening to a thumping beat in a pair of headphones. My pulse is a techno throb.

Underneath me everything moves to the rhythm. Even the pine trees want to bump and grind. I crawl on the dance floor in slow circles, reminded suddenly of a drunken Augustus breakdancing for the ladies in that club before we left for bigger and better things. It seems so long ago, distant as lunchtime school milk, Saturday-morning cartoons, video games, pennies on railway tracks. Suddenly I can no longer see. My eyes are covered in a thin white shroud. My ears are stuffed with cotton. I'm gasping for air, but I can't breathe any faster or deeper no matter how hard I try. I feel Augustus standing on my chest. Choking me with his beautiful hands.

TWENTY

They look at first like faraway angels, flitting among giant trees through the fog, but perspective is a funny thing. You can block out the entire sun with a raised fingertip even though the sun's big enough to swallow Earth in its roiling surface without causing a ripple. My mind clears, my eyes adjust, perspective returns, and I see that it's not the trees that are giants but the angels that are tiny. Eventually I notice that the angels aren't angels at all but butterflies separated from me by a pane of dirty, humid glass. Little orange and yellow candle flames flicker in the air, will-o'-the-wisps. Others are black as fighter jets. A few are blue. I recognize swallowtails and monarchs, a few viceroys pretending to be deadly. They wing through the branches of orange and avocado trees, ignoring the fruit, after nectar, probing flowers with straws. None stay for long.

It's a greenhouse, only feet away from my bed. Hundreds of bright flowers, the mechanical splash of artificial ponds stocked with slow-moving gold-fish. Bright sponges probably soaked in sugar water as snacks. There are bees. A few of the branches are bent against the glass that forms my west wall. A newly hatched butterfly is drying its wings. It clings to its pupal shell, which hangs from a silk mat to a leaf. The branch is close enough to touch the glass, near enough that I can see the scales and membranes of the insect's wings, its chitinous body, the blood coursing through unfamiliar wings. Its antennae are home to the chemoreceptors that will tell it where all the good stuff is, or where it can get lucky. I read somewhere that butterflies don't see the world as a continuous picture but as a series of still photographs. I wonder what it's like not to have eyelids. To keep one's eyes open all one's life. Not one of these butterflies will live longer than a year.

Another butterfly is resting on a branch, its wings frayed from days of beating against glass. Butterflies can hear sound through the veins in their wings. I wonder if, through wet glass and ripped wings, he can still hear me breathe.

Not far from the foot of my bed there's a door of sorts leading into the greenhouse. The door's just a sheet of slitted plastic, the kind that leads to supermarket receiving bays. Some butterflies have managed to escape. They glide overhead like vultures, or flutter by like lashes. Many stray close enough for me to grab, but I can't seem to move. I hope they haven't acquired a taste for meat.

When I wake again, I'm strong enough to throw back the covers and scratch at the spot I was thinking about for what seemed like hours. I'm wearing what appears to be an evening gown. I take it in stride. It's not the first time I've put on a dress. I wore one to launch Hosie Martin's fall collection to great acclaim. I wore one to my high-school graduation on a dare. I wore one to bed once because Melody said it would turn her on, but it didn't. I wore one when my mother wasn't home, years before I would learn in how many ways that was wrong. I wonder what Simien would think if he could see me now. I smile and drift back to sleep.

Now there's a very short man at the doorway, looking as though he's not quite sure he should come in. His skin's the colour of chocolate powder. His arms are covered in smudged blue-black tattoos. His face would be crunchy if bitten into. I try to speak, but my voice is still in its cocoon. Even I can barely hear it, and I'm standing right next to it. He disappears before I can try again.

Minutes later an extremely large woman bustles in. She has a palisade of greying blond hair, the sad kind that almost sweeps the ceiling. The woman carries a tray, which she sets before me. It holds cutlery, a napkin, a small bowl of cold almond soup, and some grilled sardines. And two tiny pills. She glances at me and smiles. Neither of us seems to be surprised to see the other, though I don't remember ever meeting her before. She tucks my dress under my legs, folds the blankets back onto my chest, reaches under my bed, removes a sloshing metal bowl, and walks out. Eventually I drink the soup without the spoon, eat the sardines without the knife, and swallow the pills without water. I ease the tray onto the nearby bedside table and stretch. I suppose the time has finally come for me to wonder in earnest where the hell I am and what I'm doing here.

I'm propped on a bouquet of pillows, high enough that I can see through the far window, which looks onto the opposite side of the house. It appears to be a centuries-old Spanish *cortijo*, with a shaded patio and a lush garden. Past the garden is grass, then sky. Though the big blond woman had the feel of a nurse, this building doesn't have the dull gleam or the sharp smell of a hospital. This may, in fact, be the very bed and breakfast I was aiming for before I was struck by the sun. And that's, I'm willing to guess, exactly what happened to me. In retrospect the signs of heat stroke are unmistakable: headache, vertigo, fatigue, disorientation, unconsciousness. I'm familiar enough with the chain of progression to know that circulatory collapse, brain damage, and death are usually not far behind. But unless St. Peter is a short man with tattoos and God a blond woman who cooks a mean bowl of soup, someone must have done something. But who found me, and how? And how many days has it been since I was boiled in my shell? Today the sun has fled the country. Rain streams through the trough at the side of the house, splattering onto the brick walkway like horse piss. I watch the water drown worms and rot grass. I'm comforted. I grow drowsy. The two pills have dissolved and are starting to shut me down. Soon I'm floating with the butterflies and stinging with the bees.

My dry mouth and cardboard limbs tell me time has gone by. Someone is standing near my bed. I squint, but my eyes are busy shooting low-budget independent films, neither of which is comprehensible or in focus. I raise my head. It feels as if I have more than one.

"Do you know how they saved you?" It sounds like B.

"No," I croak.

"They filled a bathtub with ice cubes and threw you in. Chilled you like a bottle of wine."

"Who found me?"

"A couple on vacation. I think they were staying here."

"Are they still here? I'd...I'd like to thank them."

"They were gone by the time I got here."

"How...did you find me?"

B waves a bit of coloured cloth in front of my face. Her card.

"They found it in your pocket and called me."

"In Alicante? But you were in Granada."

"I was checking my messages every hour." She squeezes my arm. "I was worried. How do you feel?"

"My skin is sore. I guess that's what sunburn feels like. And I'm very tired."

"I'm not surprised. You boiled away most of your brain." B shakes her head. "Why did you run away?"

"I...it doesn't make any sense now." I can't go on. B smiles as though she understands. We sit and listen to the rain, which is getting worse. I hope it doesn't stop. I never want to see the sun again.

"So what will you do now?" B asks.

"I don't know." What *can* I do? There's no support group for disfigured models. I would have served my craft better by being left for dead, a *risus sardonicus*—death's sardonic grin—carved on my face. A fitting picture. My only useful contribution to my profession, an indictment of an industry fuelled by teenage angst and surgically implanted dreams.

"You could go back to modelling," B says.

"I don't think so."

"Sure. Scarifications are hot right now. Supermodels are cutting themselves up left and right. And once they find out about your disappearance and the drugs and everything, you'll be unstoppable. Think of the buzz. You'd be the ultimate model to launch a campaign that's trying to tell kids what to wear while convincing them that no one can tell them what to wear."

"It's not the scar," I say, touching the crack in my face. How can I explain to her that modelling's flawless illusions no longer seem real. My dreams were sublimated in the mountain sun.

One of the most precious qualities a model can possess is the chameleonlike power to transform herself, seemingly at will, to suit the requirements of each and every job. This is not accomplished by merely changing makeup, clothes, or hairstyle. It requires the capacity to express and project a wide variety of attitudes and personalities.

That's from *Modelling Made Easy*, page 18. I remember because it's the only page I agreed with. All good models are good chameleons, but I'm neither a good model nor a good chameleon, and I'm finally ready to admit it. My only consolation is the earnest hope that the things I failed to get weren't really worth having, anyway.

"They liked your work, by the way," B says.

"What work?"

"The shots I used in my exhibit. They wrote about it in the paper." She shows me a small article in a local Spanish newspaper. Above it is a shot of B and me getting out of a limousine outside the art gallery. I take a closer look. It's hardly a flattering picture—I have pixels for eyes, and my inky skin is rubbing off in my hands. But of all the pictures I've ever done, this dirty black-and-white—overexposed and underlit—is one shot I'll never forget. My eyes won't stay still long enough for me to read the caption.

"Someone even wants to buy the piece," B says.

"Good for you." I smile to myself, remembering the man with the Cockney accent and hit-man hands.

"If I sell it, I'm willing to split the money with you," B says.

"It's your work."

"They were your photos. Just think, this could be the start of a whole new career for you. It sure beats smuggling smack in your crack."

I laugh until I remember Tube. Even if I went to the police, I know he could reach me from anywhere. Tube has contacts on most planets.

"Don't worry," B says. "We'll find a way."

Whether it's her lopsided smile, or the way she touched my shoulder, or a desperate need to have faith in someone, or simply sheer exhaustion, I believe her.

"That would be nice," I murmur.

She takes my hand. "You look tired. Shall I let you sleep?"

"That would be nice."

B pats my hand and walks over to the window. The only sounds are the scraping and banging of love from the room upstairs, and the squawking and flapping of the chickens outside fighting for shelter from the rain.

I rack focus from B to the butterfly, the last one left in my room. It's on the underside of the bedside table. This butterfly is the colour of margarine. It's not moving. Resting. Or dying. It's hard to tell whether it's attempting to hold on or trying to let go. Its compound eyes look past me, through me, as it readies itself for its next metamorphosis.

I nestle farther into the blankets and think that yes, indeed, life is truly coming together quite nicely. I have a friend who won't evaporate at dawn. The rarest of creatures—a woman who I can recognize during the day. Really, all along, I should have had faith that the mean happiness quotient would kick in at some point. After all, no matter how hard you jump on the scale, no matter how wildly the needle swings up and down, it eventually evens itself out every time. I'd like to believe that the way I feel right now isn't merely the work of two little pills, that I really am happy for the first time in as long as I can remember. This moment, like almost all others, will probably be forgotten unless I learn to see the world through compound eyes.

B is still at the window, staring out over the mountains. The greenhouse is backlit and reflects onto her. There's a garden in her face. I expand the picture, broaden it 360 degrees to include me. That's it. The first shot. I raise the loupe, hold the picture to the light, examine it from all angles. This single photograph almost makes up for everything that went into the taking. I close my eyes. For a beginning, it's not a bad start.

ACKNOWLEDGEMENTS

I'd like to thank Beach Holme Publishing, CJOH-TV, the Canada Council for the Arts, DJ Norts, Garfield, Gordy, Houdini, Icy C, Ichi Wu, MLZ, Natty D, Nino, Prince Rupert, Rock, Seb, and Wasir. And a special thanks to Tom Henighan.

KIM BARRY BRUNHUBER is a writer, television reporter, and documentary filmmaker who lives in Ottawa. His news stories have been broadcast around the globe and he also hosts a nationally distributed book review segment. Born in Montreal, he has a master of journalism from Carleton University.

MORE NEW FICTION
from Beach Holme Publishing

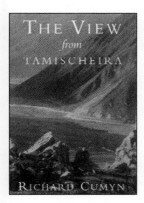

The View from Tamischeira
by Richard Cumyn
NOVELLA $15.95 CDN $11.95 US ISBN: 0-88878-441-4

"Richard Cumyn has created a fabulous tale....
The reader is also swept away into the current of fully
lived life and imagination, the wellspring of all our
mythologies and our science."—*Quill & Quire*

"...a jolly Victorian romp full of adultery, exotic locations,
and wild ideas..."—*Ottawa Citizen*

The Moor Is Dark Beneath the Moon
by David Watmough
NOVEL $18.95 CDN $14.95 US ISBN: 0-88878-434-1

After decades in Canada, Davey Bryant returns to Cornwall,
England, for the funeral of a mysterious relative and lands
in the middle of a property-inheritance squabble that
threatens to escalate into something far worse.
Distraught by the changed landscape of his beloved
homeland, Davey wanders the lonely moors and is soon
sleuthing his way through a farce of megalithic proportions.

Cold Clear Morning
by Lesley Choyce
NOVEL $18.95 CDN $14.95 US ISBN: 0-88878-416-3

Taylor Colby and his childhood sweetheart, Laura,
abandoned their Nova Scotia coastal village home for a life
in the high-octane world of rock music in California. Now,
after Laura's drug-related death, Taylor has returned to his
roots to live once again with his noble but isolated boat-
builder father. Complicating matters further, Taylor's mother,
who has been battling cancer, attempts to reconcile with both
her husband and son whom she deserted decades earlier.

BEACH HOLME PUBLISHING • WWW.BEACHHOLME.BC.CA